LILY'S CHOICE

MAY ELLIS

Boldwood

First published in 2020 as *Mine*. This edition first published in Great Britain in 2024 by Boldwood Books Ltd.

Copyright © May Ellis, 2020

Cover Design by Colin Thomas

Cover Images: Colin Thomas and Alamy

Every effort has been made to obtain the necessary permissions with reference to copyright material, both illustrative and quoted. We apologise for any omissions in this respect and will be pleased to make the appropriate acknowledgements in any future edition.

A CIP catalogue record for this book is available from the British Library.

Paperback ISBN 978-1-83633-903-8

Large Print ISBN 978-1-83633-902-1

Hardback ISBN 978-1-83633-901-4

Ebook ISBN 978-1-83633-904-5

Kindle ISBN 978-1-83633-905-2

Audio CD ISBN 978-1-83633-896-3

MP3 CD ISBN 978-1-83633-897-0

Digital audio download ISBN 978-1-83633-898-7

This book is printed on certified sustainable paper. Boldwood Books is dedicated to putting sustainability at the heart of our business. For more information please visit https://www.boldwoodbooks.com/about-us/sustainability/

Boldwood Books Ltd, 23 Bowerdean Street, London, SW6 3TN

www.boldwoodbooks.com

For my parents.
This is my imagining of their story. It is written with love and gratitude.

1

BOW CHURCH, EAST LONDON, OCTOBER 1968

A jangling siren broke through into the quiet interior of the church, disturbing hushed conversations.

'What's all that noise?' asked Lily's mum. 'It sounds like it's going to come through the flipping door.'

Lily kept her attention on the stained-glass window behind the altar, watching as the soft autumn sunlight made the blues and yellows glow. She felt so alone in the midst of her extended family as they gathered for her youngest sister's wedding. Her husband Jack was driving the wedding car, so Lily sat beside her mother in the pew reserved for the close family of the bride.

'It's an ambulance,' she said as its strident warning got louder and louder and then dwindled away as it sped past the building on its way to save some poor soul's life. 'Or maybe a police car, I don't know. Either way, someone's in trouble.'

She felt like rushing out of the church and chasing after it – to get them to take her away and lock her up in a ward or even a prison cell. Maybe then she might find some peace. Instead she had to stay where she was, acting as though everything was all right. But it wasn't. There was nowhere she could go to forget about what a mess her life had become – at home she was losing every battle, and at work she was terrified everyone would find out what a bloody mess she'd made of everything. She was so ashamed. It wasn't supposed to be like this.

She hadn't been happy when her daughter Beverley had decided to hide at the back of the church with her three-month-old baby. If she had to come to the wedding at all, they ought to stick together, hold their heads up high and brazen it out. By hiding in the back, Beverley was accepting that her illegitimate child was something shameful. If she was determined to keep the baby, Lily had told her, she should be prepared for the stares and the comments because they weren't going to go away. But she'd lost that battle with her daughter as well. *She's mine,* Bev had said, *and I'm not giving her up.* Now everyone would be whispering about how the teenager and her baby had been banished to the back of the church.

Anyone looking at Lily at this moment would think she was a model of calm. Pride wouldn't let her show just how spitting mad she was, but her hands shook as she smoothed out an imaginary crease in her new tailored dress, then fiddled with the carnation pinned to the matching jacket. Lily knew she looked good. She worked hard to make sure she always did. But she couldn't find any joy in it today. She took a deep breath, trying to dispel the huge knot of butterflies in her stomach.

She had a headache. It had been there for weeks, squeezing her temples, making her eyes hurt. From the back of the church she heard a baby's faint cry. Her mother sighed.

Oh God, give me strength, thought Lily. *Why can't I get through one single day without wanting to kill Beverley for being so stupid? I am sick to death of my own parents acting as if this is all my fault. My daughter is not the only unmarried mother in the world.*

She closed her eyes, clenching her jaw against the urge just to let go and weep. But she couldn't. Not today. Today was her sister's day.

'You all right, Lily?'

She opened her eyes. Her mother was looking at her with concern. Lily was tempted to tell her all the reasons why she was definitely *not* all right, but she knew now was not the time or place.

'I'm fine, Mum. Just a bit tired, that's all.'

'I hope you're not getting up for that baby every night. If that girl wants to keep her, she's got to learn to take responsibility.'

Lily sighed. 'She's doing fine. I'm not getting up for her.'

She wasn't about to confess that Jack was the one who rushed out of bed the moment he heard the baby cry every night. 'This place hasn't changed much has it, Mum?'

Even though years had passed since her own wedding day, the old church still looked the same. The walls were just as cracked and dull as they had been back then, contrasting sharply with the gleaming cross on the altar table and the brightly polished brass candlesticks.

'Mmm. It could still do with a coat of paint. And the traffic outside is getting worse. Fancy building the flyover right behind the church. They come shooting down off there and barely miss it. Mark my words, someone's going to end up driving right through the railings into the graveyard one of these days.'

Lily could hear vehicles rumbling around the building, rattling the stained-glass windows. The church had been there for hundreds of years, and the increasingly busy A11 traffic turned it into an island. When she and Jack got married there in 1949 there had been fewer cars around, and the church, sitting majestically in the middle of the road, had been quiet. This afternoon, with the new Ilford flyover spewing traffic just yards from the building, they'd taken their lives in their hands getting across the road to the church.

Someone came over to greet her mother, and Lily felt her tension grow. She really wasn't in the mood to talk to anyone, especially well-meaning relatives keen to give her advice on how to deal with her wayward daughter. For a moment, she wished she was hiding at the back with Beverley.

'Hello, Lil love. You look nice. I just seen your little Caroline outside with the bridesmaids. Bless her, she's jumping up and down, all excited.'

Lily felt a pang of guilt as she realised she'd forgotten all about Caroline, her younger child, a bridesmaid for the first time. She'd been so wrapped up in all this trouble with Beverley and the baby that lately the poor kid had virtually been ignored. The nine-year-old had been so good about it. Thrilled about being an auntie; even more thrilled about being a bridesmaid. She'd been a bit quiet about moving house so quickly, but she hadn't complained. All she worried about was that her apple-green bridesmaid's dress didn't get wrinkled in the move.

'Yes, this is her first time as a bridesmaid. It's all she's talked about for months.'

'Aw, sweet. They're lovely at that age, ain't they?'

Not like when they're older and come home pregnant!

Lily could see the thoughts forming in the woman's mind. She knew that if the cow so much as mentioned her elder daughter's name, Lily would smack her, whether they were in church or not.

'The flowers are lovely, aren't they?' she said, determined to move the conversation away from her children.

'Oh yes, I do love them purple things – lovely smell. I 'aven't got a clue what you call 'em, but I do like 'em.'

'Freesias,' said Lily. 'They're called freesias.'

She knew what they were called because she'd wanted them for her own wedding. Looking back, she should never have agreed to get married on Boxing Day. It had been a nightmare finding enough flowers for the bouquets. She'd ended up with some hothouse tulips and bits of fern. She'd wanted freesias and roses.

Don't think about it. This is another day. A happy day. One more deep breath – that's it.

The music began and the guests moved out of the aisle to take their places. Everyone stood as the bridal party started its slow procession into the church.

Lily looked around.

There, among her equally excited cousins, Caroline glided along behind the bride, a huge grin lighting up her little face. The circlet of flowers in her hair was slightly askew, her posy held tightly against her chest as if it might fly away.

Lily felt tears burn at the backs of her eyes. Her little angel. She remembered when Beverley had been as sweet and innocent as that.

What happened? Was it her fault? Was she really such an awful mother?

She turned away, eyes front, unable to bear it. Everything was going wrong! Why? She worked so hard. Years of evening classes to get herself out of the sweatshop where she'd been a machinist since the age of fourteen. Now she had certificates for shorthand, typing and book-keeping. She'd learned French before they went abroad for the first time a couple of years ago.

Oh yes, her in-laws might think she was getting above herself, going to work in the City, in an office. But she didn't care; she was proud of what she'd achieved. It meant she and Jack and the girls had holidays abroad, nice furniture, a car. She now wore smart clothes to work instead of making them for other people to wear. And high heels. She had respect. She even had a season ticket!

Was this the price she had to pay? Her eldest daughter an unmarried mother, her nerves on edge, everyone laughing and talking about her behind her back? *That Lily, stuck-up mare, thinks she's something special. Didn't stop her girl getting a bun in the oven though, did it? Moved they did. The pram was the first thing in the van, so the neighbours wouldn't see. Been telling the new neighbours the girl's married to a soldier who's stationed abroad. Would you believe that? The girl's only sixteen.*

What a mess. What a bloody, bloody mess!

Jack wasn't much help. He'd been devastated when he'd found out about the baby. But he'd taken one look at little Kerry and fallen in love, just like he'd done with both of their girls. As far as he was concerned, there had been no question of Beverley giving her up if she didn't want to. It didn't matter to him that that baby was going to drag their daughter down. No decent man would want to marry her now. They would be a laughing stock.

Lily's dreams of making a better life for her and Jack and the girls were melting away, and there was nothing she could do about it.

* * *

Jack pulled the Jaguar to a halt outside the church gates, confident that the traffic flowing around them towards the new flyover would give a wide berth to the luxury saloon decked with white ribbons. Everyone respected a Jag.

He pocketed the keys and jumped out smartly to open the door for the bride.

'Here you go, Kath, darlin'. I said I'd get you 'ere on time. We don't wanna give the groom any excuse to hop it, do we?'

'He wouldn't dare,' said Jack's father-in-law Ken, as he got out first and turned to help his daughter.

'He wouldn't want to.' Kathy slid across the leather seat and grasped her father's hand. 'Why would he want to? He's marrying me.'

Jack laughed. 'Yeah, well, I've had a little chat with him about taking on this family as in-laws. Might have worried him a bit.' He winked at his father-in-law.

The photographer arrived to take a picture of the bride's father helping her out of the car, with the smiling chauffeur standing behind them holding the door open.

There was a flurry of activity as the bridesmaids spotted them, and more photographs had to be taken. Latecomers were still going into the church, calling greetings and good luck to the bride.

Jack locked the car. No point in taking chances. A Jag, British racing green. Company car. If this beauty got nicked outside the wedding he'd be in a right bother. He was due to drive the boss to the airport first thing Monday morning.

A jangling siren broke through the chatting and giggling of the bride and her attendants. Jack watched as an ambulance sped past and turned right to disappear into Old Ford. He wouldn't mind driving one of them things one day. He'd done the buses and lorries. He was enjoying the chauffeuring lark, but it was almost too easy. There was too much hanging about. He fancied a bit of high-speed stuff. A bit of excitement. Lily wouldn't like it though.

The photographer took a few more shots. The bridesmaids were getting restless. Jack walked over to the little ones and squatted down between Caroline and her cousin Patsy.

'You all right, girls?'

Caroline beamed at him. Patsy didn't look so sure.

'Don't you both look pretty? Just like little princesses.' He leaned in closer, lowering his voice. 'Here, you'd better let Granddad take Auntie Kathy in first, 'cos you girls look so beautiful. If Uncle Steve sees you he'll want to marry you two instead.'

Patsy giggled. Caroline shook her head and huffed, just like her mum.

'Daddy, don't be silly. Uncle Steve can't marry two people, and he's too old for us.'

'You're right, my darlin'. Much too old for my princess.'

He kissed her on the cheek and stood up. 'You be good girls now. I'll see when you get out.'

'Aren't you coming in to see the wedding, Daddy?'

He gestured to the Jag standing gleaming at the kerb. 'I've got to keep an eye on the boss's car, darlin'.'

'I like the ribbons. Can we keep them on?'

'Girls!' Ken's gruff voice summoned them. 'Keep up.'

They rushed to join the others as inside the organ played 'Here Comes the Bride'. Jack watched his father-in-law lead the bridal party into the church. When they were out of sight he fumbled in his pocket for his fags. He lit up, taking a long drag and exhaling slowly. They'd be a good hour, so he could relax. He'd check out the gee-gees in the paper. He might even have time to put a bet on. Lily didn't need to know. If he won, he could treat her to a night up town.

Maybe that would get a smile out of her. Bugger-all else did these days.

2

'Daddy! Daddy! You have to dance with me.' Caroline tugged at her father's jacket. 'You promised.'

Jack laughed and took a quick sup of his pint before surrendering the almost empty glass to his brother-in-law.

'And you promised not to tread on my toes, Princess. D'you think I can trust her, Uncle Tony?'

Tony laughed. 'She's a right little mover, mate. I've got the bruises to prove it.' He stood on one leg and wiggled his foot.

She pouted. 'But I had to stand on your feet, Uncle Tony, because I'm not big enough and I don't know how to dance like Mummy does.'

Her uncle laughed and said something about getting another round in, then disappeared into the crowd.

'Where is Mum?' Jack asked.

'She was talking to Auntie Sheila. She's having another baby. Do you think her baby will play with our baby?'

Her father shrugged. 'Probably, when they get a bit bigger.'

'Has Beverley gone home? Auntie Sheila wanted to see baby Kerry.'

'Yeah. She got a minicab. Littl'un was getting restless.' Caroline sighed. 'Babies make a lot of fuss, don't they?'

Jack laughed and agreed.

'Me and Patsy will have to make sure they don't fight.'

The music changed from The Tremeloes to Frank Sinatra.

She tugged on Jack's sleeve again. 'Come on, Daddy! I want to dance!'

'All right, keep your hair on.'

Jack allowed her to lead him to where other guests were dancing. He picked her up and held her so that her feet dangled above his own, spinning her around the room as though she were a real princess at a ball.

* * *

Lily took a sip of her second port and lemon and watched as Jack danced with Caroline. For the first time in days she felt herself relax as the alcohol soothed her nerves.

It had been a good day. The bride had looked lovely, and little Caroline had been in her element as a bridesmaid.

She smiled as her daughter was spun higher by her father, then he caught her in his arms and bowed over her like a Latin lover in the throes of a tango. Caroline squealed and clung to him, then giggled as he straightened and put his cheek against hers, pointing their joined hands out in front of them. Jack caught Lily's eye across the room and winked. She laughed as the pair stepped purposely towards her, the big man holding the child with her legs dangling in mid-air.

'Mummy! Look at me and Daddy dancing!'

'I can see. What sort of dance is that?'

'It's grown-up dancing, like you do, 'cept I can't touch the floor 'cause Daddy's too big.'

'Or you're too short, squirt.' Jack laughed, reaching out a hand. 'D'you want to dance with us, Gorgeous?'

For a moment Lily saw the doubt in his eyes, as though he expected her to give him grief. She couldn't blame him. She'd been a cow lately. Guilt made her smile brighter as she stood and took his hand.

'I thought you'd never ask.'

Old Blue Eyes gave way to The Beatles. Caroline sang along to the chorus of 'All You Need is Love' as the three of them moved around the dance floor, with the child held between her parents.

Lily laughed, enjoying the feel of Jack's arms around her and their little girl wriggling in between the two of them. She could see the relief in his eyes, and feel it in the relaxed shift of his body as they danced. He'd always been good on his feet. That was one of the things that had attracted her to him all those years ago. He was a big bloke. Not over-tall at just under six feet, but with a broad chest and an aura of strength that gave the impression of a much larger man. In contrast to her dad and her brother Tony, who were both well over six feet and skinny as hell, Jack was built like a brick outhouse, whilst her old granddad had often described her father and Tony as *'long streaks of piss'*.

Caroline stopped singing, her attention caught elsewhere. 'Daddy, put me down please. I want to get some lemonade.'

They lowered her to the floor and she scampered off, the smooth soles of her silver shoes slipping on the dance floor. She nearly tripped over the hem of her dress. Lily gasped and felt her heart leap as the child floundered then regained her balance. She let out a long breath as Caroline made it safely to the edge of the treacherously polished floor and joined her cousins as they queued up for drinks.

'I swear that child has a death wish, the way she runs everywhere at full tilt. One of these days she's going to go flying. It's a miracle she hasn't broken something already.'

'She's all right.' Jack swung Lily back into his arms and back into the dance. 'All kids are like that at her age.'

'I suppose. Let's hope she grows out of it.'

They danced on in silence for a while, Lily trying to find that carefree feeling she'd had just a few minutes ago.

'I need another drink.' She stepped back, giving up.

'Aw, come on, Lil, I've hardly seen you all day. I'll get you one in a minute, love. Listen, they're playing our song.'

Perry Como's voice filled the room. 'Some Enchanted Evening'.

Jack pulled Lily close, singing softly against her hair. His warm breath soothed her. Memories of happy times and other dances crowded her mind, and she gave herself up to them. She was filled with longing for those uncomplicated days. She wanted to feel now what she'd felt then. Jack was still the same man she'd married; it wasn't his fault she felt so... so unsettled.

The song came to an end, and Lily clung to him. 'You all right, love?' he asked quietly.

'Yes. I'm fine.' Jack was a good man. No matter how unhappy she felt, she wouldn't hurt this man. He didn't deserve it. She needed to work it out – to come to terms with the fact that now they had another mouth to feed, and the future she'd dreamed of for her and Jack and their daughters was disappearing under the shame and anger she'd felt lately.

She smiled at him, trying to convince both of them that things would be all right. But the lead weight of disappointment made her feel like weeping again. She took a deep breath. Today was not the day to be having these thoughts.

'Where's that drink you threatened me with?' she asked.

3

On Monday morning, Leonard Warwick was sitting at his desk at the offices of Alder & Powney, Solicitors, waiting for Lily Wickham to arrive. He planned it that way, telling his wife that he needed to be in early to finish up some urgent work before the partners' meeting. Daphne had complained that she didn't have time to make his sandwiches, and why hadn't he said anything last night? He shrugged off her complaints, kissed the children and departed before she could get a loaf out of the bread bin.

He enjoyed a rush of excitement when he reached the station in time to catch the early train, but was disappointed to discover Lily had yet to arrive at the office.

Leonard had spent the weekend trying to act normally, when in reality he felt as though his whole world was spinning on a different axis from the rest of the population. Had he imagined the brief but intense look they'd shared on Friday?

All he could think about was Lily. Beautiful, fragrant Lily.

Just the thought of her made him feel quite giddy.

The building was quiet when he arrived. The old cage elevator groaned and squawked as it slowly carried Leonard up to the fourth-floor offices of Alder & Powney. He unlocked the door and turned lights on as he made his way through the reception area and typing pool to his office, still hoping that he would find Lily there.

Surely she had felt it too? Surely she would be as eager to see him?

But her office, just a few feet from his own, was dark and empty. He paused in the doorway, remembering. It had been gone five o'clock. They had been the only ones here – both reluctant, for their own reasons, to pack up and go home.

He'd gone over their conversation in his head so many times during the past forty-eight hours. It all started so innocently: a polite chat about their respective plans for the weekend – his to take the family to the cinema, hers to attend her youngest sister's wedding. Her nine-year-old daughter was to be bridesmaid. She'd smiled as she described the child's excitement.

From the first time he saw Lily Wickham, he'd been captivated. He remembered feeling crushed when he realised she was a married woman, even as he told himself that of course she would be taken. And it was just as well, because he, too, had a wife. But that realisation never dampened the thrill he felt whenever she smiled at him. Nor did it stop him wanting to touch her...

He looked at his watch. It was a quarter to nine. Lily usually arrived by half past eight. Where was she?

* * *

Lily was sitting in the crowded café around the corner from the office, cradling a cup of frothy coffee she didn't really want. She should be in the office by now, but she was hiding like some guilty kid. What the hell was she playing at?

The truth was, she was hiding from her boss. She had a feeling she was developing a crush on him. Not that he'd given her any encouragement. Not really. He was nice, polite, respectful. If he fancied her, he'd been subtle about it – not like some of the partners in the firm. Some of the older chaps thought nothing of patting her knee or copping a look at her bust while she took dictation, the dirty old sods. If she said anything, they'd act all offended. But she knew how they operated. At least she managed to stay out of reach of them most of the time. She felt sorry for the girls in the typing pool; they got the worst of it.

She'd believed Mr Warwick, the office manager, had been different. None of the girls had ever complained about him like they did the others. She'd enjoyed working with him. It didn't hurt that he was quite dishy, in a stuffy sort of way.

She'd often wished she could get Jack to go for an office job, to be more like Mr Warwick, but it just wasn't him. He'd go stark-raving mad being cooped up in an office.

She sighed as she thought about her husband this morning in his chauffeur's uniform, giving the Jag a final polish before leaving to pick up a man who would be dressed just like Mr Warwick – in a Savile Row suit and carrying a leather briefcase. Lily remembered feeling so proud of Jack when he'd got that job. Wearing a smart uniform and having a posh car he could bring home had been such a big improvement on driving a bus up and down the Mile End Road. But she couldn't help comparing him to her boss, who had people working for him and saw clients in a book-lined office. Lily realised that Jack was still a lowly driver, a servant, at his boss's beck and call. No better than a bus driver, really. Dreaming about him becoming a professional man, of them buying a nice house and getting away from their lowly council house, wasn't going to happen, so the sooner she faced that the better. Maybe what she was feeling about Mr Warwick was just a wish that Jack could've been more like him and that Beverley hadn't just ruined things.

The door opened, letting in a gust of autumn wind as a couple of office workers hurried out. Lily glanced at her watch. Five to nine. She couldn't put it off much longer. She hated being late for work, and there was a pile of accounts to get through before the end of the month. With any luck Mr Warwick would be busy too, and she could avoid seeing him. Whenever she saw him, she couldn't help wondering what it would be like being married to someone like that.

Silly thoughts. Dangerous thoughts. She had to stop it.

Well, sitting here isn't going to help.

Lily took a deep breath and let it out slowly. Leaving the now cold coffee, she slipped on her jacket and gathered up her handbag and gloves. As she left the café she heard her name being called. Maureen from the typing pool caught up with her as she reached the kerb.

'Morning, Lil. How was the wedding?'

'It was lovely, thanks. How was your weekend?'

'Oh, same old same old. I washed me smalls and Trev went to see West Ham get hammered again.'

Lily laughed. 'Jack wasn't too happy about missing the Millwall game. By all accounts it was their best result this season, and he was stuck with his in-laws.'

Maureen chattered on about Trev and her own family as they dodged the rush-hour traffic. Her story lasted until they reached the fourth floor and Lily was smiling as they walked into reception at exactly nine o'clock.

She made it to the sanctuary of her office without seeing anyone else, grateful that Maureen's mindless chatter had helped her get this far. After taking off her jacket, she hung it on the hook behind the door. Her high heels clattered over the linoleum flooring. Only the areas where clients went, like the reception area and the solicitors' offices, were deemed good enough for carpet. She put her handbag on the battered old desk and rooted through it for her keys. She unlocked the filing cabinet, deposited her bag into the bottom drawer and slammed it shut.

Lily sat at her desk, taking in the beige walls and brown wood, and the draughty old sash window, which never got cleaned. Alder & Powney's offices were too high up for window cleaners to reach with ladders. All the partners had plain net curtains up at their windows to hide the grime clinging to the outside, but a lowly cashier had to put up with it. Most of the time Lily was too busy to look out of the window, and the view across the inner void to the offices in the opposite corridor wasn't up to much anyway. But this was *her* office, the only room she'd ever had that was just for her. People knocked when they came in, except the partners of course, but even they treated her with respect. Yes, this grotty old office was everything Lily had worked for, and more. Usually it welcomed her and gave her confidence. But today, she couldn't relax.

This bloody business with Beverley and the baby was driving her mad. She felt so helpless. Her heart was breaking for everything her daughter was throwing away. Didn't she see that if the father – whoever he was – couldn't be bothered to hang around and marry her, she'll be regarded as a loose woman for the rest of her life? Bev had said she didn't care, but she hadn't hung around for Kathy and Steve's reception, had she? Lily had felt like running home as well. But her mother wouldn't have forgiven her if she'd left.

Lily had stuck it out, her head held high, but it had left her exhausted. It didn't help that Jack had been determined to have a good time. Was he really oblivious to the whispers? The sniggers behind their backs? She'd tried to keep up with him, but she didn't think she'd ever get over the shame of it.

With a sigh she opened her desk drawer and brought out her

notebook. There was lot to do today. She couldn't afford to make mistakes. She loved this job and her grotty little office. And now, more than ever, she couldn't afford to lose it.

She was sitting at her desk a few moments later, head in hands, trying to make sense of the notes she'd made on Friday, when Mr Warwick walked into the room without knocking. With a start she sat up straight as he shut the door behind him.

'Good morning, Lily.' He smiled. 'I thought I'd get a head start on everyone beating a path to your door this morning. Do you have a few minutes to go through my completions for this week?'

She pasted on a smile but couldn't meet his eyes. 'Yes, of course.'

He sat down opposite her and laid a handful of files on the desk between them. Lily turned her notebook to a fresh page and rummaged through her drawer for a pencil.

'Is everything all right, Lily?'

She glanced up, surprised. His brown eyes, dark and unfathomable, held hers. She should look away, but found she didn't want to. He was taller than Jack, leaner. His hair was just as dark, but finer, beautifully cut. Lily doubted he paid two bob to a barber down the Roman Road like Jack did. She wondered how two men with the same colouring could appear so different: one a solid, dependable bloke, the other a more refined, elegant gentleman. She nodded, then felt herself blush. When she was a girl, she'd dreamed of meeting someone like Leonard Warwick. When she met Jack, she thought she'd found her dream man – or at least, the best a girl from the East End who worked in a factory could do. If only... 'Are you sure? You looked quite pale when I came in, but you seem quite feverish now. You're not coming down with something are you?'

Lily shook her head, shaken by the concern in his expression. He was such a nice man. 'No. No, honestly, I'm fine, thank you. I...

It's been a busy weekend, that's all. I'm afraid I'm still trying to get into work mode. I'm sorry.' What on earth had made her admit that to her boss? Did she have a bleeding death wish? She took a restorative breath and made a more successful attempt at a smile. 'What can I do for you?'

He studied her for a few moments more. 'If something was bothering you, I hope you'd feel that you could talk to me about it,' he said gently. 'I hold you in high regard. You know that, don't you?'

Oh God! The last thing she'd expected was this. Or was it? 'Thank you. But everything's fine. Shall we go through your completions? I'll need to check the accounts and schedule the bank draft orders.'

For a second, she thought he was going to push it, but he gave a slight shrug and opened the first file. For the next hour, they worked steadily through the various transactions that were due to complete at the end of the week. All the time, Lily was aware of his warm gaze, but she kept her focus on the papers in front of her, trying to keep her hands from shaking. It didn't help when he occasionally pointed a well-manicured finger at a line of figures. She doubted he ever got his hands covered in motor oil like Jack did. She was always nagging him to scrub the damn stuff off.

'I think that's everything,' he said eventually. 'I'll get one of the clerks to deal with the out-of-office completions. I'll sign the bank draft orders when you've got them ready.'

'I'll have them for you later today. We won't be able to take them to the bank until the mortgage cheques arrive, of course.'

'Right.' He stood up and gathered up the files. 'Thank you, Lily. I'll leave you to get on.'

She smiled, watching him leave the room. As soon as he closed the door she let out a shaky breath. Of all the solicitors and clerks she had to deal with, Mr Warwick was the only one who made her feel like this. It was pathetic, really. A woman of her age, having a schoolgirl crush on a man – a married man, her immediate boss, in fact. He wasn't a partner yet, but he was a busy solicitor as well as the office manager.

When he'd said that he held her in high regard, Lily had almost burst into tears. Of course, he hadn't meant it as she'd have liked him to. Why would he? No, he was just being professional, looking out for his staff. Why on earth did she get the silly idea that he meant it in a more personal way? After all, he was married. And so was she. For Christ's sake, she was a grandmother! As if her life wasn't in enough of a mess, the last thing she needed was to let a silly crush get the better of her.

She shook her head and forced herself to concentrate on real life. These accounts wouldn't sort themselves out. It didn't help that she was blinking back tears when one of the partners walked into her room unannounced.

* * *

Leonard reached the sanctuary of his office and closed the door behind him, leaning back against it as he ran a shaking hand through his hair.

'Oh bugger!' His fingers were coated in Brylcreem. Why on earth did he use the foul stuff? Daphne bought it, and he dutifully combed it through his hair every morning. He hated it. But it was part of the uniform of a professional man, along with the suit and the briefcase. He'd thought Lily was impressed by the image, but maybe not. She never gave any hint that she saw him as anything more than her boss. Much as he wanted to impress her, he realised he shouldn't. He'd almost given himself away this morning, but thankfully she hadn't noticed.

He used his other hand to reach for his handkerchief and wipe the offending muck from his fingers. Now the damned hanky was covered in grease as well. If he put it back in his pocket he'd end up with a mark and a dry-cleaning bill. He went to his desk and threw it in the drawer. He'd have to remember to take it home so that Daphne could launder it.

The door opened and Gerald Irwin walked in. As an equity partner in the firm he had the right to enter Leonard's office unannounced. If ever Leonard was made a partner, he'd give Gerald a dose of his own medicine. But right now, as a lowly salaried solicitor and office manager, he had to put up with it.

Maybe in another year or two... 'Morning, Warwick. Good weekend?'

'Irwin.' He nodded. 'Not bad, thanks. You?'

'Splendid. Rugger match on Saturday – London Irish and the Harlequins. Plenty of blood! Talking of which, what have you done to upset our lovely Lily?'

For a moment Leonard felt his whole body freeze in shock. Irwin went on. 'I just popped my head in to say good morning to her and asked if she'd seen you. She was all smiles until she heard your name. So, what have you done at...' he consulted his watch, '...half past ten on a Monday morning to already be in the sainted Lily's bad books? I walked in just after you left and she looked like she'd lost five pounds and found a ten-bob note.'

'Nothing I can think of,' he said. *But if only you knew that I've been dreaming about her,* he thought.

That brought him up sharp. For years he'd been chasing a partnership. He'd worked bloody hard. He'd played the game. He'd even joined the Masons, for God's sake. If word got out that he was having improper thoughts about a member of staff – a married one at that – his career could be over. With blinding clarity he realised what a lucky escape he'd had when Lily chose to ignore his clumsy declaration this morning. He'd been so wrapped up in his infatuation that he hadn't even considered the risks.

He cleared his throat and gave a half-hearted laugh.

'Ah, yes. I'm entirely to blame.' *That much at least was the truth.* 'I'm afraid I asked Lily to work overtime tonight to get ahead of the end-of-month accounts,' he lied, 'not realising she'd promised to be home in time to take her daughter somewhere. She said she would work her lunch hour instead. I didn't realise she was upset about it. I'll go and talk to her.'

'Good idea. No point in upsetting her unnecessarily. Not only is she a good worker, she's also damned good to look at. Not like that old crone that used to run the accounts. Lily is a breath of fresh air.'

Leonard felt his insides clench even as he willed his hands not to form into fists. It seemed he wasn't the only one who'd recognised Lily's charms. Was Irwin after her as well?

'Steady on there, Irwin. People will think you have a thing for her.'

He laughed. 'Yes, I suppose they will. I'd better watch out. Don't want to be hauled up before the Law Society. Not that a dalliance with Lily wouldn't be worth it. I think I've fancied the woman since the day she started here. Delicious knees. Have you noticed the freckles there? I've never shown such an interest in clients' accounts before.'

'I really think—'

'Oh, don't go all puritan on me, Warwick. I'm not stupid. I'm a respectably married man and not about to risk my reputation for one of the staff, as tempting as she is. But a man's got to be dead from the neck down not to want to look occasionally. Got to have some dreams to keep the world from being eternally dull, haven't we, old boy?'

As the other man left the room, Leonard sank into his chair, stunned.

Is that what he'd been doing? Allowing himself to become obsessed with a member of staff because his life was dull? Had his own respectably married state become so boring that his dreams of Lily had got out of hand? Had the risks been part of the attraction?

He tried to imagine Daphne's reaction if she ever found out about how much he thought about Lily Wickham. Would she be angry? Would she cry and wail, or make him pay for his guilt with reproachful silences? Could he bear it? Losing his wife's trust? And what about the children?

He shook his head and got up, striding out into the typing pool where Sally, his secretary, was busy at her desk. 'Morning, Mr Warwick.'

'Sally.' He nodded, distracted. Lily's door was open and he could see her working. She concentrated on a ledger in front of her, running a finger from her right hand down a line of figures whilst using her left hand to key the numbers into an adding machine. She pulled the lever to subtotal the figures, her wedding and engagement rings catching the light. Another set of numbers; fingers flying, hitting the right keys with ease of long practice; again the lever was pulled, again her rings – the symbols of her husband's ownership – flash, mocking him, accusing him.

'I've finished typing the lease for the shop premises in Battersea, sir. I've just got to check it and sew it up. I'll have it on your desk in time for your eleven o'clock appointment.'

'What?' The spell was broken. He focussed on his secretary. 'Oh, good. Thank you, Sally. Have you seen my post yet?'

'Not yet. The new office junior starts today, so I expect the post will be a bit late while they show him the ropes.'

'Of course. Never mind. I've got plenty to be getting on with.'

He turned, intending to go back to his room, but unable to stop himself from walking into Lily's office instead.

'Lily.' He spoke quietly, but she immediately looked up, her fingers stilled.

'Yes, Mr Warwick?'

She looked guarded, as though not sure what to expect from him. He wanted to shut the door behind him and talk to her – really talk to her – about anything and everything. To find out what it was about this woman that made him forget everything else.

But Gerald Irwin's comments had hit home. He was respectably married. He could look but he couldn't touch. To do so was to risk too much. He shook his head.

'I'm sorry,' he said. He slipped his hands into his jacket pockets. *What the hell was he doing here?* He pulled out his fountain pen and held it up. 'Didn't mean to interrupt. Thought I'd left my pen in here earlier, but here it is.'

He returned to his office and tried to get on with his dull, respectable life.

4

On Wednesday evening, Caroline rushed into the hall as soon as Lily put her key in the door.

'Dad, Mummy's here! Can we go now, pleeeease?' she begged. 'We're going to be late and I'll be in trouble.'

Lily came through the front door as Jack came out of the kitchen with baby Kerry in his arms. She was crying. She'd clearly been crying for ages.

'What's going on?' Lily asked.

'I'm late for my dancing, because Beverley went out and left me with the baby. When Daddy came home he said we couldn't go until someone gets home to see to her. She's been sick so she can't go in the car with us in case she's sick again on Daddy's boss's leather seats.'

'Why didn't you take the Anglia?'

'We couldn't find the keys.'

Lily looked at the bunch of keys in her hand and grimaced. 'Oh! Yes. Sorry, darling. I've got them.'

Caroline was nearly in tears. Kerry wailed again. Jack tried to shush her. Lily felt her anger grow.

'Where is she?'

'Bev?' Jack shrugged. 'Dunno, love.'

'When did she go out?' Lily asked.

This time Caroline shrugged. 'As soon as I got home from school.'

Lily looked at her watch. 'Did she tell you where she was going?'

Caroline frowned. 'Mummy, I really need to go to dancing class. We're practising for a competition and Mrs Moyes will be really cross if I'm late. If I miss it she might not let me go to the competition and I really, really wanted to go now you've finished making my new dancing dress, and—'

'Caroline!'

She jumped.

'Concentrate. Answer my question. Did your sister say where she was going?'

She shook her head. 'No, Mummy, she just said she needed a break and she wouldn't be late. Then she got in a car with a boy.'

'What boy?' Lily asked.

'Don't know. I've never seen him before.'

'What sort of car?' Jack wanted to know.

'I think it was a Mini. A white one, but not like Granddad's one with all the wooden bits on it.'

Lily closed her eyes. Jack swore. Kerry cried louder. Caroline looked ready to cry too. Why did Beverley always have to ruin everything?

'Please can we go now?' Caroline asked. 'Mrs Moyes will be really cross.'

Lily could see the tears welling up in Caroline's eyes. She felt like crying too, she was so angry with Beverley. How could she do that? Just dump Kerry on a nine-year-old and go swanning off, to God knows where, with God knows who?

Jack looked grim as he soothed the fractious baby. His white shirt was open at the neck and stained with vomit and tears. She hoped he'd taken his tie off before he'd picked her up, otherwise that would need sponging clean pretty soon if it was going to survive.

'Do you want me to take her?'

'The baby, or Twinkle-Toes?' he asked.

'Well, you're in no fit state to be seen in public, so why don't I take Caroline? Or do you want a break?'

'Nah, I'm all right. No point in both of us getting puked on.'

Lily shook her head. She didn't know where he got the patience, but Jack never lost his rag like she did about this sort of thing. If Beverley walked in right now, Lily would gladly shake the girl. She walked over to her husband and laid the back of her fingers against the baby's cheek.

'She's hot.'

'Course she is, she's been bawling for a couple of hours. I reckon that's why she's been sick. I'll do her up a bottle and she'll settle down – don't worry. You go. Get her to the class. She'll never let us forget it if she misses it.'

He nodded in Caroline's direction. She had her bag with her dancing shoes in her hands and looked desperate to get out of the house.

'Come on then, love. Let's go. Are we picking up Wendy on the way?'

'No. Daddy rang her mum and she's going to meet us there. But you have to take her home afterwards. Daddy promised.' She rushed out of the door and up the garden path. 'Hurry up, Mummy. We're really late.'

* * *

Lily got back with Caroline at half past seven. Jack had fed and changed the baby, and as predicted she'd settled down. She was now sleeping peacefully in her cot upstairs, and Jack, in a clean vest, was watching *Z-Cars* and nursing a glass of beer.

Lily came in to the living room and sat down on the sofa, resting her head back against the vinyl.

'All right, love?'

She sighed. 'Yeah. Caroline's happy. Mrs Moyes has partnered her with Wendy for the competition. She was worried she'd get Hazel.'

'The fat one?'

Lily nodded. 'The dumpy, clumsy and nasty-tempered one. Getting paired with her best friend, who's a much better dancer than Hazel, has made our little girl happy as Larry. She reckons they'll be a cert for a medal.'

Jack laughed. 'Never expected one of our kids to take up Old Tyme dancing.'

'No, you wanted a footballer.'

It was true. His girls were his world, but he couldn't deny he'd have loved a son too.

'Yeah, well. Even me brother Fred can't claim to have a decent footballer, even with all them boys of his.'

'Is Beverley home yet?'

'Course not. She won't show her face until she thinks we're in bed.'

Lily let out a long breath. She looked tired.

'You hungry?' he asked. 'D'you fancy a sandwich?'

'For God's sake, Jack! Your teenaged daughter has buggered off with some boy in a car, leaving her baby with a nine-year-old, and you think a bloody sandwich will make me feel better?'

Jack held up his hands in surrender. 'All right, love, keep your hair on. You ain't had any tea. I just thought you'd want something to eat.'

'Well, I don't.'

'Want a drink?' he asked. 'A port and lemon might calm you down. The beer's taken the edge off it for me.'

'No.'

He shrugged and took a sip of his beer. He couldn't be doing with this. The *Z-Cars* music blared out of the telly. He'd missed the ending. Oh well, the coppers always got their man in the end, so it didn't matter.

'Can't you see how serious this is?' Lily wouldn't let it go.

'What d'you want me to do?'

'You could go out and look for her, for a start.'

'Be reasonable, Lil. If they're in a car they could've gone anywhere from the West End to Southend Pier.'

'Oh, I like that, calling me unreasonable. Were you reasonable when you took her side and said she could she keep the baby? A fine mother she's turning out to be. She didn't care what happened to that child today, just so long as she could go out with some Herbert who probably thinks she's a dead cert to open her legs, seeing as how she's already got one fatherless kid!'

Christ, here we go.

'That "fatherless kid" is our granddaughter,' he said, his voice dangerously low. 'I'm not letting some stranger take her away.'

'Why not? If she'd been adopted you can bet she'd never have been dumped on a little kid just so her mother can go out on the town. She doesn't deserve that. We don't deserve that. If we don't do something about Bev, Jack, she'll end up pregnant again.'

'Don't be daft! She's learned her lesson.'

'Has she? Has she really? So where is she? And if she gets away with it this time, how many more times are we going to come home to the same thing? You've got to put your foot down, Jack.'

He hated it when she got like this. As far as she was concerned, it was all his fault. Lily couldn't see that there was no way he could have let Kerry be adopted. She was family. She was beautiful. Even if Beverley had wanted to give her up, he would've fought it. Why didn't Lily understand?

'She'll come round,' he said. 'She's just kicking over. All young girls want to go out and have fun. She's been good with the baby up to now.'

'Don't give me that. You get up every bloody night to that baby while she ignores it. She's a selfish little cow.'

'She's with her all day.'

'And you're out at work. You need a good night's sleep.'

'Lily—'

'No, Jack, you've got to stop defending her. She's got to take responsibility. It's not fair on anyone else – you, me, Caroline. That child was in a terrible state on the way to dancing. Why should she have to pay for Beverley's selfishness?'

Oh no! Lily obviously knew the thought of his little Caroline getting upset would get to him. It was bad enough that Lily was so worked up about everything, but Caroline too... He shook his head. *Why the bloody hell can't life be simple?*

'I don't know, love. I just want some peace and quiet for a change. We'll have a talk with Bev when she gets home. I don't want any of my girls being upset.'

'Well, you should have thought about that before you lumbered us with her little bastard.'

Jack stood up, his breathing erratic, his fist clenched. 'That's enough, Lily. Don't you ever call Kerry that again, d'you hear?'

She froze, clearly recognising that she'd gone too far. 'All right, I won't,' she said, her voice shaking. 'But I won't put up with Beverley acting up like this, Jack. I won't. It's tearing this family apart and I won't have it.' She got up. 'I'm going to bed.'

'Right. You do that.'

As she left the room, Jack slumped back into his chair. The news was just finishing. He hadn't even noticed that the telly was still on. They were saying something about that oil tanker that ran aground a few months back. He knew how it felt. In bits, and bloody messy.

* * *

Lily crept in to check on the baby before she got ready for bed. Kerry was sleeping soundly. The golden curls framing her face made her look like one of the little cherubs on her mother-in-law's brass clock. Lily reached out and stroked the baby's soft cheek.

Jack didn't understand. He thought he was the only one who loved this baby. But she did too. So much.

She sniffed as she felt tears build up in her throat.

This sweet, innocent child deserved so much better than a mother like Beverley – still a child herself, no matter what she thought. Her behaviour today only proved what Lily had said all along. She should have given Kerry up. By keeping her, she was ruining both their lives. And Lily's and Jack's too.

Everything Lily had worked for had been within reach. They both had decent jobs. Beverley had left school and started training to be a hairdresser, before the baby arrived and put paid to all that. Caroline was doing well at school, going to dancing classes, Brownies, and swimming club. Lily and Jack had even talked about buying a house instead of renting from the council.

But now they had another mouth to feed, a teenager who only wanted to be a mother when it suited her; and the shame of having an illegitimate child in the family. Instead of buying a nice house and in a nice area, they'd ended up exchanging one grotty council place for another, and poor Caroline had been sent off to a new school, away from her friends.

The tears Lily had been fighting spilled down her cheeks. She stood back, frightened they'd drip on the baby and wake her up. She rubbed a hand over her face, smudging her make-up and wiping the moisture from her skin.

She was so tired.

She left the room and walked slowly down the hall to the bathroom, where she locked herself in and finally allowed herself to cry.

5

'...Two and nine, twenty-nine.'

'House!'

A collective groan rose around the crowded room at the Bryant & May Social Club as a blousy woman with peroxide hair jumped to her feet and waved her bingo ticket in the air. One of the floor-walkers checked the winning numbers, and the caller declared that the next game would start after a ten-minute break.

Lily and her sister-in-law Maggie both threw down their marking pens in disgust.

'I don't know about you, Maggie, but I'm beginning to think someone's put the mockers on us. We haven't had a win here for weeks.'

'Yeah, it's about time our luck changed.' She stood up. 'Want a drink?'

'I'll get it,' Lily offered, knowing Maggie didn't have much money. With five kids to feed and clothe, Maggie was always struggling. Her old man – Jack's brother, Fred – earned good money, but with a big family it didn't go far.

'Don't be daft,' her friend said. 'I'm up now, and you paid for the tickets, so it's my round.'

Lily subsided into her chair and looked around the room. She and Maggie had been coming here for donkeys' years. It had been their escape as teenagers, a fun night out, their chance to daydream – winning a full house meant extra money to spend on clothes and make-up. Then after Maggie met Jack's brother Fred at Lily's wedding, the friends had used any winnings that came their way for little extras for their marital homes and their kids.

Maggie had been her best friend for as long as she could remember, and had been her sister-in-law for a good few years now as well. They had grown up in houses on the same street, they'd gone to school together, worked alongside each other as machinists, and married the two youngest Wickham brothers. Lily and Maggie had always been there for each other, sharing everything that happened in their lives. The only time they'd been separated had been when they'd been evacuated during the war.

But recently, things had changed. When Kerry was born, and Lily had poured out her shock and hurt to her friend, Maggie and Fred had offered to take the baby. Their youngest, a little girl after four boys, had been just a year old.

'She'll have a sister to play with, and brothers to look out for her,' Maggie had said. 'And you'll be her aunt. Beverley can get on with her life knowing how her baby's getting on, and she'll be her cousin.'

It all sounded so reasonable, but Lily had been reluctant. She hadn't been able to say why, but she knew it would be a disaster. Jack might have been persuaded – his brother Fred was the only person he'd allow to take the baby – but Beverley had kicked up and refused point-blank. In the end it had left everyone feeling awkward, and for a while things were a bit difficult between the brothers and their wives.

On the surface they were okay again, and right now Lily really needed someone to talk to. It hurt to know that, for the first time in her life, she couldn't rely on her best friend. How could she tell Maggie that she felt more and more unhappy at home, that she and Jack seemed to be getting more like strangers to each other, and every time she let herself think about Leonard Warwick she got as giddy as a schoolgirl? How just seeing him every day at work was driving her round the bend? How she couldn't help comparing him to Jack and finding her husband wanting? What was she to do?

She'd been strong so far, keeping her distance and trying her best to act as if she didn't feel anything. It was bloody hard though. He was always so nice to her. She'd even thought about changing jobs, but how could she explain that to Jack when he knew she loved it at Alder & Powney?

She really needed to confide in someone right now. But they weren't teenagers any more, and a wife's loyalty was to her husband rather than her oldest friend. Lily could guarantee that Maggie would tell Fred, and Fred would be straight round to tell Jack.

Oh Christ, what a mess!

'Here you go, Lil. I got you a port and lemon.'

Lily smiled and accepted the drink, forcing her errant thoughts to the back of her mind. She thought for a moment that Maggie might comment on her preoccupation, but as the other woman took a sip of her own drink something occurred to Lily and she blinked in surprise.

'You drinking lemonade?'

Maggie pulled a wry face. 'Yeah, I'm thirsty.'

'Don't give me that. Come to think of it, you haven't smoked a fag tonight either. The only time you drink that stuff or stop smoking is when... Oh, Maggie! Again?'

Maggie laughed. 'It took you long enough to work it out. You're slipping.'

Lily shook her head. 'When's this one due?'

'I reckon in six months.'

Lily wondered how she'd missed the signs for three whole months. She supposed it was hardly surprising; she'd been so wrapped up in her own problems lately.

'I thought you said Samantha was your last one?'

'I thought she was.' She shrugged. 'But you know how it is.'

Lily was silent for a moment, trying to absorb the news. They were the same age, but now she was a grandmother and Maggie was pregnant again.

'Mags, this isn't anything to do with Beverley keeping Kerry, is it?' she asked quietly.

Her friend took another sip of her drink, avoiding Lily's eyes. 'I dunno. Maybe. Or maybe I just thought Sammy needed a sister to help her stand up to all her big brothers.'

'And what if this one's another boy?'

Maggie rolled her eyes. 'Oh Christ, you know how to cheer a girl up, don't you?'

* * *

Jack pulled his Millwall scarf tighter around his neck as he turned to his brother.

'It's bleedin' brass monkey weather, and we're two-nil down. Tell me again why we support this useless team?'

Fred huddled into his jacket and grunted. 'It ain't half-time yet. The boys'll turn it round.'

'Don't make me laugh! We've already missed a penalty, and if the ref weren't blind as a bat Gilchrist would have been sent off in the first five minutes. This lot don't deserve to win.

We might as well go to the pub now, before the pitch invasion.'

He pointed to the younger element of the crowd below them on the terraces who were already jeering their own team. Beer bottles and toilet rolls were being thrown at any Millwall player who was stupid enough to get within range.

Before Fred could argue, the other side got control of the ball and their star player legged it down the wing to deliver another goal into the back of the net.

'Oh, Jesus! Where the hell is our defence? Playing sodding Ludo?' Jack shouted, as the visiting fans erupted in cheers.

Fred threw his hands up in disgust. 'Come on, let's get a beer. This is pathetic.'

The brothers made their way out of the grounds, pulling off their scarves and stuffing them in their pockets as they walked down the road to Fred's car. They weren't the only ones. A steady flow of men and boys wearing blue and white hats and scarves were walking away, all looking pissed off.

'Ain't no point staying round here,' said Fred. 'There'll be a riot before full-time. Let's head over to The Guildford.'

The Guildford in Poplar was the whole family's regular drinking hole. It wasn't unusual for Mum, Dad, all four Wickham brothers and their wives, plus sister Betty and her other half, to be found in the public bar. Their kids would sit outside on the pavement, or if the weather wasn't too special, crammed into someone's car, drinking pop out of a bottle and eating crisps. Every now and then a littl'un would stick their head around the door to tell tales on one of their brothers or sisters, or to ask for another packet of crisps, but otherwise the bar was a sanctuary for the grown-ups.

Jack and Fred greeted a few locals and retreated to a corner table with their beers to carry on moaning about Millwall's diabolical performance.

As Fred ranted on about the state of the defence and the lack of attack, Jack nodded a couple of times and switched off. He'd heard it all before.

He savoured his pint and wondered whether Lily was having a peaceful time at home with the girls. After Bev had done a runner the other week leaving Caroline with the baby, Lily had gone ballistic. When the girl had finally crept in at three in the morning, mascara smudged and reeking of smoke and gin, there'd been an almighty row.

She might have got away with it if she'd been quiet, but she'd tripped over the pram in the passage and woken everyone up. He'd had to step in and do a bit of shouting himself to get Lily and Bev to shut up. By then both Kerry and Caroline were bawling their heads off. Christ, it was a bloody mess!

There'd been an armed truce since then, for the sake of the littl'uns. Bev had agreed to be more responsible, and Lily had agreed to back off and give the girl a chance, but Jack knew that a wrong look or a snide word would set them off again. Give 'em their due, they were both trying. But it was like living in a war zone, waiting for the next shot to be fired.

Lily didn't even seem to like going to work any more. She used to come home full of it – this partner said this; that client had done that; why didn't they buy a house instead of renting from the council? If they just saved a bit, her boss could fix it for them to get a mortgage, no problem. But for a few weeks now she'd been quiet about all that. She'd been quiet about everything really, except that Maggie was expecting again. Number six.

Fred was winding down. Jack finished his pint and waved it at Arthur behind the bar. On a quiet night like this, he'd send the barmaid over with another round for them in a minute. Fred looked at his watch.

'Better make this a quick one,' he said. 'We're working down

Avonmouth Docks tomorrow. It's Harry's turn to drive, so he'll be knocking on the door at five.'

'I'm surprised he's still got his licence, dozy sod. Didn't he crash into a copper's car?'

Fred laughed. 'Yeah, and he had a load of dodgy stuff in the boot straight off a boat from India.'

One of the perks of being a ship's rigger was that you could half-inch some of the cargo before it was off-loaded. Fred was always coming home with crates of bananas, sacks of tea; you name it, and he and his mates would manage to get some off the boat before they'd finished organising the derricks for the dockers to unload.

'How'd he get away with it?'

'Gave 'em some sob story about rushing home because his sainted mother was on her deathbed.'

Their pints arrived and Jack handed over a note. By the time the barmaid had brought back his change they'd knocked them back and were getting to their feet.

'How's Maggie?' he asked as he pulled on his jacket. 'I meant to ask earlier. Lily says she's expecting again. Ain't it about time you tied a knot in it, mate?'

Fred shrugged. 'One more won't make no difference. Maggie wants another girl. She's worried Sammy's getting spoilt. The boys treat her like a bleedin' doll. If we say no to her, they just give her what she wants. Bloody little sods.'

'Another girl ain't going to solve your problems.' Jack laughed. 'Trust me, the more women in the house, the more trouble.'

'You'd know all about that, bruv,' Fred replied.

'Too right, mate. Listen and learn.'

6

A few days later, Lily had been at her desk for half an hour when she heard the outer office door open. She glanced up from the ledger in front of her and checked her watch. It was still only a quarter past eight. Jack had dropped her off this morning on his way to pick up a visiting VIP from a hotel up west. It was a nice change from trudging through the cold to the station and squeezing onto an overcrowded train.

It was still dark outside, but she hadn't bothered to turn on more than her desk light. Now someone was turning on the main lights as they moved into the main office, waking the place up.

She sighed. She'd been hoping to enjoy the peace and quiet of the place by herself a bit longer.

When Leonard Warwick walked past her open door, her heart missed a beat.

* * *

Leonard didn't notice that Lily's door was open as he made his way wearily to his office. Only her soft, 'Good morning, sir,' alerted him to her presence.

He stopped and walked back to her open door. She was bathed in the soft glow of her desk light.

'Lily, you're in early. Is everything all right?'

'Yes. My husband was passing here on his way to work this morning, so he gave me a lift.'

'Ah. That explains it. He's a driver, isn't he?'

'A chauffeur,' she corrected him. 'For one of the directors of Calico International.'

Leonard nodded. The last thing he wanted to hear about was Lily's husband, but nor did he want this conversation to end. 'So where's your little girl when you both go to work so early on a school day?'

Lily fiddled with her pen, a simple ballpoint. She had lovely hands – soft skin, well-kept nails with clear polish.

'My elder daughter is taking her to school for me.'

Of course, the wayward teenager who had made Lily a grand-mother. It wasn't something she talked about much at work, but as her boss he'd had to be told when she needed to take time off when the girl gave birth. Leonard wondered about the baby, but knew better than to ask. It wasn't a topic to raise if he wanted to have a conversation with Lily.

'Good. Good.' *Now what? Think of something to say, man!* He knew he was playing with fire, but this was the first time he and Lily had been alone together, and he was damned if he was going to just walk away.

She saved him the bother. 'You're making an early start as well,' she said.

* * *

As soon as she said it, Lily realised she'd been stupid. Now he'd stay and talk to her. She'd managed to avoid speaking to him alone for weeks now, and just when he might have walked away she'd blurted out the first thing she could think of. *For God's sake, just because I want to talk to him, doesn't mean I should!*

'Yes, my wife's mother had a fall at the weekend and needs looking after. I took Daphne and the children there yesterday.'

'I'm sorry to hear that. Anything broken?'

'Her wrist, so she can't do much for herself, and Daphne must take care of her. It means the children will miss a few days of school, but it can't be helped. We did think about bringing her over to stay with us, but it wouldn't be practical.'

'I expect they'll enjoy the holiday,' she said.

It made her feel odd, talking about their families. It reminded her that neither of them were free. She must stop having silly ideas about this man. They both had responsibilities.

He smiled. Lily thought he looked a little tired.

'Yes, I suppose they will. As I was on my own at home, I thought I might as well come in early. I can get so much more done when the office is quiet.'

'Of course. I find that too. Once the telephone starts ringing and clients start coming in, it can be bedlam.'

'Mmm. Quite.'

Mmm... I love it when he does that. His voice is so deep.

Mmm... He sounds like a big cat purring.

The thought of a big, lean jungle cat – a Jaguar – brought her up sharp. Jack's smiling face swam before her. She gulped. 'Well, I hope your mother-in-law gets better soon.'

'I'm sure she will. She's an independent old girl.'

'I suppose I'm lucky. My youngest sister and her husband live with my parents, and one of Jack's brothers lives next door to my in-laws. There's always someone around to see to them if need be.'

'You're very fortunate, Lily. My wife's an only child, so the whole burden always falls on her.'

Lily stopped herself from asking whether he was an only child too. That would be too familiar. The trouble was, she liked asking people things like that, getting to know about their families and their lives. But you didn't do that with the boss. This conversation had gone far enough as it was. She needed to keep things professional. He was too dangerous for her peace of mind. They were work colleagues, nothing more. He was the boss, out of her league.

He consulted his watch. 'Well, I must get on.'

'Yes, of course. Me too.'

Their eyes met for a brief moment and she felt herself getting warm. Then he was gone.

7

At home in Wimbledon on Tuesday evening, Leonard discovered that mashing potatoes was tedious. For a good ten minutes he had been pounding, and there were still lumps in the damned mess. Should he put some more butter in? He thought that Daphne sometimes put something else in – milk, perhaps? He tipped in a splash and carried on. Had he cooked them enough? He'd checked them with a fork and thought they were soft, but under the masher they seemed quite hard. He'd probably made too much as well. It looked like an awful lot.

Fat spat noisily from the frying pan on the stove, splashing his arm and shirt sleeve.

'Hell's bells!'

He dropped the masher into the saucepan and reached across to turn off the gas. A sausage exploded out of its skin, spraying more hot fat over his hand.

Swearing, he pushed the frying pan to the back of the stove, then strode to the sink. It was full of dirty dishes, but he managed to get his hand under the cold tap and turn it on, the cool water bringing instant relief to his stinging skin.

Leonard let out a gusty sigh as he leaned against the counter, waiting for his skin to become numb. He looked down at the pile of crockery he'd tipped into the sink and realised that if he wanted to eat this meal he'd have to wash a plate.

At first, he'd relished the quiet, and the novelty of having the house to himself. Daphne had left a shepherd's pie in the fridge, which he'd polished off on Sunday evening, and he'd had lunch with a client yesterday, so he'd made do with a sandwich when he'd got home. But tonight he'd happily set about making bangers and mash, confident it would be a simple task. Now he was faced with lumpy mash and sausages that were burnt on one side and pink on the other. And judging by the red blotches on his hand, he could be scarred for life. His admiration for his wife's cooking skills went up. He missed her and the children. It was just too bloody quiet.

Eventually he was able to sit down to eat. The meal looked unappetising, but he was hungry. Maybe he should make some gravy to go with it? He had no idea how. Or open a tin of peas? No. He couldn't be bothered.

He ate slowly, chewing on lumps of undercooked potato, miserably aware that without Daphne he would probably starve within a week. Tomorrow he'd stop for a fish supper on the way home, and on Thursday he'd see if someone from the Lodge would feed him before the Masonic meeting.

She was due home by the weekend, thank God. They were going out on Friday evening and would enjoy dinner in a restaurant before the ballet. He hoped she'd remembered to organise a babysitter. He'd take the children out on Saturday, maybe to the zoo, or a museum, to give Daphne a break. Her mother wasn't the easiest of people, even when she wasn't in pain. As miserable as it was at home without his wife and children, Leonard was grateful he hadn't had to decamp to his mother-in-law's with them.

Leonard swallowed a particularly gristly piece of sausage. He was a terrible cook, but at least he could do a decent job with the washing up. He'd better get on and do it before Daphne came home. But maybe not tonight. He was contemplating opening a bottle of claret when the telephone rang. Putting down his knife and fork with relief, he got up and went out into the hall to answer it.

'Leonard, it's me.'

'Daphne, darling, how are you? And the children?'

'They're having a lovely time. I went up into the attic and dragged down my old doll's house for Susan, and Peter brought his Lego set with him, so they've both been keeping themselves occupied.'

'Good, good. Are they there? Can I talk to them?'

'Sorry, dear, they're in the bath. Shall I get them to call you later?'

Leonard was surprised at how disappointed he felt. He'd looked forward to speaking to them. He enjoyed their unquestioning adoration, and missed them more than he'd expected to.

'All right. And what about you?'

'I'm fine, but Mummy's not so good.'

'Why? What's the problem?'

'She had another X-ray this afternoon, and the doctor's concerned that the bones aren't set as well as expected. He also suspects she's got some sort of calcium deficiency, which means it will take longer to heal. Apparently it's quite common amongst women over sixty.'

'Oh dear.'

'Mmm, she's still in a lot of pain. It looks like she'll need to keep the plaster on for a lot longer than we anticipated.'

'But she'll be getting used to that, I expect. She's learning to manage with it, isn't she?'

Daphne was silent for a moment. Leonard felt his heart sink.

'Actually, she's not managing very well at all, Leonard. I'm having to help her wash and dress, and she can't cook for herself one-handed.'

He could sympathise about the cooking. The remains of his meal lay on the table through the kitchen door, mocking him.

'Is she trying to help herself, Daphne? I know she's your mother, but—'

'Of course she is, darling. If you were here, you'd see. Poor Mummy is in agony.' She lowered her voice. 'I even have to help her go to the toilet. She hates that.'

I can imagine. He felt a moment's sympathy for his dignified mother-in-law.

'If it's as bad as that, she should be back in hospital or in a convalescent home. You can't stay there forever. The children need to get back to school, and, well, let's face it, you have your own home to run.'

She sighed. 'I know it's difficult for you, being on your own. Have you been keeping everything tidy?'

He frowned, turning away from the chaos in the kitchen to stare into the lounge. There was an empty whisky glass on the coffee table, next to an accumulation of newspapers. A lone cushion lay on the carpet, looking as though it had been ejected by its fellows on the sofa. They were lying in abandoned disarray, like drunks after a party.

'Of course. I'm perfectly capable of looking after myself, Daphne. But that's not the point. I miss you and the children, and I'm worried that your mother is expecting too much of you. You can't be at her beck and call indefinitely.'

'But what can I do? I can't abandon her, Leonard, and it's selfish of you to ask.'

Selfish? How the hell did I become the villain in this piece? 'I'm not suggesting for one moment that your mother is left to fend for herself. I'm merely pointing out that if she's in pain and incapable of looking after herself, she should be in hospital.'

'But you know how she hates hospitals, after Daddy—'

'I know, and it's admirable that you want to care for her, my darling, but you have to think about the children.' *And me.* 'Peter has his eleven-plus coming up, and if he misses any more schooling now it could affect his chances of getting into grammar school. Surely your mother wouldn't want to ruin her grandson's future?' *Even that old witch wouldn't be so selfish, would she?*

'Can't you take some time off work?'

'What on earth for?'

'You could have the children at home and they could go back to school. It might help Mummy's recovery if I can give her some more attention.'

'That's out of the question. You know how hard I'm working for a partnership, Daphne. If I just waltz in and ask for indefinite leave to take my children to school... Well, I can kiss goodbye to any chance of advancement. I'd be lucky to keep my job, and then where would we be?'

'I'm sorry, I just thought...' Daphne sounded defeated. Leonard felt guilty. The poor love must be exhausted. But there was not a hope in hell he would even consider doing as she asked. He wasn't a nanny, for God's sake!

'It's just not going to be practical. I can't afford to take time off if we're going to get anywhere, Daphne. I wish I could, but there's not a hope. Look, why don't we talk about it when I see you on Friday night?'

'Friday night? Are you coming here?'

'No, we're going out. Don't you remember? The ballet?'

'But Leonard, I can't! What about—?'

'Surely you can get someone – a neighbour, or one of your

mother's friends – to come in and sit with the old girl and the children? We've been looking forward to this for months.'

'I know, but, well, Leonard, I'm just not feeling up to it. I'm up and down all night with Mummy; and what with keeping the children busy, and running the house... And it's not likely to be any better by Friday. Couldn't we change the tickets and go in a week or two?'

'I'm sure we could return the tickets, but I very much doubt if we'll get any more. The season is booked solid, and there's bound to be a long waiting list for returns. Are you sure you can't get away? I've booked dinner. It would be just the two of us. We haven't had a night out together like this in such a long time.'

'Oh dear.' She sounded close to tears. 'I'm sorry, Leonard. I know you're being neglected, my love. But I really don't feel I can. Couldn't you go with someone else? One of your Masonic friends? Or what about someone from work?'

'I want to go with you, my wife,' he said gently.

'I know, and if it weren't for Mummy, I'd love to go. But I can't. Please understand, Leonard. It's just too much on top of everything else. But you must go. There must be someone who'll step in.'

'Well, I can't think of anyone.'

'What about Gerald Irwin?'

'He's tone-deaf and hates classical music.'

'Oh. Well, what about—?'

'I'll have a think. But it won't be the same.'

'Oh, Leonard. I'm so sorry. I'm sure you'll have a nice time without me.'

'I was rather hoping for a nice time *with* you,' he sighed. 'I miss you. But don't worry about it. I understand. I'll come over on Saturday, shall I?'

'Oh, that would be lovely. Stay for the weekend.'

He brightened at the thought of waking up next to her warm

body. Sleeping alone was hell. A spot of home cooking wouldn't go amiss either.

'Good idea.'

'So, how has your week been so far? Are you really coping without me?'

He glanced down at his hand. The redness had faded, so he wouldn't be bearing any battle scars.

'Yes, of course. I am capable of looking after myself.'

'Well bring your laundry with you on Saturday. I'll use Mummy's automatic. You'll probably flood the kitchen if you try to use the twin-tub.'

'I'm sure I wouldn't, but I'll take you up on that.' He laughed. 'I haven't got around to trying because I've been working late. It's hellishly busy at work. I don't know how we'd have coped without Mrs Wickham's organisational skills.'

'Who's she?'

'Our cashier. I'm sure I've mentioned her before.'

'Oh yes! Isn't she the grandmother?'

Leonard flinched. He'd mentioned Lily's name months ago, and Daphne had immediately wanted to know more about her. Aware of his attraction to her, he'd not lied exactly, but had emphasised the fact that Lily had a new granddaughter. Daphne had therefore assumed that Lily was an older woman. In fact, she was a year or two younger than Daphne.

'That's right. Jolly good at her job. I wish I could give her a pay rise. If we don't look after her, she might move to another firm.'

'Well then, there's your solution.'

'To what?'

'To what to do with my ticket for Friday's performance, of course. You might not be able to raise her salary, but you could take her to the ballet to show your appreciation. I'm sure she'd be thrilled! It would be a lovely gesture, darling. She'll think you're the best boss in the world!'

'I don't think—'

'Oh, do ask her. It would make me feel so much better if you were still able to go. I know you love it more than I do anyway. And we can always have another night out as soon as Mummy's better.'

Leonard was stunned. His wife was encouraging him to take Lily out in her place. Even though Daphne thought Lily was an older woman and no threat, he knew that she was quite the opposite on both counts. He was horrified at the idea of their being thrown together by his wife, albeit unintentionally. But at the same time, he felt his blood race. *Lily, alone with him; having dinner, sitting close together in the dark whilst the greatest love story ever told unfolded before them.*

'I don't know if she likes that sort of thing,' he said, weakening.

'Well, there's only one way to find out. Ask her.'

8

The next afternoon, Lily closed the last ledger and sighed. All done. The partners had a busy day on Friday with the completion of several property contracts. Lily had checked every account and done all the paperwork to make sure that the bank drafts could be drawn up tomorrow. Some of the amounts involved made her jaw drop. For a girl from the East End, it was like playing with Monopoly money.

Every time she did this, it was like rubbing salt in a wound. Her own silly dream of buying a nice semi in South London had flown out of the window when Bev had brought home little Kerry.

Unwilling to think about it, Lily leaned her elbows on the desk and massaged her temples with her fingers. Her glasses slid down her nose and she plucked them off and laid them on the desk before resuming the soothing movements. Her headache eased and she began to relax.

The phone at her side jangled, making her jump. Before it could ring again she picked up the receiver.

'Lily, it's your little girl on the line,' the telephonist said. 'Shall I put her through?' She always checked in case one of the bosses was around.

'Yes please, Joan.'

A click. 'You're through now.' Another click as Joan moved on to the next call.

'Mummy?'

'Hello, love. Everything all right?'

'Yes. I just got home.'

'Is Beverley in?'

'No. I used my key. She left a note.'

'What does it say?'

'Hang on a minute.' There was a bang, making Lily wince, as Caroline dropped the phone receiver on the table; footsteps running away and then back again, and a rustle of paper before she picked up again. 'Are you still there, Mummy?'

'I'm still here. Now, what does the note say?'

'Um... it's very untidy... I think it says, um, "*Gone to Angie's. Back for tea.*"'

Lily looked at her wristwatch. It was almost five o'clock. If she didn't get a move on, she'd miss her train and there'd be no tea for them to get back for.

'All right. I'm leaving the office in a minute. Will you be all right on your own a bit longer? Daddy should be home soon.'

'Yes. I've been playing next door, helping Mrs Simpkins weed her garden.'

Lily smiled. Thank God for their elderly neighbours. They treated Caroline like a granddaughter and kept an eye out for her. The press had been making a lot of fuss about 'latch-key kids' recently, making Lily feel guilty about not being there when Caroline got home from school. Mr and Mrs Simpkins made her feel a bit better about her decision to go out to work.

'Right then. You take care, and I'll see you soon.'

'Okay, Mummy. Love you.'

'I love you too.' She smiled. 'Now hang up or I'll miss my train!'

She put the phone down and looked up to see Leonard standing in her office doorway. As always, her breath caught in her throat at the sight of him.

She fumbled for her glasses, sliding them back on, hoping they would shield her reaction from him. His suit and hair were as immaculate as usual; but at this time of day his lean face looked different, more rugged, as it revealed a dark five-o'clock shadow. Lily wondered briefly what he'd look like waking up in the morning, before she blinked her thoughts away and took a deep breath.

'Mr Warwick. I'm sorry, I didn't realise you were there.' He shook his head almost as though he'd read her thoughts, waving away her apology. 'Not at all, Lily. I just got here.'

'What can I do for you?'

'I wanted to check that you were all set for Friday's completions.'

Lily relaxed, confident that she'd done all she needed to. 'Yes. It's all ready. We're just waiting for a couple of mortgage cheques, which should arrive in the morning.'

'Good. Well done. I was sure you'd have everything under control.'

She smiled at him, pleased that he had faith in her. Sometimes she found it hard to have faith in herself – to separate the seamstress with no qualifications that she'd been from the new career woman she'd become. When her boss praised her, even after all these months, she still felt herself glow with pleasure and pride.

'Thank you.'

'Are you heading off now?'

'Yes, if that's all right? It's five o'clock.'

'Of course, Lily.' He smiled. 'I'm not a slave driver. You go along. I'll see you tomorrow. Have a good evening.'

'I will, thank you.'

She slid the ledger she'd been working on into her desk drawer and locked it. Leonard stayed where he was.

She stood up and moved to the filing cabinet. Retrieving her handbag from the bottom drawer, Lily was sure Leonard's eyes were on her backside as she bent over, but when she straightened and turned to face him he was looking at the spider plant in a lurid pink and green pot on top of the filing cabinet.

'That's quite a pot,' he said, smiling.

'Yes, my youngest daughter gave it to me for Christmas. She made it at school.'

'How sweet.'

She laughed. 'It's pretty awful, isn't it? She's not the most artistic child, I'm afraid. She got a prize for reading her first year at school, but has never got the hang of making things. Now if she was writing a description of a flower pot, she'd be much better at it.'

He laughed too. Lily smiled, enjoying the moment of shared understanding, before she started to feel awkward again.

She realised she would have to get him to move – her coat was hanging on a hook on the back of her door. Her smile faded a bit. She hoped he'd just go. Being in the same room without a desk between them was... difficult.

Lily stood in front of him, waiting. 'Excuse me,' she said. 'I need to get my coat.'

For a moment he looked blank.

'It's behind there,' she explained, raising a hand to point at the open door.

'Oh. I'm sorry. I was miles away,' he said, moving out of her way.

She retrieved her coat and struggled into it, self-consciousness making her uncoordinated. At last the coat was on, buttons fastened. Lily ran nervous fingers over the fur collar, for once not taking sensual pleasure from its softness.

She picked up her bag and finally looked him in the eye. 'Well, I must be off. Have a good evening, Mr Warwick.'

'Are you heading for Liverpool Street?'

She hesitated. 'No, Moorgate. I need the Northern Line to get to London Bridge.'

'Of course. You're out at Eltham, aren't you?'

'Yes.' *And I'll never get there if you keep talking to me. I want to leave, but I can't. I want to stay, but I shouldn't.*

Just listening to his voice gave her the collywobbles. Walking away, halfway through a conversation she never expected to have, wasn't possible.

He glanced at his watch. 'I'm sorry, I just wanted a quick word, but I won't keep you. Your family will be waiting for you.'

Lily felt the familiar guilt heat her cheeks. *Yes. Train, family, cooking, duty.*

'If you need me to work—'

'No. It wasn't work I wanted to talk to you about. It was something my wife suggested.'

'Oh?'

'She's still at her mother's, you see. My mother-in-law's wrist is taking longer to heal than expected,' he explained. 'And we had, or rather, have, tickets for the ballet on Friday night.'

Lily blinked. 'Do you want me to look after your mother-in-law?' she asked.

Leonard laughed. 'Good Lord, no! It's incredibly kind of you to suggest it, but I wouldn't dream of imposing that on you. No, Lily, my wife wondered if you might like to go.'

'Me?'

He nodded. 'As a thank-you for all your hard work. I should have thought of it myself, of course, but, well, I'm just a man.' He smiled and shrugged. 'But I agree with her – it's a good idea. You always work jolly hard. The partners have had a tremendously busy month and you've kept up with all their transactions. Just look at how many completions you've prepared for this week. And you do it with no fuss at all.'

Lily wasn't sure how she felt about Leonard discussing her with his wife, but she glowed with pleasure at his praise.

'So, would you like the tickets? It's Prokofiev's *Romeo and Juliet*. I'm told it's an excellent production.'

'I'd love to, but...' She sighed. Ever since Margot Fonteyn and Rudolf Nureyev had first played the doomed lovers three years ago, she'd been wishing she could see it. 'I won't get my husband within a mile of a ballet. My mother would come, but her brother is visiting from Canada and I think they've already got something on. It's a bit of a late night for my daughter Caroline.'

'Mmm. And you might find it a rush getting home to collect her and back into town for the first act.'

Lily shook her head. 'You're right. It's not practical. It's a lovely idea. But—'

'Can I make a suggestion?' He stopped her.

She nodded. She didn't want to seem ungrateful, but she couldn't see any obvious solution.

'Would you mind awfully if I escorted you? I rather enjoy Prokofiev, and it would be a shame to waste the tickets just because neither of us wants to go alone.'

Bloody hell!

'I don't—' She was shaking her head when he put up a hand to stop her.

'Please, Lily, don't say no until you've had time to think about it. It's all perfectly respectable. We'll be in the company of hundreds of other people, and I'm hardly likely to be considering anything untoward if my wife has been the one to suggest this, am I?'

'But... I thought you were offering me both tickets.'

'I was. But if you can't use both of them, I'd be delighted to go too. I'm rather tired of my own company in the evenings.'

Lily still wasn't sure. She'd love to go to the ballet. She'd been to see the Red Army dancers with her mum, and that had been a thrilling night. They'd got dolled up to the nines and were still talking about going up town to see an opera or ballet one day. But Mum was busy and she wouldn't get Jack within a mile of a man in tights. Millwall, yes. But ballet? Not bloody likely!

Could she go with Mr Warwick? Was it a good idea? Of course it wasn't. It was a stupid idea. But... She needed to think about this without having his gorgeous dark eyes smiling into hers. He was a devil who could persuade her to do all sorts of stupid things if she wasn't careful.

'Can I think about it and let you know tomorrow?'

Leonard was heartened by the fact that she wasn't saying no outright. If she knew that Daphne thought she was a lot older than she actually was, she might well be suspicious of his motives. It wasn't his fault that his wife had assumed Lily must be in her fifties or older. He doubted whether Daphne would have been so keen on him offering her ticket to a beautiful woman in her late thirties.

He knew he ought to be feeling guilty. Maybe he should retreat. But he didn't.

What was the harm in spending a little time with Lily away from work? They could hardly get up to anything inside a crowded theatre. And he wasn't deceiving his wife, not really. Lily was a valuable member of staff and she deserved a treat.

The poor woman had had a difficult time of it recently. Daphne wouldn't begrudge her an evening's entertainment. Would she?

Lily was looking at him, waiting for a response.

'Of course. Let me know what you decide. If you don't want them, I may go anyway.'

'All right. I'll let you know in the morning. Thank you for thinking of me.'

'Yes, well, off you go. Don't miss your train.'

'Goodnight.'

He nodded and watched her cross the main office and disappear through the door into reception. A moment later he heard the outer door shut and the whine of the old elevator.

'Goodnight, sweet Lily,' he whispered, before turning towards his office.

9

'Any tea in the pot?' Jack called out as he let himself in the front door. 'Me throat feels drier than the bleedin' Gobi Desert.'

'Daddy! Daddy's home!' Caroline bounded out of the living room, nearly knocking him over. 'Hello, sweetheart. Where's your mum?'

'In the kitchen.'

'Getting the kettle on, I hope.' He picked her up and swung her round. 'So what have you been up to today, Princess?'

'After school I helped Mrs Simpkins with her weeding.'

'Oh no! You haven't dug up all her prize flowers, have you? She'll be round with her shears to chop your hands off. I'd better hide you in the cupboard 'til she's gone.'

She giggled and squirmed, trying to get down. Jack simply tucked her under one arm and walked into the kitchen. Lily was at the sink, peeling spuds. Ignoring the wriggling child, he went over and kissed the back of his wife's neck.

'All right, love? Got the kettle on?'

'Mummy! Tell Daddy! He's going to put me in the cupboard!'

Lily turned her head to look at them and gave them a tired

smile. She carried on peeling. Jack wondered how she managed it without slicing her own fingers. Years of practice, he supposed.

'Don't be daft,' she replied. 'You're too big to go in a cupboard now. It'll have to be the shed.'

Jack laughed. 'Yes, the shed! With a great big bolt on the door!'

Caroline screamed. 'No, Daddy! I didn't dig up the flowers! You're being silly. Now put me down!'

For a minute there he could have sworn she sounded just like Lily. He had a photo of the two of them on holiday years ago, before they had the girls, when he'd picked Lily up and dangled her over a swimming pool. She'd never liked water since she'd fallen in a river as a kid, so she'd been right pissed off with him. *'You're being silly, Jack! Now put me down!'*

Lily dropped the knife on the drainer before putting her fingers to her temples and pressing hard. 'Jesus Christ, Caroline, what have I told you about screaming?'

Jack let the child slide down to the floor. 'But Daddy was—'

'I know. But I've got a headache and I've told you before not to scream. The neighbours will think there's a murder going on in here.'

'Sorry, Mummy,' she said, looking miserable.

'It's all right. Just remember, no screaming next time Daddy plays silly beggars, all right?'

Caroline nodded. Lily patted her cheek. 'Now go and play in the living room 'til tea's ready. It won't be long.'

Caroline ran out of the kitchen, leaving Jack to face the music.

'Sorry, love,' he said, pulling her into his arms. 'Got one of your heads?' He kissed her forehead. She nodded, relaxing against him. 'Have you taken anything?'

'I've had a couple of aspirin. I'm just too tired, I think. It's been a busy day.'

'D'you want me to do the tea? What we having with them spuds?'

'There's chops in the oven. I was just going to boil the potatoes and open a tin of carrots.'

'I could do chips instead. It won't take long.'

Lily sighed. 'If you want. I'll put the kettle on.'

'No, you go and sit down. I'll sort it out.'

'You sure?'

'Yeah, go on.'

She reached up and kissed his cheek. 'Thanks, darling.'

When Jack brought a cup of tea into the living room five minutes later, Caroline was sprawled out on the floor reading a book and Lily was fast asleep, curled up in his orange leather swivel chair.

* * *

It was the jangling of the telephone that woke Lily. For a minute she didn't know where she was. Her neck was stiff and she had tucked her feet under her, so when she tried to get up she nearly ended up face first on the carpet.

'Buggeration!'

Caroline giggled. She seemed to find it hilarious when Lily forgot herself and swore. No doubt, the sight of her mother tumbling head first out of the armchair added to the comedy.

The phone was still ringing as Lily righted herself and gave Caroline one of her looks. The child subsided, still smiling. Lily sighed. Her famous 'look' wasn't so effective as Caroline got older and realised her mum was all bark and no bite.

Jack was singing off-key in the kitchen, oblivious to the noise in the hall. He'd burst an eardrum as a kid, so his hearing was never as good as he claimed it was. God knows how he heard the baby cry in the night. He seemed to have some instinct that Lily had lost.

It was Beverley on the phone.

'I'm still at Angie's. Her mate'll drop us home about eight.'

'What mate? And what about your tea? We've got chops cooking now.'

'Oh. Sorry. We've had beans on toast.'

'What about the baby? You can't keep her out all hours.'

Lily heard Beverley sigh. 'She's all right. I brought a couple of bottles, and I scrounged some more milk off Angie. Her baby has the same stuff. And I always bring loads of nappies with me, just in case. Don't fuss, Mum. Kerry's been playing with Zoë all day, and now she's fast asleep. She ain't bothered where she kips.'

Lily gave up. Short of starting a world war by demanding Bev should come home straight away, there wasn't anything she could do. It would also mean driving over to get her, which she just couldn't face.

'All right. But next time, let me know if you won't be back for meals.'

'Yeah, 'course.'

Lily gritted her teeth. *How many times did she have to tell her girls to say 'yes', not 'yeah'? Or 'isn't' instead of 'ain't'?*

'I might be going to the pictures Friday night,' Beverley said. 'You'll be all right watching Kerry, won't you?'

Just like that? No 'Please will you?', or 'Do you mind?' Bloody typical!

'No, actually, Beverley, we won't. I've got plans, and after Brownies I think your dad's taking Caroline over to Uncle Fred's.'

Jack had emerged from the kitchen just in time to hear this.

He raised his eyebrows.

'Can't Dad take Kerry as well?'

'You'll have to ask him yourself. I thought you didn't want her going over there,' Lily pushed.

'How would you feel, if someone wanted to take your baby off you?'

'No one was going to steal her, Beverley. We were trying to do what was best.'

'Well, she's my baby, so I'll decide that.'

'Fine. And you can look after her Friday, while we have a night out. I'll see you later. Dad can have your chop.' She put the phone down, furious. 'I swear I'll swing for that girl one of these days.'

'I take it she's had her tea out?'

'Yes, round at her friend's. She's getting a lift back later. Some young Herbert with long hair and no job, no doubt.'

'Ah, let her get on with it, love. Come on, it's ready. Looks like I'm getting seconds.'

* * *

'How's your head?' Jack asked when they sat down to eat.

'Better, thanks. Or it was, until Beverley phoned.' She rubbed her temples.

'Don't let her get to you. She's just pushing her luck. You know what she's like.'

'I suppose. She just caught me at an awkward time. I nearly fell off the chair when the phone rang. I was out like a light.'

They ate their meal on trays in the living room in front of the telly. Lily had taken to watching *Peyton Place*. Jack thought it was a load of rubbish, so he read the paper; and the littl'un just stuck her nose back in her book and read while she ate.

When Caroline finished, she took her plate out to the sink and went upstairs for a bath. She'd be down soon in her pyjamas, wanting to carry on reading her book. Lily had put a stop to her taking books in the bath with her after one she'd borrowed from school had fallen in. It had cost them a few quid to buy a replacement because it was a hardback.

'So, what was all that about Friday night?' Jack asked. 'I didn't think we were doing anything.'

'I know,' Lily sighed. 'She just bloody annoyed me, expecting us to babysit without a please or thank you.' She paused, picking at a piece of thread on her skirt. 'But I have been offered some free tickets to the ballet on Friday by someone at work. D'you fancy taking me?'

'God no! It ain't natural, blokes in tights. You go if you want; I'll go over to Fred's, like you told her. There's a good film on telly. We were talking about it the other day.'

'Another war film, I expect, if Fred's going to watch it.'

'Course it is. Reminds him of his glory days.'

'Well, I'm glad you were too young to serve. I'm fed up with hearing all his old stories. You'd think he won the war single-handed.'

Jack laughed. 'Come on, Lily, he's not that bad. I've heard a lot worse from other blokes down the pub. And his ship was alongside the Yanks' when they took the surrender from Japan. I reckon that's something worth showing off about.'

'Maybe he should write it down. Not tell it to us every time we see him. It must drive poor Maggie mad.'

'Fat chance of that. The only writing Fred does is betting slips and pools coupons. Anyway, if you're off to the ballet, madam, you'll be watching blokes prancing round, instead of Alan Ladd and his big guns.'

Lily pulled a face. She knew if she tried to argue that male dancers were strong enough to lift a woman over their heads, it would fall on deaf ears. Jack just didn't understand that sort of thing. Ballet was girls' stuff, not for real men.

'So you don't mind if I go, then?'

Would you be so easy-going about it if you knew who I was going with? she thought. *Why don't you ask who I'm going with? Give me a chance to do the right thing?*

He shook his head. 'Nah, you go, love. Enjoy yourself. Just so long as you ain't expecting me to go.'

'I'll have to take some clothes and change at work. I won't have time to come home.'

'D'you want a lift Friday morning, save you getting your frock creased?'

'Mmm, could you manage that? It'll be awkward on the train.'

'I'll take you in, then. The boss don't want picking up 'til ten. He's got some do on tomorrow night that'll keep him out till late.'

'It's all right for some, being able to pick their hours. I suppose that means he'll expect you to hang around late and take him home.' She paused when she realised how sharp that had sounded, but Jack just shrugged it off.

'Yea, but don't knock it, 'cos it's getting you a free lift to work.'

'Sorry, you're right. It'll be nice, thanks.'

'How you getting home? Want me to come and get you?'

'No, don't. I'll be all right on the train.'

'You sure?'

'Yes. You'll need to get Caroline home to bed anyway. It'll be a late night for her, without you dragging her off to get me in town.'

'I could drop her off with Bev first.'

'Oh, I can just hear her – "*No one'll babysit for me, why should I have to look after her?*" Honestly, Jack, it's not worth the trouble. I'll get the train. I can always get a minicab from the station if it's really late.'

'All right, darlin'. We'll see you when we see you then.'

Lily sat back and closed her eyes. She felt excitement course through her veins, washing away the remnants of her headache.

She was going to the ballet. And she was going with her boss. Tall, dark, handsome, *married* Leonard Warwick.

10

On Friday afternoon, Jack let himself into the house and whistled. The only response was a soft tap-tapping from the kitchen.

He walked down the passage and opened the door. Bev was sitting at the kitchen table with Lily's old typewriter, a book open beside her. She was looking at the book and typing, a frown of concentration on her face.

'Hallo, love.'

She jumped a mile. 'Bloody hell!' she yelped. 'Don't do that!'

'What? Walk into me own kitchen? What you doing?'

'Baking a cake, what does it look like?'

'Then you're a lousy cook.' He grinned.

Bev giggled. Jack knew she could never resist her old dad's jokes.

'Any danger of a cuppa?'

She rolled her eyes and got up to put the kettle on.

'Where's the baby?'

'Upstairs in her cot. She finally decided she was tired.'

He walked round the table and looked at the paper in the machine.

The quick brown fox jumps over the lazy dog. The quick brown fox jumps over the lazy dog. The quick btrim

'What's a b-t-r-i-m?'

'It's an old man what sneaks up on you.'

'Ah, I thought so.' He sat down. 'So, you're learning to type?'

'Yeah. I'm using Mum's old book. It's easy. Or it was till you scared the living daylights out of me.'

He held up his hands. 'Sorry, love. So, how long's this been going on?'

She shrugged. 'Not long. I got bored, so thought I might as well do something useful.'

'Something useful, eh? Like doing some housework to help your mum out?'

She leaned against the sink and gave him a look, just like Lily. What was it about his girls and those stroppy looks?

'Something useful for me,' she said. 'So I can get a job.'

He frowned. 'There's plenty of time for that. You've got Kerry to think of first.'

Bev huffed and turned away, spooning tea into the pot, muttering to herself.

'What?'

'Nothing. When's Mum getting home?'

'Not till late.'

'How late?'

'I dunno. She's going out straight from work.'

Before she could say anything else the front door slammed. 'Daddy?'

'In here, Princess.'

Out of the corner of his eye he saw Bev throw her hands up before she grabbed the kettle off the gas as it whistled.

Caroline came skipping down the passage. 'Where's Kerry?' she asked.

'She was asleep until you came banging in like a bloody elephant,' Beverley snapped. 'Can't you ever be quiet?'

'Sorry,' she said, looking sheepish. 'I didn't know.'

'Well, next time think before you slam the door and start shouting.'

'All right, Bev,' said Jack. 'The baby's still asleep. So, any chance of that cuppa?'

Caroline sidled up and he slid an arm around her. Bev glared at both of them, then got the milk out of the fridge. A minute later she pushed a cup and saucer across the table.

'Thanks, darlin'. You having one?'

'No. I'd better put this away.' She picked up the typewriter.

'Oh, can't I play with it?' asked Caroline.

'It's not a bloody toy. Go and find a doll or something.'

Jack sighed. Whatever was wrong with Bev, she had no right to take it out on her sister.

'Bev,' he said firmly. 'That's enough.'

'Ooh, sorry,' she sulked. 'I forgot we all have to be nice to "the little princess".'

'Don't push it. Whatever's got your knickers in a twist, she's just walked in the door. Leave her alone.'

She stood glaring at him, holding the typewriter to her chest. 'So I've just got to let her play with anything she likes? Even if it's Mum's?'

'No. I didn't say that. Just stop being so snotty with her.' He took a sip of his tea. 'Now,' he said, turning to Caroline. 'How was school?'

'All right,' she said, shrugging. 'Can I have a biscuit?'

'Go on then. Are you swimming tonight?'

'No, Daddy, not tonight. Swimming is on Tuesdays and Thursdays. Wednesdays is dancing.'

'Oh yeah, and Fridays is Brownies, right?'

Caroline nodded. Beverley picked up the book she'd left on the table and took it and the machine out of the room. Something was up with that madam. He'd have to have a chat with her later. He never could work out how his daughters could be so bloody bitchy to each other. He thanked God he only had one sister. At least with his brothers he knew where he stood. If he upset one of them, he got a bloody nose and then they were mates again.

He glanced at his watch. 'Right. You'd better get your Brownie uniform on, and we'd better get going. I'll pick up fish and chips for tea on the way back.'

Bev had calmed down by the time they got back, and cheered up no end when she sat down to a paper-load of cod and chips with a wally (or 'gherkin', as Lily insisted he call it). The baby was awake again and bouncing in her chair. Jack let her have a lick of his wally, laughing when she screwed up her face at the vinegary taste. He would have given her a chip to suck on, but Bev whipped her out of his way and gave her a bottle.

Caroline must have been hungry, because she just about inhaled her meal before going upstairs to get her pyjamas on. She stayed up there, reading her latest story from the Puffin Club. Jack would go up later and tuck her in. She'd probably be fast asleep with her face in the book. Right now, he'd clear up the chip papers and get himself a beer. The great thing about a chip supper was no washing up. Mind you, if Lily was about, she'd insist on using plates. *'We're not tramps,'* she'd say.

'But they taste better in the paper,' he'd argue.

'Don't be daft,' she'd tell him, and give him a plate.

Bev came in and sat down just as he was about to turn the telly on.

'I thought you was going to Uncle Fred's,' she said.

He shrugged. 'He rung. He's had to go over to Aunt Maggie's mum's. Her toilet's blocked.'

Bev pulled a face. 'Dad,' she said. 'What time will Mum be back?'

'Search me, love. She's gone to some ballet up town with the girls from work. She might go out for a gin or two after. Could be late.'

Bev looked annoyed.

'Why? What's the matter?'

She shook her head. 'Nothing.'

Jack raised an eyebrow, but didn't say anything. 'It's just... You know I've taught myself to type?'

'Yeah.'

'Well, Mum's always going on about how much it costs, having another mouth to feed, and me not working. So... I've got an interview for a job on Monday.'

'Bloody hell, Bev, you know your mum don't mean it. You need to stay at home with Kerry.'

'It'll be fine, Dad, honest. My mate Angie'll look after Kerry for me. She's got a little girl a month older, so they'll be company for each other.'

Jack sighed and took a pull on his beer. For all her moaning, Lily wasn't going to like this. But if the girl had gone to all the trouble to teach herself to type and get an interview, well, maybe there was more of Lily in her than they gave her credit for.

'How much is it going to cost you, to pay this Angie?' he asked.

'Not much. A few quid a week.'

'You won't be earning much more than that.'

'It's not about the money, Dad,' she said, sounding older than she should. 'It's just, I need to get out the house. I'm going mad in here.'

'But you've got a baby.'

'Yeah, and so did Mum – she had two of us, and she still went out to work, and to evening classes, and now she's out at the soddin' ballet.'

Caroline walked in the room in time to hear the last of that. 'Who's at the ballet?' she asked.

'Our mother,' declared Bev, looking fed up. 'Gone with her posh friends to some la-di-da do up town, while we have fish and chips out of yesterday's paper.'

Jack winced at her bitterness. He'd always been a bit bothered by Lily going out to work, especially when she got this office job and with Caroline being so young. But it had made Lily happy, so he'd gone along with it. It sometimes struck him that if she'd been home for the girls, Beverley might not have got herself into so much trouble.

But what was done was done. It made it more difficult to argue when Bev wanted to go out to work, though.

'That's not fair!' Caroline stamped her foot and crossed her arms over her skinny little body. 'Why can't I go to the ballet?'

Jack rolled his eyes.

'Because you ain't posh enough,' said Bev with a sneer. She got up. 'I'm going to have an early night.' Jack waved a hand at her as he reached for his beer with the other. 'I'll leave you to tell Mum about my interview then. Night night.'

Jack sighed. 'Don't let the bed bugs bite,' he said and took another drink.

11

While Jack was acting as referee between the girls, Lily and Mr Warwick arrived at a restaurant a couple of streets away from the theatre.

He held Lily's chair as she sat down. She could feel his warm breath on her neck for a moment, sending shivers down her spine, before he straightened and moved round to sit opposite her.

Lily couldn't remember when she'd felt so nervous. As he sat down, he caught her eye and smiled. He looked nervous too. For some reason that made her feel a bit better.

'This is nice,' she said, trying to look as though she was used to coming into fancy restaurants. The last time she'd had a meal out with Jack had been at the pie and mash shop down Roman Road. The one by the betting shop. He'd had a win on the dogs. *No expense spared,* she'd sighed.

'Yes. It hasn't been open for long, but it already has a good reputation,' he said, picking up the menu. 'Let's see what the fuss is all about.'

Lily followed suit, trying not to panic when she saw the prices.

Bloody hell, she thought. *I could get a week's shopping for the price of one of these dishes.*

'Would you like me to translate?' Leonard asked softly. She gave him a cool look, thankful she'd taken those French classes. 'No, thank you. I can manage.'

'Oh, good.' He didn't look too sure, but Lily just smiled and concentrated on the menu.

A waiter approached. 'Would you like an aperitif?'

'Lily? A sherry, perhaps? Or a gin and tonic?'

'A gin and tonic would be lovely.'

'Make that two,' he said.

They ordered their food. The waiter gave a little bow and walked away.

Lily looked at Mr Warwick through her lashes. He was smiling.

'A bit pompous, don't you think?' he said, nodding in the direction of the waiter.

She smiled, giving a soft laugh. 'I suppose people coming here expect it.' She looked around at the other diners. Mostly couples, the men in dinner suits, the women in cocktail dresses and pearls. They oozed middle-class confidence. Lily knew that she looked the part; she'd worked hard to make sure she did. But she couldn't help thinking that any minute now someone would see through her disguise and throw her out on her ear.

Their drinks arrived in beautiful cut-crystal tumblers. Lily picked up her glass, surprised by its weight. Mr Warwick followed suit.

'Here's to an enjoyable evening,' he said, raising it to her. 'I'm glad you decided to join me.'

'An enjoyable evening,' she said. 'Thank you for inviting me, Mr Warwick.'

'Leonard, please. We're not in the office now.'

'Leonard,' she said, smiling shyly.

'You look lovely, by the way. I meant to say earlier.'

Lily was glad he hadn't. If he had, with that look in his dark eyes, before they were sitting here, trapped in full view of a bunch of strangers, she might have turned tail and run.

She took a sip of her drink, not trusting herself to respond. His quietly spoken words left her breathless. Jack was always calling her gorgeous, but she doubted he noticed much about her these days. It was just part of him – he automatically called women 'darlin', or 'sweetheart', reserving 'gorgeous' for his wife alone. Sometimes, she thought he did it because he forgot her name. He probably thought it made her feel special, but it didn't. He'd never looked her in the eye and said, '*You look lovely,*' as Leonard had done. She blinked back tears.

'I'm sorry,' he said. 'I was determined to keep things light, but you must have realised by now—'

She put her drink down, focussing on the patterns of brilliant light that sparkled from the diamond-cut crystal. 'You shouldn't be saying things like that, Mr Warwick,' she whispered.

He sighed. 'I know. But, God help me, I can't seem to help myself. I'm trying very hard to do the right thing, Lily. But right now there's nowhere else on this earth that I want to be.'

Lily looked up, seeing her own fears and longings mirrored in his handsome face. She reached across the small table, wanting to touch him. He took her hand, enveloping her cold fingers in his warm grasp, and she instantly felt better. 'Me neither,' she said.

He smiled. They sat there, oblivious to the rest of the world. Lily wanted this moment to last forever. They hadn't done anything wrong – not really, not yet. They hadn't even kissed. But she wanted to, so much. She knew she shouldn't, but she doubted she could resist him. For the first time in months, she felt alive. And she loved it.

* * *

Leonard could see that Lily was nervous, despite her outward appearance of calm elegance. Her eyes were darting everywhere, taking in the opulence of the restaurant and the calibre of the clientele. It wasn't until they sat down that he'd thought to wonder whether she'd ever been anywhere like this before. He worried that the choice of restaurant might make her feel uncomfortable. The last thing he wanted to do was to cause her distress. He'd told her how lovely she looked to try and make her feel better. She was the most beautiful woman in this place, and he'd just had to tell her, even at the risk of unsettling her. When she'd reached towards him, he'd had to touch her. In that moment, he felt like the luckiest man on earth. Only her trembling fingers stopped him from leaping in the air and shouting in triumph. Instead he smiled and wrapped her hand in his.

They talked – about the food, the weather, books, films. Neither of them mentioned their families, and they avoided any reference to the office. When they left the restaurant, Leonard took her coat from the waiter and helped her into it. He offered her his arm as they walked to the theatre. She took it, smiling. He couldn't help smiling back at her; she was so beautiful.

In a quiet street he stopped. 'May I kiss you?' he asked.

She looked up at him, and for a moment he thought she would say yes. But she shook her head and put her fingers to his lips. 'I don't think we should,' she said.

He swallowed his disappointment. Rather than be tempted by her soft touch on his mouth, he moved back. 'You're probably right,' he sighed.

She smiled. 'Let's just enjoy the evening. We can be friends, can't we? There's no harm in that.'

12

Lily paid the minicab driver and slowly made her way up the garden path. The house was in darkness, thank God. She didn't want to face anyone right now. She just wanted to hug her secrets around her. She reached the front door and stood there, unwilling to go in.

Out here in the moonlight she was a different woman: no longer a wife, a mother, a grandmother. Instead she was Juliet: a beautiful, desirable woman, caught up in a forbidden flirtation, defying her family, her duties and her obligations for the sake of love.

She turned her back on the door and raised her face to the sky. It was a clear night; she could see loads of stars. Lily hummed softly to herself, her hips swaying as she remembered the elegance of the dancers. The performance had been wonderful, far better than she'd imagined. The music! The colours! The dancing! She remembered the scents of the well-dressed women around her in the theatre. Some of their husbands had looked at her, and fancied her – she could tell. But she wasn't interested in them. Leonard was the best-looking man there. For a few hours he had been *hers*. And she had been free. Nothing else had mattered, just the ballet, and Leonard's hand in hers in the darkness.

In the house she could hear the thin wail of the baby. At the end of the road a goods train rumbled past on the railway line from Well Hall to Blackheath. Lily sighed.

'Time to get back to real life.' She turned, breathed out her dreams, and walked into the house.

* * *

Jack was half-asleep when Lily slipped into bed in the dark. He rolled towards her, the shock of her cold feet on his leg waking him up.

'Christ! You're a block of ice,' he said.

'Sorry.' She went to move away, but he pulled her into his arms.

''S'all right. Snuggle up. Soon have you warm.' He nuzzled her neck. 'Mmm. You smell nice.' She was all tense for a minute, before he felt her relax.

'Thanks.' She touched his cheek, scratching gently at the whiskers along his jaw. She liked him to have a good shave; she said it was like kissing sandpaper when he didn't have one. 'Go to sleep.'

'You've woken me up now,' he said, rubbing himself against her hip.

'Jack, it's late.'

'Aw, come on, love. We ain't done it for ages.' He stroked her back. 'And that sexy scent is driving me mad.' Her cool fingers on his skin made him hiss. 'Yesssss, that's it, sweetheart. Let's get some more skin...' He used his feet to drag his pyjama bottoms off. He hated wearing the bloody things, but Lily insisted he cover himself, first when they'd lived with her mum and dad, and then with the girls around the house. He'd soon learned to strip them off quickly when he needed to.

Lily sat up, pulling her nightdress over her head.

'Come 'ere.' He kissed her shoulder, his hands moving over her soft skin. 'Oh, yeah.'

'Don't wait,' she breathed.

'Christ, no.' He didn't need telling twice.

She was wild tonight. 'Slow down, sweetheart,' he said. 'I can't hold on much longer...' But she didn't listen. She gasped, lost.

'Jeez, Lil, you're gorgeous. So gorgeous!' He buried his face in her neck.

They lay together for a couple of minutes after, catching their breath. Jack moved to the side, not wanting to crush her under him.

'You all right?' he asked.

'Yeah,' she whispered.

'Good.' He lay on his back, content. Lily rolled away and he heard her get up. 'Whatcha doing?'

'I need the loo. Where's my nightdress?'

'Dunno. End of the bed, I think.'

'Got it.'

He heard the rustle of nylon as she pulled it on. 'Take it off again when you come back. I'll keep you warm.'

Lily's soft laugh floated through the darkness. 'Yeah, I know. But I really am tired now. Go to sleep.'

'All right. Night night.' He smiled, rolling onto his side and letting sleep swallow him up.

* * *

In the stark light of the bathroom, Lily saw that she'd pulled on her nightdress inside-out. She quickly stripped it off and cleaned herself before putting it back on the right way. In the mirror, she could see smudges of make-up round her eyes. She'd forgotten to take it off. She looked and felt awful. Refilling the basin with warm water, she washed her face, scrubbing hard.

What was the matter with her? She'd just had sex with her husband. Nothing wrong with that. It had been good, too.

She dried her face and turned off the bathroom light. She walked softly along the passage back to their bedroom. In bed, Jack was snoring.

She lay awake, listening to him, envying him his peace. She wished she could relax, but her mind wouldn't let her. She felt sick.

For the first time in months, Lily had had sex with her husband. He was happy. She closed her eyes, rolled onto her side away from him, curling herself up into a protective ball. If he'd known that she'd been thinking of Leonard – wanting it to be Leonard making love to her instead of him – Jack would have killed her.

13

'Daddy! Daddy!' Susan ran to greet Leonard as he opened the car door in his mother-in-law's driveway.

'Hello, sweetie. How are you?'

'I've missed you, Daddy. Peter's been beastly to me. And Grandmother isn't being very nice either. Mummy says it's because her arm is hurting, so we have to be patient. Daddy, can I come home with you? Please?'

She clung to his leg and looked up at him with swimming eyes. Leonard picked her up, kissing her forehead. 'Good grief, what's all this?'

'For goodness' sake, Susan, let your father in the door before you start complaining.' Daphne stood in the open doorway. 'Hello, darling. Did you have a good trip?'

Leonard kissed his wife on the cheek and followed her into the house. 'Quite smooth. Not much traffic on the weekend.' He lowered his daughter to her feet. 'Go and play for a bit, there's a good girl.'

She opened her mouth to protest, but her mother stopped her with a wave of her hand. 'Susan, your father is going to be here all day. Now go and amuse yourself for a few minutes whilst I make him a cup of tea.'

With another tear-filled look aimed at her father's heart, Susan went upstairs.

'I take it things aren't going terribly well,' he said, taking in his wife's pallor as they entered the kitchen.

Daphne sighed and shook her head. 'I don't want to burden you with this as soon as you arrive. Let's have a cup of tea and talk about something else for a while.' She busied herself filling the kettle and setting out cups, including one for her mother. 'Did you go to the ballet? How was it?'

Leonard shrugged off his jacket and put it on the back of a chair. He sat down at the kitchen table. 'Mmm? Oh, yes. I did go. Excellent production. It's a shame you had to miss it.'

'Did you take her?' Daphne got the milk out of the refrigerator. 'Your cashier?'

Leonard hesitated for a moment, reluctant to discuss Lily with his wife. She poured milk into a jug and returned the bottle to the refrigerator before looking at him again. 'Well?'

'Yes. Mrs Wickham asked me to thank you for thinking of her,' he lied. 'She had a lovely evening.' That, at least, was the truth.

Daphne smiled. 'How nice of her. I'm glad she enjoyed it. It would've been an awful waste otherwise.' She warmed the teapot. 'I hope you thought to warn her that it was black tie. I meant to mention it to you, but simply forgot.'

'I didn't need to tell her. She's not stupid.'

She looked startled. 'I didn't think she was, darling. I just wonder whether she's ever been to a top-class ballet production before. I didn't want the poor woman being embarrassed because she wasn't appropriately dressed.'

Leonard took a deep breath. Of course, Daphne was thinking of someone else's comfort. 'Of course. I'm sorry, dear.'

Her face softened as she looked at him. 'It doesn't matter. It's so good to see you.' She touched his cheek. 'I hate being parted from you.'

'When are you coming home?' he asked.

'I don't know,' she said, shaking her head. 'Mummy's wrist seems to be taking a long time to heal. I spoke to her doctor yesterday, and he suggested she might go to a convalescent home until she can manage. But you know Mummy. She wants to stay here.'

'And I want you and the children home. You've got to learn to stand up to her, Daphne. You have enough to do, without disrupting our whole family for your mother's convenience.' *And with my wife and children at home, I'll remember where my duty lies, and maybe then I'll stop dreaming about Lily.*

'I know, Leonard, dear. I want to come home, too. Lord knows, the children have had enough. But, well, Mummy—'

'Is difficult, and demanding, and needs to think of others for a change.' He sighed. 'But I don't suppose she will.'

Daphne looked unhappy. He realised he was being difficult too, but he was sick of coming home to an empty house. The kettle whistled. She turned round to deal with it, but not before he saw relief flash across her face at the diversion.

A clattering on the stairs warned him that Peter was heading their way. The boy burst into the kitchen at full pelt. 'Daddy! Have you come to take us home?' He flung his arms around Leonard's neck. 'I really need to get back to school next week.'

Leonard laughed, tousling his son's hair. 'And hello to you, too, young man. Have you been a good boy for your mother and grandmother?'

Peter stepped back nodding vigorously. His mother looked askance, but he took no notice. 'Yes, but I think it's about time we go home, now.' He swiped at his hair in an attempt to flatten it. 'Granny would really appreciate some peace and quiet.'

Leonard and Daphne shared a moment of amusement over their son's head.

'It's not like you to be so keen to get back to school, Peter,' said Daphne. 'It wouldn't have anything to do with Timmy Bradley's birthday party next week, would it?'

The boy blushed. 'Oh, is it next week, Mummy?' he asked.

'Yes, it is, as you well know. I've already told you I'll do my best to make sure you can go. Now run along and let Daddy and me drink our tea.' She poured three cups, added milk and sugar, and put some biscuits on a plate. She brought theirs to the table, and then picked up the third cup. 'I'll just take this up to Mummy, and then we can have some peace and quiet for a little while.'

Leonard sat back and nibbled on a fig roll, watching Peter through the open kitchen door as he kicked at the leaves in the garden. The boy looked unhappy. Leonard didn't blame him. His mother-in-law wasn't the warmest of women, even to her grand-children.

When Daphne returned, she sat down with a weary sigh.

'I'll have to go back up soon. She's finally decided she wants to get up, and she can't manage washing and dressing with one hand.' She took a sip of her tea, eyes downcast. 'I'm sorry, Leonard, but I don't know what else to do. I know it's wrong to keep the children off school, and I hate to think of you at home, trying to cope on your own on top of work. But Mummy can't be left alone. Maybe if the children shared a bedroom for a while, she could come and stay with us—'

'Absolutely not. We'd never get rid of her.'

'But, Leonard—'

He held up a hand. 'I mean it, Daphne. There's got to be a better way to deal with this.' He thought for a moment. 'What about that cousin of yours – Fiona, is it? Can't she spare some time? She's not married, and she looked after her own mother for years, didn't she?'

Daphne's head came up. 'I don't think...' She looked doubtful. 'No, I can't expect poor Fiona to do this. She's finally got some freedom. It would be a terrible imposition.'

'You could at least ask her. She might be glad of something to do. It could be the perfect solution.' Leonard couldn't imagine the dowdy Fiona kicking up her heels. 'She's probably bored to tears without someone to care for. It would take the pressure off you, my dear. The children really should get back to school. It's not doing any of us any good.'

Above their heads, a bell tinkled. They both looked up. Leonard felt rage building as his wife got up to answer the summons. 'What on earth possessed you to give her a bell, woman?' he asked. 'You're not a bloody servant.'

Daphne paused in the doorway and looked back at him. 'No, I'm not. I'm her daughter. I'm sorry if that's proving to be inconvenient right now, Leonard, but I don't know what else I can do. I'll ring Fiona, but I wouldn't blame her if she told me to go to hell.'

14

'Why didn't you tell me about this?' Lily asked Beverley. It was Sunday evening, and Bev had just announced she had a job interview in the morning.

'Dad said it was all right.'

Jack looked up from his paper. 'Oi, don't drag me into this. I told you to talk to your mum.'

'So you knew about it?' Lily turned on him.

Oh, bugger, he thought.

'You said you'd tell her, Dad.'

'Oh, for Christ's sake! I never said. Anyway, it's just an interview, ain't it?' He looked at Lily. 'What's the problem? If she gets a job, she can pay her way.'

'She has a baby.'

'Yeah, but she's sorted out a minder, ain't ya?' He looked to Bev for backup.

She nodded. 'Angie's going to have her for me.' Lily sniffed. 'She won't let me down.'

Jack didn't think she would either. The girl needed the money.

Lily looked at him. He knew that accusing look. There was

going to be an almighty bust-up, and neither Lily nor Bev would back down.

'Let her get on with it, love. If it don't work out, she'll have to pack the job in.'

Lily looked at Jack, then at Beverley. 'Suit yourself,' she said. 'I'll give it a month before she lets you down, or you get sacked. Let's face it, you've never stuck with anything, have you?'

She turned away from them and picked up her handbag from the counter. 'You can sort out your own tea. I'm picking Caroline up from her friend's, then I'm going to Mum's. She promised to do my hair.'

'I could've done it, if you'd said,' said Beverley.

'You could look after your baby, like a proper mother,' she snapped.

'Yeah? Like you? You're never bloody here. If you ain't at work, you're swanning off to the ballet, like Lady Muck.'

Lily slammed the door behind her. 'Oh, Gawd!' muttered Jack.

Beverley sank down onto a chair and rested her head in her hands. She was shaking. She took a deep breath and looked up.

'That went well, eh, Dad?'

He shook his head, blowing the air out of his lungs. 'Christ, Bev. You know how to wind her up. Why don't you try to get on with her for a change? She only wants what's best.'

She rolled her eyes. 'Yeah. If we all did what Mum thinks is best, you'd be an office boy, I'd be at grammar school learning how to be a posh cow, and we'd all have to lift our little fingers when we drink our tea.'

He shrugged. 'You know what? Right now, I'd try anything for a quiet life.'

'Wuss,' she sneered.

* * *

Lily was so tired. She'd deliberately stayed at her mum's until late last night, not wanting to face either of them. Caroline had fallen asleep, curled up on Kathy's old bed, while Lily's mother had coloured and set her hair. Lily had carried Caroline out to the car and the child hadn't woken until they got home. The poor little mite had been like a zombie – up the stairs, clean teeth, nightie on – and out like a light again. At least she'd been full of beans this morning.

She wandered into the general office and looked up to see Leonard watching her. She smiled. He smiled back, and her tiredness disappeared. 'Good morning, Mr Warwick,' she said.

He gave a slight bow. 'And good morning to you, Mrs Wickham.'

She felt a warm glow, knowing that this man at least thought she was something special. If someone could bottle this feeling, she'd spend every penny she earned buying it. In the meantime, she had work to do.

'If you'll excuse me, Mr Warwick, Mr Irwin asked for some bank drafts this morning. I'd better not keep him waiting.'

'Of course. Can you come and see me when you've got a minute? It's not urgent.'

Leonard stepped back. She caught a whiff of his aftershave as she passed him. It was subtle and expensive; nothing like the Old Spice that Jack used. She filled her lungs with it as she walked into her office, holding her breath until she sat down at her desk. She looked up. Leonard was still in the general office outside, watching her. For a moment she forgot everything and sat there, caught in his gaze. God, he could turn her on with just a look.

Someone walked past, blocking her view, breaking the spell. Lily quickly looked away and concentrated on her tasks for the day.

Leonard's weekend had been miserable. The children had been fractious. They had sobbed and clung to him when he left them with Daphne at their grandmother's house. His wife had been frosty, paying more attention to her damned mother than to her own husband. He'd been relieved to get back to the peace and quiet of Wimbledon.

He'd had to iron his own shirt this morning. It was a blessing he had several appointments today and would need to keep his suit jacket on. Teamed with a waistcoat, he'd managed to disguise the worst of his efforts. But if Daphne didn't come home soon he'd have to see about getting someone in to char for him and keep him supplied in freshly laundered shirts. He ought to send the bill to his mother-in-law.

But the moment he'd caught a glimpse of Lily's smile, his whole mood lifted. That's what he'd been missing for the past two days. He could put up with anything if only he could see her lovely face. His anger at Daphne was as much about being denied Lily's presence as it was about her stubborn refusal to stand up to her mother.

* * *

It was another hour before Lily had a chance to go and see Leonard, but then he was busy with clients. In the end it was nearly five o'clock before she managed to see him.

'I'm so sorry,' she said. 'You wanted to see me this morning.'

'Don't worry, it wasn't a work matter.'

'Oh.' She wasn't sure how to react to that.

He picked up his briefcase and placed it on the desk.

'This is for you,' he said, taking something out and handing it to her. 'A memento of Friday's performance.'

It was a record. '*Romeo and Juliet!*' she gasped.

'This is the 1938 recording Prokofiev made with the Moscow Philharmonic. It's a 78, I'm afraid. I hope your record player can cope with it. I know some of the new models are set up for just 45 and 33 rpm these days, but a lot of the best classics are still being produced as 78s.'

'No, that's fine. Our radiogram manages all of them.' She turned it over, studying the information on the back. 'I can't wait to listen to it.' She smiled at him. 'You didn't need to do this.'

'I know. But I wanted to. I know how much you enjoyed the music, and I wanted you to remember.'

'Thank you.' She clutched the record to her chest. Even without this reminder, she was never likely to forget. 'Er, would it be all right if I leave it in here until the others have left? It might look odd, me walking out of your office with it. Someone might ask.'

'Of course. Pop back when you're leaving.'

'I will. Thanks again.'

'You're very welcome, Lily.'

She left his office, trying hard not to smile. No one had ever given her a present like that before. An LP of the Red Army choir that she'd bought when she'd seen them with her mum was the nearest she had to a classical record. All their LPs were popular stuff, like Frank Sinatra, Tony Bennett and the like. Beverley had a few singles and long-players of the latest groups, but Lily couldn't be doing with those. And Caroline had the soundtrack to *The Sound of Music*, which she played over and over again. Lily regretted buying it for her – she was sick of bloody Maria. She knew what she'd like to do with the girl!

She waited until the office was quiet before going back to

Leonard's office to collect her present. He'd already gone, leaving it on his desk. She picked it up and hugged it. She'd tell Jack she'd bought it herself. He wouldn't know any different.

There was music playing as Jack walked in the door. Proper stuff, with violins and all that bollocks.

Lily was sitting in an armchair, her eyes shut, listening. She looked so happy and peaceful. He hadn't seen her like that for months. He didn't want to disturb her, but he couldn't put up with that racket for long, so he tiptoed out and shut the living-room door behind him.

The rest of the house was quiet, so he went into the kitchen and made himself a cuppa. He was sitting at the table, reading the *Standard* and drinking his tea, when Lily surfaced from the living room.

'Hallo, love. I didn't hear you come in.'

'I'm not surprised, with all that racket you was listening to in there.' He laughed. 'What the bloody hell was that?'

'*Romeo and Juliet.* You know, the ballet I went to.'

'Is that what brought the smile to your face, then? Remembering all them blokes in tights?'

Lily flushed, her lips tightening with annoyance at being caught out. 'Don't be ridiculous. I was enjoying the music. It's beautiful.'

'It's a load of bleeding noise to me. I like something I can sing along to.'

'You never give it a chance. That's the trouble.'

'What's the point? It ain't for the likes of me.'

'That's rubbish. Classical music is for everyone. You shouldn't just dismiss it.'

He held up his hands. 'Sorry, love. As Bev would say, it ain't my scene. I ain't posh enough for no violin music.'

'That's just typical. You both wallow in your ignorance, the pair of you. Anything you think is the slightest bit intellectual, you take the mickey.'

'Aw, come on, Lil. You listen to it if you like, darling. But we don't all have to like the same things, do we? I mean, you turn your nose up at football, don't you? I like me Millwall, and you like your toffee-nosed music. Let's live and let live, eh? Just don't try putting that stuff on while I'm watching *Match of the Day*, all right?'

Lily sighed. 'You just don't want to know, do you? There's so much music and literature and art out there to be discovered. But if I suggested a visit to an art gallery, you'd run a mile, wouldn't you?'

'Probably.' He laughed. 'The only ones I'm interested in are the *Spot the Ball* pictures, and photo-finishes at the races. At least I could win something with them.'

Lily shook her head, her smile not reaching her eyes.

15

After an early start, Jack was twiddling his thumbs. He'd dropped the boss off at his office, then taken his missus to the airport. She was heading off to St Moritz for a few days with some friends. The snotty bitch had been issuing orders all the way to Heathrow.

'I don't want my husband visiting any unsavoury establishments while I'm gone. Make sure he gets home at a decent hour. Don't let him work in the car – it's not good for his eyes. Take the decanter and cigars out of here.'

Jesus bloody Christ! No wonder the poor sod worked so hard. Who'd want to go home to a miserable cow like that? She lays down the law then swans off on holiday without him.

Well, if Jack had anything to do with it, the boss was in for a good time while she was off gallivanting. *What the old cow don't know can't hurt her.* His first stop after he dropped her off was an off-licence and a tobacconist, to top up the brandy and Cubans.

He checked his watch. Half eleven. Maybe he'd ring Lily and take her out to lunch. He didn't need to report in till two. He reached for the car phone and dialled the operator. It tickled him that the handset was just like his phone at home, complete with the curly wire. The rest of it was fixed to the dashboard – a box with a dial and some square buttons. The operator answered and he gave her Lily's office number and waited to be connected. God, he loved this job. Posh car, radio phone, and a boss who didn't mind what he did, so long as he was there to drive him when he wanted.

* * *

Mr Irwin was leaning over Lily's desk, checking the bank drafts, when her phone rang. He jumped, and she hid a smile. Serves him right, she thought. He didn't need to loom over her like that. He knew she'd checked them herself. He could've sent his secretary to get them, or asked Lily to take them to him. But he seemed to enjoy coming into her office – her sanctuary – and getting as close to her as he could without actually climbing down the front of her blouse.

She also knew that he was basically a coward who wouldn't do anything that would earn him a slap. Lily supposed he regarded himself as a gentleman. But that didn't stop him drooling over her cleavage. She kept her eyes on the file in front of her, refusing to give him the satisfaction of reacting. Let him look. But if he ever tried to touch, he'd get an earful he wouldn't forget.

In a strange way she was enjoying the game. Perhaps it was because she didn't find him attractive. He was no threat to her peace of mind.

She was delighted when the phone ringing made him twitch like a guilty schoolboy.

'Excuse me, sir. I need to get that.' She looked at him now, her expression polite as the phone rang again.

He gathered up the drafts and stepped back. 'Yes, yes, of course. These are all in order. Thank you, Lily.'

As she picked up the phone, he exited the room and closed the door behind him. She resisted the urge to giggle.

'Cashier's office,' she said.

'Your husband on the line, Lily.'

'Thank you.' There was a click.

'Hallo, sweetheart.'

Lily sighed. 'Jack.' It always niggled her when he phoned her at work. He didn't belong here. 'Everything all right?'

'Yeah, I'm fine, darling. Just dropped her ladyship off at the airport. Got me ear bent all the bloody way. Toffee-nosed mare.'

'Is that what you rang to tell me? 'Cause I'm a bit busy.'

'No, no, love. I thought you might like a nice bit of lunch. We could go to that café round the corner from you. I'm nearly there.'

'Why aren't you working?'

'I have been. But I ain't due to pick the boss up now until two.'

Lily looked at her watch. 'I've got a lot to do, Jack. I was just going to get a sandwich or something.'

'Aw, come on, love. An hour won't make no difference, will it? I thought it'd be nice to have a bit of time to ourselves.'

'Why didn't you say so this morning?'

'Didn't get a chance, did I? I thought you'd be glad of a break. We ain't had a normal conversation for bleeding ages, have we?'

Lily looked at the pile of work on her desk. She wanted to get on. But old habits die hard. The day she'd married Jack, her mum told her the secret to a good marriage: *'If your husband wants to take you out, don't ever turn him down, else he'll stop asking and start playing away from home.'* Christ knows where she got that from, seeing as how Dad never took her anywhere.

'I can spare half an hour,' she said. 'Not a minute more.'

'Well get your coat on then, girl. I've just pulled up outside.'

* * *

The waitress brought Leonard's order, slapping it down onto the table with hurried disregard. The pork chop looked dry, and even through the thick gravy he could see the lumps in the mashed potato. But nevertheless, it looked more appetising than the egg and chips he'd attempted to cook last night. He'd made the decision that, for as long as Daphne was at her mother's, he would eat a cooked lunch and make do with a sandwich or something on toast in the evening. It wasn't ideal, but needs must.

On his way home, he'd have to find a shop. He needed to buy bread and other staples. The larder had nothing but some flour and a few tins of dreadful things Daphne made the children eat. The refrigerator had yielded just a piece of mouldy cheese and some questionable milk.

As he ate his meal, Leonard made a mental list. The first item was a fresh bottle of Scotch. Even the most unappealing meal could be made palatable with a glass of decent whisky.

The bell above the café door chimed as new customers entered. He swallowed as he looked up to see Lily standing a few feet from him, a man helping her remove her coat.

* * *

It was warm and steamy in the café and Lily's spectacles immediately misted over. She felt Jack's hand on her shoulder and let him take her coat.

'Thanks. Hang on, I can't see a thing.' She pulled a hankie out of her bag and wiped her glasses. When she put them back on she looked straight into Leonard's eyes. She gasped.

'You all right, love?' asked Jack.

'Er, yeah. It's a bit crowded in here. Why don't we go somewhere else?'

'Everywhere's crowded. It's dinner time, ain't it? Here – that fella over there's moving.'

Leonard rose to his feet, still holding her startled gaze.

Jack took her arm. 'Come on, sweetheart. We can grab his table.'

Lily felt helpless as her husband led her over to her boss.

'Mrs Wickham.' He nodded.

'Mr Warwick.' She turned to her husband. 'Jack, this is my boss.'

'Hallo, sir. I'm Lily's other half.'

Lily wanted to cringe. Jack sounded so common. So bloody working class. She held her head up high as the men shook hands, wishing she was anywhere but here.

'Mr Wickham. How nice to meet you.'

The three of them stood in awkward silence for a moment. The waitress broke the spell as she collected Leonard's plate. 'You all done here? I'll need to set some fresh places. You can pay at the till.'

Leonard nodded. 'Yes, thank you.' He picked up his jacket from the back of his chair and shrugged it on. When the girl was out of earshot he looked at his watch and smiled politely. 'Well, it's been nice to meet you, but I have my next appointment in ten minutes. I wouldn't recommend the pork chops,' he said. 'I'll see you back at the office, Lily.'

'Yes, sir.'

'Cheerio, then,' said Jack. 'See you again.'

Not if I have anything to do with it, Lily thought as she sat down, in the chair Leonard had given up, feeling his warmth on her bottom. She shivered. It was like sitting on his lap.

* * *

Leonard paid his bill and walked out of the café, aware that Lily was sitting in the seat he'd just vacated. He wondered whether he'd ever persuade her to sit on his lap. Preferably naked. He closed his eyes, savouring the thought, but was brought rudely back to reality when he almost collided with a lamp-post.

His eyes wide open, he straightened his collar and made his way back to the office.

Lily's husband was a big chap. Quite affable, but not his sort. He didn't suppose he would ever be, given that he was the man who had Lily. He hadn't really thought about what sort of a man she would be married to, but it certainly wasn't this fellow. Lily was far too good for him.

She was far too good for anyone. But it didn't stop him wanting her with a passion he'd never thought himself capable of. And even though her husband looked as though he was more than capable of using his fists, Leonard knew that as long as Lily showed him the least encouragement, he couldn't leave her alone.

* * *

'He seems all right, your boss,' said Jack.

Lily shrugged. 'Yeah, he's not bad.'

'He fancies you.' He grinned.

'Don't be daft,' she snapped. 'He's a married man.'

'Well, his missus can't be much cop. Did you see the state of his shirt? Looked like he'd slept in it.'

'She's busy looking after her sick mother.'

'Is that what he told you? I reckon she must have scarpered. Probably got herself a bit of rough. Posh blokes are too much up their own arses to satisfy a real woman.'

'Do you have to be so bloody crude?' she hissed. 'He's a gentleman. He wouldn't sit around slagging off someone he's just met.'

Jack held up his hands. 'All right, love, calm down. I was only joking.'

'Well I don't appreciate it. That man pays my wages and he deserves a bit of respect. Now, are we going to eat or not? I told you I've only got half an hour.'

'Keep your hair on. What do you fancy?'

A quiet lunch with Leonard, she thought, picking up the menu. 'I'll have the hotpot,' she said.

Jack looked at Lily's set face and wished he'd kept quiet. *So much for a nice lunch with the missus.* He was right back in the bleeding doghouse.

16

A week later, Lily answered her office phone. 'Cashier's office.'

'Mummy,' said Caroline, 'I'm home.'

'Good girl. Everything all right?'

'Yes. I'm going to make scrambled eggs for my tea.'

'Well, be careful, and remember to soak the pan like I showed you.'

'Yes, Mummy.'

'And mind you don't burn yourself lighting the grill.'

'I won't, Mummy.'

Lily hoped she wouldn't. That grill was fierce, and if she didn't get the match to it quick, the gas would pop and flash. She lived in fear of Caroline burning herself. Lily would never be able to forgive herself.

'Make sure your hair is tied back before you go near it,' she said.

'Yes, Mummy,' she said. 'I promise.'

'Good girl.' Lily smiled.

'Will you be home soon? I've got swimming tonight.'

Lily sighed. 'Daddy said he'd be back just before five. Make sure you've got your costume on under your clothes so you don't waste time getting changed when you get there.'

'But, Mummy, it starts at five. I'll be late again!'

'No, you won't,' she assured her. 'They won't be in the water dead on five.'

'Yes they will, and they're choosing the team for the next gala tonight. I'll never get picked if I'm late,' she wailed.

'For goodness' sake, Caroline, stop whining. Daddy'll be there as soon as he can. Get him to go in and talk to the teacher if you're that worried. I'm too busy for all this fuss. Now go and have your tea and make sure you're ready to go. I'll see you later.'

Caroline was quiet for a moment, then she sniffed. 'Can't I walk? I know the way.'

Lily sighed. She really couldn't be doing with this. 'No. Daddy promised he'd take you. If you're not there when he gets home he'll worry.'

'I could write him a note. Please, Mummy, I'm big enough. I really don't want to be late.'

'I said no and I mean it. If you're going to argue with me, young lady, I'll have to see whether it's worth the fuss, letting you stay in the swimming club.'

Caroline made a strangled sound, as though she wanted to scream and shout, but Lily knew she wouldn't throw a tantrum. Lily wouldn't put up with that. 'I'm sorry, Mummy,' she said eventually. 'I'll be good.'

Lily sighed. 'I'm sorry too, darling. I don't mean to be cross. But I've got a lot to do. Off you go and have your scrambled eggs, and make sure you don't leave a mess. I'll see you later.'

'All right. Bye, Mummy.'

'Bye.'

Just before she put down the phone, Lily heard a little sob. She closed her eyes, feeling like a monster. She hung the phone on its cradle and rubbed her throbbing temples. Why did that child always manage to make her feel so guilty? If she didn't work, they wouldn't have two ha'pennies to rub together. Where did she think the money came from for all those swimming and dancing lessons and holidays? Jack might be a grafter, but he'd never earn a decent wage, not while he was content to be nothing more than some rich man's lackey.

Well, if she wanted to get anywhere, she'd have to do it herself. No good waiting for Jack to change his ways. Every time she thought they were getting somewhere, he'd spend time with Fred, and his brother would shoot all their dreams down in flames.

'What you wanna do that for?' he'd ask. 'That ain't for the likes of us,' he'd say. 'Getting a bit above yourself, ain't you, Lil?'

The stupid sod thought he was doing all right, with his house full of kids, and poor Maggie struggling to keep body and soul together on what was left of his wages after he'd been down the betting shop. Not that Maggie complained, but Lily could see it was wearing her down. Her latest baby would be number eight, if you included the one that had died years ago and the miscarriage before she'd had Samantha. There was nothing left of her figure, and apart from the odd night at bingo she never had any time for herself.

For a moment, Lily felt a pang of regret as she remembered how lively and pretty Maggie had been when they were girls. They'd both had such plans, but Maggie had let Fred suck all that out of her.

Well, Lily wasn't having any of that, thank you very much. She still had her plans. Two kids was her lot. Having another baby in the house was her worst nightmare. Sometimes she thought Beverley had got pregnant just to spite her. It still hurt to think that Jack had taken their daughter's side and let her keep the child. It was dragging them down again, just when Lily had started to see a real chance of getting on.

She couldn't rely on Jack any more. She'd have to work it out herself. One thing she knew without any doubt: she wasn't going to let Caroline go the same way as her sister. That child was bright. She could go far. *She will go far.* Lily would make sure of that. Even if she had to work all hours God sends, Lily was going to make a better life for herself and her little girl, even if it meant leaving Jack and Beverley behind.

Christ, did I really just think that?

Lily felt her heart race. She'd been unhappy for months, but until now she'd never thought about leaving. But now she'd had that thought, she couldn't ignore it. It scared her silly.

17

On a Saturday a couple of weeks later, the Roman Road pie and mash shop was packed. Lily couldn't be bothered to wait. 'Why don't we go to that new Wimpy for a change?' she suggested to her mother.

Caroline danced up and down. 'Ooh, please can we? They do sausages in circles. My friend Wendy told me.'

'I don't know,' said Lily's mum. 'It looks a bit fancy, that place.'

'Don't be daft, it's a glorified café, that's all. It's hardly the Ritz.'

'It'll be dearer than the pie shop.'

Lily shrugged. 'So what? My treat. Come on, Mum. It'll make a change. We'll have to wait ages for a table here, and I'm ready for a sit-down and a nice cuppa.'

'Please, Nanny,' said Caroline. 'All my friends have been there.'

'We can't let her be the only girl in her class who hasn't had a sausage circle, can we?' Lily laughed.

'Well, I suppose not. So long as they do a decent cup of tea. I ain't drinking none of that gnat's piss they serve in the coffee shop.'

Lily winced. Did no one care what they said in front of children these days? *Gnat's piss, I ask you. What kind of an example is that?*

'You're more than capable of telling them if it's not right, Mum. They'll soon get the message.'

They made their way through the market crowds, with Caroline skipping along ahead of them. The Wimpy was busy, but they managed to get a table straight away. Caroline was delighted with the tomato-shaped ketchup bottle. Their order was taken by a mini-skirted, bubble-gum-chewing girl with badly backcombed hair and far too much eyeliner. Lily and her mother exchanged looks. Why on earth did pretty girls think it was a good idea to put that much muck on their faces? And for Christ's sake, if that skirt was any shorter, she might as well not bother.

'What was her mother thinking?' Lily's mother muttered as the girl wove her way towards the kitchen.

Lily sighed. 'It's not that easy, Mum. The state Beverley goes out in these days, it doesn't bear thinking about. But girls don't take a blind bit of notice of anyone over thirty any more. The other day she had this dress on, it was right up to here.' She pointed to halfway up her thighs. 'Had a hole cut out here.' She traced a circle across her belly. She shook her head. 'Mary Simpkins from next door was round having a cuppa and she took one look at her and said, "You've forgotten your vest, love." Oh, it was priceless, the look on Beverley's face.' She laughed.

Mum and Caroline joined in. The old woman's cackle and the child's high-pitched giggle made Lily's heart sing.

'I saw it, Nanny. It was ever so funny, but Beverley got really cross.'

'Well it sounds like she was asking for it, the silly girl,' she replied, touching her cheek. 'You won't go round displaying yourself like that, eh? You're a good girl, you are.'

Caroline shook her head, then her little face lit up as the waitress put her plate in front of her. They'd taken a hot dog sausage and made diagonal cuts in it so that it twisted into a circle. Half a grilled tomato plonked in the middle had the child gasping with delight. The freshly made chips and a spoonful of garden peas added to her joy.

Lily thanked the girl as she placed her meal on the table. 'This looks tasty.'

Her mum, who'd picked the same as Caroline, wasn't so easy to impress. She poked at the sausage with her fork. 'That's not going to do my ulcer any good.'

'I said you should've had the omelette, Mum. Here, do you want to swap?'

'No, you're all right. I'll just try a bit of this. I can't eat a lot anyway.'

'Suit yourself,' she said, winking at Caroline, who smiled back and reached for the plastic tomato.

They ate in silence for a few minutes. Lily was content. It wasn't anything like the fancy restaurant she'd been to with Leonard, but it was miles better than the pie and mash shop, with its trays of live eels and white-tiled walls that reminded her of a public toilet. It was always full of mouthy women and their plug-ugly husbands. She wouldn't care if she never went near another pie and mash shop again. It was so common.

'How's Beverley getting on with her job?' asked her mother. 'Ready to give up yet, is she?'

'I don't know, Mum. She never talks to me about it. She's still there, so I suppose it must be all right. Seems to me though, if she's got enough sense to teach herself how to type, she could've at least tried to have found a position in a better sort of business. I mean, an invoice clerk in a joke factory. I ask you. Of course they call themselves a Fancy Goods Wholesaler, but it's all jokey rubbish.'

'Well I hope she's going to stop bringing samples home for her father. The bleeder put a plastic fly in my tea last weekend. I thought something was up when he offered to make it. If I hadn't drunk most of it before the thing floated to the top, I'd have chucked the lot over him.'

Caroline giggled, her mouth full of chips. Lily gave her one of her looks and the child subsided. There was ketchup on her chin. Lily reached over with a napkin and wiped it off, making her daughter squirm.

'He's not helping, that's for sure. He's like a big kid when he gets the chance.'

'Well if he tries that with your father, he'll live to regret it.'

'Oh, Mum, don't. Mind you, it might teach him a lesson, the bloody idiot. I look forward to going to work to get away from the pair of them.' *And to see Leonard, and to bask in his warmth and approval.*

'But not me, Mummy.' Caroline looked at her, her big hazel eyes so like Lily's own. 'You don't want to get away from me, do you?'

Lily felt a pang of guilt. She smiled brightly at her daughter. 'No, of course not. Now eat up those peas and I'll get you an ice-cream.'

'We'd better not take too long,' said Lily's mum. 'Granddad'll be wanting his kippers soon, and your dad'll be wanting to get off to the football.'

Lily finished her omelette and sat back. 'Let's hope Millwall win for a change.'

'And pigs might fly,' scoffed her mother.

* * *

'Tell me again why we bother with this bunch of shysters, Fred,' said Jack. 'I ain't seen a worse team in all my bleeding life. What was they thinking of, putting that idiot on the wing? He can't run; he can't kick. The stupid bastard's useless.'

Fred nodded, his expression grim. 'Waste of space.'

'It's a bleeding miracle we ain't five-nil down already. I reckon they should give our goalie a medal. King, ain't it? Poor sod's done more work than any of them today.' At that moment, the goalie slipped and the ball hit the back of the net. 'Jesus Christ!' Jack put his hands to his head. 'What is he playing at? He could've saved that. Our sodding mother could've bloody saved that!'

The half-time whistle blew. The brothers headed for the bar. They managed to find a couple of stools and sat cradling their pints, their expressions morose. They didn't speak until they were halfway through their beers.

'Family all right?' asked Jack. 'When's the baby due?'

'Not bad. The boys are being little sods as usual, but they ain't bad. Maggie's got a couple of months yet. She ain't happy. Her legs are playing her up something rotten. Doc says they can't do nothing while she's pregnant, but if they get any worse she'll need an operation.'

'What's that, her veins?'

'Yeah. Bloody ugly, all purple lumps and that. I tell you, when I think about how gorgeous her legs was when I met her, I can't believe it. Beautiful legs she had.'

'Well, what d'you expect, you silly sod? You keep getting her up the duff, the poor cow's going to be worn out.'

'Well, a man needs his oats, don't he?'

'Yeah, but ain't you never heard of johnnies?'

'Is that what Lil makes you use?' Fred sneered. 'I ain't wearing one of them. What's the point? You can't feel nothing with a bleeding rubber on.'

'Not any more. She's on that new Pill. I don't have to worry about a thing. I can get me leg over anytime.' He grimaced. 'Well, I could, until our Bev delivered her little surprise and started World War Three.'

'I'll bet. Ain't Lily calmed down yet?'

'Has she heck. She's been in a mood for months. Her and Bev can't be in the same room for five minutes without all hell breaking loose. Then she turns on me. I'll tell you, Fred, I can't win in my house these days. Did I tell you Bev's got a job?'

'What about the baby?'

'Her mate's looking after her. Bev worked it all out for herself. Taught herself to type on Lily's little portable, sorted a childminder, everything. But still Lily ain't happy.'

'Why not? She did the same, didn't she?'

'Exactly. So she ain't got a leg to stand on when she tells Bev she needs to be at home. Lil didn't like it, mate. Never expected it to come back and bite her on the arse.' He finished his beer. 'Come on, get that down you. They'll be kicking off again in a minute.'

Fred drained his glass and stood up. 'So what's this job then?' They made their way back to the terraces.

Jack laughed. 'She's an invoice clerk at a joke factory. They make stuff like plastic flies and them cushions what fart when you sit on them. Oh, and imitation dog poo.'

'No! You're having me on.' Fred laughed.

'Yeah, I kid you not. Bloody hilarious. But Lil's furious. Can't stand the stuff. She says it's common.' He rolled his eyes. 'Like I said, she's permanently pissed off these days.'

'You know your trouble, little brother? You ain't giving her enough. Get her on her back, give her bit of the other, Bob's your uncle.'

Jack shook his head. 'You really are a stupid sod sometimes, ain't you?'

'Yeah? Well it ain't my missus who's kicking off, is it? Mine's happy, and three times a week I get me end away, regular as clockwork, even when she's got a bun in the oven. Try it, mate. Even if she still ain't happy, you'll be too knackered to care.'

18

Jack made a quick stop at Covent Garden and got some nice flowers for Lily. He'd drop them off at her office on his way past. With any luck the girls there would make a fuss, and Lily would be pleased. He had to do something to get himself out of the doghouse. She'd been well fed up with him last night.

He should have known better, he supposed. Just because him and the girls thought it was funny to leave the back door open and a fake dog turd on the kitchen floor, didn't mean Lily would appreciate the joke. Christ, she'd hit the roof. It didn't help that the rest of them had laughed till they had tears running down their faces.

Yeah, delivering some fancy flowers so everyone could see should get him back in her good books. For a couple of hours at least.

* * *

Lily had been in with Mr Irwin, going over some estate accounts, when Jack arrived with a huge bouquet of hothouse flowers. He hadn't waited around, but left them at the reception desk with a note. '*For my gorgease wife*,' he'd written. She sighed. If he didn't know how to spell it, he should have written something else. She was embarrassed. The girls in the office had seen it and now they'd be laughing about it. She was sick of people laughing. Her whole bloody life was one big joke.

'Oh, Lily, they're beautiful. Is it a special occasion?' asked the receptionist.

She shook her head, trying to keep her smile from slipping.

'Not that I can think of. He just likes surprising me sometimes.'

'You're so lucky,' sighed one of the typists.

'I'll just take these into the kitchen and put them in the sink,' she said.

Leonard came out of his office as she walked past, most of her upper body obscured by the blooms. 'Lily? Is that you?'

She peered round the flowers at him. 'Yes, Mr Warwick. Did you want something?'

He raised his eyebrows. 'Where on earth did those come from?'

She tried to keep her expression calm. 'A surprise from my husband,' she said. 'I'm sorry, I know you're waiting to go through the bank draft orders. I'll just take them into the kitchen and I'll grab the files and be back.'

'Jolly good. I'll see you in a moment.' He turned and went back into his office, closing the door behind him.

Lily tightened her lips. *Damn!*

* * *

Leonard sat at his desk, waiting for Lily to come in. His hands were shaking. He'd felt hot anger when she'd told him who the flowers were from, which was totally illogical. A husband had every right to make romantic gestures. If they'd been from another man, it would have had quite a different connotation. No, he was relieved they were from her husband. What enraged him was the fact that he couldn't give her flowers, and he yearned to do so.

A soft knock at his door heralded her arrival. 'Come in,' he said.

Lily entered carrying a pile of case files. He stood up and hurried to take them from her. She looked startled when his hands brushed her arms.

'Oh! Thank you.' She gave them up, retrieving her notepad and pencil from the top and sitting in the chair opposite his own. He watched with satisfaction as she smoothed her skirt down with a nervous hand.

'Is it a special occasion?' he couldn't help asking. 'Have we missed your birthday?'

She shook her head. 'No, no. Nothing like that.' She sighed, staring into her lap. 'My husband likes to make big gestures.'

He relaxed into his chair. 'But not always the right ones?' he asked.

Her head snapped up at his soft tone. 'He means well,' she said.

'Most people mean well.' He smiled. 'But that doesn't mean we poor males get it right very often.'

She nodded, her lips closed tight, as though she didn't trust herself to speak. He longed to reach across and touch her lips, to soothe her.

He waited for a moment, but she didn't break her silence. What did he expect? That she would tell him why she was unhappy? He was a fool.

'Shall we get on?' he asked.

Her relief was palpable. She adjusted her glasses and leaned forward, her pencil poised over her notepad. Leonard opened the first file and issued instructions. Lily recorded everything in short-hand, her fingers flying over the page. Within twenty minutes they were finished, and she left, closing the door behind her.

He sat for a moment, his eyes closed, breathing in her lingering perfume. It wasn't enough. It was never enough. But it was all he could hope for.

Lily worked like a demon, focussing on her tasks, hiding from everyone. Could she go on like this? At home everything was a mess. She couldn't talk to Jack any more. He didn't understand; he probably never had. He did what he thought would keep the peace; that was all. She dreaded going home at night, so made excuses to go out, to stay away. His stupid, childish jokes were the last straw. She couldn't stand it.

Why did he think that an overblown gesture like those flowers would make a difference? She sighed. She knew why. Every time she was annoyed, he did something like that. And every bloody time she'd taken pity on him and let him get away with it. Like she'd told Leonard, he meant well. The trouble was, it didn't work any more. Their problems were too big now to solve with a few showy flowers.

The bank draft orders were ready. She needed to get Mr Warwick to sign them. She felt like a dizzy schoolgirl – dreading having to go into his office, but longing to see him. But dear God, she was asking for trouble if she went down that road.

Lily pulled off her specs. She leaned forward, elbows on the table, rubbing her throbbing temples. She was getting more and more of her heads these days. She just couldn't relax.

Maybe she should look for another job. The worse things got at home, the more she was tempted to do something stupid with Leonard Warwick. He might be the soul of discretion when other people were around, but when they were alone he didn't bother to hide the fact that he fancied her. It would be so easy to give in. But it wouldn't be enough. A few kisses wouldn't put her world right. It would make things harder than ever.

At lunchtime she would go and get a paper and start looking for a new job. She'd hate to leave here, but she couldn't stand much more of this temptation. Maybe if she got away from here, she could stop comparing her husband to her boss all the time and finding Jack wanting.

Daphne, home at last, had made Leonard a pack of sandwiches. Cheese and pickle. He grimaced. Surely after more than a decade of marriage she should remember that he couldn't stand Branston. He dropped the packet into his waste bin and put on his jacket. He needed some fresh air. It was hard to concentrate after spending time with Lily and not being able to touch her. Since she left his office earlier he'd been functioning – taking calls, studying case files, dealing with correspondence – but all the time his mind had been thinking about Lily, imagining Lily. He didn't know how he managed to get through the morning without finding excuses to go to her or to call her back to his office.

Outside, a pale sun made him think of spring, even though it was a long way off. He liked spring, after months of cold and rain. People would leave off their heavy winter coats. Women would favour pastel colours after the dull, dark shades of winter. He headed for his usual café, unable to prevent himself from imagining the sort of dresses Lily would be wearing in the spring and summer – smooth cottons in warm colours, sleeveless, but worn with a modest light cardigan in the office. He might be able to persuade her to walk with him in the park on a warm day. She'd take off her cardigan to enjoy the sun on her arms. He'd reach out and stroke her bare skin...

A large lady brandishing a furled umbrella like a sword nearly mowed him down. Brought back down to earth. He shook his head to clear it and concentrated on where he was going.

He glanced in the window as he reached the café. Lily was sitting at a table, reading a newspaper. He was about to go in and suggest they lunch together when he noticed the pen in her hand. She frowned in concentration, and as he watched she circled something.

Dear God, she's looking for another job.

His first instinct was to storm in and confront her. She couldn't leave; how could he bear it? Lily raised her head and smiled as someone approached the table, folding up the newspaper and putting it under her coat on the chair beside her. One of the girls from the typing pool sat down. She said something, and Lily shook her head. His view was obscured by the waitress delivering an order.

Leonard turned away, his appetite gone.

19

'I hate you! You're a fat, ugly pig!' Caroline screamed from upstairs as Lily walked through the front door.

'Oof, you little mare!' Beverley yelled.

Lily could see Kerry, crying, in the high chair in the kitchen.

She grabbed the baby and ran upstairs.

'What the hell is going on?' she asked, as she stood in the doorway of Caroline's room. She still had her coat on.

'That little cow punched me,' Beverley snapped, pointing at Caroline with one hand and rubbing her belly with the other.

'Mummy, she's been horrible to me. She's always hitting me.'

'You deserve it, you—'

'Shut up, the pair of you,' Lily shouted. The baby cried louder, dripping snot on Lily's coat. 'No one will be doing any more hitting in this house. Here.' She thrust the baby at Beverley. 'I suggest you pay more attention to your own child and leave your sister alone.'

Beverley took the baby, who rubbed her wet face on her blouse.

'Eugh! Bloody hell.' Beverley held Kerry away from her and walked out of the room. 'Fine, I'll sort mine out. And you'd better sort yours out, n'all. She's packing to leave.'

Lily looked at the pile of clothes and books on the bed, and then at the pale, tearful expression on Caroline's face. She felt herself go cold at the thought of her little girl so unhappy that she wanted to run away. She pressed her lips together, pushed her hands into her sides to stop herself shaking. Was she really such a terrible mother that it had come to this? She closed her eyes and tried to calm down.

'Put that lot away right now, young lady,' she said quietly.

Then she walked out and shut the door behind her. She just reached the sanctuary of her own bedroom before she burst into tears.

Jack walked in the front door as Lily came down the stairs an hour later.

'All right, love?'

She stood on the bottom stop, holding on to the banister with one hand, rubbing her temple with the other.

'Oh, everything's fine. Beverley thinks it's all right to leave the baby screaming in her high chair while she lays into Caroline, who's upstairs packing.'

'Where's she going?'

Lily shook her head, wincing in pain. 'Christ knows, but she's trying to get all her books and clothes into her little red overnight case.'

'Well she won't get far carrying all them books of hers.'

'No. Thank God for the Puffin Club, eh?' She tried and failed to smile.

Jack sighed. 'Aw, come here.' He pulled her into his arms and gave her a hug. She laid her head against his shoulder. 'Want a cuppa?'

'I'd really rather have a couple of Anadin and just get out of here for an hour. The girls can sort themselves out.'

'All right, darlin'. Where d'you want to go?'

She thought for a bit. 'There's that new restaurant on Eltham High Street. Shall we give it a try?'

'Ain't it doing foreign stuff?'

Lily rolled her eyes. 'It's Italian,' she said. 'You can have a spag bol.'

'Fair enough.' He shrugged. 'Let's go.'

'Just mind you don't get sauce all over your shirt.'

Romano's was charming, although Lily doubted there'd be much call for it round here. It was done up like something out of a Gina Lollobrigida film, with gingham tablecloths and pictures of places in Italy on the walls. Dean Martin sang in the background. On the table between them was an empty wine bottle wrapped in a raffia basket and with a red candle stuck in its neck. The waiter came over and made a big fuss about lighting it. Lily watched the drips of hot wax run down and join the clumps that had collected on previous nights. She wondered about the other couples who had sat here, laughing over the waiter's accent and trying to figure out what the names on the menu meant.

'Christ, love. I ain't got a clue what this bloody thing says.'

'Let me see.' He handed it over. 'You'd think they'd know no one round here speaks Italian,' she muttered, trying to work out what the strange-sounding dishes might be.

'What do we do?' Jack looked panicked.

'Well, either we point at something and hope for the best, or we ask the waiter to tell us what it says.'

'Have they got spag bol on there?'

She checked. *Spaghetti alla Bolognese.* 'Yeah, you're all right.'

'Thank Christ. We'll have that then.'

'Don't you fancy trying something new?'

'Nah, I'm all right. What about you?'

'Mmm. I'm feeling a bit adventurous.'

Jack laughed. 'God help you.'

The waiter approached. Lily took a breath and pointed.

'Ah, *Scallopine Milanese. Bella*. You like wine?'

'Just a beer for me, mate,' said Jack.

'I'd like a glass of white wine, please,' said Lily.

'Would you like to see the wine list, *Signora*?'

'I'll leave it up to you.' She smiled.

The waiter bowed, took the menu and headed for the kitchen.

'What did you order?'

'I'm not sure,' she said. 'I think he said scallops.'

'That'll be nice.'

Lily was sitting with her back to the wall, so she could see most of the interior of the restaurant. There were only a couple of other tables occupied, but it was still early. And it was a weeknight. It probably didn't get very busy until the weekend.

The waiter returned with their drinks. Jack looked at the tall thin glass in front of him, but didn't say anything until they were alone again.

'That looks like piss,' he said under his breath. 'I asked for a beer.'

She leaned forward. 'Jack, stop it!' she hissed. 'It's obviously Italian beer. Just drink it, and don't show me up.'

He looked at her and Lily sat back. 'I ain't stupid,' he said. 'And I ain't one of the kids. What's the matter with you, telling me not to show you up?'

She reached for her wine, but her hand was shaking so she pressed her palm to the red and white tablecloth. 'I'm sorry. I'm a bit on edge, that's all.'

He nodded. 'How's your head?'

'Still there.' She gave a weak smile. 'You wouldn't believe the bloody racket when I got home tonight. I thought they were killing each other.'

'It's just noise, love. You shouldn't let it get to you.'

'Yeah, well it does. I can't be doing with it. When I think of what Beverley could've done with her life—'

'For God's sake, Lily. Can we change the record for tonight? It ain't worth getting in a state about. It's done. She'll be all right.'

Lily felt rage building up inside her. She wanted to talk about this. She wanted to scream and rant and... and... Oh, God. What was the point?

'Fine,' she sighed. She picked up her glass and sipped the cool, crisp wine. 'This is nice. What's the beer like?'

Jack took a reluctant sip. He swallowed and ran his tongue round his lips. 'Tastes all right,' he said. 'Still looks like piss, though.'

Lily ignored him and went back to people-watching. The other diners were all couples. They seemed relaxed, comfortable in their surroundings. She didn't expect any of them had had to bluff their way through the menu. She wondered if she'd ever reach a point when she'd be able to take things like that in her stride.

She looked at Jack. His beer was almost gone. He'd probably have another in a minute. Not that he'd get drunk. He wasn't that sort of a man. He liked his pint, but she never worried about him having too many.

The waiter arrived. 'Your *scallopine*, Signora.'

Lily looked at her food as the waiter placed a steaming plate of spag bol in front of her husband. They both refused the huge pepper mill. 'Just some salt, please mate,' said Jack.

'Of course.' The waiter pointed to the salt cellar on the table. 'Would you also like some *parmigiano*?'

'Eh?' said Jack. 'What's that then?'

Lily closed her eyes. 'I think that's cheese,' she said. She usually grated some Cheddar over her spag bol.

'*Si, Signora*. How you say? Parmesan?'

'Yes, I'll have some please. Just a little.' She didn't really want any, but felt she must so that at least she wouldn't look so bloody ignorant.

The waiter made a performance of sprinkling parmesan on her plate. '*Signor?*'

'No thanks. But I'll have another beer.' The waiter bowed and left.

'What's that?' Jack pointed at her food with his fork. 'It ain't scallops.'

Lily cut into it, picking up a small piece and sniffing it. 'It's some sort of meat. In breadcrumbs.' She took a bite. It melted in her mouth. 'Oh, God, that's lovely.' She'd have to pop into the library and see if she could find an Italian dictionary. Whatever this was, she wanted to know. 'How's your spaghetti?'

Jack swirled his fork and brought it to his lips. 'It smells a bit funny,' he said, hesitating.

'That'll be the garlic. They always use garlic on the Continent. I don't put it in my spag bol because everyone moans about the smell.'

'You might have warned me.'

'Oh, stop fussing and eat it. You might like it.'

'Don't blame me if I'm stinking of this stuff later.'

'It can't be any worse than when you've had a curry. At least you won't fart. Anyway, I'm pretty sure there's some garlic in mine as well, so we'll cancel each other out.'

Jack didn't look convinced. 'Oh sod it, I'm hungry,' he said, and took a mouthful.

They ate in silence. Lily loved it, but she could see Jack was struggling. He wasn't likely to want to come here again. Maybe she could persuade one of her sisters to try it? Or maybe Leonard... Of course not! Even if Jack never set foot in the place again, she would be off her rocker to think she could bring another man here. It was too close to home.

To reinforce that thought, the door opened and a couple walked in. Lily recognised the woman. It was Mrs Baker from three doors up. She didn't see Lily as she smiled up at the man by her side. The waiter greeted them and led them to a table on the other side of the restaurant.

'What's up?' asked Jack.

'Nothing, why?'

'You're frowning.'

Lily raised her eyebrows. 'Am I? Didn't mean to. I just saw Mrs Baker come in. I thought her husband worked nights.'

'He does.'

'So who's the fella she's with then? No, don't turn round! She'll know we're talking about her.'

Jack rolled his eyes. 'I ain't got eyes in the back of me head. What does he look like?'

'Tall. Fair hair.'

'Well that definitely ain't her old man. He's dark. It ain't their son is it?'

Lily opened her mouth to say, '*Of course not, the boy's only twelve,*' when the mystery man picked up Mrs Baker's hand and kissed it. It was a romantic gesture, perfect for the seductive atmosphere of the restaurant. Only Jack seemed oblivious to the charms of the place. He was concentrating on getting his spaghetti from his fork to his mouth before it splattered all over his shirt.

Mrs Baker looked round, her face a mask of horror as she clocked Lily staring at her. Lily remembered how nervous she'd been at the restaurant with Leonard. They'd been miles from home, but she'd been convinced someone would recognise them. She felt a moment of longing for the excitement of that night, and she understood Mrs Baker's need to risk everything for some stolen moments with a man who clearly adored her. She smiled at her neighbour. After a moment, something in her expression must have reassured the woman and she gave Lily a shy, grateful smile in return.

Lily turned back to Jack and shrugged. 'Actually it's hard to tell in this light. I can see now it's someone else. She just looks like Mrs Baker.'

'Blimey, Lil, that could've been awkward. What if you'd gone and told someone you'd seen her with some fancy man? Her old man would kill her.'

'I wouldn't do that. I'm not a gossip.' She cut into her *scallopine*, her appetite gone. She forced herself to eat, and refused to let her gaze wander in the direction of the lovers. God, she envied them.

Jack finished his meal and took a long draught of beer. 'So, love. Where do you reckon our Caroline was planning on running away to?'

'I have no idea.' But she knew how her daughter felt.

'I thought we could take her out on Saturday,' said Jack. 'You know, spoil her a bit. What do you think?'

'Good idea. Only I promised Mum I'd take over some gardening catalogues so she can pick out a new climber.'

'It's a bit early for planting ain't it? We could still have frost and snow.'

'We weren't going to get it yet, just look through the catalogues and see what they've got. We might need to order it soon to make sure it arrives at the right time for planting. She wants something to climb up that old brick wall at the back of the garden. If we get a good rambling rose, it will cover it in a couple of years, and it'll smell gorgeous.'

'And it has to be done Saturday?'

'Not necessarily. But I've still got to get some shopping done.' She sighed. 'I suppose I could go round to Mum after work on Friday, but then you'll have to pick Caroline up from Brownies.'

'Can't. I promised Fred I'd help him decorate. Maggie wants the place sorted before the new baby arrives.'

'What are they doing?' Lily felt bad that she hadn't seen her friend for a couple of weeks. But the closer Maggie got to giving birth again, the less Lily felt she had in common with her. 'New wallpaper in the living room. We've got to lay some new carpet n'all.'

'Where did they get the money for new carpet?'

'They ain't paid much for it. Some geezer down the betting shop got it off the back of a lorry. Nice stuff it is – Axminster. I wouldn't mind a bit of it for our place.'

'I will not have stolen goods in my house.'

Jack held up his hands. 'I was only saying. I knew it weren't worth the grief.'

'Good. I won't have it.'

'You didn't say that when I brought home all that lovely turf from Wembley when they changed the pitch.'

'You told me you'd paid for that.'

'I did pay for some of it. But what's the point of working a weekend on a selling job if you ain't getting some perks out of it? We've got the best-looking grass in the street.'

'Are you telling me that you stole some of that turf from your firm, when they asked you to sell it? Jesus Christ, Jack. Have you no sense? If you'd *been* caught you'd have been sacked on the spot, and then where would we be?'

'All right, keep your hair on. It was only a few yards. No one noticed. It weren't like the boss was going to hang around and offload it, was he? The wanker was off playing golf. You won't see him get his hands dirty.'

'He doesn't need to. He's clever enough to earn a decent living and to be able to pay for other people to get their hands dirty.'

'Yeah, people like me. I'm the daft sod who runs round after him, delivering him from A to B, taking his missus all over the place – now that's a bloody good perk of the job, using the firm's driver to shift the old woman around so he don't have to bother. So don't you worry about him sacking me for helping meself to a couple of sods of Wembley turf, darlin'. The stuff he gets away with is nobody's business.'

Lily patted at her lips with a napkin. He just didn't understand. 'Your boss is a director of the company. He practically owns it. If he wants you to stand on one leg and sing *Dixie* in the firm's time, that's up to him. He's paying.'

'Yeah, I know. That's why I do what I'm told. But just because he's the boss don't mean he's something special, love. He sends me off to drive his missus around while he's shagging some tart, so don't tell me he's better than me just because I nicked some stuff he ain't even missed.'

She stared at him. 'He's having an affair?'

'Always.'

'Why didn't you tell me?'

'I dunno. I didn't think you'd approve.'

'Too right I don't.'

'So, what do you want me to do about it? Get another job? I thought you liked having the fancy car parked outside, and me in a shirt and tie.'

'I... I do. But, God, I had no idea the man was—'

'Oh come on, Lily, love. Them sorts are at it all the time. I reckon the wife's getting some from her hairdresser, n'all. She's always rushing over there for an hour or two, but she don't look no different when she comes out – apart from the twinkle in her eye.' He winked.

Lily flinched. 'It's all so bloody sordid.'

'That's the difference between them and us.'

Lily glanced over at Mrs Baker and her lover. She thought

about the times she'd been alone with Leonard, how she was always thinking about him, *wanting* him. Was she really so different from Jack's boss and his wife? Or from Mrs Baker? Probably not. She felt sick and dirty, even though she hadn't done more than hold the man's hand. They hadn't even kissed, but she still felt guilty. She didn't want to be like them. She wanted *love*. She wanted to be with a man who understood her, who enjoyed the same things, who saw life in the same way that she did.

'So,' said Jack when she remained silent. 'I'll take Caroline somewhere on Saturday, shall I? Then you can get your hair done and see your mum in peace.'

'If you like.' She'd do something with her later in the week. Perhaps they could go to the Wimpy Bar again. Caroline had liked that. She'd hardly seen the poor child all week; no wonder she was on the point of running away. Dear God, it didn't bear thinking about. What if she'd done it? No, she wouldn't, would she? Caroline loved a bit of drama, but she was too timid to just march out into the big wide world on her own. Lily really needed to give her a bit more attention. But she was always so busy, and so tired. She'd just have to find the time.

Jack finished his beer. His plate was clean. 'Did you enjoy it?' she asked.

He wrinkled his nose. 'It was all right, but I'd rather have something with chips next time.' He pointed at her plate. 'You gonna finish that?'

She shook her head. 'It's nice, but I'm not hungry.'

'Chuck it over here. Shame to waste it.'

'Jack!' She grabbed her plate when he would have swapped it for his empty one. 'What are you doing? Someone will see.'

'So what? I'm paying for it, so why ain't I allowed to eat it? That poncey little portion of spag bol ain't filled me up. Come on, Lily, hand it over. They're more likely to notice if you sit there glaring at me.' He grinned and held out his empty plate.

Lily had no choice but to take it before they attracted attention. She shook her head. 'You're worse than the kids sometimes,' she said. He laughed and blew her a kiss. She sat back, sipping on her wine while he demolished what was left of her meal.

'Blimey, that tasted better than it looked. I wish I'd had that now.'

'It was sheer luck we got it. Maybe I should have some Italian lessons.' At least in the French restaurant she'd understood most of the menu, thanks to her evening classes. 'We could save up and go on holiday there. I've always wanted to see Rome, or Verona – where Romeo and Juliet lived. The gardens in Italy are supposed to be out of this world.'

'Fred reckons Italy's a dump.'

'Fred reckons everywhere's a dump. He saw a couple of bombed-out ports in the war, and he's an expert on the whole world. Well, I'd rather see it for myself and make up my own mind, thank you very much.'

'I was just saying.'

'I know,' she sighed. 'Sorry. It wasn't a good idea, coming here. I thought it would be nice.'

'It's all right. Just not our sort of place, that's all.'

It was silent when they walked back into the house. Beverley was sitting in the kitchen drinking coffee and reading a magazine.

Lily shivered. 'It's freezing in here.'

Bev shrugged, not looking up. 'Is it? I'm not cold.'

Lily went to fill the kettle. There were traces of cigarette ash in the sink. She sighed. That would explain the temperature in here as well. Beverley must have had the back door open, trying to clear the air.

'If you must smoke, you could at least hide the evidence.'

'I don't see why I have to hide it at all. I'm not a kid.'

'No, you're not. Which means you should know better. What are you trying to do, Beverley? Annoy me, or kill yourself? You're a mother now. You should be looking after yourself better.'

'Oh, for Christ's sake!' Beverley slammed her hands on the table, making Lily jump. 'You do nothing but moan. You ain't even noticed I cleaned up in here, have you? There ain't no pleasing you, you miserable old cow!' She stood up, and the chair toppled over and clattered on the lino.

Lily was stunned. She turned round as Beverley pushed past her father in the doorway and ran upstairs. Jack met her gaze and raised his eyebrows. She closed her eyes, trying to calm down.

'Oh God, I can't do anything right, can I?'

'Don't worry about it,' said Jack, coming into the room. He set the chair upright and pulled Lily into a bear hug. She sank into his embrace, fighting back tears. He felt so solid, so reassuring.

'Everything's such a bloody mess. I just want what's best for the girls, and I get it wrong every time.'

'Now that's daft. You're doing fine.'

'They both hate me.'

'No they don't. Here, come on, gorgeous. You're getting yourself in a state over nothing. You know what they're like – it'll all be forgotten in the morning.'

'I doubt it. Every time I open my mouth, Beverley snaps. It's getting to the point where I daren't say a thing. I worry about her. Why can't she see that?'

'She knows that. She's just a contrary mare, that's all. If you say the sky's blue, she'll say it's pink, just to get a rise out of you. They're all like that when they're growing up.'

'I wasn't. God, my mother would have slapped me from here to kingdom come if I'd spoken to her like that.'

'Yeah, mine n'all. But it's different now. We've got to face it, Lily, life ain't the same as it was when we was her age. We was just out of the war, remember?'

'Don't remind me.' She shivered.

'I'd rather all our kids had to worry about was getting caught sneaking the odd fag.' Jack rubbed her back. They stayed like that for a few minutes, each lost in their own thoughts.

Jack kissed her cheek. 'Want a cuppa?'

'Please.'

'You go in the front room – it'll be warmer in there. I'll bring it in.'

She nodded and went into the living room, putting on the electric fire in an effort to dispel the chill that permeated her whole body. She sat in an armchair, her arms wrapped around herself, staring at the elements as they glowed orange. She felt sick, and she was pretty sure it wasn't the meal she'd eaten.

No, this sickness was guilt, pure and simple. She was a failure as a mother and a failure as a wife.

* * *

'Leonard, wake up!'

He came back to consciousness with a jolt. Daphne was standing over him, shaking his shoulder. He shrugged her off and sat upright. Damn! He'd fallen asleep in his armchair. The television was emitting a high-pitched whine. Daphne walked over and switched it off.

'What time is it?' he asked, his voice gritty.

'Gone midnight. I thought you were coming up after the news. I just woke up and realised you were still down here.'

He rubbed a hand over his face. 'I must have dozed off.'

Daphne picked up the empty tumbler from the lamp table by his chair. She sniffed. 'I really don't think it's a good idea for you to drink during the week, dear. A cup of Horlicks would be much better.'

'Don't nag, Daphne. I hardly make a habit of it.'

She sighed. Leonard glanced up. She stood in her dressing gown, her curler-clad hair covered by a silk scarf. Her discontented face shone in the electric light, a result of the layer of cold cream she slathered on it every night before she went to bed. Cold cream – very apt. It left him cold, guiltily aware that he couldn't conjure up a shred of desire for his wife.

But that didn't mean he wasn't capable of desire. God knows, he fought it during his waking hours, but he was painfully aware that his brief nap had left him in a state that he did not want his wife to notice.

'I'm sorry, Leonard. I know you've been very busy at the office, but do you really think alcohol will help?'

'Probably not,' he admitted, rubbing a hand over his face. 'Go back to bed, dear. I'll be up in a minute.'

'Why can't you come now?'

'Because I want to finish reading an article in the *Telegraph*.'

'Well, don't be long.'

Leonard watched her go, took a deep breath and unzipped his fly. His mind filled with visions of Lily. He might not be able to take his desires to her in reality, but the mere thought of her helped him to satisfy himself within moments.

20

Jack was enjoying a quiet cup of tea after work when the phone rang.

Caroline was up in her room, reading her new book from the Puffin Club. He waited for a few seconds to see if she'd run down the stairs to answer it. Nothing happened – it must be a good book. Jack went out into the hall to answer the phone. Pips squeaked noisily as whoever was on the other end of the line struggled to put coins in the slot. He thought it must be Bev.

It was Lily. 'Jack? Are you there?'

'Yeah. Where are you, love?'

'Well Hall Station. The train was late and I missed the bus. Any chance you can come and get me? I can't walk all the way home in these heels, and I don't want to wait half an hour for the next bus.'

He sighed. He'd been on the road all day and the traffic had been hell. But it wouldn't take five minutes to get Lily.

'All right, love. I'll be there in a minute.'

'Thanks, darling. You're a lifesaver.'

He put the phone down and reached for his car keys. 'Caroline,' he called up the stairs. Silence. 'Caroline!' His shout got through and she opened her door and peered over the banister.

'Yes, Daddy?'

'I'm going to pick Mum up from the station. Do you want to come?'

She shook her head. 'No, I'm reading.'

"Course you are,' he said. 'I won't be long. Bev will be back soon as well.'

She nodded, clearly more interested in getting back to her story. Jack left her to it.

It only took a few minutes to reach the station, and by the time he did the heavens had opened. He pulled up as close to the entrance as he could. Lily was sheltering under the door canopy and dashed through the rain to the car.

He pushed open the passenger door for her and she collapsed into the seat.

'Thank God you were at home,' she said, pulling the door shut. 'I'd've got soaked. I left my umbrella at the office. I should've known it would rain.'

'Yeah, Sod's law.' He smiled and leaned over for a kiss. She offered her cheek. He would rather have had a proper kiss, but he supposed the station forecourt wasn't the most romantic place round here. 'You're lucky. I'd only been in ten minutes. Didn't even get to finish me cuppa.'

'I'll make a fresh pot. Caroline all right?'

'Yeah, reading in her bedroom.'

'Best place for her in this weather. I can't believe it's nearly Easter. It's about time we had some better weather.'

Jack put the car into gear and pulled smoothly out onto the street. He allowed himself a smile of satisfaction as traffic slowed and made room for the Jag. It never failed. Everyone respected the Great British Jaguar.

'Talking of better weather,' he said. 'I forgot to tell you. Your brother rang last night while you and Maggie were at the bingo.'

'Tony? What did he want?'

'He's off to Spain with his motorbike racing. Wanted to know if I'd drive the lorry.'

'That's typical of him, isn't it? He knows full well you've got a full-time job. You can't go gallivanting off with him for God knows how long just so he can ride his bloody bike.'

Jack concentrated on the road, realising he'd messed that up royally.

He could see Lily out of the corner of his eye.

She turned towards him. 'Tell me you told him no.'

He shrugged. What could he say? Why hadn't he waited till he got her home and poured a gin inside her or something?

'Jack, you can't. What about your job?'

'It's only for a fortnight. I can take some of me work holidays.'

'What about me and the girls?'

'You could come with us.'

She sat back in her seat and folded her arms. 'If you think I'm going to spend my holidays in a stinking lorry full of motorbikes, you've got another think coming.'

Oh bugger.

He pulled into the cul-de-sac and parked smoothly in front of their gate. Lily got out without a word and ran for the front door. By the time he got there she'd left her wet coat in the hall and was slamming cupboard doors in the kitchen.

He sidled into the kitchen, keeping his back to the wall. She was mad enough to start chucking stuff, so he'd better be careful.

'Anything I can do, love?' he asked.

'Yes, you can ring that useless lump of a brother of mine and tell him to find his own driver.' She swung towards him, a frying pan in her hand. Jack opened his arms and smiled.

'Lily, darling. I didn't think you'd mind. He's going to pay me.'

She laughed, but he could see she wasn't finding it funny. 'Like he was going to pay you when you painted and decorated his whole bloody house last year?'

'He got all the stuff for that. It didn't cost me nothing.'

'Nicked it, more like. And he never paid you a penny for your time. It would've cost him a fortune to pay someone else to do it. He wouldn't get his hands dirty, the useless bugger. How can you trust him? He won't just want you to drive. He'll have you running around after him like a blue-arsed fly. You'll end up doing everything, while he jumps on his flipping bike and acts like he's Stirling Moss on two wheels.'

Jack knew that. But it would be a laugh, and he fancied a change from sitting on his arse and wearing a pretty-boy uniform.

'And what about his wife and kids, seeing as how you've already decided your family will have the privilege of being dragged round Spain like bloody vagrants?'

'She thinks it's a great idea. She's going to see her mum in Cyprus. Tony's going to take young Vince with us. He don't see much of the boy since his divorce.'

'Oh, I see. She gets to go to Cyprus, does she, and doesn't have to put up with her stepson on her holidays? I bet she won't be travelling in the back of a lorry either.'

He winced. 'Fine! You don't like the idea. I get the message, loud and clear. We'll have an 'oliday in some poncey hotel again, shall we? I forgot you were too posh for a decent camping trip nowadays.'

'I've never liked camping, and you know that. We only ever did it because we couldn't afford anything else. It's nothing to do with being posh, it's to do with being married and deciding things together, and not letting my stupid brother talk you into joining him in his hare-brained schemes.'

She turned away, busying herself with the meal preparations. Jack ran a hand over his face. He moved closer, noting how her back stiffened. He ignored her keep-off signals and put his hands on her shoulders.

'Lily, love. I'm sorry. I never thought.'

She huffed, but didn't say anything.

'It was the idea of Spain. You always get excited about travelling to new places. I thought you'd want to go.'

'I'd love to go to Spain,' she said slowly. 'But not with my brother and a load of filthy motorbikes.'

'All right,' he sighed. 'It was a bad idea. I'll let him know.'

Lily shook her head. 'Do what you like. Just don't expect me and the girls to go with you.'

He felt a flicker of excitement. Surely she wasn't going to give in this easily? 'I can't leave you girls. How are you going to have an 'oliday?'

She shrugged. 'Maybe I'll talk to Tina, and lay it on thick that as her husband is behind all this, I should take the girls to stay in that nice house of theirs that you decorated for free while they're all away. It's not exactly the Riviera, but Hastings has got a beach, and it won't cost us anything while Tony's using you for free labour in Spain.'

He grinned. *Bloody hell! I'm getting away with it! Spain, here I come!* He wouldn't mention that the beach at Hastings was all shingle. She might change her mind again. He leaned in to kiss the back of her neck, but she wriggled out of his grasp.

'Don't push your luck,' she warned, waving the potato knife at him. 'I'm not happy about it, Jack, and you'd better let my brother know. One cocky remark from him and I won't be held responsible.'

'Gotcha. I'll tell him.'

'Good. Now let me get this dinner done before we all starve to death.'

He nodded and headed for the door.

'Have you heard from Beverley?' she asked.

'No. I expect she'll be back in a minute.'

'I hope she has the sense to wait at her friend's 'til this rain stops. I don't like the idea of her walking the baby through that. Kerry's had enough colds these past few weeks.'

The phone rang in the hall. There was a thump from above and the sound of a door opening.

'I'll get it!' Caroline yelled as she ran down the stairs.

'She must've finished her book,' said Jack. 'She wouldn't move when you rang earlier.'

Lily shook her head and turned back to her cooking. Jack smiled. All was right with his world.

'Daddy! Beverley says can you go and get her so the baby won't get wet?'

Lily looked at him over her shoulder and they shared a moment of harmony. 'Looks like she's learning some sense at last,' she said.

Jack rolled his eyes. 'Or she don't want to spoil her hairdo. Tell her I'm on my way,' he called to Caroline, reaching once again for his keys.

Lily heard him go, and let out a sigh as she carried on peeling potatoes. They hadn't had a holiday last year because of the business with the baby, then moving house so quickly. Money was tight now, so she hadn't expected anything fancy this year, but she'd thought they might manage to do something nice. Of course, her dream of a couple of weeks in the sun was just that – a dream. They'd had a lovely holiday in Austria two years ago. She'd been so happy. She'd seen what their lives could be after all her hard work in night school and getting the job at Alder & Powney.

But it hadn't lasted. And now Jack was running off to play silly beggars with her brother and his racing bikes. What on earth had possessed him?

She got the dinner on, made herself a cup of tea and took it into the living room. She turned on the television, but didn't watch it. Instead she sat in the orange chair and dreamed of sandy beaches and blue skies.

It wasn't until the front door slammed, and her peace was rudely interrupted by a squawking baby, that Lily realised the man she'd been dreaming of sharing that beach with was not Jack but Leonard.

21

'Morning, Warwick.'

'Irwin.' Leonard nodded, as he came into his office.

'I wonder if I could ask a favour of you?'

'Of course.'

'I have an elderly client, a Miss Jarvis. She's instructed me to update her will and wants to sign it today. The trouble is, she's now bedridden at a nursing home in the wilds of Essex, and I have a number of appointments today that I simply can't alter. Would you be a chum and nip out to see the old girl? She's quite a character. Used to be a nurse or something; inherited piles of family money. There's a shifty nephew waiting in the wings, expecting to bag the lot, but she's determined to cut him off at the knees. She knows she hasn't got long, so she's insisting that I send someone out with the will today. You can use my car.'

Leonard nodded. It would be good to get out of the office for a couple of hours. Some days, just knowing that Lily was in the building made him restless, and today was one of those days. He'd seen her arrive, laughing at something one of the secretaries had said. His wife, on the other hand, had been sour-faced and mono-

syllabic this morning. The contrast between the two women had
left him yearning to escape his dismal routine.

'I'll do that for you. I take it one of the nursing home staff will
be the second witness?'

Irwin shook his head. 'I'd rather it didn't look like a deathbed
statement that the boy can contest. Don't want to find ourselves in
the middle of a dispute over her state of mind, do we? No, you can
take Lily Wickham. I've already spoken to her. She'll be ready to go
at eleven. I'll get my secretary to give you all the details, along with
the will and a copy. Cheers, old chap. Appreciate it.'

And with that he was gone, leaving Leonard staring at the
closed door, his heart pounding in his chest.

* * *

At eleven o'clock, Lily stood, coat on, handbag on her arm, in
Leonard's office while Mr Irwin's secretary Beryl handed over the
documents and the directions to the nursing home. She felt hot
and foolish. She shouldn't have put her coat on before leaving her
office, but was in such a state that she didn't think. Now she looked
like a silly girl, over-eager for an outing.

At last Beryl left and Leonard stood. He smiled at her. 'Ready?'

She stifled a giggle. Was he blind? Here she was, buttoned up
and sweating, feeling like a right lemon, and he had to ask? 'Yes,'
she said, trying to look professional. 'Would you like me to take
those?' She indicated the packet of papers.

He looked at the documents. 'I think I'd better take my briefcase. By all accounts this lady is a valued client, and even though
she's frail I believe she has all of her faculties. She'll expect us to be
completely professional.'

She felt herself shrink. 'Of course. I didn't think.'

He dropped the documents into his briefcase and snapped it

shut. 'I'll just get my coat.' He came and stood in front of her. She stared at him, wondering what he was waiting for. He raised his eyebrows, his eyes twinkling. 'Excuse me, Lily. It's behind you.'

She blushed and moved out of his way, remembering the time the situation had been reversed.

He shrugged into his camel coat and picked up his case. 'Shall we go?'

He opened the door and stood back for her to pass. Lily felt everyone's gaze on her as they walked through the general office and reception. She didn't breathe again until the doors of the lift closed, hiding them from prying eyes.

It took a while to get out of the City, but eventually they were driving along Commercial Road. Lily sat next to Leonard in Mr Irwin's Rover, her hands crossed on her lap, handbag by her feet. She stared out of the windscreen, seeing familiar landmarks. There was the council estate where her sister-in-law lived. They sped past the turning for Crisp Street where the market was in full swing. No doubt her mother-in-law was there, buying something for her and old Bert's dinner. Lily didn't look; she didn't want to see anyone she knew. She didn't want to have to explain to Leonard if someone spotted her and waved like a lunatic.

She wanted to say something, anything. But she was so nervous, she didn't dare. Her stomach was churning. Out of the corner of her eye she could see Leonard's fine fingers on the steering wheel. They looked so different from Jack's work-roughened, heavy hands.

At last they left the East End behind, and Lily relaxed and began to enjoy the ride.

'Do you know this part of the world?' he asked.

She nodded. 'I know bits of Essex. We've got relatives in Aveley and Canvey, and we sometimes come out to Epping Forest for a picnic.'

'I've never seen it. We usually head down to the New Forest. Is it nice?'

'It's lovely, and so close to London. It's good for a day out.'

'I'll bear it in mind.'

They lapsed into silence.

Lily wanted to fidget, but remained still. She didn't want to talk about days out with Jack. She wanted to savour every second of being alone with Leonard, even if it was only because of work and perfectly innocent.

She didn't feel innocent. She felt guilty and excited and verging on hysterics. What was it about him? Why did he make her feel so reckless? She took a deep breath and tried to bring herself under control.

'How's your mother-in-law?' she asked, not because she wanted to know, but because she was punishing herself. 'Is her wrist healed now?'

Leonard sighed. 'Just about. It's taken longer than expected. I was beginning to think she was malingering, just for the attention.'

'Oh dear. I'm sorry to hear that. I suppose she's been taking up a lot of your time.'

'Not mine. Thankfully the old girl doesn't think much of me, so is happy for me to stay away. But my wife has been run ragged by it all. I had to put my foot down in the end because the children were missing school and Daphne was exhausted. Her mother expected her to be at her beck and call all the time. As it is, we managed to persuade a spinster cousin to step in to look after her so that they could come home.'

'Oh. That's good.'

Lily subsided, wishing she'd never asked. She'd just wanted to hear his voice, and had said the first thing that came into her stupid mind.

She breathed a sigh of relief when they finally reached the

nursing home and she could get out of the car. The matron showed them into a private room where Miss Jarvis reclined in bed, propped up by half a dozen pillows. It was obvious that the old woman was very ill, but her eyes were clear and she smiled when she saw them. Someone had tidied her snowy-white hair, and she wore a pink bed jacket over her nightie.

Leonard introduced Lily and she stepped forward and took the old lady's proffered hand. She was shocked by the frailty of this tiny woman, because her gaze was direct and her voice strong when she spoke.

'I'm delighted to meet you. I understand Mr Irwin is too important these days to visit an old woman.' She sniffed. 'I remember that boy when he was in short trousers.'

Lily blinked, and Leonard raised his eyebrows.

Miss Jarvis smiled. 'I take it he didn't mention that I went to school with his mother? No, I thought not. He always was a tricky one, full of his own importance. I'm surprised he wasn't worried I'd reveal his secrets.' She looked them up and down. 'However, I assume he felt he could rely upon your professionalism and my discretion, so I'll excuse him this time.'

Leonard smiled and opened his briefcase. 'He sends his apologies, Miss Jarvis, but he simply couldn't get away today, I'm afraid. But he didn't want to let you down, so here we are in his stead. I have your new will here, together with a copy for you to keep. Mrs Wickham and I will be your witnesses.'

They sat in chairs on either side of the bed while Leonard went through the will, clause by clause, making sure Miss Jarvis understood everything. She nodded and waved him on, occasionally saying, 'Yes, yes, that hasn't changed. Go on, go on.'

Eventually Leonard finished. 'So, to make absolutely sure, Miss Jarvis, this new will leaves the sum of five thousand pounds to your nephew, and the residue of your estate to your god-daughter.'

'Correct.'

'And this is to supersede your previous will, which left five thousand pounds to your god-daughter and the residue to your nephew.'

'That is also correct.'

Leonard hesitated.

'You have a question, Mr Warwick?'

'Forgive me,' he said. 'I'm simply wondering if there is a particular reason why you've chosen to effectively disinherit your only blood relative.' He raised a hand when she would have replied. 'Of course, you are entitled to make whatever provision you wish. I'm simply trying to establish that your nephew won't have any recourse to a claim against your estate, Miss Jarvis. Such cases can seriously deplete the value of an inheritance for all concerned.'

The old lady leaned forward, pinning Leonard with a steely gaze. 'I have also read *Bleak House*, Mr Warwick. I can assure you, I am in full command of my faculties, and this decision has not been taken lightly.'

She turned to Lily. 'Tell me, my dear, do you take shorthand?'

'Yes.'

'Good, good. Would you be so kind as to take notes?'

Lily nodded, relieved that she'd had the sense to put her shorthand notebook and a pencil in her handbag. She got them out, turned to a fresh page, wrote the date at the top, and waited.

Miss Jarvis nodded. 'Having become aware of my nephew's profligate lifestyle and his frivolous unconcern for anyone other than himself, I am not prepared to finance his activities to the detriment of everything that I and the others who saw fit to bequeath their hard-earned fortunes to me have worked for.

'I feel I have been more than generous in leaving him anything, and I sincerely hope that it will be a wake-up call for the young man. He has a good brain and could go far, but only if he is forced to work for what he needs.'

She paused for a moment, her pale wrinkled face taking on a greyish hue.

'Do you want me to get a nurse?' Lily asked.

'No, thank you. I'm just a little tired.'

'Would you like some water, Miss Jarvis?' she asked.

'Yes please.'

Lily poured some water into a glass and held it to Miss Jarvis's lips. It was a measure of the old woman's weakness that she didn't attempt to take the glass from Lily, but merely bent her head and sipped. Lily caught Leonard's eye over her snowy head.

'Should we come back another time?' Leonard asked gently.

'No. I want this business finished. I don't have time to waste.' Miss Jarvis took a shaky breath and looked at Lily. 'Thank you, my dear, you're very kind. Shall we continue?'

Lily put the glass down and resumed her seat. She picked up the notepad and pencil and waited.

Miss Jarvis nodded. 'Now, where was I?'

'*He has a good brain and could go far,*' Lily read out, '*but only if he is forced to work for what he needs.*'

'Quite. As for my god-daughter, she is an honest, hard-working girl who has the integrity and intelligence to deal with the responsibility of such an inheritance. It is my wish that she enjoy the benefits of my estate, and I leave it to her in the knowledge that she will use it for good. Do you have that, dear?'

'Yes. Would you like me to read it all back?'

'I suppose I ought to,' she replied, lying back against her pillows and closing her eyes.

Again, Lily looked at Leonard. He nodded, indicating she should go ahead. Lily read out what she'd recorded.

When she was finished Lily waited, wondering if Miss Jarvis

had fallen asleep, or worse. She was just about to get up to check when the old lady opened her eyes.

'Excellent,' she said, her voice clear but frail. 'Thank you. I'd appreciate it if you would get that transcribed and placed with my will. Perhaps you'd both be so good as to sign it to say that they are my words, uttered in your presence, freely and without coercion. I suspect I don't have the time to wait for someone to provide a transcript for me to sign. How silly of me, not to have thought of it when I spoke to young Gerald.' She turned to Leonard. 'Tell me, Mr Warwick, will that be enough to prevent my nephew from getting his hands on any more of my money?'

'I'm sure it will be, Miss Jarvis.'

'Good. Now, shall we get this business over with? I'm feeling rather tired.'

The Last Will and Testament of Miss Lilian Jane Emily Jarvis was signed by a shaky hand and properly witnessed by Leonard and Lily. On impulse, Lily kissed the old woman's cheek as they left.

'God bless you, Miss Jarvis,' she said softly.

'And you, my dear. Thank you.'

Leonard followed Lily as she hurried out of the room. He caught up with her on the drive of the nursing home, where she stood by the car, rummaging through her handbag, her eyes swimming.

'Here.' He handed her a freshly laundered handkerchief.

'Th... thanks.' She took it and turned away. 'I'm sorry. She's such a sweet lady, and she's so alone.'

He wanted to take her in his arms, but was aware of the people around them: a gardener weeding the flower beds, a nurse pushing a patient in a wheelchair across the lawn, and no doubt any number of staff, patients and visitors gazing out of the windows.

'Lily, I'm sorry. I should have warned you that visits like these can be difficult.'

'It's all right. I knew it really. I just didn't expect to like her so much.' Her shoulders shook.

Leonard threw caution to the wind and pulled her towards him. She turned, burying her face in his coat. He held her while she cried. The nurse caught his eye and was clearly offering assistance. Leonard shook his head and mouthed his thanks, but he didn't want anyone else comforting Lily. He no longer cared who was watching. All that mattered was that he was here, holding her.

In too short a time she had herself under control again. She raised her head.

'I'm so sorry. I'm not being very professional, am I?'

He smiled, stroking her damp cheek. 'It doesn't matter. You were wonderful. You are wonderful.'

She blushed and ducked her head. 'Thank you,' she whispered.

Leonard let go, opening the car door for her to get in, then going round to the driver's side. He stowed his coat and briefcase on the back seat and got in beside Lily. He glanced at his watch.

'It's lunchtime. Shall we find somewhere to eat? I think we've both earned a break before we go back to the office, don't you?'

Lily gave him a shy smile and he started the engine.

* * *

All through lunch in a delightful restaurant Leonard found in one of the chocolate-box villages off the main road back to London, the ease between them grew. She knew he felt it too.

He was waiting for the right moment, and it would come soon.

At last their meal was finished. She couldn't even remember what she'd had, but it didn't matter. Leonard paid the bill and she felt his hand warm against the middle of her back as he guided her to the car. As they paused by the passenger door, he opened his arms and she went to him, breathing in his cologne, wanting to stay there forever. This time there were no tears. Instead, he tipped her chin with gentle fingers and kissed her. This time, she let him kiss her.

She kissed him back and held him close.

She couldn't fight him any more. She wanted this. She wanted *him*.

* * *

Leonard couldn't fight it any more. He wanted this. He wanted *her*.

'Lily,' he murmured against her lips. 'My darling.'

A car horn beeped. A raucous shout of, 'Oi, oi!' followed by laughter echoing across the street brought him back to reality. He jumped back, angry and embarrassed.

'I'm so sorry...'

But Lily put a soft fingertip against his lips. She looked up at him with laughing eyes. 'It's all right, Leonard. They're just silly kids.'

He let out a cleansing breath, letting her warmth wash over him. 'I wouldn't embarrass you. I should have been more circumspect.'

'No you shouldn't,' she said. 'I wanted you to do exactly what you did.' She looked around the once again tranquil street. 'But maybe this isn't the right place.'

He nodded and opened the car door.

* * *

They left the village behind and were soon driving through Epping Forest back towards London. Lily wanted him to stop the car, but he hadn't said anything since he had switched the engine on. He kept his hands on the wheel and his eyes on the road. After a few minutes, Lily was beginning to think she'd got it all wrong.

Maybe he was just trying to comfort her because she'd been such a sobbing mess. Maybe when he kissed her he'd just been taking what she'd so blatantly offered. Maybe...

They reached a crossroads. She expected him to go straight across towards the main road, but instead he turned left.

'It's that way.' She pointed.

'I know,' he said, through gritted teeth.

Lily subsided into her seat, half-afraid, half-thrilled. Before she could think about it and get herself into a state, he pulled off the road onto a track and eased the car into the trees, out of sight of the road, before coming to a halt and switching off the engine. They sat frozen for a moment, the only sound the ticking of the engine as it cooled.

'Lily?'

She jumped. His voice sounded so loud in the confines of the car.

'Yes?'

'You know how I feel about you, don't you?'

'Not really,' she said, still not looking at him. She'd die if she'd got it wrong. She needed to hear it straight from him. But she was so afraid. She wanted to tell him not to say anything, to start the car and take her back to the office. They shouldn't be talking like this. But she couldn't. She really didn't want that. What she really wanted and needed was to hear that he...

'I love you, Lily.'

She did look at him then, eyes wide. 'Do you know what you're saying?'

'Oh yes,' he said, twisting towards her, his face set. 'I mean it, and I know exactly what I'm saying. I need to know, Lily. Can you possibly care for me? Is there any chance for us?'

'I...' She was going to deny it, to protect herself. But how *could* she? 'God help me, yes!'

With a groan he closed his eyes, reaching for her. They kissed, clinging to each other. Only when Lily felt the handbrake dig into her ribs did she pull back, laughing.

'It's a long time since I've done this in a car. I'd forgotten how uncomfortable it is.'

He rested his forehead against hers, his hand caressing her neck. She shivered with delight.

'There's more room in the back,' he said, his voice low and full of promise.

'Won't they be wondering where we are?'

'Who?'

'The office.'

'I don't care,' he said. 'I need you. The office and the rest of the world can go hang.'

Lily felt power flow through her. *He loves me. He needs me.* 'You're right,' she said. 'They can all go hang.' She kissed him hard then turned and got out of the car. When he didn't move she bent down and looked into the car. 'Well?'

His smile lit his whole face. 'Right,' he said, opening his car door and slamming it shut behind him. He came round to her and opened the back door. For a split second Lily thought of Jack, smiling and doffing his cap as people got into the back of his car, ever the pleasant and efficient servant. A shadow crossed her face.

'Lily?' Leonard asked again.

She banished everything but Leonard from her mind. 'I think you ought to move your briefcase first, Leonard. It might get squashed.'

She couldn't help laughing as he grabbed it and threw it and his top coat into the boot before urging her into the back seat and joining her there.

Then there was no time for talk or laughter; no time for thinking. Just touching and stroking, kissing and sighing, and the thrill of love at last acknowledged.

* * *

Leonard couldn't get enough of her. He loved the scent of her, the feel of her skin, the sounds she couldn't hold back – little gasps and whimpers – as he learned her shape and drank his fill from her lips. Her hunger matched his own.

It wasn't enough. He wanted to possess her. He'd never been so overwhelmed with need before, not even in the early days of... No, he wouldn't think of anyone but Lily, not now. He raised his head, filling his lungs with her perfume, trying to calm the desire raging through him.

Lily looked magnificent. Her eyes were closed as she licked her lips, catching her breath. He kissed her exposed throat and felt her hands against him. He tried to shrug out of his suit jacket, but he couldn't bear to take his hands off her. Instead he groaned, his mind so addled he didn't know how he could assuage the fire.

'What's the matter?' she asked. Her eyes were open now.

'It's not enough. I need to touch your skin. Please, Lily.'

For a terrible moment, he saw doubt in her eyes. His heart faltered. She stared up at him. He fought a brief battle with his pride, wanting to beg her, prepared to abase himself at her feet, her delicious feet, just to be granted a moment inside her.

'What if someone sees us?' she whispered.

He looked around, surprised. He hadn't thought; he hadn't cared if the whole world was standing outside the car watching them. But, even in his haste to have her, his subconscious mind must have been aware of the dangers.

'No one will see you but me, Lily. We're well hidden. In fact, I'm not sure how I'm going to get the car out of here.'

She raised herself on one elbow and peeked out. 'Oh my God, we could be lost in the forest forever.' She laughed, and he joined in.

'They'll find our bones, years from now, and Miss Jarvis's nephew will be living the high life while her poor, deserving god-daughter will be living in penury.'

'Leonard, don't. What if she dies while we're...? Perhaps we should get back.'

His laughter died. 'I can't, Lily. Not now. Please, my love. Just a few more minutes.'

She stroked his face, and he turned his head to kiss her palm.

'You're going to crease your shirt. Why don't you take it off?' she whispered, so quietly that for a moment he wasn't sure what she meant. Then her hands moved to his tie, tugging it loose. He froze, hardly breathing as she pulled it off and threw it into the front seat, before slowly unbuttoning his shirt.

He looked down. Her hands were shaking.

'You are magnificent,' he said. 'Oh, Lily, my darling. I want this moment to last forever.'

Her eyes filled with tears. He took her in his arms.

'Don't cry, my love.' He kissed her, afraid that she was going to change her mind.

She shook her head. 'It's nothing. I'm just so happy. I've fought this for so long. I can't believe what a relief it is to stop fighting.' She caressed his cheek again, her gaze warm on his face. 'It is all right, isn't it, Leonard?' she asked. 'I mean, I know it's wrong, but if we love each other...'

'It's more than all right,' he said hugging her close, moulding her body to his. 'And if I don't make love to you right now, I'll die.'

She laughed, running her hand down his chest. 'We can't have that,' she said. 'What would I tell them in the office?'

'To hell with the office,' he growled. He laid her gently back on the long seat.

Lily opened her arms and welcomed him.

22

Lily didn't go back to the office that afternoon. She didn't dare. Even though her dress was crease-free, her stockings had snagged on something and they were beyond repair. If she walked through reception bare-legged, it would be round the whole office – probably the whole building – within five minutes. And everyone would know what she had done with Leonard this afternoon.

Instead he had dropped her off at the station and she'd come straight home, praying she got there before Jack did. He'd notice. He'd know.

Oh, God help me, she thought. *I can still taste Leonard. If Jack sees me in this state he'll know. But he can't know. Not ever.*

She almost stumbled in her relief as she turned the corner and saw that the Jag wasn't there. She glanced at her watch. Twenty to six. Beverley would be home at six. She couldn't let her see either. Lily had twenty minutes to get herself straight. She rushed down the road, confident that at least the neighbours couldn't see her legs through the hedges and gates.

She walked through the front door just as Caroline came clattering down the stairs in her Brownie uniform.

'Hello, love. Have you been good?' She greeted the child, giving her a quick hug and a kiss. 'You're a bit early, aren't you? Give me ten minutes.'

Caroline pulled away. 'Mummy! You forgot!' She crossed her arms across her skinny body, her bottom lip jutting ominously.

'What did I forget?'

'You said I could go on my own if I was good.'

Lily smiled. 'That's right. But you haven't told me if you've been good or not, have you?'

'You didn't give me a chance, but I have been good. I've remembered all my things for Brownies.' She opened the little leather purse attached to her belt. 'See? I've got a clean hanky, a pencil and piece of paper, four pennies for the phone—'

'What about your safety pin?'

Caroline looked distraught. 'Oh no, I forgot it! I don't know where it is.'

Before she could panic and start bawling, Lily rummaged in her handbag and found one. 'There you are. Now put it in your purse and don't lose it.'

The child's face lit up; all was right with her world again. Lily laughed and kissed her. As she straightened up she saw the clock on the wall through the open kitchen door. Quarter to.

'All right. I think you're good enough to walk to Brownies on your own tonight. Go straight there, no mucking around, and I'll pick you up when it finishes.'

'Oh, but—'

Lily held up a hand. 'Don't push your luck. It will be getting dark by then, and I'm not letting you wander around on your own.'

'Okay,' said Caroline with a sigh. 'But I really am big enough.'

'Not yet, you're not. Now go on, off you go before I change my mind.'

Caroline slammed the door behind her before her mother had

even finished the sentence. Lily saw Caroline skipping up the path through the frosted glass. She shook her head, then remembered what she had to do and ran up the stairs to the bathroom.

Leonard was sweating by the time he left Irwin's car keys on his desk. He'd tried to make sure he looked normal before he returned to the office. Lily had done an efficient job of folding his shirt, but his trousers looked as though they needed a good steam to get them right again. He could only hope that his overcoat covered the worst of it and no one would notice.

Not, he decided, that he gave a damn if anyone did. He'd had the best afternoon of his life. He'd forgotten that sex could be so wonderful – in fact, on reflection, he'd never had such incredible sex before in his life. And it had been with Lily.

He smiled. She was his now. There could be no going back, no denial, no *being sensible.*

But neither could there be any more sex in the back of a car, especially not someone else's. Thank God Lily had told him she couldn't get pregnant.

That had pleased and surprised him. He only hoped she was telling the truth. A baby would be a total disaster.

Or would it? He tried to imagine Lily heavy with his child. The image of Lily's husband imposed itself between Leonard and his musings. He shuddered. No, there could be no baby. Just Lily, his secret, perfect love.

Jack drove into the cul-de-sac just as Beverley turned the corner, pushing the pram. He could see little Kerry waving her arms in the air. Bev was laughing. That was a good sign. He parked the car and jumped out as they reached the garden gate. 'All right, my darlings?' he said, putting his arm round his daughter's shoulder and giving her a kiss on the cheek. Kerry looked up at him and gave him a lovely grin, showing off her few little teeth, and clapped her hands – her latest trick.

'Dad! Don't be daft!' Bev squirmed out of his embrace, but she was smiling.

'What's the matter? Too old to kiss your old dad?'

'As my sainted mother would say, there's a time and place for everything, so bugger off.'

Jack laughed and held the gate open so she could push the pram in.

'Since when have you ever taken any notice of your mother?' he asked.

She paused, door key in hand. 'Good point,' she said. 'But she does talk some sense sometimes. Especially about old geezers like you.'

'Charming! All right, you miserable mare, get that door open. I hope she's got the kettle on. Me throat's as dry as the bleedin' Gobi Desert.'

* * *

Lily wasn't in the kitchen, but her handbag was on the telephone table, so she couldn't have gone far.

'Lily, you here, love?' he yelled.

'I'm up here,' she called from upstairs. 'I won't be a minute.'

'Where's Caroline?'

'Brownies.'

'Ah, yeah, 'course.'

He went back into the kitchen and put the kettle on. Lily

couldn't have been home long; it didn't look like she'd even been in here. He rummaged in the fridge and found a packet of sausages. 'That'll do.'

'Where's Mum?' Bev came in, carrying the baby. 'Upstairs.'

'What's for tea?'

'Bangers and mash.'

'Lovely. I'm starving.'

'Well make yourself useful and peel some spuds.'

She pulled a face. 'Do I have to?'

'You do if you want to eat anytime soon.'

'Oh, all right.' She went to put the baby into her high chair, but Kerry let out an enormous fart and the aroma of soiled nappy wafted across the room.

'Jesus Christ!' said Bev.

'Here, let me have her. I'll sort her out while you get the tea in the pot and sort them spuds out.' Jack took the baby. It would give him a chance to check on Lily n'all. What was she doing up there?

* * *

Lily lay on the bed, trying to get up the courage to go downstairs. She'd had a quick bath and was going to get into some fresh clothes, but as soon as she'd heard Jack and Beverley come in her head had started pounding and she'd hidden up here in the dark bedroom in her housecoat.

She couldn't do it. Her nerves were shot to pieces. How could she act normally when she'd spent the afternoon having sex with Leonard? She was an adulteress, for God's sake, and with someone else's husband.

She heard Jack come upstairs. Oh God, had she put her knickers out of sight? She'd meant to shove them to the bottom of the laundry basket, but they'd arrived just as she was doing it and she panicked and ran in here. Please God, she hadn't just left them on the top for everyone to see. She'd have to put some washing on, and make sure no one would see the tell-tale stains.

The room suddenly flooded with light and she flinched away from it.

'You all right, love?'

Shielding her eyes from the brightness, she looked up to see Jack standing in the doorway, the baby in his arms.

She tried to speak, but couldn't. What could she say?

Jack frowned. 'You got one of your heads?'

Feeling like hell, she nodded. Jack turned the light off and came over to rest a gentle hand on her forehead. Baby Kerry leaned over and patted her grandmother's shoulder. 'Nananana,' she gurgled. Lily managed a feeble smile.

'Have you taken anything?' Jack asked. 'D'you want me to get you some Anadin?'

'No, I— Christ! What is that smell?'

'Sorry,' said Jack, hoicking the baby higher up his chest and moving away. Kerry started to protest, reaching for Lily. 'I brought her up to change her. Bev's peeling spuds.'

'I'll come down.'

'Don't be daft, love. You stay here. I'll bring you up a cup of tea in a minute and me and Bev'll sort ourselves out.'

'What about Caroline?'

He looked at his watch. 'She finishes at seven, right?'

'Yeah.'

'I'll pick her up.'

Lily surrendered, feeling terrible, but also feeling relieved that she could hide away up here and pretend to be having a migraine. She couldn't bear to look anyone in the eye. She knew she had to act as though everything was the same, but right now she didn't know how she could.

'Thanks, love.' She almost cringed. She felt like a hypocrite, calling him that.

'You rest. We'll be all right.'

Jack shut the door behind him, leaving her to ponder in the comforting darkness whether they would ever be all right again. What had seemed at the time to be so right, exciting and thrilling, now seemed dirty and sordid. Lily felt overwhelmed with shame. How could she have done it? Jack was a good man – look at how kind he was. He never complained. He did everything he could to make her and the girls happy. How could she betray him like this?

She couldn't bear to think about what might happen if he found out. He must *never* find out. She must never give in to temptation again. She'd have to tell Leonard. He would understand. He must be feeling the same about his wife. They owed it to Jack and to Leonard's wife to stop this madness now, before it was too late.

Her thoughts whirled around her head, driving her deeper and deeper into despair. When Jack brought her the promised cup of tea, she feigned sleep. As he closed the door quietly behind him, she finally let her tears fall.

23

'Morning, Warwick.' Gerald Irwin stood in Leonard's office doorway on Monday morning. 'How was Miss Jarvis on Friday?'

'She was fine. Well, not fine, that's the wrong word. Obviously, she's very ill, but her mind was as clear as a bell.'

'She always was a sharp one. So she signed the new will? Just in time, as it turns out. I've had a call from the nursing home. She died in the early hours of this morning.'

Leo sighed. He'd have to tell Lily. She would be upset. 'Oh. I'm sorry. But yes. I've got the new will here. She also dictated a statement as to why she was effectively disinheriting the nephew in favour of the god-daughter. Lily will transcribe it and she and I will attest it and put it with the will.'

'Good. Good. I've met the nephew. If he'd been my relative I'd have cut him off without a penny. He doesn't deserve what she's giving him. He'll piss it up a wall in no time.'

Leonard marvelled how a partner in this prestigious firm, a man with the best education money could buy, could be so damned crude.

'Would you like to read the statement?'

'No, no. I'm sure it will be adequate. If the old girl dictated it and she was of sound mind, I've no doubt it will make it quite clear why she made the decision. Just make sure it's filed with the will, there's a good chap. Oh, and if the nephew decides to challenge it, we might need you and Lily Wickham to swear affidavits about the old girl's state of mind. Come to think of it, it might also be worth asking Lily to make sure she keeps her original notes, just in case.'

Irwin wandered off, leaving Leonard's door open. The general office outside was busy as usual, everyone working with quiet efficiency. It gave Leonard a measure of satisfaction that he was responsible for the smooth running of it. He hadn't been keen on taking on the responsibilities of office manager on top of everything else, but he saw it as a sign that the partners trusted his managerial skills. At the time, he'd thought it would lead him to an early partnership, but he was realising that it might have been a step backwards in that respect. The work involved in organising the office and overseeing the accounts meant that he had less time to devote to building up his client list. Partnerships, when offered (which was rare), were going to the likes of Irwin, who not only had the right pedigree, but also brought in the larger portion of fees.

The time had come, Leonard decided, to do something about it. He'd had many a sleepless night to think about it, and the plan that had presented itself to him in the wee small hours was perfect. He'd actually been thinking of Lily when the solution had leapt into his mind. He supposed he ought to run it by someone first, but damn it, he wasn't going to take the chance of it being vetoed. No, he would go ahead, and to hell with the consequences.

He picked up the phone and dialled Lily's extension.

* * *

Lily had been waiting for him for what seemed like hours. She'd even managed to get an early train in, hoping he'd do the same. But when the office had started filling up with people and Leonard still hadn't arrived, she'd started to worry. He'd finally arrived at a quarter past nine. She'd seen him walk past her door, talking to one of the partners. He hadn't looked in her direction, and it was now gone eleven and she hadn't heard a thing from him. The thought that he might have been stringing her along just to get inside her knickers was terrifying.

She tried to concentrate on her work, but the figures were blurring in front of her. With a sigh she took off her glasses and laid them on the ledger. She massaged her temples. The pretend migraine from Friday night was threatening to become a reality any minute. No matter that she'd decided it couldn't happen again; the idea that he'd been playing her for a fool horrified her. How could she be so bloody stupid? Men like Leonard Warwick didn't end up with women like her.

The rattling of the tea trolley provided a welcome distraction.

'Morning, Lily. Here you are, dear. Nice and strong with one sugar, just how you like it.'

'Thanks, Rita. You're a lifesaver.' She smiled, putting her glasses back on.

'You're welcome. Keeping busy I see. I'll leave you to it.'

She stirred the tea and extracted two Anadin from her desk drawer. No good waiting for her head to sort itself out. If only Leonard would talk to her!

The jangling of the telephone made her jump. With a hand on her heart, as if preventing it from leaping out of her chest, she answered it.

'Cashier's office.'

'Good morning, Lily.' Leonard's voice was crisp and businesslike. 'Could you bring your notepad into my office, please?'

'Yes, sir,' she said, feeling sick. 'I'll be right there.'

Lily put the phone down carefully, willing her hands not to shake. She took a deep breath and let it out, trying to shake the butterflies out of her stomach. This is what she'd been waiting for, so why was she suddenly so reluctant to go? Another deep breath.

'Oh, get on with it, you silly mare,' she muttered to herself, standing up.

She picked up her pad, a couple of pencils and Miss Jarvis's statement, which she'd typed up first thing. Then she put them down again and reached for her cup of tea. The Anadin tablets lay on top of the open ledger. She took them and washed them down with some sweet, hot tea. She drained half the cup before returning it to its saucer. Only then did she take her things and go to answer Leonard's summons.

He was on the phone when she got there. He gave her a quick glance and waved his hand, indicating she should shut the door and take a seat. She sat opposite him, watching his lips move as he spoke, not hearing a word of what he said over the pounding in her head. He wasn't looking at her, so she was free to stare at his handsome profile, to see how he tapped his pen impatiently against the blotter on his desk, to observe the pulse beating against his throat.

She forgot to be nervous. Instead, she remembered what it had felt like to stroke his cheek and how raspy it felt in the afternoon. She remembered kissing his throat. She remembered his impatient fingers caressing her, making her gasp.

By the time he put the phone down, Lily was ready to crawl over the desk to get closer to him. The look he gave her when he finally met her eyes had her halfway out of her seat. But the brisk knock on the door sent her right back down again, her cheeks burning.

She looked down at her notepad while Leonard growled a curt, 'Come in.'

Leonard's secretary came in, apparently unaware of the tension raging around the room.

'Sorry to interrupt,' she said. 'But you wanted these documents as soon as they were ready. It's the licensing application. The client will be here in half an hour.'

'Yes, thank you. Let me know when he arrives. In the meantime, I'll be in conference with Mrs Wickham. Can you see to it that we're not disturbed, please?'

'Of course.'

Lily could hardly look at the woman, sure that her guilt would be written all over her face. At the same time, she was trying hard not to giggle like a hysterical schoolgirl. Leonard's secretary closed the door behind her and Lily let out a soft chuckle.

'In conference?' she asked.

'Well I could hardly say, "Leave us alone so I can kiss the woman I love senseless," now could I?'

'So, are you going to kiss me?' She felt a bit giddy.

'Not yet. I'm afraid if I start I'll never be able to stop.'

'We've only got half an hour.'

He nodded. 'Give me five minutes to deal with business, then I'll see what I can do.'

Lily shook her head to try and clear it. 'I was scared you'd changed your mind.'

'That will never happen.'

'Really? What if people find out?'

'We'll be careful, I promise.'

'We're both married. I can't hurt Jack. And what about your wife?'

He sighed. 'I know. I don't want to hurt her either. But I didn't expect to fall in love, nor did I ever dream you would feel the same. But it's happened, Lily, and I simply can't fight it any more.'

'If anyone finds out, we'll lose our jobs as well.'

'I promise you, my darling. I will do everything I can to protect you. We've both worked too hard to lose it all. But I need you, Lily. I've never felt so strongly about anyone or anything.'

'Neither have I,' she admitted. 'It's terrifying.'

He stood up. 'Come here,' he said.

They met halfway round his desk. Judging by the hunger in his eyes Lily thought he was going to ravage her, and she wanted that. But at the last moment they both hesitated, their bodies barely touching, their lips barely half an inch apart, before they met in the gentlest of kisses. Lily wanted to cry at the tenderness of it all.

Leonard cradled her face in his hands and deepened the kiss, taking his time, exploring her in a way that hadn't been possible in the heat of their passion on Friday. He wanted to touch her body, to strip her and enjoy her right here in his office, but he couldn't help but be aware of the sound of typewriters and telex machines just a few feet away. As exciting as it felt, he knew he could go no further.

He ended the kiss, even though he wanted it to go on for ever. For a moment he rested his forehead against hers, then he kissed her cheeks and stood back.

'Tempted as I am to rush you out of here to somewhere where we can be alone, we have to be sensible.' He sat down. When he looked up at her, still standing where he had left her, her lips swollen from his kisses, he nearly went back to her, and to hell with the consequences.

Lily blinked, let out a shuddering breath, touched her lips briefly, and moved back to her seat.

'All right?' he asked.

She nodded.

'How were things at home?'

Lily grimaced. 'I couldn't face them. I pretended to have a migraine and went straight to bed. I'm not sure I'm cut out for this sort of thing. God help me, I know we should stop, but I don't want to. Not now.'

Leonard nodded, leaning forward. 'Neither do I. I don't know how I got through the weekend without you, Lily. I sat there, listening to my wife talking about some domestic crisis – the children were bickering – and all I wanted to do was remember the feel of your skin against mine.'

She blushed. He felt inordinately proud that he could have that effect on her.

'Leonard, please, don't say things like that. We're supposed to be working. You're getting me all hot and bothered.'

He laughed. 'Me too. All right, my love. Back to business. But first. I have a request.'

'What is it?'

'When we're alone. Will you call me Leo?'

She smiled. 'Leo the Lion. Yes, it suits you.'

He shrugged. 'I don't know about that. It's just a whim. No one else calls me that. I wanted to hear it from you.'

'Maybe I should get you to call me something different. I've never liked my name.'

'I love your name. It's perfect for you – you're a beautiful, delicate flower. My precious Lily.'

'All right.' She blushed again. 'It doesn't sound so bad when you put it like that.'

'Good. Now, um...' *What in heaven's name was he going to talk about?*

'I have Miss Jarvis's statement.' Lily handed the document over, giving him some breathing space.

'Have you seen Irwin this morning?' he asked.

'No.'

'Ah. You won't know, then. I'm afraid Miss Jarvis has passed away.'

Lily closed her eyes and let out a shaky breath. 'Poor woman,' she said. 'Then this statement is really important now.'

He nodded and skimmed it, barely taking in any of the words. He signed it in the space she indicated, then gave it to Lily to do the same. She reached over and took his pen from his fingers, not touching him. As she signed next to his signature, he watched her hand, remembering how her fingers had curled around him. He closed his eyes, wondering whether his excitement from being close to her would subside before his client arrived.

'Shall I file it?' asked Lily.

He opened his eyes. His pen lay in front of him, and Lily was holding the statement.

'Yes please,' he said. 'It should be attached to her will. And Irwin has suggested that you should keep your shorthand notes. If the nephew decides to contest the will, they might be needed as evidence.'

Lily nodded and looked down for a moment. 'She didn't last long, after all.'

'It was very peaceful at the end, according to Irwin.'

'But she was alone. That's sad.'

'She didn't strike me as sad. I'd say she's had a good life and was ready to go. It's just a shame her worthless nephew caused her so much grief at the end.'

Lily nodded. 'I think I'd like to send some flowers to her funeral.'

'Yes, of course.'

'Thank you.' She smiled. 'Sorry to be so morbid, but I really liked her.'

'You're a nice woman, Lily Wickham.'

She wrinkled her nose. 'Nice? Is that all?'

'Nice is good for now, I think, or we'll never get any work done.'

She opened her notepad and waited, pencil poised. 'I'm ready,' she said.

Yes, he was ready too. More than ready. *Damn! Concentrate, man.*

'There's no need for you to take notes, Lily,' he said. 'I have a proposition for you.'

* * *

She raised her eyebrows, waiting.

He cleared his throat. 'You might not know, but I've been hoping for a partnership here at Alder & Powney. It's taking rather longer than I'd expected, so I've been looking at my situation and trying to work out the best course.'

'You're not thinking of leaving?' she asked, careless of the panic in her voice.

He shook his head. 'No, not at all. But I think the problem is that too much of my time is taken up with the office management rather than building up my client list. Unless I can bring in more fees for the firm, I won't be considered for promotion.'

'Oh,' she said. 'So are you going to get in a new office manager?'

'Not exactly. I don't have the authority to do that in my current situation. But I thought you and I could work something out that could benefit us – both professionally and personally.'

'I don't understand,' she said, frowning.

He leaned forward, elbows on the desk, his hands clasped together. 'I want to be able to give you more responsibility, Lily. You're more than capable of taking over some of the office management. It's perfect, don't you see? You'll work more closely with me – as my deputy, if you like. That will mean that I'll have more time to devote to client work. I can't promise a pay rise for you immediately, but I'll do my best. But ultimately, we'll be spending more time together. Eventually, I'll get that partnership, and you'll be able to take over as office manager.'

She sat there, blinking, trying to get her thoughts straight. 'Leo, are you doing this because we—?'

He sat back, shaking his head. 'Absolutely not. I've been thinking about this for a long time and would be having this discussion with you regardless of anything, I promise you.'

'Are you sure?'

'Completely,' he said. 'Although...' he smiled, looking a bit sheepish, '...I can't help thinking that it's the perfect solution to the dilemma of how I can get you alone in the office. I suppose it's a case of good timing.' He shrugged, grinning like a guilty schoolboy.

Lily laughed. 'I see. It's just a coincidence it's come up now that we've—'

'Fallen in love,' he said firmly. 'Don't ever imagine that my feelings for you are less than that, my darling. But regardless of my feelings, I know you're capable of doing much more professionally, and that you'll be a greater asset to the firm than you already are if you agree to take on these extra duties.'

'Including sleeping with my boss?' She wasn't sure if she was challenging or teasing him. She was flattered by what he proposed. It was a dream come true. She knew she was up to the task; it was what she'd been working towards all these years. But part of her –

that stubborn little bit of the East End girl who'd had to leave school at fourteen and hated being poor and uneducated – still thought she might not be good enough. If that was true, then the only explanation for this offer could be that Leonard was being driven by his cock, rather than his brain, to keep her close. Lily hated the idea of that. She wished he'd made this offer before they'd been together in the back of Irwin's car. Then she might not have felt she'd passed some sort of casting-couch test.

Leonard stood up, his whole body radiating outrage. 'If that's what you think of me, then I've misjudged you.'

Her heart sank. 'I – I just don't want any special favours because of what we did.'

He leaned against the desk.

She held herself still, not looking away from his fierce gaze, even though she wanted to shrink back.

'Do you honestly think I'd risk the partnership I've been working towards for years, Lily? Or that I'd belittle what we have by trying to buy your affections with a promotion?'

She put a hand to her temple, pressing against the tension there. 'No. No, of course not. I'm sorry. You're right. I – I'm being silly.'

He relaxed, sitting down again. 'Yes, you are. Silly, but beautiful. I realise that the timing is unfortunate, but believe me, Lily, this is completely separate from what is happening between us. You are good at your job, and I want to reward that while helping my own progression up the ladder. The fact that I happen to be in love with you just makes it better, because it means we'll have more excuses to be together.'

She smiled. God, she loved it when he talked about being in love! When he reached out to her she leaned forward and took his hand. The warmth from his fingers spread up her arm. He bent and turned her hand, kissing the inside of her wrist.

'Oh God,' she said. 'You're going to be the death of me.'

He raised an eyebrow, just like that actor, Roger Moore. 'Why?'

'Because you're giving me everything I've ever wanted. Love, respect, the chance of a proper career. I'm so happy I could die.'

'You forgot to mention the incredible sex, but I'll forgive you. It's no more than you deserve.'

'Really?' She felt guilt wash over her, mocking her happiness and making her feel as though she was tempting fate. 'Even though I'm an adulteress? Shouldn't I be punished?'

'For falling in love? For working hard? For being the most beautiful woman on earth? Never.'

'Then there's only one thing I can do. I accept.'

He continued to hold her hand across the desk. They gazed at each other, unwilling to move or talk. How long they remained like that she didn't know. It could have been seconds, or minutes. It didn't matter. She was so happy. She had never felt like this before. She wanted this moment to last forever.

But she was afraid too. Deep in the recesses of her heart and mind, she was scared silly that plain little Lily wasn't meant to feel like this. She wasn't meant to fly. And one day she would come crashing down to earth, and she would have to live with the consequences of what she had stolen.

24

At home in Eltham a couple of weeks later, Jack checked his watch. Half eight. Still no Lily. She said she was working late, but he'd thought she'd meant an extra hour or something. She should be home by now, for Christ's sake.

'Daddy, when is Mummy coming home?' Caroline asked from her usual spot on the floor. She lay on her belly on the carpet, yet another book open in front of her. 'I want to show her the poem I wrote in school.'

'Yeah, it's a good 'un, ain't it?'

'You should say "isn't it," Daddy, or Mummy will get cross.'

Jack rolled his eyes. 'Well I won't tell her if you don't.'

'All right,' she said, getting up and climbing onto his lap, her book forgotten on the floor.

Jack held her close, enjoying the fact that she still liked a cuddle from her old dad. Christ knows, he didn't get much affection from Lily or Bev these days. They were both too bloody busy being 'career women.'

'But when is she coming home?' Caroline asked again.

'I'm not sure, darling. She's got a lot on at work. Did you phone her when you got home?'

'Yes. I told her about my poem, but she said she didn't have time for me to read it to her. She said I could do it when she gets home. But she's still not here.' Her eyes filled and her bottom lip trembled.

Jesus, where the hell is that woman?

'Oi, don't go getting all weepy on me,' he said, trying to keep his voice jolly. 'She'll be back soon. And you don't want to have red eyes when you do your big performance, do you?'

She sniffed and rubbed her eyes. 'But I miss Mummy,' she said, nearly breaking Jack's heart.

'Aw, come on. It's not the end of the world. You've still got your old dad, haven't you?'

'Yes, but you've already heard my poem and I—'

The front door opened. Caroline shot out of Jack's arms. 'Mummy!'

And there she was, standing in the living room doorway, with Caroline clinging to her waist.

'Mummy! Where have you been?'

'You know where I've been,' said Lily, laughing. 'Here, let me get my coat off.' She looked at Jack as she unbuttoned her mac. 'All right, love?'

'Not really, no.'

That wiped the smile off her face. Even Caroline seemed to notice he was pissed off. She let go of Lily and stood back, looking from one to the other, frowning.

'What's wrong?' Lily asked, pausing.

He shook his head. She was sodding unbelievable. 'You tell me. What's wrong with a woman getting home at—' he looked at his watch '—twenty-five to nine?'

She looked down, like a guilty kid. Caroline looked worried.

Jack never usually started a row in front of the kids. He didn't see why they should get involved in fights between him and Lily. Now he felt he was in the wrong.

Lily looked up, her chin set. 'I'm sorry, but there was a lot to do. I told you I was working late.'

'They paying you overtime?'

She shrugged. 'Probably not. It's not like a factory, Jack. I get a salary. If I work hard and make a good impression, I'll get a promotion and a pay rise. I might even get a bonus.'

'You might. But then again you might be taken for a ride while they get a load of extra work out of you for nothing.'

'Well that's a chance I've got to take.' She took off her coat and handed it to Caroline. 'Will you hang that up for me, sweetheart? Then you can show me that poem you were telling me about.'

Caroline beamed as she went to do her mother's bidding.

'She was in tears, waiting for you,' he said.

'I'm sorry. I'll make it up to her,' she said.

Jack shook his head. 'You don't get it, do you, Lil? She needs her mum at home. She's just a little kid.'

'Jack, we can't manage on just your money. If I wasn't doing this job, I'd be back in that bloody factory, working just as many hours to earn a pittance. I know you don't like it, but it's a good job and I've got the chance of doing really well. I could be office manager soon.'

'Not if it means you working all hours, you won't. I won't have it, Lily. They're taking the piss.'

She opened her mouth to reply, but Caroline was coming down the stairs, her poem in her hand. Instead she turned her back on him.

'Come into the kitchen,' she told the child. 'You can read it to me while I make a cup of tea.' She looked over her shoulder at him. 'I take it you've eaten?'

'We had the rest of that shepherd's pie,' he said.

She nodded. 'I'll make myself a sandwich,' she said, going down the passage to the kitchen.

Jack stood in the middle of the living room. He could hear Caroline reading out her poem, raising her voice over the noise of the tap as Lily filled the kettle. He thought about following them, but reckoned he was likely to make things worse if he did.

He heard Lily laugh and clap, and Caroline giggling. He couldn't remember the last time Lily had laughed with him. He barely recognised her these days. She wasn't the girl he'd married. They'd laughed all the time then. Now, she was always too busy or too tired. She always wanted more – a better car, better furniture, holidays abroad.

He wanted her to be happy, but he didn't think all these *things* would make a difference. She never used to need much to make her happy. She knew he was no brainbox. He was a driver, pure and simple. He weren't ever going to be some fancy manager or office *wallah*. It had never bothered her before. But since she got this job she hadn't been happy with anything he did.

Now she was putting her job before everything. Not just him, but the girls too. It was as though she couldn't bear to be at home any more.

He sighed, and rubbed a hand over his face. He could feel his beard coming through. Lily didn't like it. Maybe he should have a shave before they went to bed. But what was the point? The mood she was in, he weren't likely to get near her tonight. Shame that, 'cause having sex with his wife would do him the power of good right now. It might even cheer Lily up.

The phone rang.

'I'll get it!' Caroline yelled from the kitchen.

Jack rolled his eyes. That kid was obsessed with that bloody thing. It wouldn't be for her at this time of night. By rights, she should be in bed. But he'd let her stay up to see her mother. He got up and went out into the hall. Caroline was already there, reciting the number.

'Eight five six, one six double three,' she said. She listened for a few seconds. Out of the corner of his eye, Jack saw Lily come out of the kitchen.

'Hallo, Uncle Fred. Did you want to speak to Daddy? Here he is. Bye!'

Jack stepped forward, taking the phone from her. 'All right, mate?'

'Yeah. Maggie's had another girl.'

'Ah, lovely! Everything okay?'

'Perfect, mate. Couldn't be better.'

'Hang on, let me tell Lil,' he said, putting a hand over the mouthpiece. 'It's a girl,' he told her.

'Is Maggie all right?'

'Yeah, no problems.'

'Thank God. Tell him I'll go round tomorrow after work. Is there anything she needs?'

'I'll ask him.'

She nodded. 'I'll get Caroline to bed.' She chivvied their daughter up the stairs, answering her questions about the baby as she went.

'No, I don't know what her name is. No, I don't know what she looks like. You can come and see for yourself tomorrow. Now up you go.'

Jack turned back to the phone. 'Lily sends her love. We'll come over after work tomorrow, mate. Is there anything you need?'

'Nah, we're cushty. Me mother-in-law's here. She's keeping us all fed and watered while Maggie lies in.' He paused. 'This one's worn her out, Jack. I reckon this'd better be our last.'

'Well what do you expect, you silly sod? She ain't no spring chicken now, is she? I told you that last time.'

'It ain't just me. She wanted this one n'all.'

Jack felt a pang of guilt, wondering whether this has all been on account of Bev's baby. 'Well, next time the subject comes up, tell her to keep her legs crossed.'

'What, and miss my oats?' He laughed. 'Sod off!'

Jack laughed. 'You dirty bugger. Leave the poor woman alone.'

'She'll be all right in a couple of weeks. Be begging for it by then, she will.'

'Yeah, well, in the meantime, tie a knot in it and give the poor woman some rest.'

Lily came down the stairs at that moment. She rolled her eyes as she passed. Jack didn't know if it was what he said that got her all disgusted, or whether she was still in a mood with him about her job.

'Anyway, we'll see you tomorrow, Fred. Shout if you need anything, all right?'

'Will do. See ya.'

Jack put the phone down and wondered what his next move should be. He could go into the kitchen and talk to Lily, or he could return to his armchair and watch the telly as though nothing had happened. He didn't reckon talking was getting him very far right now, so he went back into the living room and settled down in front of *Steptoe and Son*.

25

'Darling, do you *have* to go in so early this morning?' asked Daphne. 'You've been working such long hours lately. The children and I have hardly seen you.'

Leonard looked at his wife, resplendent in her pink housecoat, face bare of make-up or cream, her head covered by a silk scarf to conceal the rollers forcing her hair into military precision. He took a last sip of his cup of tea.

'I warned you it would be like this, my dear,' he said. 'If you want me to get a partnership, I have to make an impression.'

'But none of the partners will be there at this time of the morning, and I'm sure they don't work into the night.'

'Of course not. They don't have to now, do they?' He returned his cup to its saucer and stood up, reaching for his briefcase. 'The important thing is that I build up my client base. If I don't put in these extra hours, I'll still be nothing more than a "glorified office boy," as your dear mother insists on calling me, when I retire.'

Daphne sighed. 'Well, I hope they hurry up and take notice. You're becoming a stranger, Leonard.'

For a moment her habitually dissatisfied expression softened, and he glimpsed a hint of the woman he'd married.

'We'll do something at the weekend,' he said, kissing her cheek. 'But now I've got to go.'

'When will you be home?'

'I don't know. I'll call you.'

'I'll be taking the children to piano lessons at five.'

'I'll try to remember.'

He'd forgotten before he closed the garden gate behind him. The moment he'd walked away from his wife, his attention had been on getting to Lily as quickly as possible.

They arrived at the same time. The streets were still relatively quiet, with the main rush hour not due to get under way for a while yet. Leonard smiled when he saw her, but refrained from touching her until the lift doors closed, shielding them from prying eyes.

'Good morning,' he said, kissing her welcoming lips.

'Mmm,' she replied.

He broke the kiss as they reached the office floor and they stood side by side as the doors slid open. They still had to be careful. The building caretaker had almost caught them in a clinch one morning. He would probably have been discreet, but neither of them were willing to take the chance.

He followed Lily across the corridor to the office door. It was locked. Good, that meant no one else had arrived. She used her keys and they went in.

'Shall I leave it open?' she asked.

'No. Not yet. Let's give ourselves some time.'

She locked the door and made her way through the dark reception room and into the general office. 'Your place or mine?' she asked over her shoulder.

Leonard laughed. 'I don't care. Lead the way.'

She smiled and went into her office. He came in, put his brief-case down by the door, pulled his jacket off and slung it over a chair while she hung her coat behind the door. Then she was in his arms and nothing else mattered.

'I don't know how you keep this bleeding thing running,' said Jack a few nights later as he worked under the bonnet of Fred's old Zephyr. 'You're only supposed to use a sodding stocking as a temporary fan belt, you stupid bastard.' He pulled the offending article off and threw it at his brother. Fred caught it and flung it over his shoulder.

'Don't be such a fussy bugger. I ain't had no trouble with it.' He laughed. 'Not once I got it off Maggie's leg. Made me buy her a new pair, she did. Don't know why she needed two – I only had the one off her.'

'Well, your dad must've been a leprechaun, mate, 'cause you've got the luck of the Irish.'

'I'll tell Mum you said that.'

'Don't matter – I'm her favourite.'

'Yeah, you are n'all. Must be on account of you being the runt of the litter.'

'And the most handsome.'

Fred punched him on the shoulder. Jack ignored him and went back to his task.

'Right, you need a proper fan belt, and them spark plugs need a good clean. I ain't too sure about your head gasket. We'll have to take it apart to check it. And I reckon your exhaust is buggered.'

'How much is this lot going to cost me?'

'Dunno yet. I'll see if I can get something off me mate down the scrap yard. He sometimes has wrecks in with decent exhausts still hanging on. But if that head's gone, you might as well scrap it and get yourself a new car.'

'Ain't it bloody typical? I win a few shekels on the gee-gees and me motor packs up. I wanted that money for a little holiday down Camber Sands.'

'At least you didn't have all the kids in the back when it packed up.'

'I could've done with them to give it a shove. This bleeder don't half weigh a ton when you're pushing it. Some bloke helped me in the end. Useless Harry sat behind the wheel, moaning he had a bad back. I'll give him a bad back, the lazy bastard.'

'Well, this pile of junk ain't going nowhere now. How you getting to work?'

Fred shrugged. 'One of the others picks me up. They ain't all like Harry, thank God. Reggie's taking us down Avonmouth in the morning.'

Jack nodded, wiping his oily hands on a rag. 'You told Maggie about Camber Sands?'

'Nah, I was going to surprise her. Just as well I didn't say nothing, ain't it?' He shook his head, unhooking the prop and slamming the bonnet down. The whole car shook with the force of his frustration.

'It might not be that bad,' said Jack. 'If I can blag a few bits from somewhere, you might get another few months out of it.'

'Yeah?' Fred looked hopeful.

'Yeah, mate. But don't go expecting miracles. It was a pile of rubbish when you bought it, so it ain't going to suddenly turn into a Rolls-Royce.'

'Right. Let's see if Maggie's got the kettle on.'

Lily was sitting on her own in the kitchen, cradling the new baby in her arms.

'Where's Maggie?' Fred asked.

'Samantha needed changing.'

Jack frowned. 'I thought she was out of nappies now.'

'The little mare went right back into 'em when the new one arrived,' said Fred. 'Maggie's been tearing her hair out. We didn't have none of this with the boys. But our little princess ain't taken too kindly to the baby having any attention.'

'Poor Maggie,' Lily sighed. 'She's worn out.'

'Ah, don't worry. She'll be all right. The doc's given her some tonic. That'll sort her out.'

Lily glared at Fred. She opened her mouth to say something, but Maggie came in, with the toddler in her arms. She looked terrible – no make-up, her hair was a mess, and there was a stain down the front of her dress, which strained at the seams. Jack couldn't believe how old she looked. Maggie and Lily were the same age, but seeing the two women next to each other, you'd think Maggie was years older. The fact that Lily was so well turned out in her business suit made it even more obvious that Maggie was in a bad way. Jack couldn't imagine Lily letting visitors see her without her make-up on, or with a hair out of place. She definitely wouldn't be seen dead with stains down her front. Jesus!

'There you are, girl,' said Fred. 'How about a cuppa for the workers, eh?'

Lily's mouth dropped open. Jack moved fast to head off a full-blown row. 'You sit down, Maggie, love. I'll get the kettle on. You girls have got your hands full.'

Lily smiled at him.

He grinned back, knowing he'd won some brownie points there. As he filled the kettle and put it on the gas, Fred looked at him as though he'd sprouted two heads. Lazy bastard.

'What's the matter, bruv?' Jack jeered. 'Never managed to make your own cuppa before? Did our old mum send you out into the world as useless as you came in?'

Fred shook his head. 'I've been at sodding work all day, and then out there trying to fix that bleeding motor. It ain't asking too much to have someone make me a brew, is it?'

Lily opened her mouth again, but Maggie put up a hand to stop her. 'I'll do it,' she said, putting Samantha down. The toddler clung to her mother's legs and screamed. Maggie struggled to stand up. 'I won't be a minute, Sammy. Now get off me and let me make Dad and Uncle Jack a cup of tea.'

'For Christ's sake, Mags, sit down,' said Jack. He didn't know how she could stand the screaming. Lily looked like it was bringing on one of her heads. Their girls never screamed like that. Lily wouldn't have it. 'Just 'cause this stupid bastard can't help himself, don't mean I'm useless. You sort the littl'un out, darling.'

'Thanks, Jack,' she said, sinking into her chair again like a balloon that had lost its puff.

Samantha climbed back onto her mother's lap and silence reigned again. Thank Christ.

* * *

Lily and Jack both gave a sigh of relief when they got in the car to go home.

'Jack, I know he's your brother,' said Lily as she waved goodbye to Maggie. 'But Christ, he's a selfish bastard.' She sat back and let out a deep breath. 'You know, I can't decide who I'm more disgusted with – him for treating her like that, or her for letting him get away with it. Can't he see how tired she is? I can't remember her looking so ill.'

'He's all right. He don't mean it. It's his idea of having a laugh.'

'Well it's not funny, and it's about time he realised it, the stupid sod. You should tell him.'

'What, me? He don't listen to me, does he? If he did, he wouldn't have bought that bleeding Zephyr.'

'If someone doesn't sort him out, Maggie's going to make herself ill, and then he'll be buggered. Who's going to look after all those kids then? I haven't got time, her mother won't do it for long – you know what a miserable cow she is – and I doubt if your mother would either.'

'Our mum's busy helping down the pub.'

'There you go. Fred's heading for trouble if he doesn't look after Maggie.'

Jack sighed. 'Yeah, I suppose you're right. He won't listen to me though. I'd better see if the old woman'll talk to him.'

Lily wasn't sure that her mother-in-law would be interested. She was proud of the fact that she'd brought up her six kids single-handed while old Bert was away in the Navy, and she'd think Maggie should be able to cope. The trouble was that Fred was a lot like his mum – stubborn and quick-tempered. Oh, they were a good laugh most of the time. You couldn't beat a Wickham party for a right old knees-up. But Lily was tired of always being expected to get on with it and see the funny side of everything, and she was really worried about Maggie.

'Maggie used to be really glamorous. She looked like a film star. I used to envy her. Now I feel sorry for the poor cow. I feel responsible.'

'What you on about?'

'We introduced them, didn't we?'

'For God's sake, Lily. She's a bit tired, and he's a bloody idiot. That ain't our fault.'

'Well, it feels like it, and I won't keep my mouth shut next time. If you hadn't stepped in, I'd have told him exactly what I thought of him.'

'Fine. Start World War Three, why don't you? It's none of our business what goes on in their marriage, Lily. If you go mouthing off, Christ knows what will happen. Just leave it, all right? I said I'd talk to Mum, and I will. But that's the end of it.'

She looked out of the windscreen, not seeing the passing traffic, trying to calm her breathing. How could he think that was enough? She felt tears welling and blinked to force them back down.

'Anyway,' he went on. 'Maggie won't thank you for interfering. She's got enough on her plate without you criticising. How do you think she's going to feel with you telling everyone she can't cope?'

'Fine. I'll shut up and let her kill herself because your brother is a lazy bastard. Satisfied?'

Jack sighed, turning into their road and pulling up outside the house. 'Look, I don't want a row about this, love. Let's leave them to get on with it. They ain't kids. He'll sort himself out. He won't do nothing to hurt Maggie. We just caught them on a bad night.'

'I hope so,' she said, not believing him for a moment. Maggie hadn't been right for months now. But if Jack was going to take his brother's side, then so be it. She could hardly claim to be surprised. In Jack's eyes, Fred could do no wrong.

'It'll be fine.' He leaned over to kiss her. She turned her head and accepted his lips on her cheek. 'Right, let's see what our girls have been up to.'

As they got out of the car and went into the house, Lily wondered whether Leo would tolerate someone as boorish and ignorant as her brother-in-law. She thanked God their paths would never cross.

* * *

At the same time in Wimbledon, Daphne put down her knife and fork, making sure they were neatly arranged side by side on the plate. She dabbed at her lips with a linen napkin, then refolded it and put that on the table to the left of her plate. The same ritual, performed in the same order, for each meal. Leonard waited for her to pick up her water glass. Her hand shook a little as she raised it to her lips. She took a small sip before returning it to its place.

She hadn't looked at him since their meal began. He'd been grateful for the silence, and continued to eat quite happily while his wife sulked. No doubt she was working up a head of steam that would have to escape sooner or later. But he found he didn't care. Since he and Lily had become lovers, nothing else mattered. Daphne wasn't a bad woman, and he didn't want to hurt her. But he realised he should never have married her. Now he was trapped – by duty, by children (whom he adored, of course), by reputation. If he left her, as he longed to do, he would lose everything.

Daphne sighed and put her hands in her lap. She wouldn't leave the table until he was finished. Her manners were impeccable.

'You don't have to wait for me,' he said, his tone mild. 'Thank you, I'm fine,' she said, as though he were a stranger.

He looked at his watch. 'I thought you wanted to watch the film this evening. It's about to begin.'

She did look at him then, her eyes blazing.

'Perhaps I think it's more important to spend time with my husband than to waste it in front of the television.'

He raised his eyebrows and lowered his cutlery. 'Forgive me. I got the impression I was the last person you wanted to talk to.'

'Oh, Leonard! That's a ridiculous thing to say. We could hardly hold a meaningful conversation while we were eating, could we?'

'Most people do.'

'Chit-chat, that's all it is.'

'I happen to like chit-chat.'

She looked thoughtful. 'Very well. How was your day, dear?' she asked, pasting a bright, false smile on her face.

'Much the same as any other.'

She huffed. 'Well there you have it. I tried, and you... you simply shut me out.'

'What would you have me say, Daphne? Thank you for asking. Today I completed the purchases of a commercial lease, three houses and a block of flats. I exchanged contracts on as many properties again. A client came to see me about granting his son a power of attorney to deal with his affairs while he takes a trip to India to visit his childhood haunts. I had to discipline one of the typists who has been particularly sloppy in her work lately. It seems she's having man trouble and is letting it interfere with business. There, a summary of my day. Were you in the least bit interested in any of it?'

'Well, I might have been able to advise you about dealing with the typist. I am a woman, after all.'

'Yes, I'd noticed, thank you. But I was quite capable of dealing the matter without your advice.' He picked up his napkin and wiped his lips. He couldn't imagine why she thought she'd have any understanding of the situation. She'd never worked outside the home since the day they married. In any case, Lily had been on hand to offer help. She'd spoken to the girl and got to the bottom of the problem, and persuaded him to give her another chance. Daphne would have told the girl not to be so silly and recommended her dismissal. She had no time for nonsense, and getting into a tizzy over a boyfriend would be regarded as the height of absurdity.

'I see.'

No doubt she expected him to ask what she saw, but he really wasn't interested. He threw down his napkin and stood up.

'Well, if you're finished here, I'm going to walk to the Lodge.'

'But I thought we were going to spend the evening together. With the children asleep, we can have a proper conversation.'

'Which we have,' he pointed out. 'And now your film is on, and I need to see a couple of chaps at the Lodge. I won't be long, no more than an hour.'

'Does it have to be tonight? We've hardly seen each other. You're always working. Some mornings you're out of the house before I've barely stirred, and I never know when you're going to be home.'

He had a brief flashback to Lily – touching her bare skin, kissing her. Such delicious, exciting moments, snatched at the beginning and end of their day. Why on earth would he give that up to spend time with his constantly dissatisfied wife?

'We've had this conversation, Daphne. You know why it's neces-sary. It's also the reason I need to go to the Lodge. The chaps I'm going to see are people who can help me with my career.'

'I thought it was too good to be true, you coming home at a reasonable time this evening. So who are these mysterious men? Why can't you see them at the office?'

He hid a smile. 'Now, darling, you know better than to ask. I can't disclose the identities of fellow Masons. All I can tell you is that they have contacts, which could prove very useful.'

For a moment she slumped, defeated. Then she took a breath and stood up. 'I shan't wait up for you,' she said as she began clearing the table.

'I won't be that long,' he said, making ready to leave. She followed him into the hallway, plates in hand.

'Well, when you do have a moment to talk to me, I'd like to discuss the children.'

'What about them?' he asked, putting on his jacket. It was a pleasant evening, so he didn't bother with his overcoat.

'Peter has been selected to play cricket for the school, and Susan will be in a dance recital next week. They'd both like their father to go along and support them, if that's not too much trouble.'

'I can't possibly take time off work.' He frowned. He felt bad about it. They were both good children and he'd like to be able to watch their activities. But it was out of the question.

'Peter will be practising on Saturday mornings, and Susan's performance will be in the evening.'

'Ah. Well, in that case, I'm sure I can be there. Just let me know what dates, so that I can put them in my diary.'

'Thank you. They'll be pleased.' She swept down the hall into the kitchen and he heard the clatter of dishes in the sink.

He let himself out of the house, taking a deep breath of fresh air as he closed the door behind him. The feeling of having escaped made him smile. He found he smiled a lot these days, just not in his own home. There, the cool atmosphere that had become part and parcel of his life without him even noticing froze his features into a joyless acceptance of his empty marriage. Only when he turned his back on it and looked outward could he feel alive.

He set off across the common, wondering whether he could ever afford to move to the better side of Wimbledon. The trouble was, the sort of home he envisaged would contain a fragrant, loving Lily, not a sour, formal Daphne.

It was just a dream. But one that made him smile again as he entered the Lodge.

27

The garden gate opened and Bev watched Lily walk the few steps to the open front door. Caroline flung herself at their mother, clinging to her as though she hadn't seen the old cow for days.

'Hello, love. Shouldn't you be at Brownies by now?' she asked, looking at her watch.

'I was just about to take her, seeing as how her own mother forgot she'd promised to go and see her get her sergeant's stripes,' Bev sneered, as she watched Lily realise she'd cocked it up again. 'Found her in tears, I did.'

Lily shut her eyes and took a deep breath. When she opened them and looked at her, Bev was struck by how bleak and unhappy her mother looked. It was just for a second, but it shook Bev to the core.

'I'm sorry,' said Lily, bending down to kiss the top of Caroline's head. 'It went right out of my head.'

'I can't go now – I'll be late.'

'Of course you can go.' Lily made a visible effort to pull herself together. 'Come on, grab my car keys off the hook and we'll drive round. It will only take a minute and we'll get there in plenty of time.'

Bev took the keys down and tossed them to her mother. 'I'll start the tea,' she said.

Lily smiled at her. That was another shocker. Most of the time she was giving her that thin-lipped *'Where did I go wrong?'* look. 'Thanks, love. There's sausages in the fridge. You and Dad have yours and leave me a plate. Don't wait for me.'

Bev nodded. 'See you later, squirt,' she called after Caroline as the kid ran down the path, trying to pull Mum after her. 'Watch out for them goblins!'

Caroline was laughing as she got in the car, and Bev grinned.

It wasn't until she shut the door and looked at Kerry, sleeping peacefully in the pram, that she realised she hadn't told anyone that her baby had learned to crawl today.

The next morning, Jack drove the Jag smoothly to the kerb outside the offices of Alder & Powney. Lily fought the urge to open the door straight away and hurry into the office. It was still early – Leo might not even be there yet – so there was no point in giving Jack any reason to suspect she was rushing to meet her lover.

She felt anxiety slither up her spine and curl itself around her neck. She ignored it and leaned over to kiss Jack on the cheek. He turned his head and their lips met. When she would have pulled back, he put a hand on the back of her head, holding her there. His tongue teased until she opened for him and he took his time kissing her. Lily felt helpless, wanting to pull away, but knowing she had to let him do this, and that she ought to be responding more enthusiastically.

Eventually he ended the kiss. His hand was still holding her close. She wondered why the touch of this man – the man she had loved enough to marry all those years ago – left her so cold, when just a look from Leo made her hot and wet.

Jack sighed and planted a soft kiss on her forehead before letting her go. She sat back, touched by the tender gesture. She'd forgotten how gentle he could be sometimes.

'Here you are, darling. Safe and sound, and nice and early. You working late n'all?'

'I'm not sure. Depends.'

He sighed. 'Well, let us know. I might be heading back through at about five. I could pick you up. Save you having to get the train.'

'That would be nice. Now the weather's getting better, it's downright nasty in a packed train. I swear some people never wash from one week to the next.'

He smiled. 'Well, I'll plan on being here at five then, all right?'

'Yeah, thanks.'

He peered out of the windscreen. 'Looks like someone else is in a rush to get to work. Who's that fella then?'

Lily's heart stopped, then raced away like a runaway train. Leo was walking briskly up the steps to the entrance of the building. He gave no indication that he'd seen them.

'That's Mr Warwick. Remember, you met him in the café round the corner a while back?'

'Oh yeah. The geezer what fancies you.'

'For God's sake, Jack. Don't be ridiculous. He's my boss, and he's married.'

'Well, his missus ain't likely to be as gorgeous as you, is she, doll?'

She shook her head, her laughter forced. 'You silly sod. What am I going to do with you?'

'Well, how about we both bunk off for the day and I'll show

you.' He picked up her hand and kissed her palm. 'What d'you reckon?'

Lily sighed. Why on earth did he have to get fruity with her now? All she wanted to do was run after Leo and make sure he hadn't seen Jack kissing her. She felt guilty about it. What sort of bitch was she, more worried about her lover's reaction than doing right by her husband?

'I'd love a day off, but not today. I've got a dozen bank drafts to organise, and it's coming up to the month end.' She looked at her watch. 'In fact, if I don't get in there now, I'm not likely to be finished by five.'

'Go on then,' he sighed. 'I'll see you at five.'

This time, when she leaned over to kiss his cheek, he kept his eyes front.

As she walked towards the entrance, she felt his gaze on her back. She forced herself not to rush, but she couldn't wait to get through the doors, out of his sight. At the top of the steps, she turned and waved. He waved back before driving away. With a sigh of relief she went in, her mind already focussed on Leo.

* * *

Leonard waited in the lobby, his heart pounding as he tried to peer through the glass panel of the door without being seen. Was that Lily he'd seen in the Jaguar? He was sure it was – she'd mentioned her husband drove one. But if it was, what the hell was she doing, kissing him like that, in broad daylight?

He took a deep breath. This was ridiculous. He was shaking with rage at the thought of Lily kissing her husband. He had no right to feel like this, but he couldn't help it. Dear God, what if she had decided she wanted to end their affair? It was unthinkable. The times he spent with Lily were all that made his life bearable.

She got out of the car. Leonard jumped back, not wanting to be seen. He heard her footsteps as she approached the door, and watched as she turned and waved before walking into the building.

He stepped forward as the door closed behind her.

'Oh!' She stopped dead as she saw him, her hand going to her throat. 'Leo, you nearly gave me a heart attack!' She looked behind her, a small, guilty gesture.

'I waited for you,' he said. 'I saw you outside.'

She didn't look at him. 'Oh.'

'Indeed.' He turned and pressed the call button for the lift. He didn't trust himself to speak. When it arrived, he stood back for her to enter and followed her in. They didn't speak, didn't reach for each other as they usually did. He stared straight ahead. Out of the corner of his eye, he saw Lily take a deep breath and lift her chin. They arrived at their floor and walked to the office. It wasn't until they were inside, the door locked behind them, that the silence was broken.

'Leonard, look at me.'

He turned, reluctant to meet her eyes, bracing himself for her rejection.

'Are you angry with me?'

For a moment he wasn't sure what she was asking. 'Angry? Why should I be angry?'

'Because of what you saw.'

'What I saw? Oh yes, I saw the woman I love kissing another man. Mmm. Yes, now I come to think of it, maybe I am angry.'

'He's my husband, Leo. I can hardly stop him from kissing me, can I? I'll bet you still kiss your wife.'

'A dutiful peck on the cheek. Not, as my teenaged nephew would say, a full-on snog!' He had to ask. 'Are you still sleeping with him as well?'

'That's none of your bloody business,' she snapped. 'I don't ask you if you still shag your wife, do I?'

The crudity of her language shocked him. 'Lily! I—'

She shook her head and swept past him, entering her office and dropping her handbag onto the desk. She shrugged out of her coat, keeping her back to him. He followed her in, closing the door behind him.

'I've got a lot of work to do,' she said.

'Lily, please, darling. I'm sorry. I shouldn't have—'

She whirled round. 'No, you shouldn't. For God's sake, Leo, he's my husband. I have to act naturally, and pretend everything's all right. If he had any clue about what's going on between us, I don't want to think about what he'd do. He's a man who reacts with his fists.'

'My God, does he hit you?'

She looked startled. 'Of course not. It's not me he'd hit, you daft ha'p'orth, it's you.'

'Does that mean you care about what happens to me?' He felt the pressure around his heart lift.

'Of course it does. I love you.'

Her words made him want to weep with relief. Instead he reached for her and pulled her close. Their kiss was sweet and reassuring; the next was hot and exciting. He lifted her onto the desk and opened her legs. He couldn't wait.

* * *

An hour later, at the arrivals gate in Heathrow Airport, Jack checked his watch. The boss's plane had landed half an hour ago. It wasn't like him to take his time coming through. Must be some hold-up with the luggage. If he'd known, he'd have got himself a cuppa instead of standing around here like a bleeding lemon.

A woman beside him waved as a man walked through the gate, a battered suitcase in his hand. His grizzled features lit up when he saw her and he marched right over. Dropping his case, he enveloped the woman in a bear hug and lifted her off her feet. She was laughing and crying at the same time.

Jack felt a pang of jealousy. It must be lovely when a woman is that pleased to see you. He couldn't remember the last time Lily had looked halfway bothered when she saw him. That kiss this morning was a joke. She'd just sat there and let him get on with it. He'd thought she was warming up after a bit, but in the end she couldn't wait to get away from him. He wasn't fooled by that cheery wave at the door. Her mind was already inside, where that poncey boss of hers was waiting.

He knew that bastard fancied her. He just hoped to God that Lily meant what she said.

Finally, Jack's boss appeared. He wasn't alone. Blonde, miniskirt, false eyelashes. Now, Jack understood.

'Ah, there you are, Wickham. This is Miss... er...'

'Call me Diana,' she said, flashing a flirty smile his way. 'Morning, sir. Miss.' Jack knew better than to react. So he gave her a nod and returned his attention to the boss.

'I thought we could give Miss – Diana a lift to Pimlico. It won't take us too far out of our way, will it?'

'Right-o, sir,' said Jack. He picked up their cases and led the way to the car.

28

A few weeks later, Leo was waiting for Lily as she arrived at the office. 'He's gone, then?' he asked.

She nodded. 'They're catching the ferry this morning,' she said. 'He left home at the crack of dawn. Him, my brother and nephew'll be travelling round Spain for the next fortnight – provided my idiot of a brother doesn't go and get himself killed racing his motorbike.'

'And you're sure you can get away next weekend?'

'It shouldn't be a problem. Caroline's going on the Brownie pack holiday. She's beside herself with excitement. Beverley is self-sufficient, and she'll enjoy having the house to herself.'

'What have you told them?'

'That I'm going away with one of the girls at work. I said she had it all booked and then her friend let her down, so I said I'd go instead. What about you? What did you tell your wife?'

'She thinks I'm going to a Masonic conference.'

Lily laughed. 'The good old Masons, eh? I wonder how many other men fool their wives by claiming to be doing something for the Lodge?'

'We do actually do things for the Lodge. The brotherhood expects us all to do our bit.'

She kissed his cheek. 'I'm sure you do. But thank God for the vow of secrecy you chaps take – that's all I can say. Without it, we'd never manage to pull this off.'

'I can't wait.'

'Me, neither.'

* * *

Jack leaned his back against the railing of the cross-channel ferry, watching the other passengers wandering round the deck. Beside him, Tony and his lad were hanging over the edge, chucking their guts up.

'I told you, you should've had a bacon sarnie like me.'

Tony retched again, setting the boy off.

Jack laughed. 'You're a useless pair, you are. It's like a bleeding mill pond out here, and you can't keep down a cup of tea.'

'Sod off, you bastard,' Tony growled.

'That's the trouble with your family – no sea legs. Not like my lot.'

'Your lot are a bunch of reprobates from Poplar.'

'A bunch of *sea-faring* reprobates from Poplar,' he said. 'I come from a long line of Navy lads, me. That's why I ain't hanging over there losing me breakfast.'

'Sailors? Yeah, right. A few stupid sods who got press-ganged. You ain't related to Nelson or nothing.'

'Who knows? Might be. If he ever went down the East End for a night out... Me mum reckons the blondes in the family are on account of a Swedish sea captain who got his leg over in London about an 'undred years ago.'

'Bugger off.'

A squall of wind pelted them with sea spray. Poor little Vince got his own sick splattered all over his shirt.

Jack was still laughing when they drove off the ferry in France.

29

Lily lay in bed in the middle of the morning, her body satiated. Leo had popped out of their hotel room in Brighton to get them something to eat. She'd offered to get up and go with him, but he'd shaken his head.

'Stay there. I want to come back to you just as you are – naked and warm.' He'd kissed her, and she'd clung to him.

'Don't be long.'

'I couldn't be. I don't want to waste a single moment.'

He had gone and she stayed in bed, feeling guilty because she wasn't ill – although her body felt feverish every time she let herself think about what they'd done last night and this morning. God, it had been incredible.

It had never been like that with Jack, even when they'd first got married. They'd been stupid, naïve kids, fumbling in the dark, embarrassed by their nakedness. After the few days' honeymoon in a chilly holiday chalet in Somerset, they'd gone to live in a couple of rooms at the top of her parents' house in Bow, where they'd been frightened to make a noise because her mum and dad slept in the room below them. They'd certainly never stayed in bed like this – her mum would send her brother or one of her little sisters upstairs to get them up if they tried it – and they'd never spent the whole night completely naked.

Lily stretched, revelling in the feel of the smooth cotton sheets on her bare skin.

Looking back, she couldn't believe they'd lived like that for nearly a decade before they got a place of their own. It was a miracle they'd had Beverley at all. And once they had a kid of their own, having any sort of sex life got harder. It wasn't until they got the flat in Blackheath that Caroline had been born. By then, Beverley was nearly eight.

Lily frowned as it struck her that that was the point when Beverley had started playing up. She'd been too busy with setting up her first proper home and coping with a new baby to take much notice of the girl's stroppiness. By the time she'd tried to sort her out, Beverley was set on making life as difficult as possible for all of them, and Lily knew she'd left it too late.

School exclusions, unsuitable friends, smoking and drinking became the norm for Beverley as she entered her teens. They'd thought she'd sorted herself out when she got a hairdressing apprenticeship. Lily had breathed a sigh of relief that her eldest daughter had found something she enjoyed doing and was prepared to work at. And then the stupid girl had gone and got herself pregnant...

The door opened and Leonard came in bearing a tray. 'Why the glum face?' he asked.

She shook her head, pinning on a smile. 'I'm not used to being in bed at this hour. Too much time to think.'

'Not happy thoughts, I gather.'

'It doesn't matter. Nothing I can change, so I'm wasting my time getting worked up about it.'

He put the tray on the bedside table. There was a pot of tea, and a plateful of delicate salmon sandwiches, garnished with a sprig of parsley. He passed the plate to her and poured the tea. 'Want to talk about it?'

'Not really. I'm just thinking what a terrible woman I am.' She rested the plate on the mattress.

'That's not true. You're beautiful and intelligent and very, very sexy.' He handed her a cup and saucer and sat on the edge of the bed with his own. 'You're not regretting this, are you?'

'God, no!' She leaned forward and kissed him. 'Never in a million years.'

'Good.' He put his cup back on the tray and stood up.

Lily sipped her tea as she watched him strip. When she put the cup back on the saucer it rattled slightly, so she placed it on the table beside her before she spilt it all over the white sheets.

'Is the *Do Not Disturb* sign still on the door handle?' she asked as he climbed onto the bed, narrowly missing the sandwiches.

'Yes.'

She held up the plate between them, trying hard not to smile. 'Want some?'

He took it from her and returned it to the tray before taking her in his arms. 'Later.'

'But I'm starving.'

'So am I. Food can wait.'

Lily wondered if the other hotel guests could hear her laughter, but then he kissed her and it didn't matter.

* * *

'Mmm. It's simply perfect. I could get used to this,' said Leonard.

'What? The sea air?' Lily smiled up at him as they walked arm in arm along the seafront.

'That too.'

It had been tempting to stay in their hotel room for the whole weekend. Who knew when he'd have Lily to himself again? What he did know, with a certainty that filled him with equal measures of excitement and despair, was that now that he was familiar with how exquisite a creature she was under those sensible, *respectable* clothes, and what she looked like as she awoke after a night of love, he might never be able to look at her in the office again without sporting an enormous erection.

'It's so nice here,' sighed Lily. 'I think I could get used to it too. London is so noisy and dirty, isn't it? I love the seaside. It feels so fresh and clean.'

'It's still noisy,' he said as a gang of mods rode by on their Lambrettas, their angry little engines spewing the distinctive aroma of two-stroke oil from their exhausts. 'I don't know what's more offensive – those damn hooligans or the seagulls.'

'Sometimes I wonder if we can ever be satisfied,' Lily sighed, coming to a halt as the scooters disappeared and the shouts and whistles of the riders echoed along the seafront.

'I can be extremely satisfied,' he leaned close and whispered in her ear. 'Especially when you're naked underneath me.'

She blushed, and looked away. 'Behave.'

'That wasn't the point of this weekend,' he said.

She gave up and laughed, a full-blown, head-thrown-back, joyful sound that thrilled him.

'Well, if you want any more of that, you're going to have to feed me. Those sandwiches were a long time ago. I wouldn't mind a drink either.'

They began walking again. Leonard enjoyed the feel of her holding on to his arm, her hip moving with his as they moved. Even with their clothes on, it felt unbearably sensuous.

'Shall we order room service?' he asked.

'No. I'd like to eat in the hotel restaurant, if it's all right with you?'

'Of course.'

'I mean, we're not likely to be seen by anyone we know, are we? You said this was a good place to get away without being recognised, didn't you?'

'No one will recognise us, Lily. Stop worrying.'

She sighed. 'I can't help it. I've never done anything like this before. I don't know the rules.'

'Neither do I,' he said. Although he'd heard things – snatches of conversations at the Lodge. It had shocked him at first to realise that other men were unfaithful. Even as he'd listened to them, he'd not been tempted to reveal his own secret. He'd never told a soul about his relationship with Lily. It was too precious to be brought out and examined by others.

They reached the hotel.

'Do we need to book a table? The hotel seems quite busy.'

'I'll check. Shall we have a drink in the bar before we eat?'

'All right. I'll just nip upstairs. Give me ten minutes.'

Leonard made a reservation for dinner and then headed for the bar. As he crossed the lobby he realised that he hadn't called Daphne. He always called before dinner when he was away. If he didn't tonight, she would wonder why.

He checked his watch. Lily would be another five minutes. There was a payphone in a booth in the hotel lobby. He slipped inside, pulled some coins out of his pocket and dialled.

'Wimbledon five-four-eight-three.'

'Hello, Daphne. How are you?'

'There you are, Leonard. I was beginning to wonder if you were going to call this evening. You've missed the children. They're in the bath.'

'That's a shame,' he said. 'Give them my love.'

'They've been little devils all day. Peter actually hit Susan this afternoon. I had to smack him. If you'd have been coming home this evening I would have waited for you to do it.'

'Why did he do it?' Leonard frowned. It wasn't like Peter to be violent.

'He claims that Susan drove him to it.'

He could imagine that. Much as he loved his daughter, she was showing worrying signs of the same cunning and malice that he so often witnessed in his mother-in-law. Allowing Daphne to take the children to stay with the old woman after her accident a few months ago had been a bad idea. He'd noticed that since then Susan had begun to take delight in goading her brother.

'Perhaps she did.'

'That's no excuse for hitting a girl, Leonard. It's inexcusable.'

'Of course. However, we ought to take care that we don't encourage Susan to think that she can tease her brother without there being consequences. By all means punish Peter, but it might be a good idea to have a talk with Susan about being more amiable.'

'She's a perfectly amiable child. How can you say otherwise?' Daphne sounded shocked.

'When it suits her, yes. But no doubt she's like any other human being in this world and will test her boundaries. If she gets away with pushing her brother to his limits with impunity, she'll carry on. I'm just suggesting we both be on our guard and keep the peace between them, or in a few years' time our house will be a battleground.'

Daphne sniffed. 'I'm surprised you're such an expert on child-rearing, considering you're hardly ever here.'

He refused to respond. It made his point – it wasn't just Susan who had learned the art of picking an argument from his mother-in-law.

'How's the conference?' she asked eventually.

Caught off guard by her question, it took him a moment to remember his subterfuge. 'Fine. The usual sort of thing, you know.'

'No, Leonard, I don't know. How can I? You never tell me anything.'

'I can't—'

'Of course you can. You simply choose not to.'

Leonard felt his blood pressure rising. How could he stand this? He took a deep breath. 'I'm not going to argue with you, my dear. I rang to wish the children goodnight and to see how you are. But as you are clearly coping with everything and the children are otherwise occupied, I'll say goodbye and join my friends for dinner. I'll see you tomorrow.'

'What time will you be back?'

'I'll be late. Don't wait up.'

He hung up and stayed there, his hand on the phone as he waited for his racing pulse to subside.

A tap on the door of the booth got his attention. Lily was watching through the glass, her expression showing concern. He let go of the phone and opened the door.

'Everything all right?' she asked.

Of course it wasn't. Daphne was becoming more discontent with every day that passed. He was sure she suspected, but he wasn't about to stop seeing Lily. How could he? She was his world now. He opened his mouth to tell her, and beg her to leave her husband. They could run away together and start a new life. But he couldn't imagine walking away from his children, and he doubted Lily could either.

'Everything's fine,' he said. 'I've booked a table for dinner. We've just got time for an aperitif.'

'Lovely.' She smiled and took his proffered arm.

As they made their way to the hotel bar, Leonard couldn't help thinking he hadn't fooled Lily at all. Her glance was thoughtful, and there was a sadness about her that she tried to mask with bright smiles. He didn't dare ask, not wanting to hear her voice a single regret about what they were doing. Instead he matched her smile, and determined that tonight would be so special that when they were old and grey they would look back on it with joy and wonder at the power of their love.

At the same time, in a bar outside Barcelona, Jack raised his glass. 'Well done, mate. You did it! I never thought you'd get your scrawny arse round that track, let alone win.'

Tony gave his usual *'What-would-you-know?'* smirk, and chinked his beer against his brother-in-law's. Vince joined in, almost dancing with excitement.

'Yeah, Dad. You were brilliant.'

'The first of many, my boy,' said Tony. 'Just you watch your old dad. Watch and learn.'

Jack took a swig of his beer and pulled a face. 'Christ, I could do with a real beer. This stuff's like piss.'

'I like it,' said Vince.

'Course you do. You ain't learned to appreciate the fine art of proper beer-drinking yet, boy.'

'I drink beer at home, Uncle Jack.'

'Yeah? I bet your mum don't know, does she?' The boy blushed, looking sideways at his father.

'What she don't know won't hurt her,' said Tony. 'Leave the boy alone. I brought him with us to make a man out of him. I couldn't leave him with all them bleeding females in the house, could I?'

Jack nodded. He envied Tony. At least he had a son. Jack loved his girls to bits, but Christ, he would have been over the moon if they'd had a boy as well. He'd tried to talk Lily into trying again after Caroline was born, but she'd told him to sod off. By then, Maggie had had four boys and was desperate for a girl.

'I'm not going through that again,' she'd said. 'What if we kept having girls? No, I'm not having any more babies, Jack. You'll have to get some rubbers.'

He'd hated those bloody things, but for years she wouldn't let him near her without one. Then she'd managed to get that new Pill when it came out. Jack had been in heaven, and for a while it was just like old times. But that sodding job of hers in the City had put paid to all that. Lately, he'd hardly managed to get his leg over at all. She was always too busy or too tired. He was getting sick of the way she looked at him if he tried to get a bit fruity.

Tony nudged his arm.

'Oi, watch it.' He just managed to save his beer from spilling all over the boy. 'I know it's piss, but I ain't about to waste it.'

'Look,' said Tony, pointing to a poster on the wall. 'It's tonight. We should go.'

'Flamenco dancing? You're having a laugh.'

'No, it'll be good. All them *señoritas*, strutting their stuff.'

Vince looked dubious.

Jack shrugged. He didn't care. 'Might as well. So long as there's decent beer there.'

'For Christ's sake, a decent beer, a decent cup of tea. You've been moaning since we got here.'

'Too right. The beer's rubbish, and it ain't normal, all that coffee lark. And you'd better find me some bacon and proper sausages in the morning, or I'm on the next ferry back.'

'What, and miss seeing me beat the arse off these fellas? You ain't going nowhere. You love it really.'

Jack raised his eyebrows. 'One win, and he's Stirling Moss on a motorbike,' he told Vince.

'So, are we up for this show, or not?'

Jack drained his glass. 'Yeah, why not.' It might not be proper culture like Lily's fancy boys in tights, but it was proper Spanish. 'It should be a laugh.'

'But Dad, Mum said—'

Tony held up a hand. 'Stop right there, son. What your mother don't know won't hurt her. I'll keep schtum about you having a beer, and you keep your gob shut about everything else, all right?'

The boy nodded and followed them out of the bar.

30

Jack had been travelling all day and most of the previous night. Although he was knackered, he felt his spirits lift as he opened the front door. He whistled, and there was a shriek and a thud from upstairs.

'Daddy! Daddy's home!' Caroline shot out of her room and down the stairs. Jack just about had time to shut the door and put his case down before she launched herself at him from halfway up. He caught her and swung her round.

'Hallo, my little darling! Have you missed me?'

'Yes!'

'Have you been good?' He settled her on his hip and she clung round his neck with her little arms. 'Only I met this lady in Spain and she gave me something you might like, but she said I can only give it to you if you've been a really good girl.'

'I have been good, haven't I, Mummy?' she asked over his shoulder.

Jack turned round and there was Lily, standing in the kitchen doorway, wiping her hands on a tea towel. He put Caroline down and walked towards his wife. 'All right, love?' She smiled and raised her cheek for his kiss. But Jack wasn't having none of that. 'Come here.' He gathered her up in a bear hug and buried his face in her neck. He breathed in her scent, letting it fill his lungs, chasing away the foreign smells of garlic and dodgy Spanish cigarettes.

'It's good to be home,' he said, breathing out. 'I've missed you.'

Lily shrugged. 'I'm surprised you had time, what with all the work Tony was bound to have you doing. Did he win anything?'

Jack raised his head. It felt so good, just standing there holding her. He couldn't remember the last time he'd felt so content. It seemed like years. It probably was. He wanted to pick her up and take her upstairs and do the naughty with her, right now, in broad daylight. Just shut the bedroom door, tell the kids to sod off for a couple of hours, and forget everything except her. But he knew she wouldn't have it, not with little Caroline about. Maybe later, when the kid was asleep. He stifled a yawn, which crept up on him. Must be the heat from the kitchen. Something smelt good in there.

'Well?' asked Lily.

'What? Tony?' He lifted one shoulder. 'You know him. Started off all right, got a few wins in. Then he got cocky and the Spanish got pissed off. They brought him down a peg or two.'

Lily nodded. 'That man's his own worst enemy. I suppose he's gone off motorbike racing now, has he?'

'He's talking about cars next.'

She rolled her eyes. 'Well, just don't let him con you into helping him again.'

Jack shrugged. 'He's all bloody talk. He ain't got the money for car racing.'

Caroline was standing next to his case. 'Daddy!' She put her hands on her hips. 'You mustn't swear. It's very naughty, isn't it, Mummy?'

Lily nodded. He could see she was trying not to laugh. 'That's right. Daddy's very naughty. I should wash his mouth out with soap.'

Sod that.

'How about I show you girls what I bought you instead?' he asked.

Caroline clapped and jumped up and down.

'Where's Bev and the baby?'

Lily frowned. 'They went out for some fresh air. I expect they'll be back soon.'

'They all right?'

'The baby's fine. She's almost walking. I'm not sure about Beverley, though,' she said. 'She's been off colour all week. She barely left her bed for a couple of days, and hasn't been to work. I phoned them to say she was ill, but she hasn't been to the doctor to get a sick note. I hope they don't sack her.'

'What's the matter with her?'

'I don't know. She's got no energy, and I'm sure she's lost weight. It's like a light's been switched off. She doesn't want to do anything, she won't eat, I had to nag her to do her hair, and she's been sitting around in her pyjamas and dressing gown all the time.'

'Well, she must be on the mend if she's gone out now. It was probably her monthlies or something.'

'Don't be such a bloke. I think she's really been sickening for something.'

'Nah, she'll be all right. You always fuss.'

Lily looked ready to argue, but Caroline had clearly had enough.

'What did you bring me, Daddy? Is it in your suitcase?'

'Let's take it in the living room and see, shall we?'

They followed him in and he put the case down on the rug in front of the fireplace.

'Hang on a minute, Jack, or the casserole will dry up.' Lily nipped to the kitchen and was back in a few seconds. 'Right. Let's see what you've got in there, apart from two weeks' worth of dirty washing.'

He laughed, knelt down and opened the case. Caroline came in so close she was practically climbing into it.

'Oi! Get back,' he growled, putting a protective arm over the Y-fronts lying on the top.

Caroline giggled and settled onto the rug next to him. 'Hurry up, Daddy!'

She gasped as Jack rummaged through his clothes and brought out what at first looked like some red material. But when he unrolled it they could see that it was a shawl, wrapped around a doll in a red and black Spanish dress. The headdress and lace veil were a bit skew-whiff, but he nudged them back into place as she reached for it. As Jack draped the shawl round her shoulders, its black fringe shimmered with every tiny movement.

'Oh, Daddy, she's beautiful!' She kissed him on the cheek, then sat back and examined the doll in close detail. 'And I love my shawl.' She wiggled her shoulders, setting the fringe into motion again. 'Thank you. My friends are going to be so jealous!'

'Me and Uncle Tony saw a lady dressed just like that doll, doing Spanish dancing,' he told her.

Lily raised her eyebrows. 'I thought Vince's mother had put the kibosh on that sort of thing.'

Jack grinned. 'Well, I ain't going to tell her. Anyway, it was just a bit of fun. It ain't like we was going to get up to anything – even if we wanted to, which I definitely didn't. Young Vince followed us round like a little puppy. I expect his mum'll be giving him the third degree to find out what went on. The poor little sod'll be singing like a canary by tonight, you mark my words.'

Lily laughed. 'You're right. I reckon that's why she sent him with you, don't you?'

'Yeah. He ain't exactly keen on motorbikes. He was about as useful as a chocolate teapot.'

The front door slammed.

'Is that my number-one daughter and granddaughter, home at last?' Jack called out. 'Come and see your old dad, Bev, home from the wars.'

Beverley took her time. He supposed she was getting the baby out of the pram. Caroline ran to the door and opened it.

'Look what Daddy brought me!' She held her doll up for her sister to see. 'Come and see what he's got for you.'

Beverley came into the living room, her cheeks flushed, the baby on her hip. When Kerry clocked Jack, she let out a squeal and reached for him, leaving Bev struggling not to drop her.

'There's my little poppet!' He took the baby and cuddled her. 'Ain't you getting big? What's your mum been feeding you?' He pretended to drop her, catching her up again against his chest. Kerry's laughter got Lily and Caroline laughing too, but Bev could barely manage a smile.

'You all right, darling?' he asked, putting his free arm round her and pulling her close. Lily was right, she had lost weight. He could feel her shoulder blade under his hand. 'Mum said you've been poorly.'

Bev shrugged his hand away. 'I'm all right.'

'Yeah?' She didn't bloody look it, but he knew she would only argue if he said so. 'Come and see what I've got you.' He reached down and did his rummaging act again.

'Bloody hell, is that your dirty socks and pants?' asked Bev. 'I don't want nothing out of there, thanks.'

His fingers found what he'd been searching for. He pulled a small box out. 'You're all right. Your present's in here.' He handed it over.

Bev opened it, her eyes widening when she saw the gold hooped earrings nestling inside.

'Oh, they're lovely,' said Lily. 'Proper Spanish gold, that is.'

For a minute, he thought Bev was going to burst into tears, but she sniffed and blinked, then managed a smile.

'Thanks, Dad,' she said, kissing his cheek.

The baby reached for the shiny things, but Bev moved them out of her reach. Kerry squawked in protest. Jack jiggled her about a bit.

'Oi, oi, what's all this noise, ay? Did you think Granddad forgot about you?'

The contents of his case were getting well and truly messed up as he dived in again. 'Ta da!'

He'd had this one wrapped up in pink paper. Caroline helped the baby pull the package open. Within seconds there was paper all over the rug and the baby was cooing as she cuddled up to a stuffed donkey in a sombrero.

'We'll have to get that hat off it before she eats it,' said Lily.

'Oh God, I never thought of that, sorry.'

Caroline picked up the paper while Lily distracted the baby and whipped the sombrero away. Bev sat on the edge of the sofa, looking at her earrings.

'Can I have it?' Caroline whispered, pointing at the sombrero.

Lily handed it over. 'Take it upstairs, quick,' she said. 'Right then, what else have we got in here?'

Jack was enjoying this; it was like Christmas. He loved giving his girls nice little surprises. But he made sure he had a little fun n'all. The next thing he brought out had exactly the effect he expected from Lily. He held it up and she stared at it, trying not to look disappointed.

'What is it?'

'It's another donkey.'

'I can see that. A plastic one. It's a bit funny-looking, isn't it? I mean, the body looks like a box.'

'That's 'cause it is a box, see?' He opened the top to reveal a row of cigarettes, neatly loaded.

'Oh. A cigarette box. Nice.'

He nearly laughed out loud at the look on her face. 'I thought you'd like it.'

'It's the thought that counts,' she said.

'It's a bit special, this one. It's a Spanish cigarette box. You know why them foreign fags smell dodgy?'

'I don't know, do I?'

''Cause they come out like this.' Jack pulled on the donkey's ears, and its tail rose as a cigarette slid out of its backside.

For a moment, Lily looked stunned, then she laughed. 'Only you could find something as disgusting as that, Jack Wickham. Is that all you got me?'

'Who said this was yours? I got this for your mum and dad.'

'He'll like it, but she'll kill you.'

'Nah, she loves me really.'

'Yes, but not your jokes.'

'It's a laugh though, ain't it?' He looked from Lily to Bev, who was shaking her head. At least she had a smile on her face now.

'What's that?' Caroline spotted the plastic donkey as soon as she came back in the room.

'Pull its ears,' said Bev.

Caroline looked a bit dubious, but had a go. When the tail went up and another fag came out of the arse, she laughed so hard tears were rolling down her face. 'That's naughty,' she said.

'That's for Nanny,' said Bev.

Caroline put her hand to her mouth, her eyes wide. 'She'll be really cross with you, Daddy. But it is funny.'

* * *

Lily watched Jack laughing with the girls. He looked so pleased with himself, and his whole face glowed with mischief. He was like this on birthdays and at Christmas. He loved giving presents, the tackier the better. She wouldn't be surprised if, when he was old and grey, he grew a beard and worked as Father Christmas in Self-ridges or somewhere. He'd lap it up, making sure all the kiddies went away with a nice present and a smile on their faces. They'd all be extra good until Christmas.

She'd forgotten about this side of him. She'd been so wrapped up with falling in love with Leonard. The guilt of that had warped her mind – it made her see only the things about Jack that irritated or embarrassed her. Looking at him now, with their girls so pleased to see him home, made her heart ache.

'Daddy.' Caroline tugged on his sleeve. 'What did you get for Mummy?'

Jack slapped the palm of his hand against his forehead. Lily noticed that his hairline was receding. How had she missed that? When was the last time she'd really looked at her husband?

'I knew I'd forgot something,' he said.

'Oh, Daddy! You can't have forgotten Mummy.'

'You'd think so, wouldn't you?' He tilted his head to one side, sneaking a wink at his daughter. 'Now, did I forget to get her a present, or did I forget I'd bought her one?'

Caroline looked confused.

'Shall I check?' he asked, taking pity on her.

'Yes!'

'I'm not sure I want a present if it's anything like that donkey,' said Lily. She wasn't sure she wanted anything at all.

It hurt her to think he might have spent his time looking for a gift for her, while she'd been taking advantage of his absence to be with Leo. She didn't deserve anything.

Jack pulled up his shirt-sleeves and made a big play of searching, elbow-deep, through the contents of his case.

'No, nothing here but smelly socks,' he said. He stopped. 'Oh, and these.'

He pulled out some castanets, already on his fingers. He waved his arm in the air, clacking away like mad. Lily covered her ears.

'Don't you like 'em?' asked Jack, pretending to look shocked.

'No thanks.' She grimaced. 'They'll give me one of my heads.'

'Keep looking, Daddy.'

Jack carried on the pantomime, his eyes gleaming. Kerry, already bored with her cuddly toy, crawled over and tried to climb into the case. Caroline giggled as Beverley scooped up her daughter and sat down with her on the sofa.

'Hang on,' he said. 'I think I've found something.' He held up a small bag. 'What's this?' He peeked inside. 'Yeah, that'll do.' He held it out for Lily. 'I was going to give this to me mum, but seeing as how you don't like those lovely castanets, you'd better have this one.'

Lily took the bag, bracing herself for another practical joke.

'What is it, Mummy?'

'Give her a chance to bloody look,' said Beverley.

Lily looked and gasped. 'Chanel No 5.' She took the bottle out of the bag and held it up to the light. The perfume glowed a deep gold. 'Oh, Jack, it's lovely. I've always wanted some of this.'

'That ain't Spanish,' said Beverley.

'No, I got it in the duty-free shop on the ferry. I knew you'd like it.'

'What does it smell like?' asked Caroline.

Lily eased the stopper off and inhaled the rich scent. The musky aroma made her blush. 'Lovely.'

'Let me smell it.' Caroline leaned over and sniffed. She pulled a face. 'Ugh! That's horrible!'

Lily laughed. 'It's just as well it's for me then, isn't it? You can keep your hands off it.' She looked at Jack kneeling on the rug. He looked like an eager puppy waiting to be praised. She put the stopper back in the bottle.

'Thanks, love,' she said.

'You like it?'

She nodded. 'I love it.'

He grinned and slapped his knees before jumping to his feet.

'Good. Right, now everyone's happy, who's going to put the kettle on? I ain't had a proper cuppa for two weeks.'

'I will,' said Caroline, running out of the room.

'Go careful,' Lily shouted after her.

Jack sat down in his usual armchair, opposite Lily. On the sofa, Kerry tried to wriggle out of her mother's arms. Beverley put the child down on the floor. She crawled across to Jack and pulled herself up onto her feet, clinging to his trouser legs as she found her balance.

'Bloody hell, look at that!' Jack beamed. 'She'll be off and running before we know it.'

'It's nearly her birthday,' said Beverley. 'I can't believe she's almost one.'

'Yeah,' he said. 'We'll need eyes in the back of our heads now, won't we?' He reached down and tickled the baby until she lost her balance and landed with a whoosh on her padded bottom.

* * *

Lily let the conversation drift around her as she stroked the perfume bottle, enjoying its weight in her hand. Chanel No 5. It made her think of women like Audrey Hepburn in her chic little outfits, and Marilyn Monroe. What was it Marilyn had said when someone asked her what she wore in bed? '*Chanel No 5.*' Yes, that's what she'd said. The press had gone mad; the clergy had been outraged. Silly old sods.

Had Jack been thinking about what Marilyn had said when he bought this for her? Did he hope she'd follow her lead and go to bed in nothing but some expensive scent?

Why couldn't she want to do that for her husband? He was a good man, and she used to love having sex with him. But not now. She wasn't the same any more. He deserved a better wife than she was. One who really loved him.

She *did* love him, only not like she used to. Not how she should. She loved him for being a good father, and for letting her go to night school to get out of that bloody sweatshop. She loved the way he danced, and that he didn't mind helping around the house and was so good with all the girls. But she didn't love him like a wife should. She couldn't love him like she loved Leo. She couldn't talk to him about the things that were becoming important to her, like literature, or even current affairs. Leo understood the woman she had become. He bought her books, and listened to her opinions. He valued her intelligence. Jack just made a joke out of everything, expecting everyone to be happy. To settle.

She didn't want to settle. She didn't want to wear this perfume for him. But she didn't want to hurt him either.

31

At the offices of Alder & Powney a few days later, Leonard closed the file he'd been working on and added it to the growing pile he'd dealt with this morning. His client list was growing, and he was satisfied that he would be the next in line for a partnership. Daphne would be content at last.

He reached for the next file, a complicated probate case. The receipts were finally in, and distribution to the heirs could proceed. Some fortunate nephews and nieces of the late Reverend James Armitage, a bachelor, were going to receive cheques for considerable sums, as were a number of ecclesiastical charities. He smiled. This would require at least an hour in the company of the office cashier.

He dialled Lily's number. 'Cashier's office.'

'It's been too long since I've kissed you,' he whispered.

'Good morning, Mr Warwick. I'm just helping Mr Irwin with a completion. Would it be all right if I rang you back?'

'He's not peering down your cleavage, is he?'

'Of course.'

'Tell him you're mine.'

'That might be difficult.'

'I want you, naked across my desk. Now.'

'Thank you, Mr Warwick. I'll let you know the moment I'm free.'

She hung up. Leonard sat there, holding the phone receiver to his ear as her voice echoed into silence. In his mind's eye he could see Irwin standing over her desk, ostensibly looking at the ledger in front of her, but enjoying the view of her brassiere as he peered downwards. He knew that she would be blushing after their little exchange, and he imagined that Irwin would think he'd been the one to bring a flush to her cheeks.

He put the phone down and tried to turn his attention back to the case in hand. But though his aim had been to torment Lily, he'd managed to arouse himself as well. He shifted in his chair. When Lily called back, he'd better get her to come to him. If he walked through the general office to hers in this state, he'd be in serious trouble.

By the time Lily had completed the tasks that Irwin had set her, Leonard had managed to calm himself. Nevertheless, when she closed his office door behind her, he felt his blood rise again.

'You are a very naughty man,' she said, trying but failing to look serious. 'What if he'd heard you?'

'Then we would have been discovered and he would have been as jealous as hell.'

'We'd have been out on our ears, more like. You've got to be more careful, Leo.'

'I know. But it's killing me. I want to tell the world about us. I'm sick of all this subterfuge.'

She came forward and sat down on the other side of his desk. 'I know it's hard, darling, but we have to keep it a secret. We're both married.'

He sighed. 'Do you have to keep reminding me?'

'Yes. Because we're playing a dangerous game. We could lose everything – our jobs, our children...'

'It won't come to that.'

'It could.'

'Do you know? After that weekend, being able to wake up with you in my arms, to have the freedom to walk down the street holding your hand – I almost wish—'

She held up a hand. 'Don't. Please, my love. Be careful what you wish for. Do you really want to throw away everything you've worked for?'

He frowned. 'Lily, are you trying to end our relationship?'

'No, of course not! God, no.'

'So what is your point?'

She bowed her head, then looked up. 'We've both been married for a long time, haven't we?'

He nodded. He'd been with Daphne for seventeen years, and he knew Lily had been married for almost twenty.

'I married Jack because I loved him. He hasn't done anything wrong; it's me who's changed. He's a good man. He loves the children and he's always tried to be a good husband. The trouble is, he's not the husband I want any more.' She held up her hand to stop him when he would have interrupted. 'No, just listen. I need to say this.' She took a deep breath. 'The thing is, much as I love you, I don't think I can hurt him. I need to be with you, but I can't walk out of my marriage.'

'What if he finds out? Won't he want you to go then?'

'Maybe. I don't know. But I don't want to risk him finding out.' She got up and walked over to the window. This side of the building was in shadow, but there was a patch of blue sky above them. Leonard got up and went to stand behind her, resting his hands on her shoulders. He felt the gentle rise and fall of her breathing.

'You're wearing a new scent.'

'Yes. Jack's present from his travels. It's Chanel No 5.'

He leaned down and kissed her neck, wishing he had been the one to buy it for her. She turned and kissed him tenderly on the mouth, her hand warm against his cheek. When he would have deepened the kiss she stopped him and stepped back. She was barely a foot away from him when there was a brisk knock on the door. With lightning speed, she resumed her seat and picked up her notepad and pencil.

'Come in,' he called, still standing where she left him.

His secretary opened the door and peeked through. 'Sorry to bother you, sir, but you wanted this as soon as it was finished.' She held out a file. 'It's the Bishopsgate lease.'

He took it and gave it a cursory glance. 'Excellent. Thank you.' He sat down at his desk. 'I'm just going through the Armitage estate with Mrs Wickham. I'll need to see you after lunch to dictate the letters to go with the cheques to the beneficiaries.'

'Yes, sir.'

'Thank you. That'll be all for now.'

She nodded and shut the door behind her. Lily hadn't moved.

'Are you all right?'

She nodded. 'I am now, but one of these days we're going to get caught.'

He rested his elbows on the desk, cupping his chin in his hands. 'What if we could have a place all to ourselves?'

'What sort of place?'

'A flat, right here in the city.'

'That would be nice, but neither of us could afford something like that.'

'We don't have to. We just need the right connections.'

She looked sceptical. 'Not much chance of that, then.'

He smiled. 'There's every chance, my darling.' He dipped a hand into his jacket pocket and pulled out a key. 'Look.'

'What's that for?'

'A flat, just five minutes from here.'

'Whose is it?'

'A fellow Mason. He works for a bank and has just been given an assignment in Hong Kong. He'll be gone for at least a year. We can use the flat whenever we want.'

'Does he know about us?' Lily looked appalled.

'Not exactly. I think he suspects, but he's a good chum and very discreet. He didn't ask questions, and made it clear that so long as I arrange to keep it clean and don't have wild parties that upset the neighbours, I'm free to use it any time.'

'Five minutes from here?'

He nodded. 'Would you like to join me there for lunch?'

'What if someone see us?'

'They won't. We'll be careful.'

'No one will know?'

'No.'

Still she hesitated.

'Please, my darling.' He reached over and took her hands. 'I know we're taking too many risks here. This is our opportunity to be together without anyone finding out.'

'All right,' she said. 'Where is it?'

He kissed her fingers, then let her go, reaching for her pad and pencil. He sketched a map and wrote the address down. 'Meet me here. I'll leave the office at just before one o'clock. Give me a couple of minutes then you follow.'

She took the notebook back and studied the map. 'All right.' She turned to a clean page. 'Now, we've better get these cheques sorted out. We've wasted too much time already.'

'Time spent with you is never wasted, my love.'
'Behave!' She smiled. 'We've got work to do.'

32

Lily felt like a spy, hurrying along the street, checking over her shoulder to make sure no one was watching. She looked at the sketch map. It wasn't very clear, and she worried that she'd over-shot the turning. She was just about to retrace her steps when she spotted the road she needed just up ahead.

The flat was in a mansion block on a leafy square off Old Street. Leo was waiting for her in the lobby. He smiled when he saw her, taking her arm and leading her to the lift.

'Sorry, it took me longer than I expected,' she said. 'Your map was a bit confusing.'

'Really?'

She laughed. 'Yes, really. You have no sense of scale, and a couple of the side roads were missing. I nearly turned back.'

They reached the third floor, and within moments were standing outside a nondescript door.

'I feel as though I should carry you over the threshold,' he said.

'Oh God, please don't. We'd have a devil of a job explaining what we were doing if you did your back in.'

He took the key from his pocket and opened the door. He held it wide for her to enter. He followed and closed it behind them.

For a moment, Lily felt incredibly shy. They'd never been in a place like this together. She'd thought their weekend in Brighton had been a once-in-a-lifetime thing, never to be repeated.

'Well,' he said, seeming just as nervous. 'Shall I show you around?'

She nodded and followed him along a narrow hallway. 'There are two bedrooms, here and here.' He pointed to doors on either side. 'Bathroom.' The door was ajar, and Lily peeked inside.

'Very nice,' she said, and giggled.

He leaned against the doorjamb. 'I know. I sound like an estate agent.'

'I wouldn't know,' she said. 'We've always lived in council places. I was hoping we could buy a house, but...' She didn't want to go on and remind him about Beverley and the baby. She didn't want him to think she was a bad mother. She should have kept her mouth shut. Why the hell did she have to remind him she lived in a council house? She wanted him to see her as an equal, not be reminding him that she was working class. Christ, she'd be telling him about her years in the factory next.

Leo took her hand. 'Come and see the rest of it.'

There was a neat kitchen, and a large L-shaped room that served as a lounge and dining room. The sun streamed in through the windows, highlighting the dust motes floating in the air. Lily wandered around, stroking the leather sofa, examining the pictures on the walls – modern art, full of splashes and stark lines, not her sort of thing at all. She lingered in front of the shelves full of books. Leo came up behind her and kissed the side of her neck as she selected a slim volume.

'Ah, *The Sonnets*,' he said. '*Shall I compare thee to a summer's day? Thou art more lovely and more temperate...*'

She turned in his arms and smiled. 'Go on.'

He shrugged, looking sheepish. 'I was rather hoping you'd be sufficiently impressed to let me fade into a romantic silence. I confess that's all I know by heart.'

Lily laughed. 'You old fraud. And there was me thinking you knew everything there was to know, you being a solicitor.'

'Guilty. Forgive me?'

'Of course.'

She returned the book to the shelf, making sure it went back into the same place, and continued her inspection of the room. There was one of those complicated-looking hi-fi systems on the sideboard. She'd be too scared to use that in case she broke it. Perhaps Leo would know how to operate it.

'It that one of those new colour televisions?' she asked, pointing.

'Mmm?' Leonard looked distracted. 'Yes, I think it is.'

This place must be worth a fortune, she thought. 'Leo, are you sure it's all right for us to be here?'

'Absolutely. He made it quite clear I could regard the place as my own while he's away.'

'But you haven't told him about us.'

'I didn't have to. He's a man of the world. He said he didn't care what I got up to, so long as we remained discreet.'

'In other words, don't get caught, and don't drag him into it by association.' She shook her head. 'I don't know if my nerves can take this. How do other people manage? I keep thinking about that trial Mr Profumo was involved in. It ruined his life.'

'For God's sake, Lily, he was using prostitutes. Our situation is nothing like that.'

She didn't want to argue. 'No, you're right. Sorry, I'm just so nervous about this.'

'It's all right, my love. It's going to be fine.' He kissed her forehead. 'Now, how about a cup of tea and a spot of lunch?'

'We can't steal the man's food!'

'I have no intention of stealing anything. I came in earlier with some provisions. We've got the makings for sandwiches. There's no time for anything fancier before we have to get back to work.'

'Oh, all right. I thought we...' She blushed.

He caressed her cheek. 'Much as I'd love to take my time and make love to you right now, we have to be sensible. We have to be back at the office in less than half an hour. But we can come back here as often as we like.'

'I told Jack I'd be late tonight.'

'Good. I'll call home and tell them I've got to see a client after hours.'

'Will you put the kettle on while I make the sandwiches?'

He smiled. 'Yes, we'd better, or I might forget all my good intentions. I forgot to bring milk, I'm afraid, so will black coffee be all right?'

After they had eaten, and before they left the flat, Lily inspected the bedrooms. All afternoon, she dreamed of lying in the big double bed in the master bedroom, wearing nothing but a few drops of Chanel No 5.

33

On Friday night, Jack was round at Fred's place.

'Right, boys,' he said. 'Get that screen up. We'll have our own film show. Someone open the crisps. Fred, you got some pop for these kids?'

The living room was in chaos, with four boys fighting over who was going to put up Uncle Jack's movie screen, while he got busy sorting out his cine projector. He had taken some well nice films of Tony's races, and a bullfight n'all. The boys would love it. Caroline and Samantha were in the kitchen playing with their dolls, and the littlest one was asleep in her cot. Lily and Maggie had taken themselves off to the bingo.

'I hope you got a good 'un of Tony Adams falling off his bike,' said Fred. 'I'd like to see that jumped-up sod land on his arse.'

'I aim to please,' said Jack. 'Now get those lights off. Boys, sit down and shut up. Here we go.'

* * *

At the bingo hall, Maggie sipped on her first port and lemon of the night as they waited for the first game to start. 'Ah, that's lovely. It's been ages since we had a night out.'

Lily nodded. 'Yeah, too long. There never seems to be the time any more.'

'You still working all hours?'

'Mmm.'

'Fred said they ain't paying you no overtime.'

'You don't usually get overtime when you're on a monthly salary,' said Lily. 'But it's worth doing. My boss says I could be made office manager soon, and that'll mean more money.'

'Blimey. Office manager, eh? That's a long way from Cohen's sewing factory, ain't it?'

'Not half. I'll tell you, Mags, it's a completely different world. I love it.'

'That's nice. I don't think I'd fancy it, though, putting up with all them posh geezers.'

'They're all right once you get used to them. They're just blokes, like the rest of them – except they don't eff and blind all the time like ours do. And they talk about cricket and rugby, not bloody Millwall.'

'They're all a bit clever, though, them solicitors, ain't they?'

'Well, yeah, of course. They have to work bloody hard, passing loads of exams, learning Latin, and such like. But they had the opportunity, not like us. They didn't have to leave school at fourteen like we did. I reckon if we'd had their chances, we'd do just as well.'

'Don't be daft. What use would Latin be down Brick Lane?'

'That's not the point. If we had their chances, we wouldn't be hanging around Brick Lane any more. We'd be doing their jobs in the City, living in our own houses, sending our kids off to university.'

'Huh, fat chance of that. I'll be happy if my boys all get jobs down the docks. Pen-pushing wouldn't suit them.'

'Good evening, ladies and gentlemen,' said the compère over the loudspeakers. 'Are you ready for the first game?'

There was a low rumble of assent from the crowd.

'Right then, eyes down. And the first number is: two and six, twenty-six.'

Lily checked her cards and crossed off the number. She was glad the game had started when it did. She hadn't known what to say to Maggie. She remembered how her friend had cried when her mum told her she'd have to leave school. Maggie had been bright. She could've gone to grammar school, but her dad had just died – she'd come home and found him, dead in his chair – and after that there wasn't the money for the uniform. Instead she'd gone with Lily to the secondary school, and at fourteen they'd both had to give that up to go out to work. Now, all Maggie wanted for her own kids was a back-breaking, soul-destroying job on the docks.

'Eight and four, eighty-four.'

Lily carried on checking numbers, lost in her own thoughts, until someone called 'House!' for a line. She wondered what Leo was doing. They met at the flat every lunch time, except when he had to see a client, and a couple of evenings after work. Being able to see each other, away from prying eyes, and to have that great big bed to make love in, was so lovely.

But she still worried that they'd be found out. They'd had so many near-misses at the office. She didn't know what she'd do if—

'Lily, you all right?'

'What? Sorry, Mags, I was miles away.'

'Everything okay?'

'Yeah, I'm fine.'

'How did you get on while Jack was away? I thought we'd see you down the Guildford on the Saturday.'

'I went away, with a friend from work.'

'Did you? That's nice. Where'd you go?'

'Brighton. Caroline was away with the Brownies, and Beverley can sort herself out, so when the chance came up I thought, why not? After all, Jack was off having fun.'

'And did you?'

'Did I what?'

'Have fun, you silly cow.' Maggie laughed.

'Oh.' Lily laughed too, blushing. 'Yeah, it was lovely.'

'What did you do?'

Lily felt her whole body freeze. Her heart sped up and her brain turned to mush. What could she say? She wanted to tell Maggie, her oldest friend, that she was in love and that she was happier than she'd ever been. That she'd spent most of that weekend naked in bed with her lover in a hotel on the seafront. But she couldn't tell Maggie, the wife of her brother-in-law, any of that.

'Er—'

'Eyes down!'

Oh, thank Christ!

'I'll tell you later.'

'Here we go, ladies and gents. Legs eleven.'

Everyone whistled. Lily let out a sigh of relief and concentrated on the cards in front of her. She was aware of Maggie staring at her, but she couldn't look at her.

It wasn't until they were on their way back to Maggie and Fred's that Lily realised Maggie hadn't pursued the question of what she'd done in Brighton. As they pulled up outside the house, Maggie put a hand on Lily's, stopping her from getting out of the car.

'I don't know what's going on with you, Lil, and frankly, I don't want to know. But be careful, love.'

Lily looked at her friend and saw straight away that Maggie had seen through her. She should have known that the woman who'd known her most of her life would figure out what she was up to.

'Maggie—'

'No, don't say anything. I can't get involved in this. I don't want to. If you're doing what I think you're doing, then stop it, right now, before anyone gets hurt. Promise me, Lily.'

'Are you going to tell Fred?'

'I can't tell him what I don't know. So just keep your mouth shut. Don't you dare put me in a position where I've got to choose between my best friend and my husband.'

Lily nodded, staring out of the windscreen into the darkness. 'I never wanted this to happen.'

'Then whatever it is, stop it. Jack don't deserve it, Lil.'

'I know, but—'

'But nothing. I'm telling you now. If it comes to it, I've got to stand by Jack. He's Fred's brother.'

Lily felt a lump growing in her throat, threatening to choke her. 'It won't come to it,' she said. 'I promise.'

'Good. Come on then. Let's go and see what sort of a state the place is in with them two left in charge, eh?'

Lily fished a hanky out of her handbag and blew her nose. She took a deep, calming breath.

'Ready?' asked Maggie.

'Ready.'

* * *

Leonard felt ambivalent about the coming weekend. He was glad of the break from his ever-growing case load, but aware that the price to pay for that was two whole days away from Lily.

Their stolen weekend, then having access to the flat, had helped them to take their relationship to a new level. Yet it still wasn't enough. The more time he spent with Lily, and the more he learned about her body and mind, the more he wanted. He was beginning to think that he was reaching the point where leaving Daphne was the only way forward. If only he could persuade Lily to leave her husband, he might find the courage to do it. But she was being the voice of common sense, pointing out how much was at stake.

Much as he yearned to tell the world of his love for Lily and claim her as his own, he couldn't afford to lose his job and he didn't want to risk losing his children. And Daphne's mother would be sure to finance court proceedings to ensure that he never saw them again.

No, he couldn't leave. What would be the point if Lily wouldn't do the same?

'How do you like the pie, darling? It's a new recipe.' Daphne's question over the dinner table brought him back to reality. He looked at his wife, and then at the steak and kidney pie and vegetables he had been eating.

'It's very nice,' he said. He took another bite, but couldn't detect any difference between this and any other steak and kidney pie Daphne had produced.

Daphne gave him a brittle smile and continued to eat her own meal. As always, her movements were neat and measured. Never too much on her fork. Nothing ever spilling onto the tablecloth or – heaven forfend – onto her blouse.

'It's so nice to be able to sit down and eat together for a change,' she said, taking a sip from her glass of water.

'You didn't have to wait for me,' he said. 'I don't mind if you want to eat with the children. I know it's inconvenient for you when I have to work late.'

'I'm happy to wait. It's all in a good cause, isn't it? It won't be long now before you're made a partner, and then you can relax a little. We'll have more time together then.'

Leonard frowned. 'I'll still have to maintain a heavy caseload,' he said.

'Oh, I'm sure it won't be quite so bad, will it? After all, you won't have to bother with all that office management business. They should never have burdened you with that in the first place.'

Leonard nodded and made a non-committal noise.

They continued to eat in silence until their plates were empty. Daphne got up and cleared the table, returning with steaming bowls of rice pudding.

'I forgot to tell you, I saw Mrs Lambert the other day,' she said, sitting down again.

'Oh? Is she well?'

'Yes, she's fine.'

'Good.'

'She didn't know anything about your masonic conference, though.'

Leonard paused, his spoon halfway to his mouth. 'What?'

Daphne tilted her head and studied him. He recognised that look. It felt as though he were a bug caught on the end of a sharp pin.

'I asked her if Mr Lambert had enjoyed the conference. She said it has been six months since he'd been. She didn't know anything about the one you went to a few weeks ago.'

He brought the spoon to his mouth and ate the scalding pudding, uncaring of the pain as it burnt his lips and tongue, giving himself time to think. He swallowed against a dry throat.

'I thought I'd made it clear that you were not to discuss masonic business with anyone,' he said.

Daphne waved a dismissive hand in the air. 'Oh don't be so pompous, Leonard. Mrs Lambert is well aware that you belong to the Lodge, just as I know that her husband does. And asking if someone enjoyed a conference is hardly discussing masonic business.' She leaned forward, her expression determined. 'What I want to know is where you were if you weren't at this so-called conference.'

Leonard put his spoon down, his appetite gone. Keeping his expression neutral, he picked up the napkin lying beside the pudding bowl and wiped his lips with careful, deliberate strokes. He put it down and rested his hand on the table before he spoke.

'What makes you think that every Mason in the Lodge should attend the same conference? Arnold Lambert and I are different levels in the brotherhood. We won't always be doing the same thing.'

'But why didn't Mrs Lambert know about it?'

'You didn't know about the conference six months ago, did you? Of course you didn't, because I didn't go to it, and so had no reason to mention it to you.' He stood up and walked over to the drinks cabinet and poured himself a generous measure of Scotch. 'Really, Daphne, what on earth is wrong with you? What are you accusing me of?'

He returned to the table. He put the glass down, but didn't resume his seat. He hoped that Daphne hadn't noticed that his hand was shaking.

'What was I supposed to think? Mrs Lambert knows everything that's going on. Nothing happens in Wimbledon without her knowledge. She looked so shocked when I mentioned the conference. The way she looked at me... It was as if I was the biggest fool in Christendom for believing that you were where you said you were.'

'That woman is a busybody, pure and simple. She delights in causing trouble. I can't believe you let her undermine you in that way.'

Daphne was silent for a long time. She played with her rice pudding, but didn't eat any of it. In the end she dropped her spoon with a clatter.

'I'm sorry, Leonard. I really am. It's just that you've been so distant lately, and you're hardly ever here. Even my mother—'

'I know exactly what your mother thinks of me, Daphne. I thought by now you'd have made your own decisions and stopped listening to her poison.'

'Leonard! That's an awful thing to say.'

'But it's true, nevertheless. I've no doubt your mother would love to drive a wedge between us. She'd like nothing better than to have you return to her so that she can say "I told you so" and have you at her beck and call again.'

'Well, I don't seem to have a husband around to look after most of the time,' she snapped. 'I'm tired of making excuses for you. I want you here with me. I want you to be a real husband again.'

He turned away, unable to hide the disgust he felt at the thought of touching her.

'Really?' he asked. 'I wonder if you truly know what you want, Daphne. You expect me to get a partnership, but the harder I work the more you complain. You give other people the benefit of the doubt and accuse me of gross dishonesty. I expect your support and your trust. I will not tolerate being discussed behind my back. If you feel unable to do that, then perhaps we should consider whether our marriage can survive.'

Daphne gasped, her eyes wide. She put a hand to her throat.

Her lips moved but no sound came out. She looked so stricken that for a moment Leonard felt guilt overwhelm him. What was he doing? How had he become so cruel?

He went to her and knelt by her chair. 'I'm sorry. Forgive me. I... You...' He shook his head. What could he say?

'Leonard, please say you didn't mean it,' Daphne whispered, tears overflowing. 'I'm sorry I doubted you. I was wrong. I'll never do it again, I promise. Please say you forgive me. Darling, please!'

She clasped his head to her bosom and sobbed. He felt her tears drip through his hair and onto his neck. Guilt held him fast. Daphne was innocent in all of this. She had every reason to suspect him. He couldn't believe he was getting away with his deceit so easily. He was an awful husband. He'd told so many lies. But he had to carry on, if only to preserve the façade of his marriage.

He wrapped his arms around Daphne, soothing her. He tried to remember what it had felt like when he had loved her, but his desire for Lily had wiped everything else from his senses. He felt saddened, inadequate, guilty.

'It's all right, my dear. I didn't mean it.'

'You won't leave me?'

He shook his head, his heart denying what he had to say. 'I won't.'

Daphne hadn't always been like this. It was his fault she was so unhappy. Lily had been right. Their respective spouses were good people. They didn't deserve the hurt that the lovers could inflict upon them. Their children shouldn't have to face the prospect of a broken home and the taint of divorce and scandal. Neither he nor Lily could let their selfish love ruin the lives of others.

He wouldn't leave his wife, and Lily wouldn't leave her husband. But, God help them, they couldn't leave each other either. He tried to imagine a life without Lily, and he felt the fear and panic rising through his blood. No, he needed her in his life, just to make it bearable. God help him if she ever walked away, because he surely couldn't.

34

Having managed to steal an hour with Leonard at the flat at lunchtime on Tuesday, Lily got home in time to take Caroline to her swimming lesson. When they got back, Beverley was in the kitchen, Radio One blasting out of the transistor on the window ledge, while she danced around the table. Kerry sat in her high chair eating bread-and-butter soldiers and laughing at her mum.

'What on earth is that racket?' asked Lily.

'Eh?' Bev carried on dancing, grabbing Caroline's hands and jiving with her.

Lily shook her head, smiling. She was prepared to put up with a bit of noise if it meant Beverley was happy for a change. It was nice to see her being nice to Caroline as well. After the initial shock, her younger daughter had joined in, dancing and pouting – when she wasn't giggling.

'It's great, ain't it, Mum? It's the Stones' latest. I might buy it on Saturday.'

Lily wasn't sure she could stand it being played over and over, which is what Beverley tended to do when she got a new record.

But she wasn't about to put a dampener on things now that her daughter had cheered up.

Caroline got bored halfway through the next song, and ran off to find her book. Lily put the kettle on and watched Bev do The Twist.

'It's good to see you smiling,' she said into the lull when the record ended. 'I've been worried about you.'

For a moment, she regretted saying it. Beverley's face closed up and she turned the radio off. But then she shrugged and grinned.

'Yeah, well, I let meself get fooled for a bit, but I've sorted it now. I've packed in my job and signed up at a temp agency. I don't want to go back to that dump. Full of losers. Can't trust any of 'em.'

'Did something happen at work? I wondered if it was boy trouble.'

Beverley snorted. 'Yeah. But he weren't no boy. He should've known better.'

Lily frowned. 'What happened?'

'Nothing for you to worry about.' Beverley waved a hand at her. 'I ain't daft. One of the drivers played me for a fool. He was a liar, but don't worry, I clocked him.'

In that split second when Bev's face revealed just how hurt she'd been, Lily knew.

'He cheated on you,' she guessed, getting angry on her daughter's behalf.

'Not exactly, Mother.' Beverley suddenly seemed so much older than her seventeen years. 'He cheated on his wife.'

Lily felt as if she'd been hit in the face. 'You went out with a married man?'

'No. I was messing about with this fella for a bit, who failed to mention he had a wife and kid. He fed me some sob-story about living with his sick mum. I should've known – he kept saying we had to keep it a secret 'cause the boss didn't like no one in the firm going out together.'

Now Lily felt sick. She could feel herself shaking. She sat down at the kitchen table, and laced her hands together so that Beverley couldn't see her trembling.

'Oh, Beverley!'

'Don't go all righteous on me. I didn't know, did I? I chucked him before I found out, anyway. He was a bastard, always taking the Mick even before I found out what a filthy liar he was.'

'So why did you get so upset? Why give up your job? I thought you loved it. What did he do to you, for God's sake?'

'Leave it, Mum. I was stupid, then I saw through him – that's all. End of story.'

'But your job—'

Kerry started to kick up. Beverley grabbed a flannel and wiped her face and hands before getting her out of the high chair and putting her on the floor. The baby toddled over to the table and tried to climb onto Lily's lap.

Lily pushed her chair back to make some room and picked her up. She hugged the child, her mind racing. *A married man!* 'It weren't that good,' said Beverley. 'Let's face it, it's a bleeding joke factory!' The kettle whistled. She turned it off and made a pot of tea. 'The temp work is much better. The money's good and I can try all sorts of places. The woman at the agency says if you do well they sometimes offer you a permanent job.'

'But there's no security. You don't know whether you've got work from one week to the next.'

'Stop fussing, Mum. She said there's more work than they can handle.'

Lily subsided, not knowing what to say. Kerry tried to pull her glasses off. When Lily stopped her, she tried playing with her necklace instead. Lily felt the tug at the back of her neck. She reached back and undid it, letting the baby play with the beads.

Beverley put a cup of tea in front of her and joined her at the table. They sat in silence for a bit. The baby got tired of the beads and dropped the necklace on the floor. Lily picked it up, letting Kerry slide down and crawl around the kitchen.

She had to ask. 'Did his wife find out?'

'No. I was tempted, though. I saw her with him, down Greenwich Park. I could've. But she's got a kid and there's another on the way. I wasn't about to be the one to tell her what a bastard she'd married. She's welcome to him. I don't bloody want him.'

Lily closed her eyes. She felt her guilt, choking her. Beverley hadn't known this man was married, and she'd done the right thing by getting out of the relationship. But it had hurt her. For all her bravado now, Lily had seen how she suffered.

She realised her own daughter was stronger than she was. Lily knew Leo was married. *She* was married. They should never have started their relationship in the first place. So many people could get hurt. Every day it went on, there was a chance of someone finding out. Maggie already suspected something, and Leo said his wife had started asking awkward questions.

But she couldn't stop. Neither could he. They loved each other, no matter how wrong it was, no matter how dangerous.

Her own daughter had had the strength to walk away from someone, and recognise the damage she might have done to his innocent wife and children. Yet Lily, who had always been so sanctimonious, so condemning of people's weaknesses, was the one who was risking everything so that she could snatch a few moments of love. How could she do that?

How could she not, when the alternative was giving Leo up?

'You're disgusted with me, ain't you?'

'What?' She looked at Beverley, feeling even worse when she

realised that her daughter had taken her silence for condemnation. How many times had she wanted her to talk to her, and tell her how she felt and what she was doing? She'd yearned to have the kind of relationship she'd seen other mothers have with their teenage daughters, and for a long time now she'd thought it was impossible. But today Beverley had made the first move, and it was up to Lily to make it right. She reached out and touched her hand. 'No, love. I'm just sorry you've been hurt. And I'm bloody proud of you.'

'Bloody!' said Kerry, sitting on the floor playing with her toes.

Lily gasped. Bev grinned and pointed at her. 'Your fault this time,' she said.

When Jack walked in a few minutes later, the two of them were crying with laughter.

35

A couple of weeks later, Lily sat at the dressing table in the flat in the City, repairing her make-up. Leo brought her a cup of black instant coffee and a ham sandwich.

'We'll need to bring in some more supplies, darling. I'm afraid that's all we have. The milk was off.'

She smiled at him and put her powder compact down.

'I quite like it black,' she said, sipping her drink. 'Although with this heat, perhaps we should have something cold.'

The summer had arrived, bringing long, hot, muggy days.

Leo took a bite from his sandwich, nodding as he chewed.

'Don't eat so fast. You'll get indigestion.'

He raised an eyebrow. 'I don't have a lot of choice when you rush me into bed like that. I've got a client coming in at two o'clock.'

Lily laughed. 'It's your own fault. If you will telephone me from your office telling me all the naughty things you want to do to me, you'll have to take the consequences.'

'Oh, so it's my fault is it?'

He sat on the end of the bed and put his shoes on.

'I worry, you know,' she said softly.

He got up and came over to stand behind her. Lily watched him in the mirror as he straightened his tie.

'What about, my love?'

He put his hands on her shoulders, kneading gently. It usually relaxed her, but today she couldn't get rid of the tension, the feeling of dread that kept creeping up on her every time she let herself think.

'That we'll get caught. People are getting suspicious.'

'We won't get caught,' he said, bending down and kissing her neck. 'Mmm, I love that perfume. I'll have to buy you a bottle to keep here.'

Lily blushed. 'Don't change the subject. I'm serious, Leo.'

He sighed, stepped back and raised his hands in the air. 'All right. I'm sorry. What's got you so worked up?' He sat down on the bed again.

She turned round to face him. 'Your secretary thinks you've got a fancy woman.'

He frowned. 'How do you know?'

'She told me.'

'What did she say?'

'She asked if I'd noticed how you kept your door shut all the time now, and how you always seem to be on private phone calls when she goes in. She's also clocked that you rush off for lunch every day instead of eating your sandwiches at your desk like you used to.'

When his secretary had brought it up, Lily had thought she'd also noticed her leaving just after Leo every time. But Lily was in the habit of going out for some fresh air every lunchtime anyway, so it probably hadn't occurred to her. Thank goodness.

Leo looked askance at the plate of half-eaten sandwiches they'd been sharing. 'That's hardly evidence of an affair,' he said.

Lily let her breath out in a huff. 'No, but walking back into work with a bloody great smile on your face is! Apparently the whole typing pool is speculating what you're up to. If the partners hear about it, there'll be hell to pay.'

'Dear God.'

'It's no good appealing to him. We're heading straight to the Devil.'

She turned back to the dressing table and scooped her cosmetics back into her make-up bag.

'Why didn't you tell me this earlier?' He sounded angry.

She closed her eyes. 'Because I didn't want to spoil our time together.'

'Damn!'

She opened her eyes. Leo was scowling at his watch. 'There isn't time to discuss this now. I'll be lucky to get back before my client arrives as it is. I wish you'd said something, Lily. I'm going to have to have strong words with that woman.'

Lily got up and grabbed his sleeve before he could rush out of the room. 'No! Leo, you can't. She'll know I told you.'

He stopped and looked at her. 'If she's told you, she'll have told everyone. She's a damned gossip and she's got to be stopped.'

'I didn't tell you to get her into trouble. I just want you to be more careful, that's all.' She felt sick and wanted to cry.

Leo sighed. 'Don't upset yourself, my love. I'll be careful.'

'Maybe we should—'

He put a hand to her lips. 'Don't say it. Don't ask me to stop spending this time with you. I need you, Lily.'

She looked into his eyes and saw her love reflected there.

She turned her face towards his palm and kissed it. 'Go on, or you'll be late,' she said.

After he'd gone, she tidied up and, five minutes later, followed him back to the office. All the way, she could feel a burning in the pit of her stomach. The feeling had been growing for days now. They were going to get caught. She knew it.

But even in the face of this certainty, she couldn't stop.

* * *

Leo's first instinct on seeing his secretary was to shout at her. How dare she talk about him in such a disrespectful way? But the memory of Lily's worried face kept him silent. Instead he stalked into his office, resisted the urge to slam the door behind him, and sat at his desk. He pretended to be studying a document, but his mind was racing, trying to work out what to do.

'Mr Warwick?' His secretary knocked on the doorjamb. 'I'm sorry to disturb you, sir, but your client is here.'

He looked at her, straining to keep his expression neutral whilst his anger and loathing were fighting to get out.

'Show him in.'

'Yes, sir. Would you like me to bring tea?'

'Ask him. If he wants some, then bring it by all means.'

She nodded and turned away. Leo watched, noting that one of the young women – Doreen, wasn't it? – in the general office looked at Leo and then at her. She raised her eyebrows and smiled. Even without seeing his secretary's face, Leo couldn't fail to recognise the conspiratorial nature of the exchange.

Lily's warning had opened his eyes. She was right. People were talking. Thank God they hadn't linked her with him yet. He needed to think.

He would do something about the gossip. It had to be nipped in the bud. He would not allow it to destroy what he had with Lily. *I won't lose her,* he thought. She's mine.

'Here we are, sir.' Leo's treacherous secretary arrived with his client.

As he came around his desk to greet the man with a hearty handshake, she melted away into the general office. He made up his mind that she would be getting her cards at the earliest opportunity. But he'd have to be careful.

'Pretty girl, that,' said the client.

'Is she? I hadn't noticed,' he replied, keeping his tone light. 'She's an excellent secretary. I hope you aren't planning on stealing her from me.'

The other man laughed. Leo hoped he'd planted a seed that would see him shot of the damned woman.

36

Jack asked Beverley, 'Where's your mum?'

'I don't know, Dad. I just got in. She must be doing overtime. Ain't she always doing overtime?'

Kerry tried to wriggle out of her arms, reaching for her granddad. He ignored her.

'She ain't there,' he said. 'I went to pick her up, but the place was locked up tight.'

'Well, I don't know.'

'Is she picking up Caroline?'

'No, she's upstairs.'

He went out into the hall. 'Caroline!' he shouted up the stairs.

Bev followed him out. 'What's the matter, Dad?'

'Nothing.'

'Don't give me that. You're in a right mood. It ain't like you.'

'I want to know where your mother is, all right?' *Jesus Christ! What the hell is going on with Lil?*

'She's probably stuck on a train, Dad,' she said. He ignored her as Caroline came down the stairs.

'Yes, Daddy?'

'Have you spoken to your mother? Do you know where she is?'

'She's at Nanny and Granddad's.'

He frowned. 'You sure? She never said nothing to me about it.'

Bev watched him, looking confused. 'Dad, what's the big deal?'

'She never said.'

'Yes, she did. She said the other day she needed to go over there. She ain't seen them for a couple of weeks.'

'Don't be cross, Daddy,' said Caroline. 'I didn't know I was supposed to tell you.'

He shook his head and patted her cheek. 'It ain't your fault, sweetheart. She should've said.' He kissed her forehead. 'What you doing up there?'

'Reading my *Bunty* comic.'

'All right, darling. You carry on.'

She smiled and ran back upstairs. Jack followed Bev back into the kitchen, still ignoring Kerry.

'What's the matter, Dad?'

'Nothing,' he said again as he sat at the table. 'Put the kettle on, girl.'

Bev put Kerry down and watched as she toddled over and tried to climb onto Jack's lap. He finally noticed her and picked her up.

'Hallo, my little cherub.'

The baby blew a raspberry at him. Finally, he managed a smile, but he was still shaking. He had been since he rattled the locked door of Lily's office block.

Bev put the kettle on and got some cups out of the cupboard. She went to the fridge to get the milk. 'There's chops in here, Dad. Want me to cut some chips?'

He didn't answer. His head was spinning, remembering what he thought when he realised she wasn't there. Bev looked round. He was vaguely aware of her stare and that Kerry was playing with his tie.

'Dad?'

'What?'

'Chop and chips?'

He sighed. 'Yeah. That'll do.'

He felt shaky. How could he have forgotten she was going over to Bow tonight? Bloody hell, what was the matter with him? He'd dropped the boss off at six and decided to pick Lily up to save her the train. He'd had it in mind to give that boss of hers a piece of his mind about all these hours she was putting in. When he'd found the place shut, no lights on or nothing, his first thought was Lily was lying to him.

Christ knows why he thought that. Lily hated liars. If she knew what he imagined, she'd be furious.

Bev put a cup of tea in front of him, took the baby off his lap and put her in the high chair. He missed the warmth of her little body against him.

He put his hands around the cup, feeling the heat. He stared into the steaming brown liquid, trying to stop the little ripples running over the surface as his hand shook.

The trembling wasn't because of the anger he'd felt, standing outside her office feeling like a fool. No, now it was the sheer bloody relief he'd felt when Caroline had told him where Lily was. Because if he'd been right – if she was playing away and making a fool of him – he didn't know what he'd have done.

There was a popping sound as Bev lit the gas under the frying pan. He watched as she scraped some lard in and unpacked the chops before putting them into the hot fat. Kerry was chewing on a teething ring, humming to herself. She saw him looking and gave him a grin.

'Dadadada,' she said.

Jack felt himself welling up. He wished Lily was home, safe. He hated that he'd doubted her. It had scared the bejeezus out of him.

He took a sip of his tea. It was strong and sweet, just how he liked it.

When she got home, he'd have a word. This overtime lark was getting out of hand. She should be home at a reasonable time. It weren't just her mum and dad that was being neglected. He needed her at home. So did the girls.

'Dadadada.'

He smiled at his granddaughter, feeling a bit calmer. Look what Lily was missing. Before she knew it the kids would all be grown up and gone. The promise of a promotion weren't no substitute. Why couldn't she see that?

* * *

Lily was relieved to get home. It wasn't very late when she let herself into the house, but she wanted nothing more than to crawl into bed and sleep.

The light was on in the living room. She popped her head around the door.

'All right, love?' said Jack. He was watching *On the Buses*.

'Yeah. Tired.' She went in and sat down on the armchair opposite him.

'Tough day?'

'No more than usual. It's hearing my mother going on about Tony's new colour telly that's worn me out.'

'He got it then?'

'Of course he did. What Tony wants, Tony gets. He's not likely to worry about whether his family might need something.'

'Blimey, you ain't jealous, are ya? You hardly watch the one we've got.'

She took off her glasses and pinched the bridge of her nose, trying to ease the tension. 'No, I am not jealous of a telly.' She pointed at their own. 'God knows, watching that rubbish in colour isn't going to make it any better, is it?'

On screen the audience burst into peals of laughter at Reg Varney's latest snide remark about his brother-in-law.

'It's better than that bleeding *Forsyte Saga* you used to like. Jesus, I ain't never seen anything so stuffy.'

'It was serious drama,' she said. She wasn't about to have a row about it. 'Anyway, I missed the last couple of episodes. I don't suppose they'll repeat it for a while. I'd better read the book.' The one that Leonard had given her just the other day.

Beverley came in. 'Hello, love,' said Lily.

'Watcha. How's Nan and Granddad?'

'Fine. Uncle Tony's invited them over on Saturday to see his new colour telly.'

'Yeah? I wouldn't mind seeing that. I doubt if it'll make crap like this any better though.'

Lily was torn between telling her off for her language and laughing at Jack's face. She shook her head and allowed herself a small smile. Jack tutted and turned back to his programme.

'Baby gone down?'

'Yeah. Now she's walking, she's wearing herself out, thank God.'

'Caroline in bed?'

'Yeah, but she's probably reading. She's been going on and on about the landing on the moon. Brought back a great big book from the library about space. They've been doing it at school.'

'Oh, of course. It's in all the papers. Who'd have thought it? I never imagined we'd see the day. When are they landing – probably in a couple of days now, isn't it?'

'I suppose so. Times are changing, Mum. You've got to keep up. The place I've been working at this week reckon they're going to have electric typewriters soon.'

'Well, we're not likely to be getting them at Alder & Powney –

I'm lucky to even have a proper adding machine. If some of the partners had their way, I'd be totting everything up with an abacus.'

'Well I'm looking forward to having a go with an electric. They reckon it only takes a little tap – you don't have to bash it like the normal ones.' She looked at her fingers. 'I might be able to grow me nails a bit.'

Lily looked at her own neatly trimmed nails. 'That would be nice.'

Jack roared with laughter at some ridiculous goings-on on the telly. Lily sighed. Beverley rolled her eyes and pointed at the screen.

'I don't know how that woman can go out in public,' she said, 'let alone go on there and let that lot take the Mickey out of her.'

'Who, Olive? She's only acting.'

'She's plug-ugly.'

'Na, I bet she don't look like that in real life. It's all make-up, ain't it? If she did her hair and got rid of them pebble glasses, she'd be all right.'

'Dad, nothing will make that woman look attractive. If I ever end up like that, I'll top meself.'

'Bugger off and let me watch it. I don't stand around criticising what you watch.'

'Yeah you do. You're always moaning when *Ready Steady Go!* comes on.'

'Well what d'you expect? Bloody noise.'

Lily laid her head back and closed her eyes. She should just give up and go to bed, but she didn't have the energy.

'Well, I ain't watching this. Want a cup of tea, Mum?'

'Yes please, love.' She didn't open her eyes.

'What about me?' asked Jack.

'All right, keep your hair on.'

Lily shivered in the draught as Beverley opened the door and went out into the hall. It was already July, and despite the heat outside this house was still cold. She felt her muscles relax and the noise from the television receded.

'Lily, love. Wake up. You'll get a crick in your neck.' Jack gently shook her awake. He was kneeling in front of her, smiling.

She came to with a start. He soothed her, holding her face in his big, warm hands.

'What time is it?' she asked. She shook her head slightly, dislodging his hands. He sat back on his heels.

'Half ten. Your tea went cold.'

She rubbed her hands over her face. 'Why did you let me sleep?'

'You went out like a light. I reckoned you'd have a quick doze then wake up before now. You ain't sickening for something, are you?'

'No, I'm all right.'

'You can't keep burning the candle at both ends, love.' He leaned forward, resting his hands on her knees. 'If they ain't paying you for all this overtime. I reckon you should stop doing it.'

'I told you—' She wanted to push him away, but the look in his eyes held her still.

He put up a hand. 'I know what you said, but this has been going on for months. They're taking the Mickey – getting extra hours out of you for nothing. Are they really going to make a woman the office manager?'

'Why not? Just because I'm a woman, it doesn't make me less capable. I'm the best person for the job. I'll be bloody good at it.'

'Yeah, I'll bet you will n'all. But you've got to face it, love. Them women down Dagenham last year shouted about equal pay, but they ain't made none of them managers have they? It's still a man's world.'

Lily felt herself bristle. She wanted to tell him she was as capable as any man, but that wasn't the problem here, was it? He had no idea what she was really doing.

'I've got just as good a chance as any man. They might live in the Dark Ages in some ways, but the partners weren't afraid to take on a female articled clerk this year. Rosamund's doing very well for herself.'

Jack shrugged. 'I'll bet they won't make her partner though, will they? And by the sound of her, she'll have a rich daddy who's got the same old school tie as one of your bosses. Even posh birds don't get anywhere without some bloke backing them up.'

'She works hard.'

'So would a bloke who has to support his family. She'll marry some toff and chuck it all in, mark my words.'

Lily wanted to hit him. 'So you're saying that the likes of me and Rosamund are taking jobs from men, are you?'

He shrugged and stood up. 'I'm saying you've got your priorities wrong, both of you. You should be here, looking after the girls.'

'And having your slippers warming by the fire when you get in from a hard day's graft. Is that it?'

Jack sighed and looked at the ceiling. 'I came to your office tonight,' he said. 'It was six o'clock and I reckoned you'd welcome a lift home. The place was locked up tight.'

Lily held her breath. *Oh dear God.*

'You knew I was going to Mum's.'

'I forgot.' He looked at her. 'I forgot because you're always working late. I was ready to go in there and tell your boss to stop taking advantage, and either pay you for all this over-time, make you the manager like he's promised, or stuff his bleeding job. You don't want to know what I thought when I got there and it was shut for the night.'

Lily stood up, her movements slow and painful as her mind raced. What if she *hadn't* been going to her parents' tonight? She and Leo would already left the office and been hidden away in the flat. She'd have had no idea that Jack had come looking for her. If he'd confronted her when she got home, she knew she'd have given herself away.

'I told you where I was. You should have listened.'

'I know. I'm sorry. But you can't blame me. Any bloke would wonder. I still reckon I need to have a talk with that boss of yours.'

'Jack, promise me you won't.'

'I can't do that, Lily. It ain't right.'

She put a hand on his arm. 'Please, Jack. I love that job. Don't spoil it for me.'

For a moment, she thought he was going to argue. He looked into her eyes. She stared back, praying her guilt was hidden, and terrified he would realise she was begging for her life. Without Leo, she would shrivel up and die.

He shook his head, and her heart sank.

'If you don't do something about it, Lil, I will. I'm sick of it, love. How do you think it makes me feel? I'm more of a bloody house-wife than you are these days. Me own brothers take the piss out of me every chance they get.'

'You shouldn't take any notice of them,' she snapped. 'It's none of their business.'

'Yes it is. They're family. And they're right. I'm the man of the house. Let me do the providing for a change, all right?'

'We can't manage on your wages.'

'So I'll get another job. Bring in more money.'

'Doing what?'

'Fred can get me in down the docks.'

She shook her head, stepping away from him. 'Don't you dare!'

'What the hell is wrong with you? It's honest work for a decent day's pay.'

'I don't want to be married to a bloody docker!' she shouted.

There was silence for a moment. Jack looked at her as if she were a stranger.

'Ah, I get it. A docker ain't good enough for you. Since you've been working for those bloody snobby toffs, nothing's been good enough for you, has it, Lil? That's why Tony's colour telly has got you pissed off. Your snotty-nosed brother is moving up in the world, and you ain't, because I ain't a good enough husband.'

'They are not snobs.'

He laughed. 'Says it all, don't it? They're not snobs, so it must be me what's wrong.' Suddenly he was nose to nose with her, his nostrils flaring. 'It's me what ain't good enough for you any more, eh?'

'Stop putting words in my mouth.'

'I don't need to, do I? You're as big a snob as they are these days.'

She froze. 'I am not a snob.'

He shook his head and turned away. 'Yes you are. You used to be happy with what we had. We did all right. But then you went off to them night classes and you've been getting more and more miserable. I hate your sodding job. It's making you try to be something you ain't.'

'What are you talking about?'

He turned back, his jaw set. 'I'm talking about how we used to have a laugh. Do things together. How life was good and we was happy.' He took a deep breath and tried to take her hand. She backed away.

'See?' he said. 'I ain't even good enough to touch me own wife, these days.'

She put a hand to her mouth, her eyes filling up. 'Jack, you don't understand,' she said.

'You reckon? Oh, I understand all right. I ain't some smart Alec with a job in the City, girl. But I know when things ain't right. Well, I ain't putting up with it no more. I want things to go back to normal. I want me wife at home at night. I want us to do things with the family again, like we used to.'

He put his hands on her shoulders. Lily didn't dare move. 'Either you tell them you ain't working all the hours God sends, Lily, or I will. If that means you losing that job, well, that's fair enough. If it means I have to get work down the docks to earn more, then I'll do it. There ain't no shame in hard graft, all right?'

Lily's head was pounding, and she could hardly catch her breath. What could she do? If Jack went to the office, she'd be found out.

'Don't do this to me, Jack. Please.'

'But it's killing us, darling. It's taking over everything. It ain't just me. What about the girls? You can't ignore them, Lily. They have to come first. It ain't fair, what you're doing.'

She closed her eyes. He leaned his forehead against hers.

Tears escaped and formed slow rivulets down her cheeks. 'Aw, love, don't cry. I know it's hard.'

'I can't just walk away.'

'I know. I ain't saying you've got to do that, am I? I'm saying you need to stick to the hours they pay you for, so you can get home for your family.'

'But when I get the promotion, we'll have more money. We can buy a house, and nice things for the girls. I only want the best for them. For us.'

'All the money the world ain't no good if you ain't doing right by your family. If you ain't here, who's going to make sure them girls are all right, eh? I try to do my bit, but I can't always manage it.

Besides, girls need their mum. What's best for them is having you home. At the end of the day, Caroline would rather have you here than be in some fancy house.'

He couldn't have hurt her more if he'd hit her. She tried to stifle a sob. Jack pulled her into his arms and let her cry on his shoulder.

'Come on, darling,' he soothed. 'Look at the state of you. You're always knackered. You can't go on like this, Lil love. You'll make yourself ill.'

He held her until she had cried herself out. She was too distressed to fight when he led her upstairs and put her to bed. All the time, he talked – about how she was missing seeing Caroline at her swimming and dancing lessons; how she'd not seen Kerry's latest new trick – of turning the telly off in the middle of *Match of the Day*. That should have brought a smile to her face. Lily hated football. But she barely registered his words.

All she could think of was that she had to stop Jack from going to her office. And the only way to do that was to stick to her normal hours. And if she did that, she'd have hardly any alone time with Leo. Rushed lunch hours, that was all. What if Leo kicked up? What if he ended it? She couldn't bear it.

But she would have to. What else could she do?

Jack sat on the edge of the bed, stroking her hair. He'd run out of words. So had she. She couldn't argue this any more. He was right. She was neglecting her family.

'I'm sorry,' she whispered. 'I'll speak to my boss.'

'Good. It's only right. If he don't like it, tell him to shove his job. You'll get another one, easy. Maybe somewhere nearer home would be better anyway. I know you don't like them train journeys every day.'

'They're all right,' she said. 'I don't want to have to get another job.'

Whatever happened, she wanted to stay close to Leo, even if

they had much less time together. But then again, if he abandoned her, she might be glad to go. *No!* She wouldn't think like that. Leo loved her. He wouldn't do that to her.

'I'll tell you what,' said Jack. 'We ain't had a proper holiday for months. See if you can a couple of weeks off soon, and we'll go away. Caroline breaks up from school in a fortnight. We could go then, yeah?'

She didn't want a holiday. But her guilt was overwhelming her. If she refused, the rows would start again. She nodded. 'I'll ask.'

He kissed her cheek. 'Good girl. I'll see what I can book tomorrow. You rest now, love. I'm just going to turn everything off downstairs and I'll be back up.'

She lay in the dark, hearing him potter around downstairs.

She had been so close to giving herself away tonight.

Maybe it was time to tell him. Time to walk away from this charade of a marriage. But if she did, where would she go? Leo still had a wife, and he'd never talked about leaving her. And what about the girls? And Jack? He wouldn't just be angry, it would break his heart. No, she couldn't leave.

By the time Jack came back upstairs, Lily was feigning sleep. She couldn't bear to talk to him again, not tonight. He had won this round. She would have to tell Leo that she couldn't go in early or come home late any more. She would have to book some holiday and face a fortnight away from Leo in Jack's company. It was no more than Jack deserved. But right now, it was far more than she could bear to contemplate.

37

'What do you mean?' asked Leonard. 'Has he found out?'

'No,' said Lily. 'But he came to the office to pick me up yester-day, ready to have it out with you about all this so-called overtime.'

'But you left on time.'

'I know. He'd forgotten I was going to see my parents straight from work. He got here, saw the place locked, and jumped to conclusions.' She shook her head. 'God, Leo, if it had been any other night, he'd have been right. I don't know what I'd have said. I'm a terrible liar. Normally, I hate lying. If he'd asked me where I'd been, I'd have given the game away. I know I would.'

He came round his desk and took her in his arms. 'My poor darling. You're shaking.'

'It's playing havoc with my nerves. I seem to have a permanent headache these days. What are we going to do?'

He kissed her and tucked her head against his shoulder. 'Much as I hate the idea, we'll have to do as he says for the time being.'

'But we can still go the flat at lunchtimes, can't we?'

'Yes, of course.'

'Oh, Leonard, what are we going to do? This is killing me.'

He sighed. 'I don't know. But I suppose we've been on borrowed time so far. Daphne has her suspicions too, I'm sure. I realise it would be sensible if we held back for a while, but I don't know if I can bear it.'

'So long as we can still be together. That's all that matters to me.'

'Yes, my darling.'

He kissed her again, this time not holding back his feelings.

The opening of the office door had them springing apart.

But they weren't quick enough.

Irwin came in and closed the door behind him. He stood there, looking from Lily to Leonard and back again. There was a stillness about him that made Leonard swallow hard. Lily looked terrified, guilt written all over her face. *Damn it all to hell!*

'Warwick, Lily.' Irwin nodded at each of them. 'I trust I'm not interrupting anything important?'

'Er, no, sir,' said Lily, looking down. 'I was just asking Mr Warwick if I could book some holidays later this month.'

'Going somewhere nice?'

'I don't know. My husband's organising it.'

'Well I'd advise him to avoid the Continent in the summer holidays. Far too many bloody tourists.' Irwin laughed at his own joke.

Lily smiled. 'I'll tell him,' she said. She looked at Leonard, her face now a polite mask. Only the warmth of her cheeks gave her away. 'I'd better get back to work. I'll have those figures for you as soon as possible, Mr Warwick.'

He nodded, not trusting himself to speak. He walked back around his desk and sat down.

'What can I do for you?' he asked Irwin when Lily had gone.

Irwin sat down in the chair opposite him. He looked thoughtful. 'You can tell me that I imagined seeing you and the lovely Lily leaping apart just now,' he said.

Leonard froze. Irwin held up a hand. 'On second thoughts, I really don't want to know.'

'I...' What could he say?

'I'm serious, old chap. Don't say a word. I will forget what I thought I just saw, and you, I trust, will make sure it never happens again. Am I clear?'

'Yes.'

'Good.' He stood up. 'I came to tell you that Miss Jarvis's nephew is contesting the will. Word has it that he's up to his neck in debt and was relying on the old bird's estate to bail him out.'

'Then how can he afford to contest it?'

'Apparently an old school chum has taken on the case on the promise that he'll be paid when he wins. Damn fool! Anyway, you and Lily will be key witnesses.'

'Won't our affidavits be sufficient?'

'Possibly. It depends on how devious the fellow is.' He paused, frowning. 'It isn't beyond the realms of possibility that he might send a private detective to investigate all of the witnesses, just to see if there's anything that might undermine their testimonies. I'm sure I don't have to tell you that if anyone were to discover anything untoward going on between you and Lily, it could have disastrous consequences for the case, and your own professional credibility.'

Leonard nodded, his mind racing.

'And if that were to happen, Warwick, old chap, your position at Alder & Powney might well become untenable.'

Leonard stared into Irwin's cold disapproving face, and saw the truth behind his quietly delivered words.

'Yes indeed,' he went on. 'I suggest you put your house in order, Warwick. It isn't cricket, old chap, playing with the hired help. End it now, before it's too late.'

He left the room. Leonard sat, overwhelmed with shock and

misery. In all the time he and Lily had been together, they'd never been so careless.

What to do? What the hell could he do? How could things change so quickly?

'End it now,' Irwin had said.

Leonard shook his head. It was impossible. Theirs wasn't some sordid affair, the cliché of boss and employee. He loved Lily, and she loved him. Asking them to stop was like asking them to cease breathing. If it came to it, could he give up his job, his marriage, everything, in order to be with Lily? His head said it was foolhardy, but his heart knew that if it came to it, Lily was all that mattered to him.

Perhaps they should make plans – change jobs, and put some funds aside so that they could set up home together. It would be difficult, but not impossible. He sat up straighter and took a deep, cleansing breath.

He had been complacent, taking advantage of Lily's generosity. But, as Irwin had told him in stark tones, it couldn't go on like this. That being the case, they would have to find a better way. The alternative was unacceptable. Now that he had been presented with a choice, he knew that his only option was to leave Daphne and maybe even this job.

That decision made, Leonard felt giddy with relief. They would have to be careful for a little while longer. But soon – very soon – he and Lily would make that leap of faith and be together forever.

* * *

Lily's hands were shaking. She couldn't stop them.

What was Mr Irwin saying to Leo? He must have seen them. There was not a chance in hell that he'd missed what was going on. He wasn't daft.

Oh God!

She rested her head in her hands. Her whole body was burning with shame and guilt. What had they been thinking? They'd never been so careless before. And for this to happen so soon after Jack started getting suspicious...

She felt sick. What if they were exposed? They'd be sacked. Everyone would know.

Her phone rang. She jumped, and barely stopped herself from screaming in fright. For a moment she stared at it, but the strident ringing wouldn't stop. She picked it up, but her throat was so dry she couldn't speak.

'Your husband's on the line, Lily.'

She made a strangled sound, which the telephonist took for assent. 'You're through, caller,' she said cheerfully.

'Lil? You there, darling?'

'Yeah. What do you want?' She couldn't help her gruff words. But Jack didn't seem to notice.

'I've booked us a chalet at Brean Sands. You know – where we had our honeymoon.'

Lily closed her eyes. 'Oh Jack, it was a dump.'

'Well, yeah, it was then, granted. They still had the old Nissen huts then. But it's different now. It's all been done up. Old Mr and Mrs Simpkins over the road went there last year. They reckon it's lovely now. Loads of stuff to do, and the chalets are right cosy.'

She didn't know what to say.

'Come on, Lil. Give it a chance, love. If you hate it, we'll come home early, all right?'

'All right. When are we going?'

'A week on Saturday. You got your time off sorted?'

'Yes.'

'Lovely jubbly! We'll get ourselves some holiday clothes this weekend. It'll be great – you'll see.'

She doubted it, but what choice did she have? 'Did you tell him about the other business?'

'What?'

'Your hours, love. Did you tell him?'

'Yes.'

'And?'

'And I'll be home normal time tonight.'

'Good. We'll have a nice dinner together for a change.'

She couldn't answer.

'Right, I've got to go. I'll see you later, darling.'

'Yes. See you later.'

She put the phone down and ran for the ladies'. She just made it before she threw up.

* * *

'Mr Warwick. Lily is ill.' One of the typists burst into Leonard's room. He stood up.

'Where is she? What's wrong?'

'She's in the ladies'. She's been sick.'

He followed her out through the general office to the corridor where the toilets were located, close to the lifts. 'Can you check there's no one else in there before I go in?'

'No need, sir. I'll speak to her. If you'll wait here, I'll come and let you know.'

'Does she need a doctor?'

'I'll ask her.'

Leonard paced, imagining all sorts of scenarios. Was it the shock of being discovered by Irwin, or was she really ill? He had just made up his mind to barge into the ladies' when the girl came out again.

'She says she's all right. But she looks dreadful, sir. I think she should go home.'

At that moment, Gerald Irwin appeared. Leonard wanted to punch him. This was his fault!

'Is there a problem?' he asked.

The typist got in first. 'It's Lily, Mr Irwin. She's been ever so sick. I was just saying to Mr Warwick, I think she should go home. The poor love looks awful.'

'Well, perhaps you could go back in there and attend to her, if you will.' He dismissed the girl, who disappeared through the door again.

The two men stood in silence for a moment. Leonard wished he could tell him to go to hell, but his position was too precarious. In the end it was Irwin who broke the silence.

'I sincerely hope the lady isn't suffering the effects of your little *affaire*, Warwick.'

He closed his eyes and spoke through gritted teeth. 'She's not pregnant. For God's sake, what do you take me for?'

'I really don't know, old man. Until this morning, I'd chosen to ignore the silly gossip of the typing pool and given you the benefit of the doubt.'

Leonard stared at him in shock.

'Now,' Irwin continued, 'I suggest you take my car and deliver her back to her family. She's obviously not well enough to be here today. There'll be sufficient time on the way to end the relationship, and on the way back you can consider your position here. I'd be sorry to lose either of you, but clearly things can't go on as they are.'

'You're sacking me?'

'No, no. That would mean exposing your little dalliance, wouldn't it?'

'So you want me to jump before I'm pushed.'

'Either that, or perhaps Lily should go.'

'But we've both worked damn hard for this firm!' Leonard moved towards him, ready to have it out. His fists were clenched, his whole body on fight alert. He could feel the adrenaline coursing through his veins. He was fighting for his life here!

The door to the ladies' opened and Lily emerged, pale and shaking. The typist – what was her name? – supported her with an arm around her shoulders.

Leo went to reach for her, but a hand on his shoulder stopped him. Irwin stepped in front of him.

'Lily, my dear. I'm so sorry you're indisposed. Was it something you ate, do you think?'

Lily stared at the floor and nodded. It broke Leonard's heart to see her so fragile. He wanted to comfort her, but what could he do in front of the others?

'I've asked Mr Warwick to take you home. No, don't worry, it can't be helped. If you're ill, you're ill, and you must go. We'll see you again when you're better. Now, is there anything urgent that we must deal with today? No? Good.' He turned to the typist. 'Maureen, my dear, will you be an angel and get Lily's handbag and coat from her office? I'm sure she doesn't want to be the centre of attention through the general office when she's feeling off colour.'

The girl looked at Lily, who nodded and told her where her bag was. She ran off to get it. Leonard and Lily waited.

'I'm sorry you're unwell, Lily. I'm sure you realise that what I saw in Mr Warwick's office was unacceptable – no, please don't say anything. I want you to go home and think about the consequences of what you're doing. I can't allow this sort of thing to continue. It's not good for the firm.'

Lily stifled a sob.

'For God's sake, Irwin, can't it wait? She's not well!'

Lily shook her head. 'No. It's all right,' she said. 'He's right.'

Before Leonard could argue, the girl returned with Lily's

things. Lily turned away as Mr Irwin accepted them and thanked the girl. When she'd gone, he handed Lily's bag to her and gently draped her jacket around her shoulders.

'I'm sorry, Lily. I don't want to distress you, my dear. But it has to stop.'

She nodded. She looked smaller than usual, staring at the floor. Leonard stood there, seeing all his dreams shatter into shards of glass, piercing him, bleeding the life out of him.

'Now, I suggest you go straight down in the lift and wait in the lobby. Warwick will collect my car keys and join you shortly.'

She turned away without looking at them and walked to the lift.

* * *

They were almost out of the City before she spoke.

'Oh, Leo. What have we done?' The tears she'd been trying to hold back overflowed, and she sobbed into her hands.

'Lily, darling, please don't.'

'But it's all over, isn't it? We've been found out.'

'No, it is not over! How can you say that? I love you!'

'But we can't go on like this. Irwin knows. He'll have our jobs, won't he?'

'He won't expose us. He said so. It won't be good for the firm.'

She laughed. 'Don't so bloody naïve! He'll have us out of the door before you know it. He'll find a way, you'll see.'

He couldn't deny it. 'Let him,' he said. 'We're both damned good at our jobs. We can find new ones. God, I want to hold you, but this damned traffic.'

'Take me to Epping.'

'What?'

'Take me to Epping, like you did before. I can't go home, not like this.'

He nodded and turned the car in the direction of Essex.

He couldn't find the place where they'd made love for the first time. Everything looked so different – the trees were in full bloom now. He followed another track and found a quiet spot where they wouldn't be overlooked.

He parked and switched the engine off. They sat there for a few moments, listening to the engine tick as it cooled down. Now that they'd stopped, neither of them knew what to do.

'Come here.' He pulled her into his arms. 'I need to hold you.'

She wept – deep, ragged sobs. In one careless moment, everything had changed.

'Don't, Lily, please, my darling. I never meant to make you cry.'

'What are we going to do?' she asked. 'Everything's going wrong.'

He took her face in his hands, making her look at him. 'Do you love me, Lily?'

'How can you ask that? Of course I do!'

'And I love you,' he said, kissing her forehead. 'No matter what happens. I love you.' He kissed her lips.

Lily sank into his kiss, wanting it to wipe out the horror of that morning.

'That look in his eyes,' she said, fighting against a fresh wave of tears, when they eventually broke apart. 'I felt so dirty. I've never felt so ashamed.'

'Stop it!' He pulled her firmly back into his arms. 'I won't have you thinking this is something bad, Lily. I've never loved anyone the way I love you. I was a fool to think the ridiculous infatuation I

had for Daphne was love. I just let myself be pulled along into
marriage, and was too complacent to do anything about it until I
met you. You showed me, Lily. You made me see what love really is.
Don't you ever let anyone make you think that what we have is
something to be ashamed of.'

This time her tears were different. This time they were tears of
gratitude.

'No one has ever loved me like you do,' she said.

'And no one else ever will, my darling, because I'm never going
to let you go.'

She raised her head to look at him. 'What are you saying?'

He smiled. 'I'm saying that I want to leave Daphne and be with
you, always.'

For a moment she felt faint. She leaned forward, resting her
head on the dashboard. She was overwhelmed by the storm of
emotion flowing through her body. Leonard's warm hand, resting
on her back, was the only thing keeping her from exploding into
millions of tiny pieces. Joy was fighting with sheer terror
within her.

'We can't,' she said.

'We must, my love. You're mine. I won't contemplate a future
without you.'

'Our families—'

'Will learn to accept it.'

She shook her head. 'They'll hate us. What if they stop us
seeing our kids?'

He was silent for a few seconds too long. Lily sat up, forcing
him to move his hand away. She stared out of the windscreen. The
forest around them was protecting them from prying eyes. Last
time they'd been here they'd abandoned all common sense.
They'd risked being seen naked and committed their first act of
adultery.

'We shouldn't be here. This was a mistake. I can't think straight.'

'Tell me what you want.'

She looked at him then. He was so handsome. A real dreamboat. And he loved her. For a moment, she let herself feel the glow of being adored by him. But it wasn't right. No matter how much she wanted it to be right, now that someone knew, it felt wrong. Their beautiful love affair had turned into something sordid and shameful.

She shook her head, her heart breaking. 'We can't, Leonard. We just can't. What will people say?'

'To hell with them!'

He tried to take her in his arms, but she held her hands up, stopping him.

'Don't you see? It's our fault, not theirs. They don't deserve this.' She closed her eyes. This was so hard. 'We don't have a choice. We have to stop.'

'Lily, please. You don't mean that.'

She kept her eyes closed, feeling as though any minute now her throbbing, pain-filled head would just explode, severing itself from her body in punishment for the happiness she'd stolen over the past months. Right now she would welcome it. The idea of going on without him was more than she could bear.

'I do,' she forced herself to say. 'We have to stop. I can't bear it, but now that he knows, he'll be watching us. He'll use any excuse to sack us, and then everyone will know.'

'Dammit, Lily, do you think I care about that? Maybe it's a good thing. Maybe we should just go ahead and tell everybody. I want the world to know I love you.'

'Oh God, Leo. Please don't. My husband will kill you.'

'I can look after myself. I used to box in school.'

'Oh, Leo, you haven't got a clue. Jack learned how to fight with his brothers on the streets. He won't stick to the Queensberry rules. You wouldn't stand a chance.'

'Then let's run away together. We could go anywhere. He would never find us.'

'And what about our children? I won't leave mine behind. Could you really walk away from yours and never see them again?'

He sighed. 'No, you're right. I couldn't.'

They sat in silence. Lily was exhausted. She couldn't see any way out of this, other than to end it. And it was killing her. 'You'd better take me to a station so I can get home. If you don't get back soon, Irwin will kick up.'

He didn't answer straight away. Lily thought he was going to refuse.

'Very well,' he said at last, his voice clipped. 'It's obvious we're not getting anywhere here. Just tell me one thing, please.'

'What?'

'Are you using this as an excuse to end it because you don't feel the same as I do?'

She frowned. 'What do you mean?'

'If you don't love me, Lily, I'd prefer it if you simply told me.'

She stared at him, feeling fury burn her insides. 'Don't you ever question my love, Leonard Warwick. I've risked everything for you, and right now I feel as though I'm dying from the pain of it.'

'Oh, my darling, I'm so sorry.' He pulled her into his arms again.

This time she felt his tears on her face as he kissed her. She put a hand on his cheek. 'I'm sorry, I'm so sorry.'

Eventually they calmed down.

'You really do have to go back, Leonard. You've been gone too long already.'

'I know.' He started the car and drove in grim silence back towards London.

'Drop me near Bow Church. I can get the 108 bus through Blackwall Tunnel.'

'I'd rather take you all the way home.'

'Don't. Beverley isn't working this week. She might be home. If I get the bus I'll have time to get myself together before she sees me.'

'If you're sure?'

'Yes. It doesn't make sense for you to go all the way to South London now. You've been away from the office too long. You mustn't give him any excuse to sack you.'

'True. But right now, I simply don't care.'

Lily sighed. 'I know. I don't know how I'm going to be able to walk back in there. But I'll have to.' She pointed through the windscreen. 'That bus stop will do.'

He pulled the car out of the traffic and into the kerb just beyond the bus stop, switching off the engine.

'Did you really mean it – that we have to end it?'

'Yes. No. I don't know.'

'It's impossible.'

'You've got that right. I don't know what to do.'

He leaned against the steering wheel, watching her. 'All right. Let's put it to test.'

'What do you mean?'

'Let's see if we can live without each other. I know I won't be able to, but you obviously need time to decide.'

'What can I do?'

'You're going on holiday soon. Go to your doctor and get a sick note to cover you until then.'

'I can't. What can I tell him? That I need him to cure me of a broken heart?'

He reached out and touched her lips. 'Shhh. Don't upset yourself, my love. You can play upon the fact that you were sick this morning. Plus you've been having headaches.'

'All nerves,' she said. 'He'll think I'm neurotic.'

'It doesn't matter what he thinks, so long as he signs you off. Take the time. Think about us. Miss me. God knows, it's going to be hell for me. Go on holiday with your family. Then come back to work and tell me.'

'Tell you what?'

'Tell me that you can't live without me. Or that you can. I'd prefer the former, of course. I'm relying on that.'

'And then what?'

'If you feel as I do, then we'll have some big decisions to make about our future. If you don't...' He paused. 'If you don't, then I'll try to respect your decision. I'll leave the firm. With any luck that will satisfy Irwin and he'll keep you. You're the best damned cashier they've had in years, so he'd be a fool to let you go.'

'But... Leo, that means I won't see you for nearly a month.' She felt afraid. She didn't think she could cope without seeing him. She already missed him every weekend. How could she bear to go a whole month without seeing him?

He smiled. 'Well, that's a good sign.' His expression sobered. 'If you're serious about ending this, Lily, then the next few weeks will help you. Of course, I'm hoping that you'll realise you can't. That being the case, the torture of being without you for a relatively short time will be worth it in the long run.'

Lily sighed. 'All right.' She had a horrible feeling he was right. It was going to be torture. But they had to try. 'You might change your mind about me if I'm not around.'

He shook his head. 'Oh no, my darling. I'm never going to stop loving you.'

He kissed her then. She clung to him, knowing she wouldn't feel his arms around her again for a long time. Maybe never.

Eventually their hunger abated. Lily became aware of the traffic, of the people walking by.

'I'd better go.'

He rested his forehead on hers. 'Take care, my love.' He kissed her again, gently, briefly.

Lily pulled away, scrabbling in the footwell for her handbag. She gave him a watery smile and got out of the car.

She didn't look back. She heard the car burst into life and the squeal of tyres as he drove away.

'Goodbye, my love,' she whispered.

38

The phone rang at about seven. Jack waited for a bit to see whether Caroline would run downstairs to answer it, but she must have fallen asleep over her book. He got up and went out into the hall.

'Hallo?'

'Dad?'

'Hallo, Bev darlin'. Where are ya?'

'I'm at my mate Angie's.'

'Want me to come and pick you up?'

'Nah. I'm staying here tonight. We're having a drink.'

'Are you now? Well, better not tell your mother.'

'What's it got to do with her?' she snapped.

Jack looked at the phone. 'What's the matter with you? You and your mum had another row?' Lily hadn't said anything, but then again, she was in no fit state.

'No. I ain't spoken to her. Don't want to neither, the old cow.'

'Oi, hold on, Bev. That's no way to talk about your mother. Anyway, she ain't at all well. They sent her home from work. She's been round the doctor's and he's signed her off. She's taken to her bed.'

'There ain't nothing wrong with her.'

'Don't be daft. You ain't even seen her. She's looking rough, girl. I reckon she's been working too hard. I've half a mind to go and see that boss of hers.'

'You ever met him?'

He frowned. 'Yeah, once. Bit of a wanker.'

'What does he look like?'

'I don't know. A bloke in a suit.'

'Is he old?'

'Nah, he's about my age.'

'Old then.'

'Bugger off, cheeky mare.'

Bev giggled. In the background he could hear her mate whispering, 'Tell him. Go on, tell him.'

'Shut up,' he heard Bev say, although it was muffled, as though she'd put her hand over the phone.

'What's going on? You already pie-eyed?'

'Yeah. So?'

Jack sighed. 'So, while you two get rat-arsed, who's looking after them babies?'

'They're all right. They're already in bed.'

'You sure you don't want to come home?'

'Yeah.'

'All right. We'll see you tomorrow. Behave yourself.'

'It ain't me who needs to behave,' she said.

'What's that supposed to mean?'

'Nothing. I'll see you.'

'Here, hang on! I nearly forgot.'

'What?'

'I've booked us an 'oliday. A nice chalet down Somerset. A week on Saturday. You coming?'

'Why?'

'What d'you mean, why? Your mum needs a break. We ain't had an 'oliday in months. Thought you'd wanna come too.'

'Well I ain't going with you lot. Christ, why would I want to be stuck in a chalet with—'

'All right, I get the message. Just make sure the house is tidy when we get back, eh?'

'Don't you worry about me.'

There was another round of muffled conversation in the background. Jack couldn't make out the words, but the girls were having a right set-to.

'Bev? You sure you're all right, love?'

'Yeah. I told you. I gotta go.'

'All right. See you tomorrow.'

She put the phone down without answering.

* * *

'Leonard? Is something wrong?' asked Daphne.

He looked up from this whisky. 'No, of course not.'

'Are you sure, darling? You've hardly said a word since you came home. You barely noticed when the children said goodnight to you.'

He frowned. 'Have they gone up already?'

Daphne sat down on the armchair opposite, but she didn't relax. She was staring at him, looking worried. 'It's gone eight o'clock, dear. Are you sure you're all right?'

Leonard wanted to laugh. Of course he wasn't all right! He'd never been so miserable in his life. At best, he faced four long weeks without Lily. At worst, he'd lost her forever.

'I don't think I'm going to be offered a partnership at Alder & Powney, Daphne,' he said, before taking another mouthful of Scotch.

'Oh, Leonard! Why ever not? You've been working so hard.'

'I don't think I have the right old school tie.'

'But that shouldn't count for anything these days, surely? It's 1969. The world is changing.'

'Not in the legal profession, I'm afraid.'

She got up and poured herself a sherry. 'It's not right. They've been leading you on, dangling a partnership in front of you, for years. They might have had the decency to be honest. When I think of all the sacrifices we've made.' She slumped into her chair.

Leonard almost felt sorry for her. He almost felt guilty too. After all, Lily had been right – it wasn't Daphne's fault, or Lily's husband's. But he still couldn't bring himself to feel either of those things.

He loved Lily. She loved him. Theirs wasn't some sordid, meaningless *affaire* as Irwin had implied. He supposed he ought to feel bad about letting Daphne think he was putting in hundreds of extra hours to gain favour with the partners. But he knew that he'd worked doubly hard without resorting to the fictitious overtime. He'd taken on far more clients than he should have. If it hadn't been for Lily's help, and the efficiency of his secretary and the rest of the typing pool, he'd have been crushed under a mountain of cases.

But it had all been for nothing. Because now that Irwin knew about him and Lily, his career with the firm was all but over.

He couldn't tell Daphne that. He wanted to. He wanted to yell and stamp and shout his frustration to the roof. But what would be the point? He had promised Lily he would do nothing more to jeopardise their jobs or their marriages – at least until these damned four weeks were over.

Once Lily came back to him, he would gladly tell the world. It was just that persistent little niggle of doubt growing inside him

that warned that, in her absence, Lily might find the strength to
end it with him.

He took another swig, letting the liquid burn a path down his
throat. He couldn't contemplate losing her. If he did, he would go
mad. No, he must have faith. He must be patient. She *would* come
back.

'What are you going to do?'

Leonard started. He'd forgotten Daphne, sitting there just a few
feet away. He shrugged. 'What can I do?' he said. 'I'll have to find
another job. With a firm that isn't so bloody sanctimonious.'

Daphne frowned.

'What?' he asked.

'That's an odd word to use in the circumstances.'

'What word? What are you talking about?'

'Sanctimonious.'

He held up his now empty glass. 'Sorry, old girl. It's the Scotch
talking.' He pulled himself up and stood swaying slightly. 'Time for
another, I think.'

39

Lily must have been staring into space for a while. Her tea had gone cold. She got up from the kitchen table and poured it down the sink, leaving the cup and saucer in the bowl. No point in wasting hot water until she had a few more things to wash up.

She glanced at the clock. Ten o'clock. She was still in her dressing gown, with no make-up, and her hair a mess. She supposed she should go and sort herself out. But what was the point?

The day stretched out ahead of her. She worried about work. Who was covering for her while she was away? She had everything organised just so. What sort of chaos would she go back to after a four-week absence? Would they even take her back?

She heard the front door open and went to see Beverley manoeuvre the pushchair into the hall. The baby was fast asleep. Beverley looked rough, with yesterday's mascara smudged around her eyes. Her backcombed hair looked like a bird's nest. Lily sighed. Her daughter really didn't have the legs for those miniskirts she insisted on wearing, but she wouldn't be told.

'Hello, love.'

Beverley glared at her, her eyes bloodshot. 'Shhh!' she said.

Lily watched as she gently took the baby out of the pushchair and carried her upstairs. She went back into the kitchen and put the kettle on. She was stirring sugar into mugs of Nescafé when Beverley came into the kitchen.

'Here you go.' She handed her a drink. 'Did you have a good night?'

Beverley shrugged, not looking at her. She took a sip of her coffee.

'The baby looks worn out.'

'Yeah, well she's been up since five, playing with Angie's baby, Zoë.'

Lily grimaced. 'You didn't get much of a lie-in, then.'

'I'm all right.'

Lily sat down at the kitchen table, cradling her drink. 'Did Dad tell you I've been signed off?'

'Yeah.'

'It's nothing serious. I'm just tired. The doctor thinks I might be anaemic.' She raised her mug to her lips.

'Well that's a load of bollocks, ain't it?'

Lily nearly choked on her coffee. 'What?'

'There ain't nothing wrong with you, is there?'

She couldn't say anything. Beverley snorted.

'I saw you,' she said. 'Yesterday, in Bow. I'd been down the Roman Road market and was on me way home.'

Lily shook her head, panic rising. 'Don't be ridiculous. I never went near Bow.'

'Yes you did. Who was the fella you was snogging, eh? Someone from work?'

'I don't know what you're talking about.'

'Yes you do. He dropped you off at the bus stop. You got on the 108, so you was coming home. And don't tell me it ain't true.

'Cause I saw you, bold as brass, with your tongue down his throat.'

'No. I went to work. I was sick and I came home.'

Beverley shook her head. The contempt on her face made Lily want to weep.

'You're a bloody awful liar, Mum.'

Lily slapped her hard across the face. 'I will not listen to this! I will not have you going round accusing me of things like that. You will show some respect in this house.'

Bev held her cheek, her eyes burning. 'You always told me respect has to be earned,' she said. She got up and threw her mug into the sink. It shattered against the crockery already there. Lily flinched.

'I know what I saw,' Bev went on. 'You had that green dress on – the one you made. You can't tell me there's two women who look exactly like you, and have exactly the same dress.'

Lily closed her eyes. She couldn't speak. This was even worse than facing Mr Irwin.

'I'm right, ain't I? You're having it off with some bloke. Is he married n'all? Got kids, has he?'

Lily put her head in her hands. She should deny it. Bluff it out. But she couldn't.

'You bloody hypocrite!' Bev shouted. 'You went on about how proud you was of me, chucking my fella 'cause he was married. And all the time, you're shagging someone else's husband.'

'You don't understand!'

'Oh yes I do!' she yelled, leaning over the table. 'You're a slag. A lying, cheating tart.'

Lily was beyond tears. Her whole body burned with shame and fear. 'It's not like that.'

'No? Why not?'

'Because I love him!' she burst out.

Beverley reared back. For a moment, Lily thought she was going to hit her.

'No,' said Beverley. 'Don't you dare. Don't you dare say you're in love. It's sex. That's all it is. Dirty. Filthy. Sex. And you're disgusting.'

Lily shook her head, but she couldn't say anything. She *did* love Leonard. But she wasn't supposed to. He wasn't supposed to love her, but he did. Beverley didn't understand. No one would. The whole world would agree with her daughter. She was a dirty, disgusting liar.

She refused to give in to the urge to run and hide. There was nowhere she could go. Instead she held her head high. 'So, what are you going to do?'

Beverley didn't answer for a moment. She turned her back and went to the sink. Lily heard her pushing the shards of crockery around in the bowl. She raised her head and saw Beverley take a glass out of the cupboard, fill it up with water and drink it down as though she were dying of thirst.

When she'd emptied the glass she turned round to look at Lily. She still held the glass in her hand, her knuckles white as she gripped it tightly.

'What am I going to do?' she said. 'I don't know yet. Angie reckons I should tell Dad. He's got a right to know, she says.'

Lily held her breath. She wanted to berate her for telling her friend about this. It was none of her business. Lily was sure the girl couldn't be trusted. Before they knew it the whole world would know.

'When I found out Andy was married, I saw his wife,' Beverley went on, before Lily could think of what to say. 'I had the chance to tell her exactly what a lying bastard her husband was. I'd have enjoyed seeing him suffer, losing his wife and kids, being shown up for the cheating sod he was.'

Lily felt the air rush out of her lungs. She thought she was going to pass out. It was all over. Beverley would tell Jack, and she'd lose everything. She'd already lost Beverley; she could see that. Her daughter would never trust her again.

'But I couldn't do it, could I?' Beverley went on, her voice choked. 'She was pregnant – ready to pop – and she had a lovely little boy who was climbing all over his dad, happy as Larry.' She laughed. 'I let him get away with it. How bloody stupid am I? I should have told her, let her see what an idiot she was to trust him. She'd have been better off without him.'

'No!' said Lily. 'You did the right thing. Think about those children.'

'Like you thought about us? You're taking the piss. You didn't even see me yesterday, you was so wrapped up in him. Who is he, anyway?'

'It doesn't matter. I ended it. It's over.'

'It didn't look like you was chucking him. You was all over him.'

'I was saying goodbye.'

'Bollocks. I'm telling Dad. He's got a right to know.'

'No! For God's sake, Beverley. Please. Think about this. I swear to you, it's over. I'm getting another job. I might not even go back. Telling your dad will just hurt him for nothing.'

'Well, whose fault is that?'

'You're right, it's mine. But I've put a stop to it. It's over.' She gulped in a breath, trying to contain the pain. 'Telling your dad now will ruin everything. It will hurt him, when he doesn't need to be. For God's sake, I'm trying to do the right thing here. Hurting your dad just to get back at me is just downright selfish.'

'That's bloody rich, coming from you!'

'Maybe it is, but think about it. Don't tell him, Beverley, please.'

Bev glared at Lily, her jaw set. For a moment, Lily thought she was going to tell her to sod off.

'Please,' she whispered.

With a scream, Bev raised her arm and flung the glass at the wall behind Lily. It shattered. Lily sank back into her chair, covering her head with her hands.

'I hate you!' Bev cried. She ran out of the room.

In the distance, Lily could hear the baby crying. She felt a sharp pain and glanced down. A shard of glass had pierced the back of her hand. She watched as her blood trickled over her skin.

Nothing was ever going to be the same again. In one fell swoop, she was looking at losing both her job and her family. She'd told Leonard they must stop, but what if it was too late?

The blood continued to drip from her hand. She welcomed the pain. She deserved it.

40

A few days later, Leonard was going through some letters with his secretary when Gerald Irwin knocked, opened the door and made an ass of himself by looking around it, as though making sure he wasn't interrupting something. Leonard pasted a smile on his face, when in reality he wanted to get up and punch the man.

'Got a minute, old boy?' asked Irwin.

'Of course.' Leonard turned to his secretary. 'Leave these with me. I'll bring them through as soon as I've finished signing them.'

'Yes, sir.' She left. Irwin held the door for her and closed it behind her.

'What can I do for you?' asked Leonard.

Irwin sat in the chair opposite and brought out a silver cigarette case. He offered him one, but Leonard declined. With a shrug he took a lighter out of his pocket and lit up. He inhaled, raising his head and exhaling smoke out of his nostrils. Leonard pushed an ashtray towards him.

'Thanks.' He tapped the end of his cigarette on the marble.

Leonard waited.

'Have you spoken to Lily?' Irwin asked.

'No. You made it quite clear that it wouldn't be appropriate.'

'Right. Yes. Of course. Well done.'

'Her doctor thinks she's anaemic. He's signed her off again this week, and she's got two weeks' holiday booked starting from next week.'

'So she won't be back until the end of the month? Damn!'

'Is there a problem?' Leonard asked, knowing damned well the place was in chaos without Lily in the cash office.

'She is coming back, though, isn't she?'

Leonard shrugged. 'You seemed to imply that both of us needed to look elsewhere for employment. For all I know she may be planning a move to a new job as we speak.'

Irwin frowned. 'Now look here, old chap. I had to take a hard line. It's not done, especially with you both married to other people. The Law Society would come down on us like a ton of bricks.'

'Well you don't have to worry. It's over.'

'Good. Good. The other partners and I are aware that you're both excellent workers. We'd hate to lose either of you, so long as there's no repeat of—'

'That won't happen again. I can assure you.'

'I suppose Lily is upset?'

Leonard nodded, not trusting himself to speak. Upset? That didn't begin to describe how he felt, and he suspected – perhaps even hoped – that it was the same for Lily. Being separated from her was tearing him apart.

'Shame. Well, let's hope the break is doing her good. We need her back, Warwick. I've had to send one of the clerks down to the bank to collect a bank draft for the completion of a big property deal today. If I hadn't checked, we'd have been in breach of contract and it would have cost us a pretty penny. That's the third time it's happened since she's been gone. I hadn't realised how much Lily had taken on until she wasn't here, getting everything ready without any fuss. The temp the agency sent simply isn't up to Lily's standards.'

'Lily thought you were going to sack her.'

Irwin shook his head. 'I told you I wouldn't. We don't want a scandal. No. If you've ended it, then we'll say no more about it. Life can go back to normal, eh?'

Leonard wondered what he meant by 'normal.' He didn't want to go back to anything, except Lily.

In the first days after she'd gone, he'd continued to go to the flat at lunchtimes. There he felt close to her. But when he found himself lying on the bed, breathing in the scent of her from the pillow, weeping, he knew it had to stop. He hadn't been back since.

Irwin stood up. 'Perhaps I should drop her a note, and let her know we need her back. Yes. I'll do that. We don't want her finding another job while we sit around waiting, do we?'

'No.'

'Good. In the meantime, perhaps you could see if the agency has a better temp to see us through until Lily returns? There's a good chap.'

After he'd gone, Leonard sat for a few moments, wondering if he could bear it if she came back and told him she didn't want him any more. But he knew the answer. Of course he couldn't. It wasn't over. It couldn't be, no matter what he'd told Irwin.

They would just have to make sure that in future they weren't found out.

* * *

The phone was ringing. Lily lay on the bed, not wanting to move. But whoever was on the other end wasn't giving up. With a sigh she rolled over and stood up. For a few seconds she felt dizzy. She waited until her head cleared and went to answer it.

'Hello?'

'Lil? Where you been? I've been ringing for ages.'

'Sorry, Maggie, I was upstairs.'

'You all right, love? Jack said you're not yourself.'

She rolled her eyes. 'I'm just a bit run-down,' she said. 'The doc's given me some iron pills.'

Maggie was quiet for a moment. 'You ain't gone and done something daft, have you, Lily?'

She opened her mouth to tell her, but couldn't. She couldn't do that to Maggie.

'No. I haven't done anything daft.' After all, she'd done the right thing, hadn't she? It had sucked the life out of her, leaving her a wreck, but that didn't matter. She couldn't help wondering, though – had she done something really daft by telling Leonard they had to end it? How could she go on like this?

'Good. Everyone's worried about you, love.'

'There's no need.'

Maggie was silent for a few moments. 'Well, if you're sure. Fancy a night at the bingo? It might cheer you up.'

'I don't know. I – I'm having trouble concentrating. I might miss my numbers.'

'That don't matter. It's just a night out. Give us both a break.'

Lily swallowed the lump that was growing in her throat. She really didn't want to go out. She didn't want to see people and have to pretend. 'Honestly, Maggie, I'd be lousy company. I'm like a wet rag right now. Let's give the pills a few more days to work, eh?'

Maggie sighed. 'All right. Maybe after your holiday. That should sort you out.'

'What? Oh, yeah, the holiday. I suppose I'd better sort out what we're going to take.'

'It sounds right nice from what Jack was saying. You'll have to let us know. I might nag Fred into booking us a chalet there next year. We could all go together, like old times.'

'That'd be nice,' Lily said, wondering if Maggie could hear the insincerity in her voice. When had she started to dread the idea of their combined family outings? All she knew was that she couldn't cope any more with the noise and chaos of all of those kids.

'Well, I hope this weather holds up for you. If you need anything before you go, let me know, all right? And if you change your mind about the bingo.'

'Yeah, thanks, love. I'll let you know.'

She put the phone down and wandered into the kitchen. The breakfast dishes were still in the sink. There were crumbs all over the table. Someone had left the butter and marmalade out. The lino could do with a mop as well, especially round the baby's high chair.

The rest of the house wasn't much better. For days she hadn't done anything but drown in her own misery. Jack and Caroline had done what they could to help. Beverley had been vicious when she hadn't been ignoring her completely.

Lily put the kettle on and sat down at the table to wait for it to boil. She rested her head in her hands and realised her hair was a mess. When was the last time she'd combed it? It probably needed a wash. She'd got Jack to cancel her shampoo and set at the hairdresser's on Saturday. She hadn't put any make-up on for days, either. She must look a right state, but she couldn't be bothered to get up and check in the mirror.

The kettle boiled and she got up to make a drink. They were nearly out of Nescafé. There wasn't much sugar either. She opened the fridge. It was almost empty. The dinner that she hadn't eaten last night was sitting there on a plate, covered in tinfoil. She took it out and unwrapped it. A dried-up lamb chop, some boiled potatoes, carrots and cabbage. It made her want to retch. She emptied it into the bin.

She sat down again, forgetting she'd intended to make a coffee. She'd have to go out and get some shopping. And she couldn't let the house get any worse. What would people think?

She couldn't spend the rest of her life like this, could she? She was in such a state that she was drawing attention to herself. If she wasn't careful, her mum and dad would be round, checking up on her. She couldn't let them see her like this.

All she wanted to do was sleep. But she couldn't even do that, because when she slept she dreamed of Leo. She was terrified that Jack would hear her crying out to her lover, telling him she loved him and couldn't bear being separated from him. In her dreams, she begged Leo to do something, to turn back time to when no one knew their secret. But as she called out to him, he moved further away, shaking his head and telling her it was too late. It was her fault. She'd been careless, and now she had to live with the consequences.

She'd woken up weeping next to her husband, and realised she couldn't let herself do that again. So she lay there, night after night, rigid with fatigue, unable to sleep.

No wonder she was in such a state. If she didn't pull herself together soon, she'd really make herself ill. At this rate she'd end up in the loony bin.

Lily took a deep breath, sitting up straighter in her chair. 'No more,' she said.

She pushed the chair back and stood up. This place needed a damned good clean. There was shopping to do. She hadn't put on a load of washing for days, so the laundry would have to be next. If she didn't sort herself out and find a new job, she'd have to think about how they'd manage on Jack's wages. Maybe she should stay at home anyway. She wasn't to be trusted out there.

For a moment, she wavered, nearly sitting down again before she found her backbone and moved. She found her handbag on the telephone table in the hall, where she'd left it over a week ago. She rummaged inside and brought out a pen and an old envelope, then sat on the stairs and started writing a shopping list.

She jumped when the letterbox rattled and a pile of post came tumbling through onto the carpet.

She put her pen down and got up. She was so stiff from doing nothing for so long that it hurt to bend over to pick up the letters. There was a postcard from one of her sisters, on holiday in Clacton. The telephone bill. A letter for Caroline, addressed in childish handwriting, from her penfriend.

Lily smiled. Caroline would be thrilled. She loved getting letters and wrote great long ones back to this little girl she'd met on holiday in Scotland. She made a note on her list to stop at the post office and buy a stamp, otherwise Caroline would nag her to death.

She went to put the letter on the telephone table, but it dropped from her hand as she recognised the Alder & Powney frank on the handwritten letter below it. For a moment she thought it was from Leonard, and her whole body came alive. But then she realised it wasn't his handwriting, and she felt the blood drain out of her face. It was from Mr Irwin. If he had written it himself, it must be bad news; otherwise he'd have got his secretary to type it.

She dropped the other post on the table and went back into the kitchen, got a knife out of the cutlery drawer and took her time slicing the envelope open. She leaned against the worktop.

With shaking hands, she drew the letter out slowly, unfolded it and read.

Dear Lily,

I was sorry to hear that you are ill. I do hope that your doctor is looking after you, and that you will soon be on the road to recovery. I must apologise if I misunderstood what was happening on your last day in the office, and I do hope that you will forgive my presumption. I had been unaware that you were feeling unwell.

Everyone at Alder & Powney sends their best wishes for your speedy recovery, and we look forward to seeing you back in the office after your holiday. You must use the time to relax with your family and regain your strength. In the meantime, we are making do with temporary staff, although none could possibly match your efficiency!

You are a valued member of the firm, and in recognition of your hard work, the partners have agreed that you should receive a small bonus. I have added this to your salary cheque, which is attached.

Enjoy your holiday, my dear.
Yours sincerely,
Gerald Irwin

A paperclip held the cheque to the letter. There was an extra £25, and they hadn't docked any money, even though she'd been off work.

She didn't understand. She couldn't believe he wasn't sacking her. There was no hint as to whether he'd given Leonard his marching orders. She stared at the cheque, working the figures out again, just in case she'd misunderstood. She reread the letter. If only she could speak to Leonard, and find out what this was really all about. But she couldn't call him. She'd have to go through the switchboard, and she didn't trust them not to listen in.

On the face of it, she still had her job. It looked as though they were having trouble getting a decent temp, and Irwin wanted to make sure she was coming back. She felt a glow of pride. After so many days of feeling worthless and ashamed, it was enough to make her weep with relief. Yes, she still had her job. And even better, the partners thought enough of her to give her a bonus. It would be a bit of spending money for their holiday.

She wouldn't think about Leonard, or about how hard it was going to be. Instead she tucked the cheque into her bag and picked up the shopping list. She'd go the bank and stock up with provisions. If she got a move on, she could have a nice dinner ready for the family when they got home.

41

'I'm not kidding,' Jack told the couple sharing their table. 'That Flamenco dancer had no knickers on.'

They burst out laughing, shaking their heads at his story. Jack lapped it up. He loved to put on a show and see people laugh. It was the first night of their holiday at Brean Sands, and even Lily was cracking a smile.

'Don't believe a word he says,' she said. 'You'll only encourage him.'

'Oh, Jack, you're such a card.' The woman laughed. 'Isn't he a card, Geoff?'

'God's honest truth,' Jack went on. 'She was flicking her skirt up, and strutting about, brazen as anything. Mind you, considering the bleeding price of their poxy beer, she was probably trying to take our minds off that.'

They roared again, fuelled as they were by their own drinks. 'Same again?' Jack asked.

The fella held up a hand. 'My turn, mate.' He stood up. 'What you having, Lily?'

'Port and lemon, please.'

'Right. Mavis?'

'I'm in the mood for a Babycham,' she said. 'After all, we're on our holidays, ain't we?'

Geoff rolled his eyes. 'Jack? What's your poison?'

'I'll come and give you an 'and.' He got up and followed him.

There was a crowd around the bar, but Geoff was even bigger than Jack, and the two men managed to shoulder their way through. Both of them leaned against the counter, admiring the two barmaids. The women were blonde and wore the same uniform of frilly blouse and tight miniskirt. With their hair done up like Dusty Springfield, and all that black eyeliner and false eyelashes, they looked like twins. As they pulled pints, they were jiggling along to the music playing in the background. Jack was impressed – they didn't spill a drop.

'You're a lucky man, Jack,' said Geoff, his eyes never leaving the swaying backside of the girl nearest them.

'Why's that then?'

'There's not many blokes whose wives would let them off the leash to go abroad on their own.'

Jack smiled. 'Like you said, mate. I'm a lucky man.'

'Mind you,' Geoff went on. 'If my Mavis was as tasty as your Lily, I don't think I'd leave her alone. I bet blokes are around her like flies, ain't they?'

Jack frowned. He knew Lily was gorgeous and he knew blokes looked at her. But he didn't take kindly to Geoff reminding him. 'They can look, but God help anyone who thinks he can touch,' he said, his voice low and deadly.

Geoff held up his hands. 'I was just saying, mate. I didn't mean nothing by it. I've got my Mavis. I ain't that sort of fella. She'd kill me.'

Jack laughed. 'What, that sweet little thing? You have to know how to handle 'em, mate.'

* * *

While the men were at the bar, Mavis rattled on about nothing in particular. Lily smiled and nodded but didn't listen.

One of the Bluecoats came on stage and approached the microphone. It squealed in protest as she spoke. Everyone groaned and covered their ears.

'Sorry, sorry.' She tapped the end, which echoed like explosions around the room. 'Can you hear me?'

'Here, it's the cabaret!' someone shouted. 'Give us a song, darling.'

The girl blushed. 'No, I'm sorry. The show will be starting soon. But I have a message from the baby patrol. There's a crying child in Chalet Number 234. Will the parents please return to their room to see to it as soon as possible.'

There was a moment of silence while everyone tried to remember their chalet number, then a woman stood up and there was a collective sigh of relief that it wasn't their kids. She looked anxious and her husband looked furious. He stayed where he was, drinking his pint, while she scurried off, red with embarrassment. The buzz of conversation and clinking of glasses resumed.

'Phew, I'm glad it wasn't any of ours,' said Mavis. 'Mind you, I told our little'uns that if we heard a peep out of them before morning, I'd tan their backsides. We've been running round after them all day, and I deserve a night out. It's my holiday as well.'

Lily sipped what was left of her drink and wished the men would hurry up with the next round.

'You've just got the one, have you?' Mavis went on.

Lily shook her head. 'Two. Our other girl's seventeen now.'

'And you left her at home?'

'She's working,' said Lily. 'She couldn't get the time off.' Not that it was any business of hers. She wasn't about to tell her life story to a stranger just because this woman had already given her and Jack chapter and verse of hers.

'What does she do then?'

Lily sighed. She really wanted to tell her to mind her own business, but she'd promised herself she'd do her best to make this a good holiday for Jack. If she started a row on the first bloody night, it would go from bad to worse.

'She works in an office,' was all she was prepared to say. She hoped to God Jack wouldn't let slip about the baby in front of Mavis. The woman would have a field day.

'Oh, nice. Better than working in a shop, ain't it? I used to work in C&A – on me feet all day I was. But I gave it up when the kiddies came along. Of course, now that Geoff's a manager, we can manage very nicely on his money. We might even have a holiday abroad next year. I fancy the Isle of Wight.'

Lily had to struggle to stop from laughing out loud. The men arrived with their drinks. Lily beamed at Jack. He sat down next to her and put an arm round her shoulder. She froze for a moment, then forced herself to relax, leaning into him.

'All right, love?'

She nodded, not looking at Mavis, who was complaining loudly that she didn't have a cherry in her Babycham. Jack kissed Lily's cheek.

'Good. It ain't bad here, is it?'

'It's nice.' Not as nice as a proper hotel on the Continent might have been, but he was doing his best, and Lily had to accept that.

The floor show finally got going. The dance band started with a foxtrot.

'Want to dance?'

She hesitated.

'Don't worry if you're still feeling poorly, love,' he said.

How could she tell him that she didn't want to be in his arms?

She looked into his face and saw beneath the cheeky chappie who'd got the strangers at their table chatting and laughing, to the man who cared about her and wanted her to be happy. It broke her heart that he wasn't the man who could make that happen. The least she could do was to try to make him happy. He deserved that much.

'I'm all right. I'd love to dance,' she said.

* * *

'That's it, darling,' said Jack, as he and Caroline stood at the edge of the swimming pool. 'Stand up straight, arms up, bounce on your toes and—'

Caroline launched herself off the side, leaning forward and pointing her fingers at the water. She didn't get the angle right and landed flat on the water. She came up choking, tears running down her face.

Lily was standing next to her deckchair. 'Are you all right, sweetheart?' she called.

Caroline nodded, ducking her head under the water again to wash away her tears.

'Do you want to get out now?'

The child shook her head. 'No, Mummy.'

Jack put down a hand and pulled her out of the water. 'You're all right, ain't you, Princess?'

'I did it wrong again, Daddy,' she said. 'Show me again.' He stood by the pool edge. 'You have to push yourself up, then aim for the water. Watch.' He bounced on his toes, then performed a perfect dive.

Caroline clapped. 'Look at that, Mummy! I'm going to do it like that.'

'Of course you are. I've got the camera ready, see?'

She turned around. Lily was holding the cine camera, ready to film. Jack pulled himself out and sat on the side, dripping.

'Reckon you can do it like that?' he asked.

She nodded, positioning herself on the edge. She took a deep breath, bounced on her toes and dived. She flew through the air, curving her body at just the right angle to cut through the water.

She came up laughing. Jack had two fingers in his mouth and he was whistling loudly. Everyone turned and looked. Lily had the camera running. Caroline waved. Lily smiled. The child grinned at the camera.

'I want to do it again,' she said, as Jack pulled her out of the water once more. 'Do it with me this time, Daddy.'

Lily continued to film as Jack stood beside Caroline and they dived into the pool together. Caroline didn't get this dive quite as perfect as the last one, because she was so excited, but it was a good effort. They came up smiling, and Jack gathered her in his arms and dunked them both. Lily carried on filming their antics, tears filling her eyes.

Jack was such a good dad. The girls adored him. Why couldn't she still love him? She wished she could, but even after weeks away from Leo she ached for him.

Eventually Jack pulled himself out of the pool. He was a big man, and strong. By rights he should be clumsy, but he was light on his feet. She noticed a few of the other women around the pool watching him. She tried to remember what it felt like to fancy him, but that feeling was long gone. For a moment, she wished he would see those other women and maybe find one who would love him as he deserved. Then she'd be free.

'All right, love. Sure you don't want to come in?'

She sighed. 'How many years have we been married?'

'Coming up for twenty.'

'And have I ever been in a swimming pool?'

'This one ain't deep, love, and I'll keep you safe.'

She shook her head. She'd fallen into a river when she was evacuated, and a bigger lad had had to dive in and hoick her out before she drowned. She'd never forgotten the fear of being swept under the cold, fast-flowing water, unable to breathe, and sure she was going to die.

'I know you would, but I don't want to. I'm happy here on my deckchair.'

He bent over her, bracing himself with his hands on either side of the chair, dripping cool water over her sun-heated skin. She yelped, as Jack laughed and gave her a kiss. She pushed him away.

'Behave,' she said. 'People are watching.'

'So what? A man's entitled to kiss his wife, ain't he?'

'Daddy!' Caroline called from the water. 'Can I have an ice-cream?'

'Not in there you can't,' he replied, standing up.

She scrambled out of the pool and ran over. Jack wrapped her in a towel as she stood there, grinning and shivering. Lily smiled. It did her heart good to see her little one so happy.

She reached for her bag and pulled out her purse. 'Right,' she said. 'Who wants what?'

* * *

'How's your little girl enjoying her holiday,' Geoff asked the next night at dinner.

'Oh, she's having a great time,' said Jack. 'She's made a little friend, and they've been doing all sorts. They're going to the indoor pool tomorrow night, to do some distance badges. I reckon Caroline could do a mile if she didn't get bored.'

'A mile? But she's only nine, ain't she?'

'Yeah, well, nearly ten. But she swims like a fish. We can hardly get her out of the water.'

'I saw you teaching her to dive the other day,' said Mavis. The cabaret started. A Bluecoat crooned one of Frank Sinatra's hits. Lily had her back to the stage, so she moved her chair round to see. She hadn't seen this man perform before. Mavis had raved about him.

When Lily saw him, she gasped. For a minute, she could have sworn the man singing was Leo – he had the same build, the same haircut. But when he turned his face towards her, he looked nothing like her lover. Lily felt her heart sink. In those moments, even though she'd known it was impossible, she'd been filled with joy. Now she felt lost and shaken. She put a hand to her temple, trying to massage away the sudden tension that tightened around her head.

'You all right, love?' Jack asked, his lips close to her ear.

She jumped. She'd been so wrapped up in this feeling of loss, of wanting – needing – it to be Leonard, that she'd forgotten about her husband sitting beside her.

She nodded, afraid to speak.

'You ain't getting one of your heads, are ya? He's a bit loud, ain't he?'

She nodded again.

'Want me to take you back to the chalet?'

'I can go. You stay.'

'Nah, it's all right. He ain't exactly Ole Blue Eyes, is he? Jesus, our Fred could do better than that.'

Lily forced a smile, but she was too miserable to make much of an effort.

Jack stood up. 'Come on, love. Let's get you some aspirin and a nice warm bed, eh?' He helped her up.

'Going already?' asked Mavis. 'I was hoping for a dance later, Jack.'

He smiled. 'Sorry, love. Lily ain't feeling too good. Next time, eh?'

Geoff raised his pint glass. 'Look after her, mate. We'll see you tomorrow.'

* * *

The next day, Jack knew he'd been right. Caroline was well on her way to swimming a mile. Other kids had done a hundred yards, some a few hundred, and the last one had given up after half a mile. Now it was just Caroline in the pool, going up and down, slow but steady. She only had a few more lengths to do. Jack was walking along the poolside, his cine camera in his hand, keeping an eye on her, while Lily sat up on the spectator benches. He knew she wanted to be close – she worried about Caroline swimming all that way – but her fear of the water kept her in her seat. He'd told her she didn't have to stay. Caroline was all right with him and the lifeguards there, but Lily had shook her head and stayed put.

Another length finished, Caroline turned and swam back the other way. One of the lifeguards took over from Jack, walking along, cheering her on.

Lily was at one end of the pool, and Jack turned the camera in her direction. She was looking away from him, towards where Caroline was swimming. She looked lonely, sitting there all on her own, and there was something about her that kept Jack filming.

Yesterday he'd thought things were getting better, and that she was perking up. But last night it was as though someone had turned off a switch, and all the light had gone out of her again. He couldn't understand it. One minute she'd been fine, then her head had come on, and...

Lily shifted on the hard wooden bench. She was still looking away from him, but he realised she wasn't watching Caroline, because the kid was halfway back up the pool. No, she was just staring into space, as if she was a million miles away. And wherever she was, she weren't happy about it. He'd never seen her look so miserable. Like her heart was broken.

He wanted to go to her, to take her in his arms and tell her it would be all right. But it wouldn't, would it? He didn't even know what was making her so unhappy. He'd do anything to make it right, but he didn't know what was wrong, or how to fix it. She never talked to him any more, not really. Not about what she was feeling. She never planned the future no more, either. Lily had always been making plans – holidays abroad, getting a house, taking another evening class. But lately she hadn't done any of that. As though she couldn't see the point.

As he filmed, she sighed and closed her eyes, her head dropping as she took a deep breath, as though she was trying not to have a good cry. He felt his heart break. His Lil, the woman who meant the world to him, was sitting there, a few yards away. But the sheer misery surrounding her meant that she might well have been on another planet, because Jack just couldn't get anywhere near her. Why wouldn't she tell him what was wrong? God knows, he'd do anything to put it right for her.

'Come on, Caroline!' shouted the lifeguard. 'Two more lengths. Good girl, keep going.'

Jack looked round. Caroline caught his eye and gave him a tired smile as she turned round and pushed off on the last lap of the pool. Jack sent a quick glance at Lily, but she hadn't moved. He turned back to his daughter and filmed her final lengths, before putting the camera down and pulling her out of the pool and cradling her exhausted little body in his arms.

'That's my girl,' he said, holding her tight, not caring that she was getting his shirt wet. 'That's Daddy's clever girl.'

42

After a holiday that had restored her body but not her heart, Lily sat in the café near the offices of Alder & Powney trying to gather up the courage to go into work.

She stirred her frothy coffee, wondering whether she was doing the right thing. When she'd gone off sick, she'd never imagined being able to go back. It was too dangerous, too painful. It was clear she and Leo couldn't be together; there was too much standing in their way. The thought of working with him, day after day, without being able to touch him – to have to ignore her feelings and pretend he was just any man instead of the one she loved – no, she couldn't do it.

Then the letter had arrived from Mr Irwin. She'd been grateful he hadn't sacked her, and at the same time shocked that he'd practically begged her to come back. It had made her feel proud, knowing that the partners valued her work so much that Mr Irwin was prepared to forget what he'd seen. She'd worked damned hard all her life. Thank God she had, otherwise she definitely would have been out on her ear.

But... could she go back in there? This morning she'd thought she could, but once she got there, she'd bottled it. So, here she was, sitting with a coffee she didn't want, trying to decide whether to go in or go home.

If she went home, she'd never come back. She'd have to start again. And she'd never, ever see Leo again. She caught her breath on that thought.

These past weeks had been hard. She imagined the pain she felt was like the agony someone went through when someone they loved died. Only hers was worse, because she hadn't been able to let it out or tell anybody. She'd had to pretend her heart wasn't broken. When everyone was expecting her to perk up after her 'illness,' she'd been feeling worse and worse.

And now, here she was, yards from the office. Could she walk away? God knows, she'd tried. But it was killing her. Even if Leo had decided he could live without her, she couldn't live without him. She needed to see him, to know he was there. She wouldn't make a fuss. She wouldn't expect anything. She just wanted to see him. And she'd have to be content with that. At least, she hoped she could be. She couldn't go on like this.

The clock on the wall showed five to nine. She drank her coffee down, hoping it would soothe the knots in her stomach, then stood up. She paid her bill, took a deep breath and left the café. At least she would know, one way or another. One look at him and she'd know.

43

At lunchtime on Wednesday, Lily let herself into the flat and there he was. He opened his arms and she ran into them. It had taken them this long before they'd had the courage to slip away at lunchtime to meet.

There was no need to speak. They kissed, drinking in the feel and taste of each other after so many weeks apart. Within moments, he had picked her up and carried her into the bedroom.

She ought to tell him to stop; they didn't have time. But she couldn't. God knows, she'd tried to live without this, but it was no good. *She needed him.* Without Leo and his love, she was nothing – her life was reduced to a dull, grey existence – and she couldn't bear the thought of going on like that.

* * *

The moment she'd walked through the door of the flat, he'd been ready for her. He should have slowed down and given her more time, but he simply couldn't. He'd been without her for too long.

These past days, when she'd been so close and they'd had to be so careful, had been heaven and hell.

They lay on the bed – in their haste they hadn't even pulled back the eiderdown – a tangle of arms and legs. He kissed her temple and pulled her close.

'Dear God, I've missed you,' he said.

She kissed him on the lips, a gentle hand cradling his face. 'I've missed you too. I thought I was going to die. I can't ever go through that again.'

'Agreed.' He kissed her again. 'We must make plans.'

She frowned. 'What kind of plans?'

'To be together, my love. We can't go on like this. Not now that Irwin knows.'

'But if we're careful—'

He shook his head. 'Darling, think about it. Do you really want to go home at the end of each day and pretend? I don't. I want to spend every night with you for the rest of our lives.'

'What about our families? Beverley is grown up, but I can't leave Caroline behind, Leo. She's still so young.'

'Then you must bring her.'

'And what about your children?'

He sighed. 'I've thought long and hard about them. I'll miss them, but I hope that Daphne will be reasonable and let me see them often.'

'But what if she doesn't? I'd never forgive myself if you lost your children.'

He felt slightly sick at the thought. 'It won't come to that, I'm sure.' He rolled over, pulling her on top of him. 'I simply can't carry on without you, Lily. You're mine. Nothing else matters.'

'What do you have in mind?'

He took a breath, relieved that she wasn't saying no. 'We find new jobs. Preferably together, but that may not be possible at first.'

He grinned and kissed her. 'But I'm sure I will eventually be able to get you on my payroll.'

She smiled. 'Then what?'

'I was thinking of contacting the chap who owns this flat, to see if he'd be willing to let it to us. His contract in Hong Kong is for another year at least.'

She frowned. 'I'm not sure if there are any schools around here.'

'We'll find somewhere. It will only be temporary.'

He didn't want her to change her mind, for the want of a damned school. She was still frowning.

'What are you thinking?' he asked, praying she wasn't finding further barriers to his plan.

'It's all so scary. I don't know how I'm going to be able to tell Jack. And my mum and dad. What are they going to think?'

'They're your parents, darling. They love you. They'll want you to be happy.'

'I hope so.'

'Well, don't worry about it now. We'll make our plans, and then decide how best to tell everyone.'

'Beverley already knows,' she said, her voice shaking 'She saw us.'

'Good God!' He frowned. 'When?'

'At the bus stop in Bow. I didn't even see her.'

'Has she told your husband?'

'Not so far,' she said, pulling on her knickers and reaching for her stockings. 'But she's got a temper on her, and I keep waiting for her to... She's hardly spoken to me since she found out. I'm treading on eggshells every day.'

Damn, he thought. If Lily's daughter let the cat out of the bag, it could all blow up in their faces. At least with Irwin, he knew the man would put the firm's reputation first.

'Oh my God!' Lily cried. 'Look at the time.'

He rolled over and saw that they had about ten minutes before they would be missed back at the office.

'Where's my bra?' She scrambled round, searching for her clothes.

He got up, finding the bra on the dressing table, where he'd thrown it as he'd undressed her.

'Calm down, my love. Stop at a call box and ring the office. Say you forgot you have a dentist's appointment.'

'That won't cover you being late, though, will it?'

He shrugged. 'I've already told them I've got a meeting with a potential client, and that I might go straight there from lunch. I'm not expected back until three.'

She rolled her eyes. 'You're far too devious for me, Mr Warwick,' she said.

He zipped up her dress at the back and kissed the top of her head as she sat at the dressing table and repaired her lipstick. 'I'm learning, my love. Until we can start a new life together, I'm willing to tell whatever lies are necessary to be with you.'

She stilled for a moment. 'Leo, are we really doing the right thing?'

He sighed. He took her hand and pulled her round to face him. When she would have spoken, he placed his finger on her soft lips. She was so beautiful.

'I love you, Lily. I've tried to be a good husband to Daphne, but I don't love her. I need to be with you. Whether it's right or not is irrelevant. My love is too strong to deny any longer.'

'Your wife – does she know?'

He shrugged. 'I don't know, but she's not happy being married to me any more. She'll probably be glad to see the back of me.'

She looked at him, her brown eyes solemn. 'Jack's not happy either. He doesn't want the same life I want.'

'Well, I do.' He kissed her. 'It's all I want.' He kissed her again. 'I want to wake up with you every morning, to take you to the ballet and out to the best restaurants. I want the world to know how much I love you.' When she would have swayed towards him and twined her arms round his neck, he stepped back. 'But right now, you need to make that call.'

She put a hand to her hair. 'Christ, I'm a mess.'

'You're beautiful.'

She smiled, shaking her head. 'I'm in need of a comb,' she said, picking one up from the dressing table and attacking her hair. 'And you need to get dressed.'

She checked her watch. 'I've got to go.'

'What will you tell them?'

'I'll say I left my purse in a shop and had to go back for it.'

'You haven't got any shopping, my love.'

She put her hands on her hips. 'I will by the time I get there,' she said, her stern expression belied by the laughter in her eyes. 'I'll have to stop and buy myself a sandwich, seeing as how you haven't fed me. My poor stomach thinks my throat's been cut.'

She scrambled for her bag and jacket, slipping on her shoes before heading for the door.

He stopped her with a hand on her arm. She looked round. 'We will work it out, Lily. I promise. We'll be happy, my love.'

She hesitated. 'I hope so,' she said. And then she was gone.

44

Lily got home before Beverley, thank God. She needed to be there, looking normal, when her daughter arrived home. She couldn't afford to make her suspicious. She took a deep breath as she put the kettle on. God, how much more of this could she take?

Caroline was sitting at the kitchen table, reading her latest Puffin book.

'What did you do today?' Lily asked.

The child looked up, blinking away the story. 'What?'

'Pardon. You say pardon, not what.'

'Sorry, pardon?'

'I said, what did you do today?'

'Sarah's mum took us to Greenwich Park.'

'That's nice. Was it fun?'

Caroline shrugged. Lily could see that her mind was already focussing back on the book in front of her. She sighed and gave up. She made herself a cup of Nescafé, and checked the contents of the fridge. Mince or sausages? She decided on a cottage pie, and got the meat out.

As she chopped some onions and carrots, she thought about what Leonard had said. Was he serious? Could they really walk away from everything? She was torn between excitement and happiness on the one hand, and fear and guilt on the other. She didn't know if she had the courage to do it.

Beverley arrived home and Lily felt her tension rise. Since she'd gone back to work, she'd felt Beverley watching her, waiting for the chance to ruin everything. She also felt ashamed. She'd tried to be a good mother and set an example to her children. But with Beverley, she'd failed at every turn. And now that Beverley knew about Lily's affair... God, she hated that word, but what else could she call it? To her, it was so much more than some sordid indiscretion. She loved Leo. Without him her world was grey and pointless. But the shame she felt when she looked into her daughter's eyes would be multiplied a thousand times when everyone else knew as well.

'Hello, love,' she said, trying to keep her voice light. 'Had a good day?'

As usual, Beverley ignored her as she put Kerry down on the floor. The baby toddled over to Lily and wrapped her arms around Lily's leg.

'Nana!' she said, beaming up at her.

Lily smiled. 'Hello, my darling. Have you been a good girl?'

Beverley picked up her child, pulling her away as though Lily was contaminated. 'She needs changing,' she said, leaving the room.

Lily felt tears welling as she turned back to her task. Would everyone else treat her like that when they found out? She sniffed.

'Are you all right, Mummy?' Caroline asked.

She nodded, not looking round. 'It's the onions, love. They're a bit strong.'

'Oh.'

Reflected in the window, Lily watched Caroline shrug and go back to her book. She attacked the onions, chopping and chopping, as her tears fell.

45

Leo let himself into the house feeling quite ill. Lily had been back at work for a week, and the strain of trying to act normally was enormous.

'Leonard? Is that you, darling? We're upstairs. I'm supervising bath-time.'

He could hear the children giggling and splashing about. With a sigh he climbed the stairs. As he reached the open bathroom door he dredged up a smile for his wife. She was sitting primly on the closed lavatory seat, while the children sat amongst a froth of Matey bubbles.

'Hallo, hallo, hallo. What have we here then?' He did a creditable impression of Dixon of Dock Green, hands behind his back, knees bending and straightening, sending the children into gales of laughter.

'Daddy!' they cried in unison, reaching for him.

'Children, don't get soap on your father's suit,' admonished Daphne.

Peter and Susan subsided for a moment, then bombarded him with words.

'Daddy, we got our new shoes for school today,' said Susan.

Leonard nodded. 'That's nice.'

'And I had a tennis lesson and learned how to lob,' said Peter, puffing out his little chest with pride. 'The coach says I'm a natural.'

'Well done, young man!' Leonard smiled.

'Daddy, will you wash my hair?' asked Susan.

He raised his eyebrows.

Daphne stirred. 'No, Susan. Daddy's had a hard day at work. Now let him go downstairs and relax. You can see him for a few minutes before you go to bed.'

'Oh, but—'

'No arguments, young lady.'

Leonard pretended to look regretful. 'I'm sorry, darling. But I really am quite exhausted, earning money for those expensive shoes of yours.'

Susan sighed. 'It's all right, Daddy.'

He smiled. 'Now let Mummy help you, and you'll be done in a trice.'

As he went downstairs, he could hear Peter arguing loudly that he was big enough to wash his own hair.

He poured himself a Scotch and sank into his usual leather armchair, all pretence at jollity gone. It was getting harder and harder to play the contented husband and father. It was a farce. As soon as he could make the arrangements, he would be gone. He was frustrated that it was taking so long, but one day soon...

He felt a pang of regret about leaving the children. They were so innocent, so trusting. Would he ever be able to make them understand? He knew full well that Daphne and her mother would do their utmost to paint him black.

He took a sip of his drink, feeling its fiery heat spread through his chest. He'd finally heard back from Hong Kong. The flat's owner had regretfully refused to let him move in.

It's fine for you to use it on an occasional basis, he'd written. *But I'm afraid I have to draw the line at permanent occupation.*

Leonard sighed. He could hear footsteps above him as the children ran from the bathroom to their bedrooms to get their pyjamas on. He'd been naïve to think he could persuade the chap to sublet to him. Of course he would want to retain the flat. Leo would have done the same if the positions were reversed. It was in a prime position for anyone working in the City, and he could be recalled to London at any time – in fact he'd mentioned he'd be back for a week in September for meetings. No, he and Lily would have to find somewhere else. And anyway, if she wanted to bring her younger daughter to live with them, they'd need somewhere more suitable for a child.

The high-pitched whine of the hairdryer floated down the stairs. Soon his peace would be shattered.

Would he miss this when he was gone? Would Daphne let the children spend holidays, or the occasional weekend, with him? Could he bear it if she didn't? Would his children get on with Lily's little girl? He got up to refill his glass, and noticed that the decanter was almost empty. He'd have to make a stop at the off-licence on the way home tomorrow. No doubt Daphne would say he drank too much, but he knew his limits.

He had put out discreet feelers for new positions, but so far nothing had come of them. Perhaps he and Lily would be better leaving London and starting again somewhere new, where they would be anonymous. In truth, he didn't really care where they went, so long as they were together.

And so long as it was soon. Being apart from Lily was killing him.

46

On Friday Jack let himself into the house after work. He whistled. Caroline ran to meet him.

'What have you got, Daddy?'

He grinned and held up a dish. 'One of Nanny Wickham's apple pies.'

She wrinkled her nose. 'Did she put cloves in it?'

''Course she did. You can't have an apple pie without cloves.'

'I would,' she said. 'I don't like them.'

'Well, you can pick yours out, darling. Just don't let your mother see you poking around in your food.'

'What shouldn't I be seeing?' Lily stood in the kitchen doorway, wiping her hands on a tea towel.

'All right, love?' he asked, moving forward to kiss her.

She stepped back, turning away from him. 'Is that one of your mother's apple pies? I expect Caroline's planning on picking the cloves out.'

He laughed at Caroline's face. 'Yeah. She ain't got the taste for them just yet.'

'I'll never like them – they're horrible. Like sticks.'

'You don't have to eat any pie,' said Jack. 'More for me then.'

'But I like the rest of it,' she protested.

Lily sighed. She looked tired. 'Let's get it in the kitchen first, shall we? I've got tea cooking, and the kettle's on for a cuppa.'

'Lovely.'

Caroline lost interest and went back into the living room. He followed Lily into the kitchen and put the pie on the table. He wanted to have a cuddle, but she was bustling about again, as though she was trying to avoid him. She was always like this these days.

'I've got some more pies in the car. I told the old woman I'd take them round to Fred and Maggie.'

Lily nodded. 'Are you going now? I can keep your tea warm. It's only spag bol. I'll do your spaghetti when you get back.'

'I'll have me tea first. I'm starving. We can all pop over there later.'

Lily shook her head. 'I'm not going anywhere. I've got too much to do.'

'Like what?'

'A pile of ironing for starters.'

He waved a hand. 'Leave it, love. You've got all weekend.'

'No. I'll do it tonight.' She handed him a cup of tea. 'I'll be doing laundry again tomorrow, so there'll be more to do. I should've done this lot days ago.'

He took it. 'Come with me, love. The ironing can wait. You ain't seen Maggie in weeks.'

'Not tonight.' She shook her head.

He frowned. 'Have you and her had a falling-out?'

'Of course not,' she said, too quickly for Jack's peace of mind.

'Then having a chat for half an hour won't hurt, will it?'

'Have you told them we're coming?'

'No. But that don't matter, does it? We're family.'

Lily glared at him. 'Just because someone's related doesn't mean they can barge in at any time. If people did that to me, I'd be bloody annoyed.'

'What are you on about? We always pop in. They don't mind.'

'Well I do. We walk in there and it's a tip. Poor Maggie doesn't get any warning. And your brother does nothing to help. She must be so embarrassed. Last time I ended up doing all the washing-up for her. It looked like she hadn't sat down all day.'

Jack rolled his eyes. 'So come with me and give her a chance for a sit-down and a natter.'

'I don't want to. I'm sick of it. I can't bear to see her like that.'

'For Christ's sake, what is the matter with you?'

She turned away again, pouring herself a cuppa. 'Nothing.' He put his tea down on the table and approached her, resting his hands on her shoulders. She stiffened. She did that a lot lately. It was beginning to really annoy him.

'What's this all about?' he asked, trying to keep his voice calm. 'There's more to it than you washing up round there.'

She shrugged his hands off and turned round. 'Maybe Maggie and I don't have anything in common any more.'

He frowned. 'Don't talk daft. You've been mates all your life, and family for nigh on twenty years.'

'Granted, but look at us now. We're different. We want different things.'

'You mean you do. I ain't seen Maggie change much.'

'What do you mean by that?'

'She's got six kids. Of course the house is going to be a tip with all them running around, ain't it? It's never bothered you before, and I've never known Maggie to worry about when we turn up. No, it's you. You're getting so toffee-nosed you can't even put up with a bit of mess.'

'I didn't say that.'

'Yes, you did. Listen to yourself. That woman has been your best friend all your life, and suddenly you can't stand to go round there because she ain't got round to tidying up after a day running round after her kids.'

Lily looked away. 'You're twisting what I said. I just think it's rude of us to just go round there without giving her any warning.'

'Well ring her up then. Tell her we're coming.'

'No. I told you, I'm busy.'

He looked at her set face, trying to work out what this was all about. But it was like staring at a brick wall. She was a stranger to him these days. They lived in the same house and slept in the same bed, but she might as well have been miles away. If he touched her, she flinched. If he tried to make her laugh, it annoyed her. She was always busy. But never with him.

'It ain't just them, is it?' he said.

'What are you talking about?' She still didn't look at him. Instead she busied herself filling a saucepan with water and setting it to boil.

'What's going on with you and Bev?'

She straightened up, as though someone had stuck a poker up her arse. 'Nothing.'

'Don't give me that. I've seen how the pair of you are squaring up. If you've got a problem, have a bloody good row and get it sorted. I'm sick of treading on eggshells round the two of you. Want me to talk to her?'

She closed her eyes and shook her head. 'Just stay out of it, Jack. Promise me.'

He frowned. 'Why?'

'Because it's nothing to do with you, all right? It's... She's growing up, trying to assert herself, I suppose. Just leave her alone. She'll come round.'

He stared at her, noticing the slight tremor in her hands. No, he could see there was more to it than that. What was going on between her and Bev that she didn't want to tell him about?

'Mummy, is tea ready yet?' Caroline stood in the doorway, her latest Puffin Club book in her hand. 'I'm really hungry.'

Lily smiled at her. 'I'm just waiting for the spaghetti. Five minutes, all right?'

Caroline nodded and went back into the living room. As she opened and shut the door behind her, they got a blast of *Crackerjack*.

'I swear I don't know how that child can read and watch the television at the same time,' said Lily as she adjusted the gas under the saucepan.

Jack realised the moment had been lost. He wasn't going to get any more out of her tonight. Maybe it was for the best. If he pushed, who knows what might come out? He just wanted it to be like it used to be. But it was so long since she'd been happy, since they'd really talked and had a laugh together. They used to be a team – a united front – the pair of them against the world. But these days he felt as if he was watching his wife across a great big canyon, out of reach, impossible to understand. It was like living with a stranger. And he bloody hated it.

'Leave mine,' he said. 'I'll have something later.'

She looked at him then, startled. 'I thought you were hungry.'

'Yeah, well, I ain't now. I'm going to me brother's. I'll see you later.'

He walked out, feeling pissed off and (though he'd never admit it to anyone else) scared. She was turning her back on everything, even her best mate, and he didn't know how to stop her.

* * *

Lily sighed as Jack slammed the front door behind him. She shouldn't have been such a bitch about going to Maggie and Fred's, but she couldn't face it. Maggie had suspected long before anyone else, and now that things were so precarious, Lily wouldn't be able look her friend in the eye. What could she say?

Jack was right; she and Maggie had been lifelong friends. They'd been able to talk about anything. But not this. This was different. She longed to be able to talk to Maggie about Leo, but he was the one thing she never could reveal to her. She couldn't put Maggie in the position of having to choose between loyalty to her or to their husbands. Not that it would be much of a contest. Family came first with Maggie.

Lily felt so alone.

47

On Monday morning, Leonard stared at the letter in his hand.

Damn!

There was a soft tap on his open door. He looked up to see Lily standing in the doorway, a notepad and pencil in her hands.

'You asked to see me, Mr Warwick?'

'Yes, Lily. Come in.'

She entered and at his nod closed the door behind her.

'Is everything all right?' she asked, sitting in the chair opposite him.

'Not really, my love. Our sanctuary is about to be breached. The flat-owner is coming home. He'll be back in London by next weekend.'

'Oh no! We'll have to get our bits and pieces out and clean up.'

'Yes, I'm afraid so. It looks as though he'll be back for a while, so we'll have to look elsewhere now.'

'Where are we going to put our things? I've got a whole set of make-up, and there's our spare clothes. And the books and records we've bought each other.'

'I know. I'll buy a suitcase to put everything in and leave it at the left luggage office at the station for now. We can't take it all home without causing suspicion, and we certainly can't bring it here.'

'How long have we got?'

'Until Friday. I can sort it out after work one day before then.'

'So soon,' she sighed.

He nodded. 'I wish I could take you there now. Can you meet me there later?'

'All right. I might shed a few tears, but it will be worth it to have you to myself for a little while.'

He smiled. 'I love you so much, my darling. We'll be together soon, I promise. I've had some interest from a firm in Sussex. Near Hastings.'

'My brother lives there.' She hesitated. 'We haven't always got on, but I think he might actually be one of the few people who will understand – you know – when we leave. He left his first wife. There was an awful to-do about it, but he's very happy now, with his new woman.'

'I look forward to meeting him.'

She nodded, looking uncertain.

He reached a hand towards her, wanting to reassure her, but before he could touch her, his phone rang. He picked up the receiver. 'Yes?'

'Mr Warwick, sir, your wife's here.'

'What? Here?'

'Yes, sir. Shall I bring her through?'

He frowned. Lily raised her eyebrows, questioning. He held up a hand to stop her when she would have got up and returned to her office.

'Give me five minutes. I'm in the middle of something.'

'Very well, sir. Would you like me to bring some tea then as well?'

'Er, yes. Thank you. Five minutes.' He put the phone down.

'Leo? What is it?'

'Daphne's here.'

'Your wife?' She half-rose.

'Sit down. We've got a few minutes.'

'But what's she doing here? Has she found out?'

He shook his head. 'No, I'm sure she doesn't know.'

'Then why—?'

'I have no idea. Darling, I'm sure there's no need to panic. You go back to your office and I'll see what she wants. You don't need to see her.'

Lily nodded and stood up, clutching her notepad to her chest, her knuckles white as her grip tightened on the pencil in her hand. Leo thought she might snap it. He knew how she felt. His head was spinning. What the hell was Daphne doing here? Was something wrong with the children? No, she would have called and stayed with them. He tried to give Lily a reassuring smile.

'I'll get rid of her as soon as I can, and we'll meet at the flat as arranged, yes?'

She hesitated. 'Are you sure?'

'Absolutely. Now go, my love. Don't worry.'

She nodded again and opened the door, walking quickly to her own room.

Leonard rose as he saw his wife being escorted through the general office to his open door. She seemed happy, smiling and chatting to the receptionist. She paused at his secretary's desk, no doubt having asked to be introduced. Daphne liked to play the part of a professional wife, and would regard it as her duty to make herself known to her husband's staff. He felt his jaw tighten as the women talked, wishing he could send Daphne packing. This was his world, the one he inhabited without her. It was separate from his home and family – that was her domain.

He went and stood in the doorway. Daphne took the hint and ended her conversation with a smile before making her way towards him. She raised her chin, her eyes cool, as he kissed her cheek and led her into his office.

'Daphne. This is an unexpected surprise. What brings you to the City? Is everything all right?'

'Yes, darling. I'm meeting an old schoolfriend for some shopping this afternoon, and thought I'd come in early in the hope that we could have lunch together. It's been so long since we've had time to ourselves without the children.'

'Why didn't you say so this morning? I'm not sure I can get away.'

'It was all very last-minute. Celia rang after you'd left for the office. The poor girl needs cheering up. Her husband has run off with his secretary.'

Leonard swallowed a lump in his dry throat as Daphne sat down in the chair recently vacated by Lily and put her handbag on the desk. 'I see,' he said, his voice cracking. He coughed. 'And you decided to check up on me?'

'Oh no, darling.' She waved a hand in dismissal. 'You're nothing like Celia's philandering old goat – her description of him, not mine. I told her at the time she shouldn't have married him. He was far too old for her, and obviously had an eye for pretty girls. She wouldn't listen, of course, so now I'm going to have to help her pick up the pieces. Thank goodness they didn't have any children.'

A discreet knock heralded the arrival of tea and biscuits. 'How kind,' said Daphne. 'Thank you.'

'You're welcome, Mrs Warwick. Is there anything else I can get you?'

'Thank you, that will be all,' said Leonard, trying to maintain the impression of a professional office rather than a Lyons Coffee House.

When they were left alone again, Daphne poured the tea.

'I didn't notice the grandmother,' she said, handing him a cup and saucer and wrinkling her nose as she offered him a Rich Tea biscuit, which he declined. 'I don't blame you. I hope you offer something better to your clients.'

He put the drink down on his desk, not trusting himself to keep his hands from shaking. He hoped the poor standard of biscuits had distracted her, but it was too much to expect. Daphne rarely got side-tracked.

'Is it her day off?'

'Whose?'

'The grandmother – now what was her name – you know, darling – the woman you took to the ballet. Mrs Wickham, wasn't it? I wanted to say hello.'

'She's not here.'

'Oh, has she retired? You didn't say.'

'I'll have one of those biscuits after all,' he said, ignoring her question as he reached for the plate.

He bit into a dry biscuit, chewing it slowly, unwilling to make any further comment. He hadn't lied – not in the strictest sense. Lily wasn't *here*, in this room. And with any luck she would remain behind the closed door of her office until Daphne had left the premises.

The next ten minutes were agony. Daphne prattled on about her stupid friend and what a mess she'd made of her life. Leonard drank his tea and ate far too many biscuits, nodding and making sympathetic noises, barely listening.

'What do you think?' said Daphne.

Leonard blinked. 'About what?'

She sighed. 'You're not listening, are you?'

He bristled. 'Well, I have got rather a lot to do.' He gestured towards to the pile of files on the table beside his desk. 'And I have clients arriving in...' he looked at his watch, '...about twenty minutes.' He put down his cup again. 'I need to check some documents before they get here. Won't you be late meeting your friend?'

Daphne looked at her watch. 'I've got plenty of time.' She stood up. 'But I can see you're busy, so I'll leave you to it. Will you be home late?'

'I don't know. I'll call you later. I assume you'll be home in time to pick the children up from school?'

'No, Mrs Fanshawe very kindly agreed to collect them and give them tea with her children. I was going to get the 5.15 train. Maybe we can travel together?'

'Possibly. I'll look out for you at the station.' He stood. 'I'll see you out.'

They were almost through the general office when Lily walked out of her office with Gerald Irwin. Leonard's heart sank as Daphne pounced.

'Mr Irwin, how nice to see you again!'

Gerald looked blank for a moment.

'My wife, sir,' Leonard mumbled, aware that Lily had frozen just behind their boss.

'Ah, yes, of course!' He shook Daphne's hand. 'How are you, Mrs Warwick?'

She held on to him, putting her other hand over his in a far too-familiar fashion.

'I'm very well, thank you.' She beamed. 'I was early for a meeting with a friend, who I'm hoping to persuade to avail herself of your services.' She leaned in, whispering, 'Marital problems.'

Leonard closed his eyes. He didn't dare look at Lily. She still hadn't moved.

'So,' Daphne prattled on, 'I thought I'd pop in to see if Leonard was free for lunch. But he's far too busy, of course. It was silly of me.'

'Oh, I'm sure we can spare him for an hour.' Irwin smiled.

Leonard shook his head. 'I've got the Templeton directors coming in to go through their leases for the new office development. I'm sure Daphne can manage without me.'

'Mr Warwick, sir?' His secretary approached. 'I've just had a call to say Mr Templeton and his colleagues are going to be delayed. I've rescheduled them for three o'clock.'

'There you go, Warwick.' Irwin clapped him on the back. 'Now you can enjoy lunch with your wife.'

Daphne giggled like a schoolgirl. 'How lovely!'

Leonard felt trapped. His wife finally let go of Irwin's hand and turned to Leonard. He knew the exact moment his wife noticed his mistress standing quietly by her office door. 'Oh, I'm sorry,' she said. 'We haven't met. I'm Mrs Warwick.'

Lily's smile was strained as she took Daphne's proffered hand.

'It's nice to meet you,' she said softly.

'And you are...?' Daphne asked, smiling encouragement. She obviously thought Lily was painfully shy, whereas Daphne was full of her own importance, having been able to manipulate a senior partner into giving her husband time off to take her to lunch.

'Lily,' she said.

Daphne nodded, apparently losing interest. They would have been fine if Irwin hadn't spoken.

'Lily is our treasure,' he said. 'She and your husband are an excellent team, organising the office and keeping the finances on track.'

'Oh?' said Daphne. 'Did you replace Mrs Wickham when she retired?'

There was absolute silence for a moment. Then Irwin cleared his throat, sending Leonard a sidelong glance. 'Well. I must be off. The work won't do itself, what? Enjoy your lunch, Mrs Warwick. Lovely to see you again.'

Daphne smiled at Gerald's back as he made his escape. As she turned back, Lily was slipping through her door, seeking the sanctuary of her office. Leo caught a glimpse of her pale cheek as she turned away, and he felt an aching sense of loss. He was hardly aware of Daphne as she stared at the closing door. It wasn't until she put a hand to her throat that he realised what she was looking at: the name plate. *Mrs Lilian Wickham.*

'Daphne,' he said, not sure what else to say.

She turned and looked at him. Her smile trembled but remained in place. 'I need to powder my nose. I'll wait for you outside.'

Leonard watched as she walked away. He was torn between rushing into Lily's office to see if she was all right, and running after Daphne. She knew. He'd seen it in her face when she turned away from Lily's door. He expected to feel dread, or shame. But in truth he felt an enormous sense of relief. He didn't have to pretend any more.

He checked his jacket pocket to make sure he had his wallet, then walked slowly out of the general office to meet his wife in the reception area. The next hour was going to be difficult, but he was glad that it had come to this. Now that Daphne had seen Lily, she would understand that their marriage was over.

* * *

Lily was shaking. *Oh God, oh God, oh God! His wife!* She sat at her desk with her head in her hands, taking deep breaths, trying to calm down.

She nearly jumped out of her skin when her phone rang. She stared at it for a few moments, frozen with fear. What should she do? She was in such a state that she wanted to grab her bag and run. But even as she formed the thought, she knew that she had to pull herself together. She had to act normally, even if her whole world had been turned upside down by the sight of her lover's wife just inches away from her.

She grabbed the phone. 'Yes?' She sounded shrill to her over-sensitised ears.

'Ah, Lily.' She recognised Mr Irwin's voice. 'In all the confusion of meeting Warwick's missus, I completely forgot that you were coming with me to check the Dalrymple Trust accounts. Can you pop into my office now? I'd like to get these settled before I go to my club for lunch.'

'Yes, I'll be right there, sir.'

'Good, good.' He put the phone down without a *thank-you* or a *by-your-leave*. Lily picked up the file she'd abandoned on her desk and went to do his bidding.

* * *

Leonard waited for Daphne to make a scene, but he'd forgotten how much his wife loathed that sort of thing. Instead, they ate their meals and she carried on chattering about inconsequential things – the children's homework; her mother's latest aches and pains; whether they should buy one of those new automatic washing machines that they'd seen advertised on the television.

'It would save me so much time, darling. It takes me all day to do the laundry with that ancient twin-tub of ours.'

'Daphne—'

'I'm sure we can afford it. They offer very good hire-purchase rates.'

'Stop it. This is more important than a damned washing machine.'

'No, it's not.'

'What the hell do you mean by that?'

She looked around the crowded restaurant. 'Don't shout, Leonard. You're drawing attention to yourself.'

'I don't care,' he said, but lowered his voice nevertheless.

'You've made that perfectly clear. However, I will not have this discussion at full volume. Don't you think I've been humiliated enough for one day?' She kept a smile on her face, but her eyes were blazing with fury.

He subsided, satisfied that she was facing reality at last. 'We have to talk about this.'

'Very well,' she said, putting her knife and fork down carefully on her plate. 'Better here, I suppose, than at home where the children might hear us.' She dabbed at her thin lips with a paper napkin. 'How long has it been going on?'

'A few months.'

She closed her eyes. He waited. When she opened them she gazed past him, as though she couldn't bear to look at him. 'Does anybody else know?'

He shook his head. If she knew that Irwin suspected, it would destroy her.

'Good. Then it will be easy for you to end it, and no one will be the wiser.'

He frowned. 'I have no intention of ending it. I love Lily.'

She flinched. 'Don't. I will not have you speak that woman's name. And as for love...' Her lip curled into a sneer. 'It's sheer nonsense. What you feel for her is lust, Leonard. You can't possibly love her. And don't for one minute think I will forgive the lies you told me. A grandmother indeed! Why, she's barely any older than I am.'

'I didn't lie about that. Lily's daughter has a child.'

Daphne narrowed her eyes. 'I take it the girl doesn't have a husband. Like mother—'

He shook his head. 'Stop it. Listen to me, Daphne. Our marriage is over. Lily and I—'

She slapped her hand on the table, making the cutlery rattle on the plates. 'No, Leonard, I will not listen to this,' she hissed between clenched teeth. 'I am your wife, the mother of your children. You made me a promise. You said you would never leave me. I will not allow you to ruin my life because you've wrapped up your sordid little *affaire* in some silly, romantic notion about love.'

He sat back, looking up at the ceiling, trying to control his temper. He blew out a breath. 'I'm sorry, Daphne. I love her and I want to be with her.'

'And I suppose she's been encouraging you. Has her husband left her? Is that it? Or is one man not enough for her, so she has to steal someone else's?'

'She's going to leave him.'

'She can do as she pleases, but not with you. I will not let you go.'

He looked at her, shaking his head. She sat, stiff and proud and cold. He wondered how he had ever thought he could love her. Now that he had Lily, he found it hard to imagine what he must have been thinking when he decided to marry Daphne. The feelings he'd had for his wife were so tepid compared to the steaming heat of his love for Lily.

He looked away. Around them people came and went, enjoying a quick lunch before rushing back to work, getting on with their lives. Leonard and Daphne sat at their table, cocooned in a casing of ice, frozen in their misery, whilst life went on around them in all its colour and variety. He wanted to join the throngs, to feel the sun on his face after trying to make the best of things. He'd made a mistake. It was time to put it behind him.

'You can't stop me.'

'I can stop you seeing your children ever again,' she said.

'You can try. But I warn you, my dear, Peter and Susan will never forgive you if you do.'

'Huh! What sort of a father abandons his children for some – some floozy? It's you they'll never forgive. I'll make sure of that.'

Leonard signalled to a hovering waitress. Daphne was silent as he paid the bill. He stood up. She remained where she was.

'Go and see your friend, Daphne. I'll see you at home this evening.'

'You're coming home?'

'For now, yes. I'll sleep on the settee.'

'You will not,' she bristled. 'You will sleep in our bed with me. The children are not to know that anything is wrong.'

His immediate reaction was to tell her to go to hell. But she was right. It would confuse the children if they were to begin sleeping apart. Better that they keep the charade going until he could make a clean break.

'Very well,' he said. It wouldn't be for long. If the flat wasn't being occupied again at the end of this week, he'd have moved in there immediately. But now he needed a few days to make arrangements. He would also find a way to make the children understand. He would not tolerate Daphne turning them against him.

She reached out and grasped his arm. He was surprised to see tears in her eyes. He looked away.

'Think about what you're giving up, Leonard. Seventeen years. Until this woman came along we were happy. We can be again. I'm willing to overlook this for the sake of the children. But it has to stop. I want that woman gone. If you won't do it, I'll speak to Gerald Irwin. Think about it. I won't give up. I won't let you do this.'

He looked at her hand, saying nothing until she let go and sank back into her chair. 'I'm sorry,' he said. 'But my mind is made up.'

He left the restaurant and was halfway down the street when she called after him.

'You promised me, Leonard. You promised!'

He shook his head and carried on walking.

* * *

Lily worked doggedly, refusing to give in to the hysteria growing within her. Her guts burned with tension, but she ignored everything but the columns of figures in front of her. If she stopped, she'd fall apart, and she doubted she would ever be able to put herself back together again. She'd spend the rest of her life in a loony bin. They'd have to put her in one of those awful straitjackets to stop her tearing her hair out.

She stopped, taking a deep breath, shaking her head slightly.

This was silly. She couldn't carry on like this. Mr Irwin hadn't sacked her. He hadn't said anything. Leonard's wife didn't have a clue who she was. Nothing bad was going to happen. They would carry on, being careful, and soon they would be together and no one could do anything about it.

A knock on her closed door sent her nerves into orbit, like that bloody Apollo space rocket. The door opened and Rita the tea lady stuck her head in.

'Want a cuppa, Lily?'

She swallowed, her throat painfully dry after what seemed like hours of open-mouthed breathing, trying to settle her racing heart. She couldn't speak if her life depended on it, so she nodded and forced a smile.

'Right-o. Won't be a minute. I'll bring you a biscuit as well.' Rita shut the door behind her.

Lily took off her glasses and pinched the bridge of her nose, squeezing her eyes shut. It seemed like only seconds later when her door opened again.

'Rita, thanks.'

'Lily.' It was Leo.

She opened her eyes to find him leaning against her desk, his expression full of loving concern – and something else. She frowned. He seemed to be lit up. He looked younger, somehow. As though he didn't have a care in the world.

'Leo? What happened?' She stood up, stepping away from him, holding up a hand. 'No, on second thoughts, don't say anything. Rita's bringing me a cup of tea. She'll be back any minute. If you start telling me and she comes in, I'll go mad. I need to hear it all, but I don't want anyone else hearing that your wife is going to kill me.'

He smiled. 'Don't worry. It's all right. Now that she knows, we—'

Rita chose that moment to come in with a mug of tea and a couple of digestives on a plate.

'Here you go – oh! Mr Warwick. I thought you were out. Would you like a cup too?'

Leonard straightened up. 'No thank you. I just need to speak to Lily about tomorrow's completions.'

Rita shrugged slightly and put the drink and plate down on Lily's desk. She caught Lily's eye and winked at her before leaving the room and shutting the door behind her. Lily realised she hadn't even thanked her. The other woman must think her terribly rude, but she couldn't worry about that now.

'Leo? Did I hear you right? Your wife knows?'

'Sit down, darling, and don't panic. Yes, she knows.' He laughed. 'God, I feel liberated! We don't have to live a lie any more.'

'What did she say?'

He sobered. 'Well, she's not thrilled, of course. But she'll get used to the idea. Don't worry, my love. Daphne's not the type to make a scene. She'll rail against me in private, but it wouldn't occur to her to kick up a fuss in public. She's too aware of her social status to do anything to jeopardise it.'

'What did she say?'

He shook his head. 'Nothing much. She was intent on ignoring it until I made her face facts. I told her I love you and that I'm leaving her.'

Lily felt equal measures of excitement and fear at his words. 'You mean it then? You really do love me?'

He took her cold hands in his, and she knew that he could feel her trembling. She pulled away.

'Someone will see,' she protested.

'I don't care. Now that Daphne knows, I can tell the world that I love you.'

She sat down, sure that her legs wouldn't hold her if she tried to remain standing. 'Have you really left her?'

He shook his head. 'Not yet. I told her I would be home this evening. I want to speak to the children, and make sure she can't poison them against me.' He checked his watch. 'She's gone to see a friend – no doubt to compare notes on their bastard husbands.' He laughed.

Lily flinched. 'Dear God. I never meant to break your family up.'

He sat down, watching her. 'Lily, darling. You haven't done anything except give me the greatest happiness I've ever experienced.'

'But, Leonard, your children?'

'They'll be fine. You know how resilient they are.'

'They'll miss you.'

He nodded. 'I know, and I'll miss them. But it's not the end of the world. We went for months – years – without seeing our parents in the war, didn't we? I never saw my father again. The Luftwaffe made sure of that. But I coped. They will too. At least I'll be able to keep in touch with them.'

She was overwhelmed by how much he was prepared to give up to be with her, but her guilt over his children made her hold back. Being evacuated had been a revelation for Lily. She'd experienced things she'd never known before – living in the country with a family so different from her own large Cockney crowd had shown her that the path she took through life wasn't set in stone. It was because of this that she had taken evening classes and worked her way out of the factory. Before the war, she'd expected to be a seamstress like her mum, and she'd tried to be a good daughter and do what they wanted. Being separated from her parents and being evacuated had shown her that a different life was possible.

'But the war's over, Leonard. This isn't the same.'

'Lily, darling.' He touched her hand. 'I promise you, I will do everything in my power to make sure Peter and Susan don't suffer. If I stayed with their mother, we'd all be miserable, believe me. They'll soon see that being with you makes me happy.' He laughed. 'I'll probably be a better father because of it.'

Lily tried to smile. She loved him and wanted nothing more than to be with him. But it had all come to a head so quickly that she couldn't help but feel afraid.

'I haven't told Jack yet.'

'Do it tonight,' he urged. 'Let's get it over with.'

'But once I've told him I won't be able to stay. Where can I go? I thought we were going to get a flat or something first. What about Caroline? I can't leave her behind, Leonard. Don't ask me to.'

'Calm down, my love. I wouldn't.'

Her panic subsided a little. 'I want to tell him, but I need to get myself organised. Give me a couple of days. If it was just me, I'd walk out today, but I have to think of Caroline. I've got so much to work out.'

'Lily, it will be all right. I promise you. I'll move heaven and earth to find somewhere for us. But in the meantime, can't you both go to your parents for a few nights? I don't like the idea of you staying with him any longer.'

She didn't want to stay either. If she was going to do it, she had to get on with it.

'A couple of days, darling, I promise. Then we can be together.'

48

Jack didn't see Lily arrive home on Wednesday night. He'd taken Caroline and her friend to their dancing class in Chislehurst.

Bev met them by the front door as they came back, the baby on her hip. As soon as Kerry saw him she wriggled and whined, her arms out for her granddad. Jack smiled and took her, holding her high above his head until she giggled.

'Where's Mummy?' asked Caroline. 'I need a new dancing dress. Mrs Moy wants me to be in the synchronised dance team with Wendy, so I have to have a lilac and lemon dress with a purple cape.' She held up a packet. 'Look, I've got the pattern so Mummy can make it for me.'

'Yeah? That's good.' Bev smiled at her sister.

Jack frowned. *Blimey! What's up with her? She normally takes the Mickey out of Caroline's dancing.* 'Well, Mum's a bit busy at the minute. Let's go in the living room and you can show me, eh?'

Caroline skipped off, and straight away Bev's smile slipped. She glanced at Jack briefly, then looked away quickly.

'What you up to?' he asked.

'Nothing,' she said, still not looking at him. 'Here, let me have her.' She took the baby. 'Go and see Mum. You need to talk to her. I'll keep Caroline down here.'

'She all right?'

'No she ain't, but it ain't up to me to tell you.'

He started up the stairs.

'Dad.' Bev's voice stopped him.

'What?'

She looked as though she was going to say something, but then shook her head and looked away.

He took the rest of the stairs two at a time. Lily wasn't in their room, but there was a suitcase on the bed. He opened it. It was full of his wife's clothes. He felt his stomach tighten.

A noise drew him out onto the landing. Lily was leaving Caroline's room with another suitcase. She froze when she saw him.

'What's going on, love?' he asked.

For a moment, she didn't say anything. Then she took a deep breath and pushed past him into the bedroom. She locked the case and picked it up from the bed, then turned round towards him, put the luggage on the floor and straightened up. She didn't look at him. Instead she stared at the wall behind him.

'I'm leaving. Beverley won't come with me, but I'm taking Caroline.'

'What have I done now?' he asked, trying to laugh. She never meant it. Lily wouldn't really leave him.

'Nothing. It's not your fault. It's mine.'

'Don't be daft.' He moved towards her. She stepped back, putting her arms round herself.

'Lily, love. What's the matter? If I've pissed you off, I'm sorry. But if you don't tell me what I've done, I can't put it right, can I?'

She shook her head, turning away from him. 'Stop it, Jack. I just can't do this any more.'

'Do what?'

'Be married to you. I don't want it any more.'

'What the hell are you talking about?' He grabbed her arm and spun her round. 'Just look at me and tell me what this is all about.'

Lily closed her eyes, her breathing fast and shallow. She shook her head.

He took her by the shoulders and gave her a little shake. 'Lily. For God's sake, talk to me.'

She gasped, as if she'd been running. When she opened her eyes he could see she was trying not to cry. 'I'm sorry, Jack. I'm really sorry.'

'Aw, come here, you daft cow.' He pulled her into his arms, wanting to comfort her. 'What's got your knickers in a twist, girl?' He kissed the side of her neck.

She whimpered and pulled away. 'Don't. It's not going to work this time. I'm leaving. I want a divorce.'

He reeled back as though she'd punched him in the balls. 'No! What you talking about? We ain't getting a divorce. For Christ's sake, Lily. Tell me what I've done and I'll put it right. But don't go talking about bloody divorces.'

'You're not listening to me,' she said, her voice quiet and deadly as she spoke through clenched teeth. 'It's not you. I'm the one at fault. I don't love you, Jack, and if you really thought about it, you don't love me either. We've just played along with this farce of a marriage for so long it's become a habit.'

His legs gave way and he sat down heavily on the bed. 'No, Lil. You're wrong. I love you to bits, darlin'. You and our girls mean the world to me. I don't understand. What are you talking about?'

'I'm sorry, Jack. But I'm going.'

'Where?'

'We'll stay at Mum and Dad's for a bit.'

He frowned. *No. This ain't right. She's mine. She's my wife!*

'Why don't you go to Maggie instead? You can talk to her.' She turned on him then.

'Why would I go to your brother's house? I'm leaving you, Jack, and that includes your bloody family as well.'

'Oi, don't bloody talk like that! It ain't on.'

She shook her head. 'I don't know why I'm even trying to have a conversation with you. It's always been the same. You and your family. You being Jack the Lad. You'll never change.'

'Why should I? I'm still the same man you married.'

'That's the bloody point,' she snapped. 'I'm not the same woman you married. I've changed. I want different things. I want to travel, go to the ballet, own my own house. All you want is to go to Millwall and moan about it to your brother. You're happy to live in a council house, and if it wasn't for me taking charge we'd have all our holidays in a crappy caravan in Margate.'

'There ain't nothing wrong with that. Plenty of people are happy like that. Why do you always have to want more? It ain't like you've gone without. I work hard, and don't waste me money or nothing. Why can't you be happy with what we've got?'

A movement at the door had them both turning in that direction.

Bev stood there, her face like thunder. 'You lying bitch,' she said, her voice shaking with anger.

'Don't talk to your mother like that,' he snapped. 'What's the matter with everyone in this house today? Why don't you go downstairs and keep the girls occupied? Me and Mum have got to talk.'

'Ain't no point if she's going to tell you a pack of lies, is there?'

'What are you talking about?' He looked from his furious daughter to his wife, who stood frozen like a rabbit in headlights. 'What's she talking about?'

They stayed like that for a while. The two women glared at

each other, as though they were squaring up for a fight. But no one said anything.

'Lily? What is she talking about?' he demanded in the end.

'You tell him,' Bev told her. 'Or I will. He's entitled to know.'

'To know what?' he yelled, standing up, wanting to punch something. *Why couldn't they just say what they meant and be done with it?*

Lily took a deep breath and let it out again. 'There's someone else,' she said, her voice barely above a whisper.

His legs gave way again and he landed on the mattress, his head spinning.

'No. You're winding me up, ain't ya?' He looked from his wife to his daughter, waiting for them to burst out laughing and tell him it was a joke. But they didn't. He closed his eyes. He felt sick, and his chest hurt. 'Stop it. This ain't funny.'

'It's true, Dad.' Bev was all choked up. 'I saw her. She was so busy snogging his face off, she didn't even see me walk right past them.'

He looked up at Lily, expecting her to deny it. But she stood there, her chin in the air while her shoulders sagged. She still couldn't look at him.

'Get out, Bev,' he said.

'But—'

'Just get out and leave us alone, all right?' he yelled.

She turned and slammed the door behind her. Jack looked at Lily. She hadn't moved.

'Who is he?'

She shook her head. 'It doesn't matter.'

He stood up and went to stand toe to toe with her. She flinched, but didn't back down.

'It does to me. Who is he?'

'Why do you want to know?'

'So I can punch his lights out, why else?'

'Well that's a good reason not to tell you, then, isn't it?' She went to pick up the suitcases, but he put out a hand to stop her.

'I've got a right, Lily. You're my wife. You stood in that church and made promises. I won't let you do this.'

She looked at his hand on her arm. Her whole body was shaking, but he could see she wasn't about to back down. He wanted to shout and curse and make her stay, but for the first time he realised she meant it. He squeezed her arm. She gasped in pain, but still didn't flinch. He wanted to puke, fighting the urge to really hurt her. But he'd never raised a hand to a woman, and even though she was ripping his heart out and chucking it away like a bit of rubbish, he weren't about to start now.

Jack stepped back, letting her go. She stooped and picked up the cases and headed for the door. She had to stop and put one down to open the door. As she did so, he spoke up.

'How long, Lily?'

She looked at him over her shoulder, but didn't say anything.

'How long has it been going on?'

She picked up the case and straightened up before she shrugged. 'A few months.'

'And have you shagged him?'

'Don't be crude,' she snapped.

'Why? I ain't the one playing away, am I?'

'Look, I know you're upset—'

He laughed. 'Upset? No love, I ain't upset. I'm livid,' he snarled. 'You've been playing me for a fool, and just fed me a load of bollocks about our marriage, when the truth is you want out because you've got yourself a fancy man. You made me feel like I'd let you down, when truth be told it's you what's let me down, ain't it?'

She nodded. 'Yes, you're right. I tried to tell you it was my fault.

Now, thanks to our dear daughter, you know why. You would've found out sooner or later, I suppose, but at least I tried to spare you that.'

'Spare me? Sod off! You was trying to make yourself look good, like you always do.' He ran a hand over his face. She stayed where she was, looking at him with those beautiful eyes of hers. He felt as if he was looking at a statue of a stranger. 'Go on, run to your mother's. But this ain't over by a long chalk, Lily. I ain't giving up on our marriage, no matter what you've done.'

Her face crumpled then, but he was having none of that. 'Bugger off, Lily. I love you, girl, but right now I can't bear to look at you.'

He turned his back on her, staring at the ceiling as his eyes filled up. He didn't know how long he stayed like that. He heard Lily call Caroline, and the little girl asking if they were going on holiday again. Lily's voice was too low for him to hear her reply. Below him, in the front room he could hear the baby crying and Bev trying to shush her.

He didn't move until he heard the front door shut and Lily's car engine start up. He walked to the window and watched through the nets as his wife and youngest daughter drove away. He could see Caroline peering out of the window, looking for him. He pushed the curtain away. As soon as she spotted him, Caroline grinned and waved like mad.

He raised a hand and forced a smile until the car turned the corner and vanished from sight. Only then did Jack let the curtain fall back over the window. Only then did he give in and cry like a baby.

49

At her parents' house hours later, Lily left the upstairs landing light on for Caroline and went back downstairs. The poor kid was confused, but at the moment Lily was in no fit state to help her. She hoped a good night's sleep would make things a bit clearer in her own mind before she had to explain to the child that they weren't going back.

She paused outside the parlour and took a deep breath. She wished she could have gone to bed with Caroline, but her parents had made it quite clear they expected to have a few words once her daughter was safely out of the way.

Hoping her face looked calmer than she felt, she blew out the breath, opened the door and went in. Her father was ensconced in his usual chair by the fire, engrossed in the *Express*, like he always was. She sat at the table with her mother, accepting a fresh cup of tea.

'Thanks, Mum.'

'She go down all right?'

'Yeah. She forgot her book, so she's a bit antsy, but she's tired. She'll drop off in a minute.'

'You must have been in a rush to get out if you didn't give her time to pick up her book,' said her father from behind his newspaper.

'Yeah, well, I didn't think there was much point in hanging around.'

'What's he done?' asked her mum.

'Nothing. It's not Jack's fault.'

'Bloody hell, he's thrown you out!'

'No! For God's sake, Mum. Do you want me to tell you, or are you going to keep jumping to conclusions?'

Her father lowered his paper, but her mother got in first.

'Well, what are we supposed to think when you turn up here with your suitcases? You wouldn't do anything stupid like leave him, would you?'

Lily sighed. 'Why not? You're always moaning about him, saying I could have done better. Maybe I've come to my senses.'

'Don't talk daft, girl,' said her father. 'He's your husband.'

'And me moaning about him for twenty years never did no good before, did it? Anyway, like Dad says, he's your husband. For better or worse.'

She shook her head. 'I'm getting a divorce.'

'What?' They both spoke at once.

Lily's heart sank at their expressions. Dad looked like thunder, while Mum clutched at her chest. She looked appalled.

'I'm sorry if it's a shock, but I've left him for good.'

'You can't do that,' said her dad. 'What about the girls?'

'Beverley is staying with him. Caroline is coming with me.'

'And is he all right with all this?' asked Mum.

She lifted her chin. She didn't want to think about the look in his eyes when she'd left. She had to stay strong. 'He'll get used to it.'

'What's brought this on?' asked her father.

Lily hesitated. She had to tell them. The longer she kept her secret, the harder it would be. She looked down at her hands clasped round the teacup, holding it so tightly that she half-expected it to shatter. 'I've met someone else.'

'Oh my God.' Her mother went quite pale. Lily wondered if she was going to faint. She reached out, but her mother reared back, as though unwilling to be touched by her. Lily dropped her hand.

'I'm sorry. I know it's a shock. But I love him, and we're going to be together.'

'Who is he?'

She'd kept her secret so long, it was hard to say it out loud. But people knew now. She and Leo were going to be a real couple. He loved her enough to leave his wife and children.

She couldn't hold back a tiny thrill of excitement. No one had ever loved her enough to risk everything for her. No one but Leo. She'd just have to learn to live with the guilt.

'His name is Leonard. He's my boss.'

'Good God!' Her father shook his head. 'I knew no good would come of that fancy office job.'

'It's nothing to do with it.'

'Course it is. You wouldn't carry on like this if you was still sewing at the old place.'

'Oh, Lil.' Her mother started to cry. 'All that overtime. You lied to everyone, didn't you? What were you thinking?'

Lily felt herself shrinking, her heart breaking as she took in her father's disgust and her mother's distress. 'I'm sorry. I didn't... We tried to do the right thing, Mum. But I love him and he loves me.'

'What sort of a man carries on with another man's wife? He's not to be trusted.'

'He loves me.'

Her father sneered. 'Until the next silly floozy comes along.'

She felt her temper rise. 'Dad, it's not like that. We're getting divorces and are going to get married. Neither of us asked for this. We didn't want to hurt anyone.' She raised her hands, helpless to make them understand. 'But it happened. Now that it's out in the open, it's best to make a clean break and make a fresh start.'

Her mother sat quietly sobbing into her hanky. Her father threw his newspaper on the floor and stood up. At well over six foot, he filled the small parlour. Lily held herself rigid although her whole body wanted to shrink into a ball.

'So he's got a wife too? And kids?'

She nodded.

'So you're not only breaking up your own family, but his as well.'

'We didn't mean to—'

'Then don't.'

She shook her head. 'I'm sorry, Dad. It's too late. It's out in the open now.'

He looked at her, and she felt tears welling at the disappointment she saw in his gaze.

'Dad, please. He's not a bad man. I do love him and he really loves me. Let me bring him round to meet you. You can see for yourself.'

He shook his head.

'Please, Dad. Don't judge him until you've met him.' She turned to her mother. 'Mum?'

Her father remained silent as her mother blew her nose. Lily waited. If they wouldn't meet Leonard, they wouldn't just be rejecting him, but her as well.

'I don't know,' said her mother. 'What about Jack?'

'Oh for God's sake!' Lily snapped. 'You didn't worry about Tony's first wife when he brought his new one round, and he'd left her and their kids high and dry!'

'Don't you talk to your mother like that!'

Lily opened her mouth to scream her hurt and frustration at her dad, but caught herself. It wouldn't do any good. There'd always been one rule for her and her sisters, and another for their brother. The sod could get away with murder, and he'd still be the blue-eyed boy. But not Lily.

She leaned her elbows on the table, putting her head in her hands. 'I just want you to meet him,' she said, suddenly so weary she could hardly think straight. 'Please.' She closed her eyes. She wished Leonard was here now. She felt so alone.

'I suppose we should,' said her mum eventually. She didn't sound convinced, but it gave Lily hope.

'I'll think about it,' said her father. 'I'm going to bed.' He left the room, stomping up the stairs.

Lily finally gave in to her tears. Her mother touched her shoulder, and Lily turned and wrapped her arms around her.

'I'm sorry, Mum. I never meant to upset you,' she sobbed.

'I know, love. I just hope you know what you're doing. Jack's a good man.'

Lily nodded. He was. But that didn't mean he was the right man. Not any more.

50

The next morning, Lily and Caroline sat in the car outside the girl's school. Lily had got her up early to make sure she could get her there. She'd have to find a new school for her soon, but until they found somewhere to live it was better she carried on at Haimo Road Primary.

'Please, Mummy,' Caroline pleaded. 'I'm going to get two badges tonight. My swimming one and my hostess badge.'

'I thought you'd done those.'

'Yes, I have. That's why I'm getting the badges. Brown Owl had to order them.'

Lily shook her head. 'I'm sorry, love. We need to get to Nanny's.'

'I don't want to go to Nanny's. I want to go to Brownies.' She crossed her arms over her chest and lowered her head, pouting. 'We went to Nanny's yesterday.'

Lily sighed. 'Look, Caroline, we're going to be staying at Nanny's for a while.'

'Why?'

She looked at her watch. 'I don't have time to explain right now. I need to get to work, and you need to get into school.'

'Is it because you and Daddy had a row last night?' She frowned.

'Yes.'

'We usually go to Aunty Maggie's when you have a row. Ricky says it's so you and Aunty Maggie can moan about men.'

Lily laughed, but she didn't feel amused. 'Well, your cousin Ricky should mind his own business,' she said. 'Anyway, we're staying at Nanny and Granddad's, and that's the end of it. Wait here when you finish school and I'll pick you up.'

'Why can't I go home? I want to get my book, and I left the pattern for my new dance dress in the front room, and I need my swimming things and my school project.'

She covered her face with her hands, but Lily knew she was crying. She sighed and pulled her onto her lap to give her cuddle. Caroline was getting a bit big, and there wasn't much room in the car, but Lily felt so horrible, she needed to hold her child for a moment. Caroline buried her face in Lily's neck and cried.

'Shh, it's all right,' whispered Lily, rubbing her back. 'Don't, darling.' She kissed her hair.

'But if I don't go to Brownies, I won't get my badges, and Brown Owl will be cross because I'm Seconder and she'll make someone else Seconder if I – I'm not reliable. If I don't turn up, she won't let me help put out the toadstool next time.'

Lily took a deep breath and let it out again. 'All right,' she said. 'You can pop home and get your things and take yourself to Brownies. I'll pick you up from there, all right? Bring everything with you.'

'Can't we go home and get them after Brownies? It would be a lot to carry.'

'No.' Lily shifted her onto the seat next to her. 'Put them in your red overnight case and bring it with you. Now, we're both in danger of being late, so let's wipe your face and get you into school.' She got a hanky out of her bag and mopped up the tears. Lily held her chin. 'All right?'

Caroline nodded. Lily could see it wasn't really all right, but it was the best she could hope for.

'Now don't forget, bring everything with you. I won't have time to chase round.'

Lily kissed her and Caroline got out of the car, slamming the door behind her. Lily noticed that she didn't bother with her usual wave before running into school.

* * *

At the same time, Beverley was knocking on her parents' bedroom door.

'Dad? D'you want a cuppa?'

Jack opened his eyes and groaned. The curtains were drawn, but the morning sun was spilling through the gap. He was lying on top of the bed in yesterday's clothes, his face buried in Lily's nightdress. His head felt as if it was full of cotton wool. He blinked, and rubbed his eyes. They felt sore and puffy. He looked to Lily's side of the bed. It was empty. He closed his eyes again, wishing he could go back to sleep and forget the pain. Where was Lily?

Beverley knocked again and opened the door. 'Dad? Dad!' She nudged him. 'Here, I brought you some tea.' She put it on the bedside table. 'You'd better get a move on or you're going to be late for work.'

He rolled onto his back, rubbing his hands over his face. He needed a shave. 'Has she come back?' he asked.

'Don't be daft, Dad,' she said. 'It's only been a few hours.'

He dropped his hands and stared at the ceiling. 'Why didn't you tell me?'

She shrugged. 'She told me it was all over. Weren't no point upsetting you, was there?'

'You should've told me,' he said, still not looking at her. 'I had a right to know.'

She sat on the edge of the bed. 'I wanted to, but I was stupid enough to want to believe her, the lying cow. I can't believe she's done this.'

He didn't respond.

She put a hand on his shoulder. 'Come on, Dad, we'll be all right. We don't need her.'

He shrugged away, rolling over to the other side of the bed. 'She's my wife and your mother. Of course we need her. We love her.' It hurt like hell, but God help him, he did still love her.

'I bloody don't,' she said.

'Watch your mouth,' he snapped. 'She's your mother. I won't have you talking about her like that.'

'Why not? She's a bloody hypocrite, she is. Went all holier-than-thou when I had Kerry, didn't she? At least I wasn't shagging someone else's husband.'

He did look at her then. He sat up, his eyes blazing. 'He's married n'all?'

'I don't know, but I bet he is. Let's face it, most blokes your age are. If they ain't, they're either plug-ugly or homosexuals. He's bound to be married.'

He narrowed his eyes. Even that small movement sent pain shooting through his head. He never thought he was the type to blub. But last night he'd cried like a baby. He'd sobbed into Lily's nightdress until he'd washed away her scent from it and he'd fallen into an exhausted sleep where he carried on crying and begging her to come home.

'What's he like?'

She shrugged. 'I don't know. I never saw his face.' She thought for a minute. 'I dunno. He had dark hair, posh suit. The car was expensive. That's how I spotted them. It looked out of place.'

'Where was it?'

She told him.

'What was she doing there?'

'Dad, you don't want to know.'

He waved a hand. 'I didn't mean that, you silly mare. What was she doing in Bow when she was supposed to be at work?'

'I don't know, do I? I didn't ask.'

'Why not?'

She rolled her eyes. 'Do me a favour. I just saw me mother with another bloke. I was surprised. By the time I decided to face up to her, she'd got out of the car and jumped on a bus and he'd driven off.'

'You should've told me,' he said again.

'I know. I'm sorry, Dad. But I told her I'd seen them and she said she'd already put a stop to it. She said you would only be upset when you didn't need to be.' She stood up. 'How was I to know she was lying through her sodding teeth? How many bloody times has she said she's always hated liars?'

'All right, girl, no need to shout.' He put a hand to his throbbing head. *Christ, what a mess! What the hell was he going to do?*

Bev closed her eyes. 'Sorry, Dad.' Her shoulders slumped, and she looked dead miserable. 'I just can't believe she did it.' Wailing from her bedroom warned that Kerry was awake, but Bev didn't move. 'What are you going to do?' she asked him. 'If you don't get a move on, you'll be late for work.'

'I ain't going in,' he said. 'I can't be doing with any of it.'

'Want me to ring them? I'll say you're ill.'

'Do what you like. I don't care.'

'Dad, don't be like that. You can't lose your job.'

'It don't matter. Nothing matters.'

'Well, thanks a lot,' she said, hands on hips. 'At least I know where me and Kerry stand. We don't matter.'

'I didn't mean it like that. I've got to talk to Lil. Get her to see sense.'

'Why would you want her back? She's played you for a fool.'

'I know. But she's still me wife. I ain't letting her just walk away from twenty years of marriage. There ain't going to be no divorce. The sooner she realises that and comes home, the better.'

Beverley shook her head. The expression on her face was hard and cold. 'You're mad. Let her go. We don't need her.'

'I do, Bev. And I know you think you don't, but you do n'all.'

She snorted. The volume from her bedroom was rising. Any minute now Kerry would fling herself out of the cot.

'Well, good luck with that. But as far as I'm concerned, she can sod off and never come back.'

Jack sighed. 'Go and see to the baby. I need a wash and shave, then I'm going to ring your mum. She'll be back. I'll make sure of it.'

'Won't you be late for work?' Daphne eyed Leonard suspiciously as he sat calmly at the breakfast table the next day. 'They haven't found out and sacked you, have they?'

Leonard shook his head. 'Why would they do that? I'm an asset to them.'

'Maybe,' she said. 'But I sincerely hope they won't continue to employ that woman. I won't be happy until she's gone from our lives.'

Leonard clenched his jaw to prevent the words he wanted to say from spilling out. Just a little longer...

He glanced at his watch. 'In answer to your question, I've a meeting with a client at his offices. I'll be on my way shortly.'

She picked up her handbag. 'Right. I'm taking the children to school. Will you be here when I get back?'

'No.'

She went into the hall and called the children. Peter and Susan ran down the stairs, looking so sweet and innocent in their school uniforms. He stood up and followed her, bending down to kiss and hug them, ignoring Daphne, who stood, stiff and uncompromising by the open door.

'Goodbye, my darlings. Be good,' he said.

As they left, he took an envelope out of his jacket pocket and placed it on the kitchen table, then loaded his suitcases into the car and drove away. His hands were shaking on the steering wheel. He had no idea where he would stay tonight. If that meant sleeping in his car for a night or two until they found somewhere, so be it. But Lily should be at her parents' with her daughter Caroline. If she had found the courage to walk away from her marriage, the least he could do was the same. If she'd not left her husband yet, he hoped and prayed she would do so now that he'd taken this leap of faith.

He had an appointment to view some offices in Battle next week. If they were suitable, he and Lily could resign and move immediately. The sooner they were out of London the better.

He felt a leaden lump of guilt settle in his stomach as he thought about Peter and Susan. He would make it up to them. As soon as he and Lily were settled, he would have them come for a weekend. He hoped they would get on with Caroline.

As he drove closer to the offices of Alder & Powney, his mood lifted and his thoughts were filled with Lily and their new life together.

51

'I've done it,' Leonard told Lily. 'I've left.'

Lily felt light-headed with relief. 'So have I.'

Now they were both free. All right, so they weren't out of the woods yet – they still had to find somewhere to live and sort out their divorces – but they'd both taken that first, frightening step of breaking away from their marriages. The hard bit was over.

She wanted to run to him and feel his arms around her, but she didn't dare. Instead, she stood to one side of his desk, notepad and pencil in hand, while he sat there, smiling, his eyes shining.

'It feels marvellous. I had no idea how liberating it would be, stacking my suitcases in the car and driving away.'

'What did she say?'

He shrugged. 'Nothing. She refused to talk about it. In the end I had to resort to leaving her a note.'

She frowned. 'Oh dear. What if she makes a fuss? We could still lose our jobs.'

He shook his head. 'Don't worry, darling. She wouldn't dream of doing that. No, she'll maintain her dignity at all costs. When the news finally reaches her circle, she'll play the wronged wife elegantly.'

'Leonard, don't. I feel sorry for the poor woman. She must be devastated.'

'She'll be less concerned about missing me than about how it will affect her status,' he said. 'Honestly, Lily. How could I not love you? Here you are worrying about my wife when she'd cut you dead in a heartbeat.'

She shrugged. 'I wouldn't blame her for that. She can't be all bad. After all, you married her.'

'I suppose so,' he sighed. 'But over the years she's become more and more like her mother.' He shuddered. 'They say you should look at the mother before committing to the daughter, don't they?'

'Well, you'll get your chance to look at mine tonight. I'd better warn you, though, neither of my parents are happy about this. It's not going to be easy.'

'I'm sure it will be fine. They're just worried about you. I'll do my best to reassure them. I only want to make you happy.'

'I know,' she said, her smile a little strained. 'It will be all right, won't it, Leonard? I mean, I'm not exactly what your friends will be expecting – an East End girl who used to work in a factory.'

'They'll love you. Not that I care what anyone thinks.'

'But I'm not like what you're used to. I left school at fourteen, I don't read the newspapers – mind you, the only one that came into our house was the *Racing Times* so that Jack could study the form. I wouldn't be surprised if some of your friends own the horses he's been betting on.'

He shook his head. 'I don't move in such exalted circles, Lily. I'm a simple man.'

'Who knows Latin and Shakespeare,' she muttered. 'I'm going to show you up; I know I will.'

He laughed. 'Never. Look, you must try to stop worrying. You are a bright, beautiful woman. They'll be charmed. They won't be able to help themselves.'

She didn't look convinced. 'Have we done the right thing, Leo?'

'Of course we have. It's difficult right now, but everyone will adjust. I can't wait to get on with the rest of our lives together, my love.'

'Me too.' She closed her notebook. 'But in the meantime, we both have work to do. I just wanted to see you.'

'You're right. What's the plan for this evening?'

She sighed. 'It's a bit tricky. I was going to see if I could leave early to pick Caroline up from school, but she got herself in a tizzy about missing Brownies. I've told her she can pop home and get her things, and I'll pick her up from the church hall when Brownies is finished. I left my car at my parents' so I'll need to go and get it first.'

'Instead of doing that, why don't we meet at the café in Bishopsgate for an early supper, then head over to Eltham in my car? What time are your parents expecting us?'

'I'll ring Mum and tell her we'll be there after we've picked up Caroline.'

'Good. I'm looking forward to meeting them.'

She nodded and headed back to her office. Leonard was taking this all in his stride, which was just as well because she was a bag of nerves. One minute she was so excited that she wanted to dance, and the next she was filled with such dread that she couldn't think straight. They *had* done the right thing. *They loved each other.* That was all that mattered, wasn't it?

She just hoped that Jack was all right. She couldn't simply dismiss the twenty years they'd been together. She knew he was hurting right now. But if he thought about it, she was doing them both a favour. They'd grown apart. They wanted different things. Once he accepted that, she was sure he'd find himself someone who would suit him better. He deserved to be happy, and Lily wasn't the woman who could make him happy any more.

52

Jack came downstairs an hour later. He'd washed and changed his clothes, but he didn't feel like himself. He felt old and grey, as though his life was over but his body hadn't got the message yet.

He ignored the baby in her high chair, making a mess of herself with Weetabix.

'All right, Dad?' asked Bev, her voice soft, as though he was sick or something. After a quick glance he looked away. He couldn't bear to see the pity in her eyes. 'Do you want some breakfast?'

'Nah. I'm all right. You get off to work.'

'I ain't leaving you like this. I've called in. Told 'em I've been throwing up all night. I rung your place, n'all. Told them the same thing. Said it must have been something we ate.'

'Don't be daft. I'm all right. I don't need a baby-sitter.'

'No? Well prove it and eat something. You missed your tea last night. You've gotta eat.'

He shook his head. 'Leave it. I said I'm all right. I just need to talk to her.'

'She's probably at work.'

'With him. It's gotta be someone at work, ain't it? I knew she should've given up that job. It ain't for the likes of her. She don't belong there. She belongs here, with us.'

'Dad, don't. She ain't worth it.'

He sighed. 'She is to me.' He sat at the table, holding his head in his hands. 'I just don't understand it. I've done me best to make her happy.' He looked up, his eyes feverish. 'We've done all right, ain't we? We've got a nice house and a lovely family. I've tried to give her everything she wanted.'

'She's an ungrateful bitch,' she said, sitting opposite him, reaching across and touching his cheek. 'Dad, it ain't your fault. It's hers.'

He turned his head away. 'She said she loves him.'

'She don't know what she's talking about, Dad.'

'No?' He looked at her then, and he knew she could see the despair on his face. 'But if she really believes that, I ain't got a chance, have I?'

'We'll be all right, Dad. You'll see. I'll bet she'll come crawling back in a couple of days.'

Jack stood up. 'I've got to talk to her.' He went out into the hall and dialled Lily's office number. A couple of minutes later, he came back in, slumping down on the chair. 'I couldn't get through. They said she was busy and she'd ring me back. That's bollocks! I always get put straight through. What's she playing at?'

'Leave it, Dad.'

He stood up. 'I'm going round there.'

'Don't be stupid! If you do that and embarrass her, you won't get nowhere, will you?'

'She's with him. That's what's keeping her busy!' His hands formed fists. 'I'm going to have him. See if I don't.'

Kerry chose that moment to start whining. Bev looked torn. Her daughter was reaching out, wanting to be picked up. She laid a hand on the baby's head but she kept her concentration on Jack.

She looked ready to burst into tears. Jack felt that n'all, but more than that, he wanted to smash something. Or someone – preferably the bastard who was stealing his wife from him.

'Dad, listen to me. You need to calm down. If you go in there and thump him, you'll end up in the nick and Mum won't never talk to you.'

He stared at her, breathing like he'd run the four-minute mile, feeling like he was ready for the fight of his life. The baby let out a shriek and banged her hands on the high chair tray. Her breakfast bowl went flying, landing upside down on the lino. Neither of them took any notice.

'She's *my* wife. Mine.'

'I know. And God knows why you want to keep it that way, but if you go there now, you'll just make it worse.'

Kerry was crying, wriggling to be let out. Bev went to pick her up, but then stopped.

'Look, I really need the loo, Dad. If don't go now I'll wet meself. Will you sort the baby out? She'd rather have her granddad than me, anyway.'

'What?' He looked round, as though he was coming out of a trance. When he saw the state Kerry was in, all covered in cereal and tears, it seemed to bring him to his senses. 'Yeah. You go. I'll sort her out.'

Bev ran upstairs, Jack picked up the baby. She cuddled into his arms and he felt a wave of love roll over him, bringing more tears to his eyes. He couldn't believe Lily would walk away from little Kerry or one of her own daughters. Thinking of little Caroline, of some other man taking his place and bringing her up, he wanted to howl in pain. He couldn't let his Caroline go. No. Lily weren't taking her. He wouldn't let her. His arms tightened around the baby, who squirmed and started to cry again.

Taking a deep breath, Jack made himself relax, loosening his grip on the child. 'It's all right, my little darlin'. Granddad's here.' He kissed her cheek, not caring that it was crusty with Weetabix. 'Don't you worry, my angel. I'm gonna go and get Nanny and Auntie Caroline and bring 'em back home. That's it. Everyone's coming home and we're all going to be all right. I promise.'

53

'Daddy!' Caroline called out as she opened the front door.

Jack had been slumped on a chair at the kitchen table. At the sound of her voice he stood up, his chair scraping on the floor. Then she was there in the doorway, and he scooped her up in a big bear hug. She giggled and wrapped her arms round his neck. Beverley stood in the living room doorway. Kerry was trying to push through her legs to toddle towards them.

'Where've you been, Princess?' he asked. His voice sounded hoarse, his throat was sore, but he was so bloody happy to see her he was ready to weep again. He buried his face in her hair, fighting the tears. He didn't want to upset her.

'To school, silly!'

'No, last night.'

'We went to Nanny's. Didn't Mummy tell you?'

'Oh, yeah. 'Course she did. I forgot. Where's Mum now?'

'She's at work. She's going to pick me up from Brownies.'

She leaned back and looked at him. 'Daddy, are you poorly?'

He shook his head, but didn't smile. 'I missed you,' he said, his voice barely a whisper.

'I missed you, too,' she said, kissing him and patting his cheek, like he did when she was upset. 'What's for tea?'

'What would you like, my angel?'

'Can I have fish fingers and chips?'

'For you, anything.' He squeezed her tight and she giggled.

Beverley blew her nose and went back into the living room. 'Has Beverley got a cold?' Caroline asked. 'Nanny said she'll catch her death of cold with all those short skirts she wears.'

Jack laughed. He couldn't help it. He was so happy.

His baby was back. 'Nah, she's all right. Don't you worry.'

Kerry was pulling on Caroline's leg, demanding to be picked up too. Jack laughed again and scooped her up. Kerry gave them both slobbery kisses as he carried them into the kitchen.

54

Outside the church hall, Jack didn't notice Lily at first; he was too busy looking for her car. He hadn't expected her to bring *him* with her.

Lily got out of the estate car and stood on the pavement as the girls came pouring out of Brownies. Just as she spotted Caroline and waved, her fancy man got out of the driver's side and came round to stand with Lily. Jack recognised him. Her boss! *Jesus Christ! All that overtime. All them nights when she came home too tired to even look at me, she'd been opening her legs for him.* He felt the rage growing within him. *I'll kill him.*

Jack saw Caroline stop running, suddenly looking shy. She obviously hadn't been expecting the fancy man. Jack had tried to get her to tell him everything she knew, but it was obvious she didn't know anything about the other fella. That had been some comfort, at least. But now here he was, large as life, and Lily was ushering Caroline into the back seat of his car, talking to her, telling her God knows what lies.

Jack stepped out of the shadows, determined to stop them taking his daughter away.

'Dad.' Beverley appeared next to him, her sleeping baby bundled up in the pushchair, grabbing his arm tightly.

He tried to shake her off, but she hung on. 'Don't, Dad. Not here. There's too many people around. We don't want strangers knowing our business. I spoke to Nan. They're going there. She don't like it any more than we do. Go there. Nan and Granddad'll back you up.'

'She's got no right, bringing him here. Who the hell does he think he is?'

They watched as the estate car drove away. Bev finally let go of him. 'Do you want us to come with you?'

'No. Get the baby to bed.'

'All right. But don't get your hopes up, eh? And don't do anything stupid.'

* * *

Lily and Leonard were shown into the front parlour, the room reserved for visitors, while Caroline watched the telly in the room next door. Lily's mum had used her best tea set and put biscuits on a plate – Bourbons and custard creams – but none of them were hungry. Lily's father sat in one armchair, glowering. Mum had been to the hairdressers and had a blue rinse. She was perching on the edge of her seat, dressed up in her Sunday best.

Lily sat beside Leo on the sofa. She felt the warmth of his leg against hers and longed to reach out and hold his hand and rest her head on his shoulder, but her father's stern expression stopped her.

Leo cleared his throat. 'I'm very pleased to meet you. Lily has told me a lot about you.'

Her father grunted. 'She told us nothing about you.'

'I'm sure you understand, Leonard,' her mum said. 'This is all a bit of shock. I mean, Lily and Jack have been married for nearly twenty years. And there's the girls to think of.'

Leo nodded. Lily didn't dare look at him. 'I quite understand. We really didn't intend for any of this to happen.' He gestured with his hands.

Lily nodded too. 'We tried not to,' she said. 'But we couldn't help it. It just happened.'

Her father grunted again and muttered under his breath.

'I can assure you,' Leo tried again. 'I love Lily with all my heart, and I would never do anything to hurt her. As she said, we neither of us took this lightly, but...' He shrugged, helplessly. 'We just can't deny our feelings any longer. We want to be together. I know you're not happy about the situation at the moment, but I swear that I'm going to devote my life to making your daughter happy.'

The doorbell went. From the other room, Caroline yelled, 'I'll get it!' None of the adults moved as they heard her running down the passageway and opening the door.

'Daddy!'

Lily gasped. Leo reached over and took her hand. 'It's all right,' he whispered. 'Stay calm.'

She could hear Jack's low voice and Caroline's happy responses. The child had been quiet since they'd picked her up from Brownies. Lily's heart broke as she realised how pleased her daughter was to see her father. She squeezed Leo's hand, drawing strength from his presence.

The door opened and Jack stood there holding Caroline's hand. The child beamed. 'Look Mummy, Daddy's here. Can we go home now?'

Lily's father stood up. 'Not yet, love. Come and help Nan make some more tea while they have a chat.' He looked at Lily and Leonard, daring them to disagree.

Lily nodded, and her parents ushered Caroline out and closed the door behind them.

Leo stood. She got up too, and they stood side by side, facing Jack. She moved closer to Leo, holding on to his arm. She was shaking, but he was calm. She clung to him. He patted her arm, comforting her. She saw Jack notice the gesture and his jaw tightened.

'Get your hands off my wife,' he said, his voice low and deadly.

'Jack,' she said, not knowing what to say. He ignored her.

Leo held out his hand towards her husband. 'I'm sorry. I know this is difficult,' he said.

'Difficult, is it?' Jack stepped forward, grabbing Leo's hand and swinging him round, pulling him away from her, and slammed him against the wall. 'There, that weren't difficult at all, was it?'

'Stop it, Jack!' she cried.

'You stay out of this. I want a little chat with the man who's been sleeping with my wife.'

'It's all right, Lily.' Leo's voice remained calm, even as Jack held him pinned to the wall with his forearm across Leo's throat. 'Let's just all talk about this, eh?'

'I'll talk, you listen, you bastard. Keep your hands off my wife. You stay away from her and my daughter, you hear? Or I swear I'll kill you.'

'Jack!'

He turned to glare at her. 'Shut up!'

'No, I won't. You leave him alone, or so help me I'll never speak to you again!' She stepped forward to pull him off, but he swung his free arm and knocked her back onto the sofa. She cried out as Leo took advantage of his distraction to push Jack away and punch him in the gut.

All hell broke loose. Lily screamed as the two men fought,

knocking over her mother's best furniture. She screamed with every new blow.

The door slammed open and her father ran in, his face red and furious. He grabbed Leo just as he was going down, pulling him out of Jack's reach.

'Enough!' he roared, shoving Leo behind him as Jack went for him again. Rather than hit his father-in-law, Jack pulled back, his fist raised.

'What the hell d'you think you're doing?' roared her father. 'This is my house, not a bloody boxing ring.'

Both men were gasping for breath. Jack wiped blood from the side of his mouth.

'I'm sorry, Ken, but do you know what this bastard's been doing with Lily?'

'I know, son. But if you want to fight, you take it outside. I won't have this under my roof.'

'You shouldn't have come, Jack,' Lily snapped. 'You've got no business here. Not any more.'

* * *

Jack turned to see Lily clinging to her fancy man, using her hanky to pat away the blood streaming from his nose. Bile rose up Jack's throat, along with his rage.

'Don't touch him.'

'I'll do what I like.'

He would've gone for the pair of them, but a movement out of the corner of his eye stopped him.

'Daddy?' Caroline stood with her nan, peering round the old woman's skirts.

'Your father's just leaving,' said Lily's dad.

Jack closed his eyes. 'She's my wife.'

'I know, son, and believe me, we're not happy about what she's doing. But I want you out. I won't have brawling in my house. You're out of order.'

Jack let out a long breath. He couldn't bear to look at Lily and that bastard. 'Caroline,' he said. 'Get your things, darling. We're going home.'

Lily moved like lightning. She ran to Caroline and grabbed her, pulling her close. 'You're not taking her.'

He went to the child and knelt before her. She clung to her mum.

'Come on, darling,' he said. 'You want to come home, don't you?'

She looked at him with big, frightened eyes.

'No, she doesn't,' said Lily. 'She wants to stay with me.'

'Shut up,' he snapped. 'I'm talking to my daughter, not you.'

'She's mine too.'

He raised his head to look at Lily. For the first time in his life, he felt utter hatred. 'I said, shut up.'

Lily lifted her chin. He could see her shaking. Good, the bitch should be frightened. He turned back to Caroline, pasting a smile on his face. He felt his cut lip pull, but he ignored the pain.

'It's up to you, darling,' he said, trying to keep his voice light and his breathing even. 'Do you want to go with me, or with that man?' He pointed at the bastard who had caused all this, never taking his eyes off Caroline.

She looked at the other fella and back at him, then up at her mum.

'Well, darling?' Jack reached out a hand and stroked her cheek. 'Shall we go home?'

Caroline's bottom lip wobbled as she turned her head and buried her face in her mother's skirt.

'There's your answer,' said Lily. 'She wants to be with her mother.'

55

Caroline lay under a blanket on the back seat of Leo's car, crying quietly as they drove through the dark streets. Lily knew she was trying to pretend she wasn't, but she could hear tell-tale sniffles. It was a heartbreaking sound, bringing Lily to the edge of tears too. She felt so damned guilty, yet it had been Jack who had reduced everything to a sordid brawl in her parents' house. She should be spitting mad at him, showing her up like that. Yet the memory of his shattered face when her dad had told him to go would haunt her for the rest of her days.

Leo drove in silence, concentrating on the road. His nose had stopped bleeding. She hoped to God it wasn't broken. She'd been so frightened. If her dad hadn't stopped them, she was sure Jack would have killed Leo. She stifled a sob, bringing her hand up to cover her mouth in an effort to stop it from escaping.

Leo turned to look at her. He held out a hand and she took it, clinging to him, but as they pulled up at a red light, she had to let him go so that he could change gear.

'It's all right, darling. Don't worry.'

She glanced over her shoulder. Caroline was still under the

blanket. 'I'm so sorry,' she said, keeping her voice low so that she didn't disturb her daughter. 'I can't believe he did that.'

'In all fairness, I hit him first,' he said softly. 'I just couldn't let him treat you like that. I'm only sorry I seem to have caused trouble for you with your parents.'

She shook her head. 'I should never have taken you there. We should've waited. Once we're settled we'll try again.'

'I'm happy to apologise,' he said. 'Do you think they'll forgive me?'

She was quiet for a moment, staring out into the evening traffic, not seeing anything. 'Well, it might take a while. But if they don't, that's their loss. I'm with you now. They accept us as a couple, or...' She shook her head. 'Where are we going now?'

'Not sure. I just started driving. I wanted to get you away from there. I suppose we should look for a hotel. Shall we try the West End?'

'Won't that be expensive? I mean, we don't know how long we'll have to stay, do we?'

'Let's just find somewhere for tonight, and we can worry about where we go from there in the morning.'

'All right.'

'Try not to worry, my love. It's going to be all right.'

'I know. I just wish—'

'Shhh. We must look on the bright side. We'll get to spend tonight in each other's arms. I'd have gladly taken a few more punches to achieve that.'

She laughed. 'Well, thank God you didn't have to. Oh, look, there's a hotel. Why don't we try there?'

Leo pulled up at the kerb. He turned to her. 'Am I presentable?' he asked.

She peered at him. They'd managed to wipe the worst of the

blood from his face, although there was some swelling on his jawline.

'I think so. It's difficult to tell in this light.'

He shrugged. 'Oh well. I'll live, I'm sure. You wait here and I'll go and see if they've got a couple of rooms.'

She nodded and watched as he got out of the car and walked towards the hotel entrance. Caroline was silent now. Lily twisted round to see if she was asleep, but didn't want to disturb her by pulling the blanket away to see her face. She turned back and closed her eyes.

She jumped when Leo opened the door and got back into the car.

'No room at the inn, I'm afraid. It's still peak season, apparently. The place is full of American tourists.'

It was the same story at the next hotel, and three more they tried, before someone told Leo they had vacancies at one of their outlying hotels.

'It's at Blackheath. D'you know it?' he asked Lily as he drove across the river into South London.

'Yes. On the heath,' she said. 'It's a bit close to home. Caroline was born not far from there.'

'Do you want to try somewhere else?'

She shook her head. 'No, it's all right. It's getting late. We can't drive round all night.'

Caroline roused when they stopped. As she got out of the car she looked around. 'This is Blackheath, isn't it, Mummy?' she asked. 'There's the pond where me and Daddy sailed a boat.'

'That's right, sweetheart. We're going to stay here in the hotel tonight. It's like being on holiday, isn't it?' Lily smiled.

Caroline held on to Lily's hand as they walked into the hotel lobby behind Leo. He approached the desk and spoke to the woman there.

'All right, darling?' said Lily. 'Tired?' Caroline nodded. 'Leo's just checking to see if they've got any rooms for us in this hotel.'

'I want to go home.'

Lily sighed. 'I'm sorry, sweetheart. Not tonight.'

'...two rooms,' Leo said.

'Certainly, Sir. And the name is?'

'Warwick.'

'Mummy,' Caroline whispered. 'That's not our name.'

'Shh!' Lily squeezed her hand but didn't look at her. She smiled at the receptionist, hoping she hadn't heard what her daughter had said.

Keys were handed over, and Caroline followed them upstairs. They stopped at the first room and opened the door. There was a double bed in there.

'You go in. I'll see you in a minute,' said Lily, taking the other key from Leo.

'You're sure? The single room is three doors down. Do you want me to—?'

Lily shook her head. 'No, it's all right. She's tired. She'll be asleep in a few minutes.' She looked at him and wanted to kiss his swollen jaw. 'I be back soon and we can talk.'

* * *

Leo nodded. He looked at the little girl. She stared up at him with suspicion. She hadn't said a word to him. It was clearly going to be a while before she accepted the situation. But that was all right. They had time. He could wait. So long as he had Lily, he could weather anything.

'Goodnight, Caroline.' He smiled.

She didn't respond until Lily said her name quietly. ''Night,' she said, looking down at the carpet.

Lily sent him an apologetic look and took the child down the corridor. Leo closed the door and leaned against it with a sigh. He was dog-tired and his face felt sore. He touched his nose tentatively, not wanting to start it bleeding again. He didn't think it was broken, but it hurt like hell. He moved his jaw from side to side, grateful he hadn't lost any teeth. Jack Wickham knew how to throw a punch.

* * *

Lily used the key Leo had given her and opened the door further along the corridor. Inside was a single bed.

'Right, let's get you to bed,' she said. 'We won't bother with unpacking. I can't be bothered to go all the way down to the car to get our bags. We're only here for the night. Just sleep in your vest and knickers, all right?'

Caroline didn't say anything as Lily helped her to get undressed.

'In you get now. Don't worry about your teeth. It won't hurt for one night.'

She slipped into bed. Lily tucked her in tight and sat on the edge of the bed to kiss her.

'Aren't you coming to bed, Mummy?' she asked.

'Yes, I'm going now, sweetheart. You remember where the other room is if you need me, don't you? I'll be there, just down the hall.'

'But that man's in there,' she said.

Lily sighed. 'That's right, I'll be there with him.'

'But he's not my daddy.'

Lily took a deep breath. She was exhausted and just wanted to crawl into bed and let sleep wash away everything that had happened at her parents' house. *It's all such a bloody mess!* But it wasn't Caroline's fault. The poor child was the innocent in all of this.

'I know,' she said, gently. 'But, well, the truth is, I've left your father. Daddy and I aren't going to be together any more. We're getting a divorce and I'm going to marry Leo.'

Caroline stared up at her mother, her eyes filling with tears. 'I don't want you to marry that man. I want my daddy.'

Lily closed her eyes. 'I'm sorry, darling. You'll see your daddy, I promise. I'd never keep you from him. I know how much you love him and he loves you. But we're not going to live with him any more. He'll still be your daddy, though. You know that, don't you?' She kissed her cheek.

'But Mummy, what if Daddy's angry with me because I've come with that man instead of going home with him? He might not want me any more.'

'Oh, darling, don't cry. Of course your daddy wants you. He's not angry with you. He loves you so much.'

'I don't like that man,' she whispered. 'Please can we go home to Daddy?'

Lily shook her head, trying hard not to let her own tears fall. 'Please give it a chance, Caroline. Leo wants us to live together in a lovely house by the seaside. Won't that be nice? He's left his own little girl at home just so he can be with you and me. I'm sure once you get used to him you'll see he's a very nice man.'

Caroline's bottom lip trembled as she tried to stem her tears. Lily got her hankie out of the purse on her Brownie belt and handed it to her. She kissed her forehead.

'Now get some sleep, there's a good girl. It's very late. We're just down the corridor, room number ten. I'll see you in the morning, and everything will be all right, I promise.'

Lily left the bedside lamp on so that Caroline wouldn't get scared if she woke up in the night, and quietly closed the door behind her. Outside, she waited for a moment, listening to her daughter's quiet sobs. She was torn. Should she go back in and stay with her until she fell asleep? Or would that make it worse? The sooner Caroline got used to Lily being with Leo, the sooner she would adapt. Lily wiped away her silent tears and took a calming breath before walking down the corridor to the room where Leo was waiting.

She'd never in her wildest dreams imagined it would be so painful. She hoped to God everyone would forgive her one day.

56

When Jack let himself back into the house, Bev and the baby had gone to bed. The place felt cold and empty. He'd lost them. Lily and Caroline. Everything was ruined.

In the kitchen, he opened a bottle of gin and drank straight from it. The first mouthful burned its way down his throat, and he coughed, fighting against the urge to gag. He hated gin, but it was the only booze in the house. He took a couple of bottles of pills from the cupboard. Lily's headache tablets and some aspirin – that was all they had. He tipped them out onto the kitchen table and sat down.

With the next slug of gin, he swallowed a handful of pills. And the next. He kept going until all the pills and booze were gone.

He waited, just wanting to die. What did he have to live for? He slumped in his seat, resting his head on his arms. He felt awful, but he could still feel, so it wasn't working, was it? He sat up. He was getting pissed off now. Why hadn't he passed out yet? When was he going to die? That'd show her. She thought he was a lightweight; she'd never understood how much he loved her, just 'cause he liked a laugh. He wanted to make her happy, that was all. No one should be serious all the time; life was too bloody short.

He laughed. That was right, life *was* too bloody short now.

He was topping himself. He'd had enough.

'Why ain't this working?' he shouted.

He got up and stumbled to the cutlery drawer. He opened it and pulled out a knife and pulled it across his wrist. It barely made an impression.

'For Christ's sake!' He rummaged through the drawer, pulling out the knife sharpener. It took him a couple of attempts to fit the knife against the sharpener. 'Too sodding pissed,' he muttered, as he slowly and carefully sharpened the blade.

Eventually he was satisfied. 'There you go, you bugger.' He tried again, this time splattering blood all over the counter. He tried to put the knife into his other hand to do the other wrist, but he dropped it. As he grabbed for it he knocked against the open drawer and it fell with a crash onto the floor. Woozy, Jack fell too, knocking the kitchen table back against the wall. The empty gin bottle rolled off and smashed onto the floor beside him.

He was barely conscious when Beverley opened the door and screamed.

'Sorry, love,' he whispered. 'Made a mess.'

57

'What the hell happened to you?'

Fred stood by his brother's hospital bed. Jack raised his left hand so his brother could see the bandage.

'Couldn't get the knife sharp enough,' he said. His voice was raspy, his throat sore. They'd pumped his stomach last night, making him gag and puke 'til he thought he'd turned his guts inside out.

'You stupid sod. What you do that for? You frightened the life out of poor Bev. She rung us in a right state.'

Jack shrugged and looked away. 'She'll be all right.'

'Yeah, but what about you? Why d'you go and something like that? For Christ's sake, Jack, they could lock you up in the loony bin.'

'Don't be daft.'

'Me? That's a laugh. I ain't the one who tried to top meself.' Fred leaned over him, forcing Jack to look at him. 'Why, Jack? If you'd done it, it would've killed our mother.'

'Sod off. She'll be all right.'

'You reckon? You're her baby. You'll break her heart, mate.' He shook his head and sat down, resting his forearms on the bed. 'Why didn't you talk to me?'

Jack shrugged. 'Weren't no point. She's gone. Taken Caroline and buggered off with her boss. She ain't coming back, Fred. Reckons she loves him.' He swiped at the tears running down the side of his face. 'I've lost her, Fred. I can't do this without her. She's me life.'

Fred patted his shoulder. 'Here, don't, mate. You'll make yourself ill. We'll sort it out. Don't you worry.'

'You ain't listening to me,' he shouted. 'She's gone! I ain't good enough for her no more. There ain't nothing left, Fred.'

'What about the girls?'

'They'd be better off without me. Everyone will.'

'Don't talk so stupid,' Fred yelled back. 'You're their dad, and worth a dozen of her, the slag. If you top yourself, you're letting her and her fancy man win, ain't you?' He punched Jack on the shoulder. 'It ain't you what should be in here, it's them. Make them pay!'

Jack's head was still throbbing from the gin and the puking, and he couldn't be doing with Fred going on at him. He lashed out with his good arm, catching his brother on the side of his head.

A nurse pulled back the curtain around the bed. 'What on earth are you doing? If you don't stop this noise at once, I'll get the porters to remove your visitor. This is a hospital, not a public house.'

Fred looked shamefaced. 'Sorry, Nurse.'

She looked down her nose at him, then she turned and went back the way she'd come, shutting the curtains behind her with a swish.

The brothers looked at each other. Jack turned away first.

He was just so tired.

'I don't know how to put it right, Fred. What the hell can I do?'

Fred tutted and leaned in, holding Jack's face in his big docker's hands. 'You can stop taking it out on me, you bastard, and think! If you're going to punch anyone, punch him. He deserves it, messing about with a man's wife. Who does he think he is?'

'I already did. I got him right in his face. Would've done more if me father-in-law hadn't pulled me off him.'

'Good on ya, mate. He deserved it. Old Ken should've lumped him one n'all.'

Jack couldn't stop a laugh bubbling up from his belly. 'He picked the sod up by the scruff of his neck. I swear he lifted him clean off his feet.'

'Good. I reckon hanging's too good for the bastard.'

Jack felt the smile slip off his face. 'It don't matter, though, does it? He's got my Lil. And Caroline. Christ, Fred, I just want to die.' The tears fell again, and he couldn't help it. His whole body was shaking from great racking sobs.

His brother sat on the bed and pulled Jack into a bear hug, holding him while his heart broke.

* * *

At the same time, Caroline was eating breakfast with her mother and Leonard in the hotel dining room.

'Guess what, sweetheart,' said Lily. 'We're going to the seaside to see Uncle Tony for the weekend!' She smiled, trying to look full of the joys of spring, when in fact she was sick with nerves.

Caroline shrugged. The child looked as if she'd lost her spark. Even the selection of individual cereal boxes in the hotel breakfast room did nothing to persuade her to smile. Normally she would have been squealing with excitement.

'Can Daddy come?'

Lily caught her breath, guilt lashing at her gut. She swallowed, sending a worried glance towards Leo. He raised his eyebrows and took a sip of his tea.

'Not today. Perhaps he'll take you another time.'

The child sighed. 'Will you ask him?'

Lily frowned. 'You can ask him yourself, can't you?'

Caroline shook her head. 'I don't think Daddy likes me any more.'

Lily reached for her, pulling her onto her lap. 'Don't be silly. Of course Daddy likes you. He loves you.'

The child looked at her with big, wounded eyes. 'I want my daddy,' she said, and buried her face into Lily's neck.

Lily looked at Leo, guilt making her feel quite faint. He reached over and stroked her arm. She gave him a shaky smile. *It will be all right. It has to be.* Gathering her child close, she rocked her, stroking her hair.

'It's all right, darling, don't worry. We were all a bit frightened last night. Everyone was angry, but that doesn't mean we love you any less. Of course Daddy loves you. Don't you ever doubt that. He was just cross with me, not you.'

'And Granddad chucked us out,' she sobbed into Lily's neck. 'I didn't like it when Granddad shouted. And Nanny cried.' She was gasping and weeping now, and all Lily could do was hold her and try not to cry herself.

What had she been thinking, leaving Caroline alone all night? She'd obviously been festering about all this and getting herself into a right state. Lily closed her eyes, pain filling her head and chest. She'd been so anxious to spend time with Leo, to feel his arms around her, to lie beside him in bed and let him comfort her, that she'd forgotten how confusing this must all be for her own sweet child. *Dear God!* How could she have been so blind and selfish?

'Look, the waiter's coming with some nice warm toast,' she

said, kissing her cheek. 'Let's pop to the ladies' and wipe your face, shall we? Then you can pick out one of those lovely little jam pots to go on it.'

Caroline's whole body juddered as she took a breath before she loosened her grip on Lily's neck. She didn't look round, but slipped off her mother's lap and stood, head bowed. Lily sent a helpless look towards Leo, who gave her an encouraging smile. She knew he was trying to reassure her, but it didn't make her feel any better.

'We won't be a minute,' she said, standing and taking Caroline's hand.

Leonard watched them weave their way through the tables towards the lavatories. The waiter deposited a rack of toast and assured him their cooked breakfasts would be with them shortly.

'Thank you. There's no rush.'

'Is your daughter unwell, sir?'

'What? Oh, no. She's fine. Just tired, I think.'

'Very well, sir.' The waiter finally moved on.

Leonard sat back and sighed. This wasn't how he'd expected it to be. He rubbed the side of his nose. Thank God it wasn't bruised, although his jaw still ached. He had an almighty bruise on his arm where he'd managed to block one of Wickham's punches, and another on his stomach where he hadn't.

He supposed he shouldn't have been surprised by the man's violence. But taking a few blows was a small price to pay for winning Lily. Hopefully by now Wickham would have had a chance to ponder his actions, and that would be the end of it. With luck, he'd feel sufficiently ashamed of his behaviour to let the divorce go through without contesting it. In fact, Leo smiled to himself, the fight had given them ammunition to use in court if need be – the fellow obviously had violent tendencies.

He topped up his teacup from the pot, wondering how long Lily would be. The child had been quite distressed. All normal, he supposed. He could imagine his Susan acting like this in the circumstances. For a moment, he had an overwhelming urge to see his own children. God knows what Daphne had told them by now. But he couldn't allow himself to worry about that now. *What's done is done. The children will be fine,* he thought. *They'll learn to adjust. We all have to.*

He took a piece of toast from the rack, spreading it with butter and marmalade. He wished Lily would come back, but he didn't begrudge the child some time alone with her mother. Last night he'd fully expected Lily to return to their room and tell him she had to stay with her daughter, but she hadn't. She'd come to him and kissed his wounds. She'd clung to him, letting him know that he was the only man she wanted, even when he was battered and bruised and had brought the wrath of her own father down upon her.

As soon as they'd eaten and checked out, they would head out of London. Lily had made an early morning call to her brother in Hastings and he'd offered them refuge for the weekend. He would understand what they were going through, having been through a divorce himself.

Leonard bit into the toast, enjoying the bitter tang of the marmalade on his tongue. *It would be all right. It had to be.*

58

An hour after they arrived at Tony's house in Hastings, the phone rang. Lily's brother answered.

'Hallo, darling, how are you?' he said. There was a pause. 'All right, love,' he went on. 'Don't get your knickers in a twist. I'll get her.'

He called Lily and handed her the phone. 'It's Bev.' She took the phone and waited until her brother had gone back into the living room before she spoke.

'Beverley? How did you know where I was?'

'Nan told me. She said Uncle Tony told her.'

'Oh.' Her brother hadn't mentioned that. 'Are you all right? What do you want?'

'You've got to come home. Dad's in hospital.'

She sighed. 'What's he done now?'

'It wasn't his fault, it was yours.'

'What are you talking about?'

'You did it. You nearly killed him.'

'Beverley, you're not making sense. Now, stop messing about and tell me what this is all about.'

'He took pills, and – and he slashed his wrist.'

Lily gasped, putting a hand to her throat. 'I don't believe you. That's a horrible thing to say.'

'He did! I found him. There was blood everywhere and it's your sodding fault! You've got to come home. He needs you.'

'Don't be ridiculous. He wouldn't do something like that. You must have misunderstood. It must have been an accident.'

'I'm telling you, it was no accident. He had a bottle of gin and all your pills and then he... he cut his wrist. I'm not kidding.'

Lily felt sick. She couldn't believe it. Jack wouldn't, would he? He never took anything seriously. It must have been staged. A big, sick joke, aimed at making her feel bad enough to go back. Well, she wasn't having any of it. It was hard enough without all this.

'I'm sorry, Beverley. I think you're exaggerating this to get me to come home. Did he put you up to it?'

'No he bloody didn't. He's in the hospital. He nearly died. And it's because of you, what you've done to him. It's your fault.'

'Don't you dare blame this on me,' Lily snapped. 'Your father needs to grow up. What was he thinking? This won't solve the problem.'

'*What was he thinking?* What do you think? You've buggered off with your fancy man and taken Caroline. You've broke his heart. He weren't thinking right. He was in such a state he didn't see the point of going on. He tried to top himself! What's the matter with you? He's your husband.'

'Not for much longer, he isn't. And if he carries on with this ridiculous behaviour, he'll make it that much easier for me.'

'You're unbelievable, you are. Why are you being so nasty? He loves you.'

Lily sighed. She didn't know what else to say.

'Mum, please. Come home. I can't cope with this on me own. I'm frightened he'll try again.'

Should she? Could she? She closed her eyes and remembered the anger and hatred on Jack's face. She knew deep down that Beverley was right. *It was her fault.* But that didn't mean that rushing to his bedside would make it all right. She still wanted a divorce. She still wanted to be with Leo. She and Jack were finished. There was no going back.

'I'm sorry, Beverley. I can't. Talk to Uncle Fred and Aunt Maggie. I'm sure all the Wickhams will be round and they'll help you. But I can't. It's too late.'

'Uncle Fred's already at the hospital. For God's sake, Mum, they pumped Dad's stomach out!'

'Well, that's the best place for him, and Fred will sort him out. Maybe a few days there will give him a chance to calm down and see sense. But seeing me won't help. I'm not about to change my mind.'

'Well good riddance to you, you old cow! If he dies, I ain't never going to forgive you. I hope you and your poxy fancy man can live with what you've done.'

'For God's sake, calm down!'

'Don't you tell me what to do! Not ever! You're a bitch and I hope you drop dead! Dad's worth ten of you!' She slammed the phone down.

Lily sank onto the stairs, staring at the phone receiver in her hand. She could hear the low hum of the dialling tone as the force of her daughter's anger continued to vibrate through her whole body.

59

Beverley had just finished giving Kerry her tea when she heard the key in the front door and Jack walked in.

'Dad, what are you doing here?' Beverley stood in the hallway, the baby on her hip. 'They said you'd be in for a few days.'

'I'm all right, don't fuss.' He shut the front door behind him and walked past her into the kitchen. He sat heavily at the table. 'Put the kettle on, girl. I'm parched.'

She put Kerry down and went to make some tea. The baby toddled over to her granddad, holding out her arms. Jack patted her head, but didn't pick her up. The baby started whining and tried to climb on his lap. In the end he pushed his chair back to give her some room and let her.

'Why didn't you ring and say they were sending you home? Did you get Uncle Fred to pick you up?'

'No. I wanted to come home, so I got dressed and found a cab.'

'So they don't know you've gone?'

'Yeah, they do. The sodding ward sister got arsy and told the porters to get me back to bed, but they didn't have the balls to try.'

He shrugged. 'I wanted to come home, so I did.' He looked around. 'Thanks for tidying up, love. Is your mum home?'

Bev shook her head. 'Not yet, Dad,' she said.

'Nah, I didn't think she would be,' he said.

60

By Sunday, Leo began to relax. After the strain of the past few days, Lily's brother's attitude was like a breath of fresh air.

'Don't worry about Mum and Dad,' said Tony. 'They'll moan – any excuse, you know? But they'll come round in the end. You should've heard them going on when Lily wanted to marry Jack. They didn't like him, thought he was right common. They did everything they could to talk her out of it.' He laughed at his expression. 'I know, you wouldn't believe, would you? Now they reckon he's the best thing since sliced bread, and you and Lil are getting it in the neck. It won't last. They'll be all right.'

'I hope so,' said Leo. 'I don't want Lily upset. She was terribly distressed when her father sent us away.'

'Trust me, I had the same with them when I left my first missus. Dad shouted for a bit. Mum cried. But once they know you're serious, they come round. I reckon it'll be easier for Lily, seeing as I done it first.'

'Uncle Tony, can I have a drink?'

Caroline had come into the kitchen where they were talking. Lily and her sister-in-law were upstairs doing something with their hair, and the child had been in the lounge, watching her uncle's colour television.

Leo smiled at her, but as usual got no response whatsoever. *Oh, well. At least she's silent in her disapproval. I couldn't have borne it if the child had been a whiner.*

"Course you can, sweetheart,' said Tony, springing into action and opening the fridge. 'What do you fancy? Lemonade?'

'Yes please,' she said.

She waited by the door. She didn't smile, or look around.

She was the same age as Peter, but she stood there like a little old woman. His son would have been bouncing around, asking questions, wanting to touch things. From what Lily said, Caroline was normally full of beans. But all Leonard had seen had been this quiet little wraith, who would burst into tears at the slightest excuse.

Tony found a glass and filled it with pop. 'There you go, Princess.'

'Thank you,' she said, taking it in two hands. She took a couple of sips so that it wasn't over-full before turning and leaving the room.

Leonard sighed. He hadn't realised he'd been holding his breath until she left.

'How's she taking it?' asked Tony, pointing in the direction his niece had gone.

'Not well,' said Leonard. 'She acts as though I don't exist.'

'Yeah, my kids are still like that with us.' Tony nodded. 'Mind you, they don't see much of us; their mother sees to that. The oldest boy's all right. He came to Spain with me and Jack when I was racing a few months back.'

Leo nodded. He remembered it well. The memory of that magical weekend made him smile.

'Caroline'll get used to you,' Tony went on, apparently not noticing. 'She's a good kid. Don't you worry.'

'I hope so,' he said. 'I'm also hoping she'll get on with my children when we get the chance to introduce them.'

That might take a while. It all depended on Daphne.

61

At six o'clock the next morning, Jack sat at the kitchen table, a cold mug of Nescafé in his hands. He hadn't slept. He hadn't even bothered to go to bed; he couldn't face going into their bedroom. He couldn't remember the last time he'd had any rest. His body ached, but his mind wouldn't stop. All he could think about was her and what she was doing with her boss.

Fred was right. He'd been stupid, trying to top himself. He glanced at the bandage on his wrist in disgust. What had he been thinking? Why should he just roll over and leave her free and clear after what she'd done to him?

He'd give her one more chance. If she came home now, he'd do his best to forgive her and they could get back to normal. It wouldn't be easy, but they would manage. They couldn't throw away twenty years just like that.

But if she didn't, she would have to pay. And so would he. Oh, yes. Definitely. Whatever else happened, he was going to nail that bastard good and proper.

Bev wandered in, yawning, with the baby on her hip. 'Morning,' she said. 'Any tea in the pot?'

He shook his head. She put the baby in her high chair and gave her a Rich Tea biscuit to keep her quiet for a bit. The baby looked at him, wary. Jack realised he'd hardly taken any notice of her these past couple of days. He felt guilty. It wasn't her fault, the poor little bugger.

He got up and picked Kerry up gave her a hug. She squealed and pushed him away, leaning over towards her high chair, wanting to get back in there. Jack felt himself welling up. He put her back and patted her head. It wasn't the baby's fault. It was Lily's. She'd ruined everything.

'Don't worry, Dad. You know she's like that with everyone when she wants her food. She'll be ready for a cuddle as soon as she's eaten. You know she will.'

He looked at Bev. He'd forgotten she was there. He felt as though he was moving through thick fog. He wished he could wake up from this nightmare.

'Yeah, I know,' he said. 'I forgot.'

Bev nodded. 'You'll be all right, Dad. It's just been a shock, that's all.'

He nodded and sat down again.

'D'you want a fresh one?' Bev asked, pointing at his mug. 'No.' He got up. 'I've got to go out.'

'You going to work?'

'No. I'm going to see your mother.'

Bev frowned. 'Don't, Dad. Leave it a few days, eh?'

'I've got to talk to her.'

'It won't do no good.'

'How do you know?'

'I just know, all right?' She looked shifty.

'What ain't you telling me?'

She shook her head. 'Nothing.'

'Bollocks! You're a useless liar, so you might as well tell me.'

'I need the loo,' she said, running out of the room and up the stairs. 'Watch the baby,' she yelled from the landing before slamming the bathroom door.

Jack sighed and gave the baby another biscuit. She grinned at him, forgiving him anything for a biscuit, her mouth already caked with crumbs. He gave her another pat and tried to smile, but couldn't.

This can't go on.

He opened the cutlery drawer. The knife he'd used to cut himself had been cleaned and put back in its place. He picked it up and closed the drawer. He heard the loo flush upstairs. With the knife in his hand he went out into the hall and took his jacket off the peg. He put it on and slipped the knife into the inside pocket.

Bev came down the stairs. 'Dad, please don't go.'

'What ain't you telling me?'

She sighed, rubbing her eyes. 'You won't like it.'

'Just tell me.'

'All right,' she snapped. 'I rung her when you was in the hospital. I told her what you'd done and said you'd nearly died. First she said she didn't believe me, then she said you needed to grow up.'

Jack felt as if he'd been punched in the gut. 'She said that?'

Bev nodded. 'I asked her to come and she wouldn't. She's a bloody cow and she ain't worth all this grief, Dad. Leave her alone. We don't need her.'

He reached for the door. She ran after him, but he shook her off.

'Dad, come back! Please, Dad!'

He raised a hand, looking at her. She didn't deserve all this. Neither did Caroline or the baby. Lily and that bastard would have to pay.

'Stay here,' he told her. 'Don't go out, you hear? I need you to stay at home.'

He got in the car and drove away.

* * *

Jack sat in the car outside the offices of Alder & Powney, waiting. At about half past eight a bloke in a suit arrived. Jack followed him in and stopped him at the lift.

'Excuse me, sir, are you from Alders?'

The bloke looked round, surprised. 'Yes, I'm Gerald Irwin, one of the partners. May I help you?'

'I'm Lily's husband.'

He smiled. 'Ah, Mr Wickham. How nice to meet you. Isn't Lily with you?'

Jack shook his head. 'They haven't told you then?'

'Told me what?'

'That bloke she works for – Warwick. She's left me for him, and taken our daughter.'

That wiped the smile off Irwin's face. He looked round, checking if anyone was listening. 'I think we should continue this conversation in my office, Mr Wickham.' He pressed the call button for the lift. The doors opened, and he gestured for Jack to enter. 'Shall we?'

'I appreciate your wish to speak to your wife, Mr Wickham,' said Irwin after Jack had poured his guts out. The lawyer was talking slowly, as though he was having to choose his words carefully. 'But I can't force her to do so. I can merely let her know that you've been here and would like to talk to her. If she's willing, I'm happy for you to use my office in order to have a private conversation.'

'She's got to talk to me,' said Jack.

'Actually, she doesn't have to do anything. It has to be her choice. If she doesn't want to see you, I'm afraid that will be that. I can't force her to do something she doesn't want to.'

'Why not? It's one of your staff what's seduced her and stolen her from me.'

'I can assure you, Mr Wickham, we take a very dim view of this kind of behaviour. That being said, I still can't force your wife to speak to you if she doesn't want to.'

'You're protecting him, ain't you? I should've known. Your sort always stick together.'

'Not at all.'

'Yes you do. I see it every day.' He put his head in his hands. *They'd never let him see her. She was one of them now.* 'I can't compete with the likes of you.'

'Mr Wickham, please calm yourself. I assure you, I will speak to Lily and ask her to talk with you. No one is trying to prevent you from speaking to your wife.'

'Nearly twenty years we've been married. Twenty years. I've been a good husband. I've never let her down. Two lovely girls, we've got. I never thought something like this would happen. I mean, I love her. She's mine. Why would she do this?'

Irwin cleared his throat. 'I'm very sorry, Mr Wickham. I will speak to Lily at the first opportunity. Now, why don't you go home, and I'll call you as soon as I can?'

Jack looked at him. He seemed straight up, but he wasn't giving much away. Jack nodded and stood up. Irwin walked him back to the lift and waited until the doors were closing.

'I'll be in touch. Now go home – there's a good chap.'

* * *

An hour later, Jack was still outside, sitting in the car and watching people arrive. Everyone except those two. He looked at his watch. Maybe they'd taken Caroline to school first. But then again, maybe they'd arrived while he was talking to Mr Irwin.

'Sod this,' he said, reaching for the door handle. Then he saw them.

Caroline was with them, clinging to Lily's hand as they went up the steps to the building entrance. The fancy man was on the other side of Lily, his hand on the middle of her back. Jack wanted to run after them and break the bugger's arm. *Who does he think he is, touching my wife? MY WIFE?* Only the worry that he'd frighten Caroline again stopped him from going after them and finishing what he'd started the other night.

He watched as they went into the building. He waited five minutes, then got out and followed them.

62

In the lift, Lily squeezed Caroline's hand. 'Now remember what I said. If anyone asks, they've had to shut your school for a few days because the roof's leaking.'

'But Mummy, that's a lie. You said I mustn't lie.'

Lily closed her eyes. She was right. She supposed it was a testament to her influence over her child that Caroline didn't want to lie.

'I know, sweetheart,' she said, getting impatient as the lift approached their floor. 'But we don't want people to know our private business, do we? Just tell them what I told you. It'll save a lot of bother.'

'Why can't I go to school?'

'Because we didn't have time to get you there,' she snapped. 'And I thought you liked coming to work with me.' The lift stopped. 'Now just do as you're told and don't show me up.'

Caroline subsided. Lily felt even more guilt gnaw at her insides.

'I'm sorry, love. Look, we'll have a nice lunch and see if we can get you a new book later. All right?'

Caroline nodded, but didn't light up like she usually did when treats were offered.

Lily looked helplessly at Leo. He smiled and mouthed, '*It'll be fine,*' over the child's head. Lily smiled back, even as she felt shaky and out of sorts. Being with Leo was what mattered. Everything else would work itself out. She just felt so bloody sad that it had to cause so much hurt and anger first.

They left the lift and entered the offices. Leo held the door for them, but didn't touch her once they were on the premises. Lily nodded at the receptionist, who was busy with a client.

She ushered Caroline through into the general office. Gerald Irwin was there, talking to Leo's secretary.

'Ah, Warwick. Can I have a word?'

'Yes of course,' said Leonard. He headed for his office, but Irwin stopped him.

'My office would be best, I think.'

Leonard nodded and changed direction. Irwin turned to Lily and Caroline.

'And what have we here? A new member of staff?' he said, smiling at Caroline.

The child stood silently by her mother. Lily forced a laugh. 'Yes, I'm sorry, Mr Irwin, but there are problems with the roof at Caroline's school. I'll keep her out of the way. She's got some books and colouring pencils, so she won't be a bother to anyone.'

'Good, good.' He nodded and patted Caroline on the head as he spoke to Lily. 'When you've got her settled, could you join us in my office?'

She felt her heart sink. Although he was smiling and keeping his tone light, she could tell by the look in his eyes that he wasn't happy. *What does he know?*

'Shall we say ten minutes?'

She swallowed hard and nodded, trying to keep her expression calm. 'Yes, sir.'

'Excellent.' He turned and marched after Leo.

Lily took Caroline into her office and closed the door.

* * *

In his office, Irwin didn't waste any time on pleasantries. 'Lily's husband has been here, after your blood.'

'Ah. You know, then.'

'All I know, Warwick, is that I had to deal with a distraught husband who claims you have seduced his wife and stolen his child. Given that you arrived here a few moments ago with said wife and child, I assume he is correct.'

'Yes. Lily has left her husband to be with me, and she brought the child with her.'

'I see. And what of your own wife and children?'

Leonard didn't say anything. What was the point?

Irwin frowned. 'This does not reflect well on the firm at all. What were you thinking, man?'

'It has nothing to do with the firm,' he said, trying to keep his temper.

'I beg to differ. You've clearly been conducting an illicit affair on our premises. And now you've compounded your sins by leaving your own family in favour of another man's wife. If he makes a fuss, the Law Society will have your guts for garters. You'll never work in the profession again.'

'It hasn't affected our work.'

'That's not the point and you know it. There are standards of professional conduct to be adhered to. For God's sake, don't you see? You could lose everything for the sake of an ill-advised romance.'

Leo felt the anger drain out of him. He even managed a lopsided smile. 'It might be ill-advised, but we both think it's worth the risk. You see, we love each other. Everything else...' He held out his hands, unable to explain. 'None of it matters.'

Irwin stared at him, shock and confusion etched on his face. 'It's that serious, eh?'

'Yes.'

He sighed and shook his head. 'Well, God help you. Just try to keep it quiet, or we'll all be for it.'

Leonard nodded, relief flooding him. *It will be all right. I have Lily, and we're going to work it all out.*

There was a knock at the door. 'Enter.'

Lily came in, her usual notepad and pencil in her hands, and stood uncertainly by the door.

'Lily, come in,' said Irwin. 'Warwick's told me what's going on.'

She looked worried. Leo stood and held out a hand to her. She gave him a brief smile and touched it before sitting down next to him and focussing on their boss.

'I'm sorry, sir,' she said.

'Yes, well, it's a bit late for that now. Your husband was here earlier. He wants to talk to you.'

Lily went pale. She glanced at Leo. He put a hand on her shoulder, wanting to reassure her.

'You don't have to,' he said, his voice low.

'I'd rather not,' she said, looking at Irwin. 'The last time I saw him he got rather violent.'

'He hit you?' he asked.

'No, not me.' She looked at Leo.

'Ah. Well, you can hardly blame him for that. Any husband would do the same in the circumstances.'

She looked down at her hands, clasped tightly round her

notepad. 'I suppose so,' she whispered. 'But I still don't think talking to him will do any good.'

Irwin was silent for a minute or two, watching them.

Neither moved. Eventually he sighed. 'Look, I can't force you to do anything you don't want to, Lily. But the man's in a great deal of distress. I think it would be the decent thing to do, to at least give him a few minutes of your time. If the meeting takes place here, you'll be in a safe place. You've nothing to be afraid of.'

Leo wanted to argue. The damned brute had said all he wanted to with his fists the other night. But as he opened his mouth to speak, Irwin sent him a warning glance and shook his head.

Lily knew Mr Irwin was right, even though she didn't want to hear it. She needed to talk to Jack, but she was being a bloody coward. He couldn't do anything to her here. Not that he would anyway. He would shout and bluff, but he'd never lay a hand on a woman. Jack wasn't like that. Never had been, never would be, no matter how angry he was with her. She was more worried about everyone hearing him effing and blinding when he realised that talking wasn't going to make any difference.

She wasn't going back, and the sooner she could make him see that, the better. They could get on with their lives. Once he calmed down and got used to the idea, they should be able to get on – if only for Caroline's sake.

'It's not his fault,' she said. 'I just don't love him any more. I'm not the same woman he married. I've changed, and he hasn't. I can't go back to him, even if I wasn't with Leo.'

Irwin raised his eyebrows at her shortening of her lover's name. 'You must do what you think best, Lily,' he said. 'But I think you know that it will be better dealt with swiftly, rather than keep the poor man hanging on.'

'Yes. I will talk to him soon. But I don't think I can cope with him today. I'm still in a bit of a state.'

'Well, you need to let him know.' He looked at his watch. 'Now I suggest we all get some work done.'

They got up and headed for the door.

'Oh, and try to be discreet about all this, please. We don't want the whole office to know what's going on. There'll be time to fill people in when you've worked out what you're going to do.'

'Yes, of course,' said Leo, guiding Lily out into the corridor with a hand at her back.

'Are you all right?' he asked her.

Lily nodded. 'It's just all so bloody at the moment. Jack's making it seem so sordid.' She shivered.

'We must stay strong, my love. You don't have to talk to him if you don't want to. Irwin's just hot air.'

'I know, but I probably should. You know – clear the air. We're the ones at fault, Leo, not Jack.'

But Jack was certainly to blame for his abominable behaviour at Lily's parents' house.

'Well, to my mind, the way he spoke to you has negated any consideration he might have been due. I refuse to accept that falling in love is a "fault." However, whatever you decide to do, I'll be here for you, my darling.'

'I know. Now, let's go and do some work, before we end up jobless as well as homeless!'

Lily went back to her office and sat at her desk. Caroline was in her visitor's chair, reading *The Lion, the Witch and the Wardrobe*.

'Mummy, your phone has been ringing,' she said.

'You didn't answer it, did you?'

'No. You said I wasn't allowed.'

'Good girl.'

'I could have taken a message.'

'No, you couldn't. You're not supposed to be here, remember? Don't worry, someone on reception would have dealt with it.'

'Okay.' She sighed. 'Mummy, can we go home today?'

Lily got up and came round her desk. She picked Caroline up off the chair and sat down again with her on her lap.

'I'm sorry, darling, but we're not going back there. We're going to find somewhere nice to live, with Leo.'

'But I want my daddy. I don't like that man.'

'Oh, Caroline, please. I'll try to arrange for you to see Daddy soon, I promise. But you've got to give Leo a chance.'

'Why can't that man go back to his little girl?' She pouted. 'I want *my* daddy...'

Lily rested her forehead against Caroline's. 'I'm sorry,' she said. 'When you're older, you'll understand.'

'I don't want to wait till I'm older. I want to understand now. Why can't we go home to Daddy?'

Lily wiped a stray tear from her daughter's cheek. 'Don't cry, sweetheart. It will be all right, I promise.'

Caroline looked as though she wanted to argue, but then someone knocked at the door. Lily got up and put her daughter down into her warm seat. Caroline looked round when the door opened and she squealed with delight.

'Daddy!' She flung herself out of the chair, and looked as though she would run to him, but then stopped. Leo came and stood behind Jack. Lily felt her throat tighten with fear.

'Jack. What are you doing here?'

'I want to talk to you.'

'I'm working. You need to go. We can talk later.'

'It won't take long.' He looked over his shoulder at Leo. 'You can sod off. I ain't got nothing to say to you.'

Leo shook his head 'You're on my turf now, Wickham. I'm not leaving Lily alone with you.'

Jack clenched his fists, but at that moment Irwin arrived. 'Ah, Mr Wickham,' he said. 'I see you've found Lily. Can I suggest we adjourn to my office where we can have some privacy?'

'Mr Irwin, I'm sorry—' Lily began.

He held up a hand. 'Don't worry, my dear. Best to get this sorted out before it takes up any more of our working time.'

After a moment's hesitation, Lily nodded. Jack nodded too. They started to go out of the room, so Caroline jumped up to follow them. Irwin turned round and looked at her.

'Stay here for now; there's a good girl. Your parents need a little chat.'

Jack looked at her, then dropped down onto his knees and opened his arms. Caroline ran to him and he held her tight. He kissed her and looked at her. Caroline touched his cheek.

'I love you, Daddy,' she whispered. 'Can we go home now?'

He sat back on his heels and held her face in his hands. 'I love you too, Princess. You know that, don't you?'

She nodded and he kissed her forehead. 'You wait here.'

'But I want to come with you.'

'This won't take long, my dear,' said Mr Irwin. She looked at her mother.

'You can see Daddy in a minute, all right?' said Lily. 'Now stay here and be a good girl.'

The child watched them until Mr Irwin closed the door, leaving her alone.

* * *

'We don't need no guards,' said Jack. 'I just want to talk to my wife.'

Lily stood by the desk, her arms crossed, not looking at him.

She didn't look like his Lily. She was a stranger. A stranger who had shagged the wanker standing next to her, who was now looking down on him just because his suit weren't from Savile Row and he didn't talk posh.

'That's as may be, but it's up to Lily, not you,' said the bastard.

Jack wanted to punch his head in. And he would. But he would talk to Lily first. Give her a chance to put things right.

'Bugger off. This is between me and my wife.'

The other fella, the one he'd seen earlier, stood by the door. Before the fancy man could take a swing at Jack, Irwin stepped forward. Like the toffee-nosed coward he was, the fancy man backed down, too scared to show himself up in front of the boss.

Jack was a bit disappointed. He'd have enjoyed sorting him out, and if he'd thrown the first punch, Jack would have had to defend himself. If it meant breaking every bone in the tosser's body, that was just bad luck, weren't it?

Lily took a shaky breath. He could see she was scared.

Good. She should be. She should be bloody ashamed. 'Jack, what do you want?'

'Tell them to go.'

She shook her head. 'Anything you want to say to me, you can say it in front of them. Mr Irwin knows what's going on.'

'Yeah?' Jack turned to look at him. 'How long have you known about this? Seems like I was the last to know.'

'I'm afraid that the injured spouse usually is,' said Irwin. 'Now, can I suggest we all sit down and try to be civilised?' He pointed to the big table by the window. There were about a dozen chairs around it, and there were leather blotters at each place, as if it was ready for a board meeting. Lily moved round so that her back was to the window. Jack followed her, almost treading on the fancy man as he elbowed him out of the way.

'I'll sit with my wife, if you don't mind.' He didn't give a toss if he did mind.

The fancy man looked annoyed, but backed off and sat opposite, next to the boss. Out of the corner of his eye, Jack saw Lily give him a smile, as though she was saying, *'Don't worry, we'll get rid of the bugger in a minute.'*

Well, they weren't getting rid of him that easily. He sat down next to Lily and turned his chair so he faced her. He ignored the other bastards.

She waited, not looking him in the eye. 'Lily,' he said.

'What?'

'Come home. I miss you.'

She swallowed and welled up. 'I'm sorry, Jack, but I'm not going back.'

'Why not?'

The fancy man leaned forward. 'Because she loves me,' he said.

Quick as you like, Jack reached across the table and had him by his scrawny neck. 'Shut. Up,' he said, their faces so close he could smell the bastard's fear. He shoved him back in his seat and let go. The pathetic sod sat there, gasping for breath, holding his throat. Jack ignored him and turned back to Lily.

'Why not?' he asked again.

Lily had her hands at her own throat. She looked at him as though she'd never seen him before. 'You know why,' she said.

'If it's because of him, forget it. If you come home now, we won't say no more about it.'

She shook her head. 'Jack, stop this, please. Our marriage has been over for a long time, and you know it. There's no point pretending any more.'

She didn't mean it. 'You don't have to say that just because they're here.' He waved a hand in the direction of the lawyers.

'Don't be embarrassed, darling. You made a mistake. You just need to admit it and come home, and we'll sort it out.'

'It won't work.'

'Course it will, sweetheart. I love you.'

She looked away.

This weren't right. 'Lily. Look at me.'

She shook her head.

He pushed his chair back. She flinched.

'Steady on,' said Irwin.

Jack ignored him. 'Did you see me just now, out there, with Caroline?' he asked.

'Leave her out of this.'

'For God's sake, I'm trying to make a point here! Did you see me?'

'All right, yes! But I don't see what that's got to do with anything. I won't stop you seeing her, I promise.'

'Lily, that's not what I'm saying. Look at me.' His voice was low. He could feel himself shaking. He was so wound up he thought he might explode into a thousand little pieces.

She turned slowly, until she was finally facing him. She stared at his chin, not looking him in the eye.

'Just now,' he said, 'out there, I could see Caroline was worried. I know I scared her the other night and I shouldn't have. I was out of order. So I had to put it right, didn't I? Let her know I love her. So I got on my knees. Did you see?'

She nodded.

'Yeah? Well, I love you too. And if I have to get on my knees and beg, then that's what I'll do.' He dropped to his knees and put his hands on Lily's knees. 'See? I'll do anything for you, darling. Anything. So please, come home.'

* * *

Lily had never felt so terrible in her life. This man, this big, strong man who had been her friend and her husband for so many years, was crawling on his knees to her, begging.

She pushed his hands away. 'Stop it, Jack. Get up.'

'Come home,' he said, touching her again.

She shook her head. How could she make him see? 'I don't want to hurt you, Jack. But it's over. I'm not coming back.'

'But I love you,' he said, welling up.

She couldn't bear it. She looked at Leonard, wishing they were both far, far away from all this. Would they ever get the chance to be happy, or would they spend the rest of their lives paying for what they'd done to their families?

She stood up, pushing his hands away again, putting the chair between them. 'I'm sorry, Jack, but I don't love you any more.'

He dropped his hands. His chin rested on his chest. She saw a tear drop onto his lapel.

'Get up. Please. Just get up and go home,' she begged.

Mr Irwin stood up. 'She's right, old chap. Give yourself some time. Nothing's going to be resolved like this.'

Jack raised his head and glared at him. 'I ain't going nowhere. She's my wife.'

'Not for much longer,' said Leo. He rose and came round the table towards her.

Before he could reach her, Jack grabbed her arm and pulled her backwards. She nearly fell over the chair, but he held her up. She cried out and tried to get away, but he held her fast against him, with his forearm across her throat, kicking the chair towards Leo.

'Get away from my wife,' he growled.

Lily shivered. He'd never been like this before. She felt the pressure of his arm, blocking off her air. She was suddenly very afraid.

'Don't be a fool, man. Let her go.' Leo pushed the chair out of the way and continued to move towards them. Out of the corner of her eye she saw Mr Irwin move round the other way.

'I said back off!' Jack shouted, his arm tightening.

Leo held his hands up and froze, his face going pale. She saw the flash of a blade in Jack's other hand. He waved it around, pulling her round so they faced both men.

'Jack,' she whispered. 'Please.'

'Put the knife down,' said Irwin. 'Come on, old chap. This isn't the way to deal with things.'

'She's my wife. Mine. He ain't having her.'

She dug her fingernails into his arm, trying to pull it off her. She couldn't breathe. She was getting dizzy. Why was he doing this? He never hurt her. Not Jack.

'Don't,' she gasped.

Jack kissed the side of her face. 'I'm sorry darling,' he said.

'No!' Leonard dived at them, but he wasn't quick enough. She felt the blade pierce her back. Jack let go of her and she fell. As she went down, she felt the knife go into her chest. Above her she saw Jack take the force of Leonard's body and roll him away from her. Leonard went flying, knocking into Gerald Irwin so that they both went down.

Lily could feel her lungs filling up with blood. *Oh God, Jack, what have you done?*

Jack bent over her, stroking her cheek. She grabbed his arm, silently begging him to save her.

'I'm sorry, my darling, but you didn't give me no choice,' he sobbed. 'He ain't having you. You're mine. If I can't have you, no one can.'

* * *

Leo got up, pushing Irwin out of the way. He had to save Lily. He reached out, trying to get Wickham away from her. An elbow in his face had him reeling back again as pain exploded from his broken cheekbone.

His vision blurred by pain, he staggered to his feet. This time, he managed to grab Jack's arm and haul him off Lily. Jack swung round, the knife in his hand, red with Lily's blood. With a roar Leo went at him, punching, kicking and gouging. The blade flashed. He saw his own blood splatter, but he didn't feel anything. He fought with every ounce of his strength, but it wasn't enough. A punch to his gut had him doubling over, and a kick to the side his neck knocked him to the floor. Before he could recover, Jack Wickham was standing over him. Leo looked at the knife and knew he was going to die.

'For God's sake, man!' Irwin cried. 'Haven't you done enough? She's dead! You've killed her!'

Leonard felt the pain then. He turned his head to look at Lily. Her lifeless eyes stared back at him.

He looked up at Jack. 'Go on then,' he said. 'Finish it!'

* * *

Jack looked at Lily, so silent and pale. She was gone. No one else would have her now.

He looked down at the man who'd really done this to her – who'd stolen her from him. He should kill him. He deserved to die.

He was tempted. God, was he tempted. But there weren't no point. If he topped him, he'd be with Lily. He weren't going to give the bastard the satisfaction. Lily was his. He weren't going to have her, not in this life or the next.

What's mine, I keep.

Jack dropped the knife. 'Go to hell,' he said, and walked out of the room, closing the door behind him.

There were some stairs by the lift. They were lit by a big window that looked out into the light well in the middle of the building. Jack ran towards the stairs as people appeared from the other offices. But instead of going down he took a running dive towards the window.

As he fell in a shower of glass, he called his wife's name.

63

SEPTEMBER 2019

The letter came out of the blue, postmarked London.

Dear Mrs Everett,
I am the executor of the estate of Leonard Warwick, my late father.

Caroline felt her heart racing. Leonard's son. Why now, after all these years? His father's executor. So Leonard was gone. She didn't know how she felt about that.

I believe that you are the surviving daughter of the late Mrs Lily Wickham. Would you please confirm this? On receipt of proof of your identity, I am instructed to pass on a letter addressed to you by my father.

A letter? What could Leonard Warwick possibly have to say that would make a difference after all these years? Sorry? It was fifty years too late for that.

She read the rest of the letter, noting the signature: Peter

Warwick. She hadn't known his name before. Had he known hers all those years ago? They were about the same age, or so her mother had told her. How had it been for him and his sister – the scandal, the shame? How did he feel about having to deal with this now?

She folded the letter carefully and put it back in the envelope. She had no idea what to do.

She wondered how Peter Warwick had found her. After all, she wasn't Caroline Wickham any more – hadn't been for decades. She went in search of her husband. He was in the garden, reading.

'Look at you.' She smiled. 'Anyone would think you're retired, lazing in the sun all day.'

He looked up and laughed. 'Best job in the world,' he said. She sat beside him on the wooden bench. 'I've had a letter.'

She handed it to him. 'I don't know what to think.'

He opened it and read it. 'Warwick. Isn't that—?'

Caroline nodded. 'It's a bit freaky that they found me after fifty years, isn't it?'

He shrugged. 'Not really. Social media and all that.'

'But I changed names when we married, don't forget.'

'Ah, yes. Well, why don't you ask him how he found you?'

'I'm not sure I want to have anything to do with him. I mean, his dad...'

He put his arm round her shoulder and kissed her cheek. 'You don't have to do anything you don't want to, darling. But you know it will bug you now until you've talked to him and found out what this is all about.'

She sighed. He was right. It might mean opening the door on some awful memories, but she'd not rest now until she found out what that letter from Leonard Warwick said.

'I thought I was done with all that,' she said. 'Do you think he even knows who I am?'

'For all we know, he might not know anything about you or what happened. He's probably just fulfilling his father's last wishes. Don't make problems for yourself, love. You've done really well. Most people would've been dragged under by what happened. But you faced it head-on. I'm so proud of you. It was tough, but you worked your way through it and made a good life for yourself. Whatever this is about won't make a difference to all that.'

'I hope not. But what if...? Oh, I don't know! It took me years to make sense of it all. I used to blame Leonard Warwick, you know.'

He nodded. She fell silent. He waited, as though knowing she needed to work this out for herself.

Eventually, she nodded. Her mind was made up.

'I'd better write back,' she said, getting up and going back into the house.

64

A week later, in an office in London, Caroline shook hands with Peter Warwick, hoping her palms weren't too clammy. She tried to keep her breathing calm, but it was hard. He looked like his father, although she realised the son was a lot older now than his father had been the last time she saw him.

'Thank you for coming,' he said, indicating that she should take a seat. She sat, smoothing shaking hands over her skirt as she stared at the envelope waiting on the desk. He took the chair opposite her and cleared his throat. 'Can I offer you tea or coffee?'

She shook her head. 'No thank you.' She'd only spill it.

'Right. If you're sure?'

She nodded.

'Very well. As you know, I'm the executor of my late father's estate.'

'Yes. I... I'm sorry for your loss.'

His jaw tightened – the only sign of any emotion in the man. 'Thank you.' He cleared his throat again. 'As I explained in my letter, my father requested that this letter...' he indicated the sealed envelope, '...be passed to you following his death.'

She nodded, her eyes on it as though it might be a bomb. When Peter Warwick picked it up and offered it to her, she flinched.

He frowned. 'Are you all right?' he asked.

She blinked rapidly, taking a deep breath before she nodded. 'I'm sorry. This is all a bit... unexpected.'

'I'm sure,' he said.

She glanced at him, trying to work out what he meant by that. 'Do you know what it says?'

'No. It's sealed. It's for your eyes only.' He continued to hold it out, waiting for her to take it. She didn't move.

'Do you know who I am?' she asked, her voice barely above a whisper.

'Yes.'

His quiet response brought forth more questions in her mind. *Did he hate her? Did he hate her mother? Had it been awful for him, having his father's affair plastered all over the papers? Was his mother still alive? Did she—?*

'I realise you may not wish to be reminded of my father's association with your mother,' he said. 'But it's my duty to fulfil his last wishes. What you choose to do with this letter is entirely up to you.'

'I tried to find him,' she blurted out. 'Years ago. I wrote to Mr Irwin.'

'I see.'

'He said he'd gone back to your mother. After that, I didn't think I should... interfere.'

'Thank you. That was thoughtful. I don't think my mother would have been able to cope with that.' Again, that jaw tightening.

Caroline felt the tightness in her chest ease a little. 'It must have been hard for her. And for you.'

His eyebrows rose, as though she'd caught him unawares.

But he didn't say anything.

'I didn't look for him to cause trouble,' she said, wishing she could crack his professional demeanour.

'Then why did you?' he asked, as though he couldn't help himself.

More pressure eased. 'I wrote to Mr Irwin after I got married. Falling in love made me realise how it takes over your whole world. I realised that your father must have loved my mother very much to have risked everything – his marriage, his family, his job – to be with her. I thought I should tell him.'

'I'm sorry, I don't understand. Tell him what?'

She leaned forwards and put her hands on the desk between them, ignoring the letter he still held in his hand.

'I wanted to tell him I didn't hate him for loving my mother.'

He closed his eyes, his face taut.

'Oh!' She put a hand to her mouth. 'Oh, I'm so sorry, Mr Warwick. That was... I'm... I shouldn't have... Your mother...' She shook her head. 'I didn't think. It must have been awful for her. And for you. Has this upset her?'

He opened his eyes but was silent for a moment, his sharp gaze searching her face. Eventually he nodded briefly before looking at the letter in his hand.

'Thank you. It was difficult when it happened, and my mother would have undoubtedly been upset if you had contacted my father at any time. However, she died a few months before my father. I believe it was after her death that he wrote this letter.' Again, he held it out. Reluctantly, she took it.

She looked at it, unwilling to open it. Instead she put it down and turned to him again. 'Again, I'm sorry for your loss. It must be hard, having to deal with the loss of both of them so soon after each other.'

Finally, his shell cracked. He grimaced and ran a hand down his face, shaking his head. 'You don't have to say that. I'm well aware that, thanks to my father's actions, you were left to deal with the deaths of both of your parents at the same time.'

'That doesn't mean I can't feel sympathy for you having just lost your mother and father in quick succession,' she said softly.

'I wouldn't blame you if you hated me,' he said.

'Do you hate me?'

'No,' he responded immediately. 'You were a child. It wasn't your fault.'

'So were you. I think we're about the same age.'

'Yes.' He looked out of the window, lost in thought. 'We have no reason to hate each other.'

He glanced back at her. 'No. You're right. We were victims—'

'No!'

'I'm sorry?'

'I said no,' she said firmly. 'I refuse to be called a victim.'

He frowned, waiting for her to elaborate.

'I learned very quickly that I had a choice. I could be a victim, or I could be a survivor. My sister chose to be a victim, and it blighted most of her life. She always needed someone to blame for whatever happened in her life. It made it hard for her to be happy, and she died in her fifties having never been truly happy. I decided to be a survivor. I've spent my life looking for the blessings in my life and celebrating them. Something tragic happened a long time ago. I've lived my life in spite of it, and it's a good one. I have never been and never will be a victim.'

Peter Warwick nodded slowly. 'Yes, I see. I'm sorry.'

She took a deep breath. 'No, I'm sorry.' She gave him a wry smile. 'I didn't mean to snap at you. It's just a bit of a bugbear with me. I hate pity. If I let myself wallow in it, I'd sink without a trace.'

He sat back and studied her for a moment. She looked down at the letter again.

'Are you going to read it?'

'I've always been too nosy for my own good.' She chuckled. 'I won't rest until I know.' She looked up. 'Do you mind if I read it here?'

'Go ahead,' he said, passing her a letter opener.

Caroline slit open the envelope. She took her time removing the sheets and reading Leonard Warwick's letter. When she finished, she passed it to Peter. He took it reluctantly, asking if she was sure she wanted to share it with him. At her nod, he began to read. A few minutes later he sighed and put the pages down onto the desk.

'He never got over her,' he said, not looking at her. 'He spent the rest of his life trying to make it up to us, but he was never the same.' He tapped the letter with his fingers. 'He made my mother happy and he was a good father, and I think – I believe – he was content with his life. But until this moment I had no idea how deeply he'd been hurting, how guilty he felt about your parents' deaths. He really did love her.' He looked at her, his face pale. 'Didn't he?'

Caroline nodded. 'I'm sorry.'

He huffed. 'What on earth do you have to be sorry about? For God's sake, your whole life changed on that day. At least I got my father back.'

'I'm sorry I didn't try harder to find him. To give him some peace. If he'd known I didn't blame him, that I'm happy, then he might have allowed himself to let go of his guilt.'

65

Caroline's husband was waiting in a coffee shop around the corner from Peter Warwick's office. He was checking his watch when she opened the door, bringing a gust of autumn wind in with her.

A waitress took her order as she shed her coat and sat down beside him.

'All right?' he asked, kissing her cheek.

'Yes,' she said. 'Everything's all right.' She took the letter from her bag and handed it to him. He read it, glancing at her occasionally.

Caroline smiled at the waitress delivering her cappuccino. 'Mum used to call this a "frothy coffee",' she mused. 'She thought it was exotic.'

He finished the letter and put it back into the envelope. She took it and put it in her bag.

'How do you feel?' he asked, stroking her hand.

She turned her hand over and linked their fingers together. 'Good. I'm good. A bit sad. Not just for Leonard, but for everyone – for me and Bev, for the rest of our family. And for Leonard's family.

It's even affected our kids and grandkids, even though they weren't even born when it happened. So many people. Mum and Dad have been gone for fifty years now, and we're still feeling the ripples it caused. We can't change it. We can't stop it hurting. We didn't just lose them, but they lost us, too. They didn't see me and Bev and Kerry grow up. Didn't meet you and our kids and grandkids. Dad didn't get to walk me or Bev down the aisle, Mum didn't get to knit booties for my babies. Peter Warwick's mum had to live with the fact that her husband had loved another woman so much he'd been prepared to walk away from her and their kids...' She shook her head and blinked away tears. 'It's just such a bloody waste, you know?'

'I know, my love.'

She sniffed. 'But I'm glad I met Peter Warwick and read Leonard's letter. I guess I always worried that he hadn't really loved Mum enough – I mean, he went back to his wife pretty sharpish, didn't he?'

He handed her a tissue and she wiped her tears and blew her nose.

'But he did love her. When she died he was in such a state he let his wife take charge and take him home. After a while he realised that walking away from his family wasn't going to bring Mum back. So he decided that, if he was going to survive, he needed to concentrate on being a good husband and father. And that's what he did for the rest of his life.' She took a sip of her coffee, savouring the warmth of the cup against her cold fingers.

'Was his son all right with you?'

She nodded. 'Yes. He was a bit cool to start with, but in the end he was fine.'

'Good. It can't have been easy for him.'

'No. I think he was as nervous as I was. But it's all right now.'

'Ready to go home?'

She nodded. 'Oh yes.' She drained her cup as he paid the bill. He held the door open for her and they walked out into the autumn sunshine.

AUTHOR'S NOTE

Thank you for reading *Lily's Choice*. This novel means a great deal to me as it is based on actual events that happened in my family in the 1960s. I have written it as fiction because there are many aspects of the real story that have been lost. I don't know how the love affair started, or how it was discovered, or what was said, other than at events I actually witnessed as a young child. Yes, I am Caroline. Some gaps have been filled in from newspaper reports, the inquest files, and the memories of other family members, but the rest comes purely from my imagination.

In the aftermath of our parents' deaths, my sister, her baby and I went to live with Aunt Maggie and Uncle Fred and their children – cousins who I now regard as siblings. Bev qualified as a nurse and went on to marry three times and to have two more children. She died of a heart attack, aged fifty-nine. I'm not sure if she was ever truly happy, but she created her own family, of whom she was very proud. Kerry and her siblings now have seven children between them. One of my great-nephews is the spitting image of his great-granddad and makes me smile every time I see him.

And me? As Caroline told Peter Warwick in the penultimate

chapter (a completely fictionalised meeting, although I did at one point exchange a few emails with Leo's son, for which I am grateful), I am a survivor. I won't pretend it has been easy, but I have lived my life determined to make my parents proud of me. I hope I've succeeded.

I've been blessed in so many ways. I've travelled the world, had more than one interesting career, been married to a wonderful man for over forty years and have two awesome children who have grown into amazing adults and given me two beautiful grandchildren. I never did get to grammar school, as my mother wanted, but I did well at school and eventually went to university as a mature student. I've been a legal executive, a registered childminder, a professional fundraiser, a teacher and a writer. One of my biggest blessings has been that both my mother's and my father's families made sure they kept in touch with me and it's a constant joy to me to still see my numerous cousins, their children and now even grandchildren at various family gatherings and also on social media.

I have so many people to thank. Family, friends and professionals who have guided me and supported me in so many ways. But most of all, I want to thank my parents for giving me life and for loving me. I still miss them every single day, but now that I've written *Lily's Choice*, I hope I have gained a better understanding of how two ordinary people followed paths that led them to an extraordinary end. No one was to blame. They just grew apart and in the end wanted different things.

May they rest in peace.

ACKNOWLEDGEMENTS

This book has been the hardest, most personal thing I've ever written and without the support and encouragement of so many people, it may never have seen the light of day.

First of all, my love and thanks go to my extended family of aunts, uncles and cousins who help me keep the memory of my parents alive. The fact that everyone has fond memories of both of my parents, no matter what 'side' of the family they come from, reminds me that they were good people and universally loved. I hope you feel I've done them justice here.

When I decided to write this story, I went to university as a mature student in order to better learn my craft. There, I found so many wonderful tutors and fellow writers who have helped me along the way. Notably, Dr Jonathan Neale at Bath Spa University and Adrian Tinniswood at Bristol University who both guided me through my research, helping me to explore avenues I hadn't thought about before and to be braver than I thought I was. My fellow students at Oxford Brookes University MA course, including authors Kit de Waal, Annie Murray and Helen Matthews, have continued, with other members of the Oxford Narrative Group, to support and encourage me.

The first person to read my manuscript was my former work colleague, Bryony Evens – the same woman who championed the first Harry Potter book when she found it in a slush pile. Thank you for your honest assessment and your encouragement, Bryony, which kept me going. I feel very blessed to have met you when I did and I'm so glad we've kept in touch through the years.

The writing community is a very special place. So many of my friends there have been my cheerleaders and I thank you all, especially Jenny Kane, my partner at Imagine Creative Writing Workshops, Rachel Brimble, Fay Keenan, Rosie de Courcy, Jane Lark, Imogen Howson and everyone at the Romantic Novelists' Association. You kept your faith in me and also kept me going, as did my famously non-writing friend, Ali Williams. I love you all.

I'm grateful to Laurence Patterson, Sue Barnard and everyone at Darkstroke Books who brought the first version of this story out into the world, and to Rachel Faulkner-Willcocks, Helena Newton and everyone at Boldwood for working with me on this edition.

One person has shared the ups and downs of my life since 1980 – my husband, Mike. His love and patience have sustained me, giving me the courage to write this book.

To our babies, George and Harriet, I'm grateful that you put up with your daft and sometimes over-emotional mother and that you grew up to be wonderful human beings anyway. I'm so proud of you both. This book is your legacy, a chance to meet the people who have gone before. I know they would both have adored you, as I do.

ABOUT THE AUTHOR

May Ellis is the author of more than five contemporary romance and YA fiction novels. She lives in Somerset, within sight of Glastonbury Tor. Inspired by her move to the area and her love of social history, she is now writing saga fiction – based on the real-life stories of the Clark's factory girls.

"Sign up to May Ellis' newsletter for EXCLUSIVE bonus content and see the wedding from the point of view of Beverley."

Visit May's website: www.alisonroseknight.com

Follow May on social media here:

facebook.com/alison.knight.942

instagram.com/alisonroseknight

x.com/Alison_Knight59

bookbub.com/authors/alison-knight

ALSO BY MAY ELLIS

The Clarks Factory Girls

The Clarks Factory Girls at War

Courage for the Clarks Factory Girls

Standalones

Lily's Choice

Sixpence Stories

Introducing Sixpence Stories!

Discover page-turning
historical novels from your
favourite authors, meet new
friends and be transported
back in time.

Join our book club
Facebook group

https://bit.ly/SixpenceGroup

Sign up to our
newsletter

https://bit.ly/SixpenceNews

Boldwood

Boldwood Books is an award-winning fiction publishing company seeking out the best stories from around the world.

Find out more at www.boldwoodbooks.com

Join our reader community for brilliant books, competitions and offers!

Follow us
@BoldwoodBooks
@TheBoldBookClub

Sign up to our weekly deals newsletter

https://bit.ly/BoldwoodBNewsletter

Printed in Great Britain
by Amazon

49493144R00253